PRINCE OF THE ANCIENTS

PRINCE OF THE ANCIENTS

G. L. PRESTON

Prince of the Ancients: Book 1 in the Stag & Hollow chronicles by G.L Preston

Editing by Emma O'Connell

https://www.emmasedit.com

Book cover by G.L.Preston

Paperback: 978-1-3999-2849-6

ASIN: B0B4BGJB98

Author Note

Prince of the Ancients is an epic fantasy. Whilst fun, the story does include some elements that might not be suitable for some readers. Mentioned death/illness of a parent/child, *reference* to homophobic/transphobic/racist views, alcohol use, discussion of SA, dismemberment and murder are present in this novel. Readers who may be sensitive to these elements, please take note.

To the survivors.
I see you; you are not alone.

RUVALON
TENEBRIS
THE SCIRES
MYTHHOLLOW
MYTHBROOK
CRYSTALWOOD
CHAEPSTOW
MORCROFT
CEFIDAN
COED
VILDSPIRE DUNES
LAUGHARNE
MISS MARGERIES
ASAPH
SOLVA BAY
TEMPLE OF THE HOLLOW
LALOW OCEAN
MERIDIUM
THE SILENT ROAD
RHUTHUN
THE STILL SEA
STILLMERE
CAFENYDD
VILDSPIRE DUNES
TOUFORT
CAREW
LACUS LORELAI
MADAIN
AION
VOLENTE
THE MARSHES
N
W
E
S
4

Pronunciation Guide

<u>CHARACTERS</u>
Eltanin: El-ta-nin
Althea: Al-thee-ah
Dracho: Dray-co
Antares: An-ta-rez
Thuban: Thoo-ban
Bastion: Bas-tea-un
Vyn: Vin
Eli: E-lie
Eliana: Eh-lee-ah-na
Connaught: Con-uh
Teyrnon: Tier-non
Roux: Roo
Bisa: Bee-sah
Azande: Ah-zan-day
Kanu: Can-oo
Jareth: Jah-reth
Jakard: Jah-card
Engel: Eng-el
Cubra: Coo-bra

<u>PLACES</u>
Tenebris: Ten-eh-bris
Mythbrook: Myth-brook
Chaepstow: Chep-stow
Laugharne: Laf-arn
Meridium: Meh-rid-ee-um
Stillmere: Still-meer

Aion: Eye-on
Volente: Vol-en-tay
Cefidan: Keh-fi-dan

<u>**OTHER**</u>
Edjer: Ed-jah
Pistwyll: Pis-tul
Gwdhŵ: Good-who
Purdue: Per-doo
Notherworld: Nuh-thuh-world
Ryu: Ri-yoo

Prologue

Boredom reminds me of what I have lost.

The emperor stared up at the magnificent mural he'd come to love for so long. The gauzy curtains fluttered back and forth in the cool spring breeze blowing through the window, tickling the exposed arms of the emperor as he rested his elbow on the marble table before him. Pinching his top lip between his thumb and finger, brow furrowed, he sat, lost in thought.

"It's your move, Your Excellency," came the steady voice of his companion.

Shaking himself free of his daydreaming, the emperor moved his gaze from the mural and towards the white chess pieces in front of him.

They were just inside one of the many nooks that adorned the sides of the vast royal library. From floor to ceiling, the shelves were filled with scripts, books, and scrolls that spanned generations. Even at his advanced age, the emperor had not the years to read such a collection. But if any knowledge were to be sought throughout Ruvalon, it was the palace library of Tenebris where it could be found.

"Are you not tired of our games, Boone?" the emperor asked after a moment, regarding the pieces of finely carved marble more closely. Although he had never lost a game in the centuries that they had played, he still liked to contemplate the individual moves of each piece. To take his time and be patient. He looked up at his royal advisor, Boone, with a smile. "With the many games we have played together, you and I, would you not have considered an alternative method of fortune-telling?"

Boone rolled his eyes. "It is certainly better than the ritualistic murder of old, I should think, Your Excellency; don't you?"

The emperor guffawed loudly. Picking up his last remaining bishop, he started twisting it between his fingers, eyeing the piece. "Hmm, quite. Mortals have always amused me with their religious ideologies. Has our friend written back yet?"

"Yes, sire. His letter arrived this morning. Still no sign, unfortunately. He seems quite beside himself; he's even offered up a reward. I will give our well-wishes, of course."

"Poor man. I can't imagine the worry he's going through. We'll have to postpone our visit until the matter is resolved—which is a shame. I was most eager to introduce everyone. I shall inform him that if he so wishes, our help is available."

"Yes, sire."

The emperor paused for a moment. "How did the Royal Guards' exploration go into the south-east border?" His eyes were sharp.

His advisor let out an exasperated breath.

"No signs at all of what is causing the..." He waved a hand through the air, searching for the right word. "Disruption. To my knowledge, the wyverns have never caused destruction like this before, nor attacked so many humans in such a short amount of time. We'll expand our efforts, but... I apologise that I cannot report anything further at this moment, Your Excellency."

"We will soon uncover what lies before us, my dear friend. Hopefully, before the humans start accusing *us* of the destruction." The emperor indicated the game before them with his free hand. "Perhaps this shall tell us what is afoot?"

Boone offered a small smile that didn't reach his eyes. "Indeed, perhaps it shall."

The emperor returned his bishop to its original position on the board, taking another few minutes to make up his mind. Finally, he sat forward, smiled, and picked it up again.

"Bishop to E2."

He placed the piece down with a tap, nodded, and crossed his arms before looking up at his friend and counsel—whose mouth was parted in abject horror.

"Y-Your—Your Excellency?" Boone whispered, a quiver in his voice.

The emperor's smile fell. It was rare to see Boone so shaken, and he looked back down at the chessboard, realising his grave error. His eyes darted back and forth, but there was no denying what the fates had foretold. In all of their bi-centennial games, the moves would change and so would the number of pieces he lost; but the emperor never lost his king.

He had never understood exactly how the game worked. The magick within it was linked to the energies residing within the planet itself. He had always known this day would come, but he hadn't realised it would be so soon.

He pinched his nose with his thumb and forefinger, closed his eyes, and took a deep breath. Opening them again, he spoke loudly and clearly. "Make your move."

"But, Your Excellency, I—"

The emperor's head snapped up, his eyes changing to reveal their true shape. "As your emperor, I command you to make your move."

Boone bowed his head, before reluctantly reaching forward to collect his knight, his fingers trembling visibly. "Knight to F4. Checkmate."

A wave of silence fell over them. At last, the emperor slumped back in his chair, roughly exhaling.

"Well, this doesn't bode well, does it?" He got up and walked over to the window. "Boone?"

Boone stood immediately. "Yes, Your Excellency?"

The emperor turned slowly and spoke with solemnity.

"Fetch my son. Fetch Dracho."

I

The day she catches me will be the day she rips my wings off.

The thought caused a deep laugh to bubble up from my chest, which I couldn't hold in as I glanced back at Althea. Her wide nostrils flared as she huffed, a scowl on her lavender face, the sun reflecting off her feather-tipped wings as she flapped furiously to try and keep up with me.

My eyes closed as I turned my head forward, stretching my wings to feel the breeze glide over them like a smooth caress from soft fingers. The skies were where I truly felt at peace, gliding and free-falling through the air. *Not a worry in the world when you're above it.* A colossal draconi I might be, but when I was free in the crystal skies of home, of Tenebris, I felt as light as the air itself.

And for the first time in fucking months, I felt *truly* free.

Tucking my heavy wings in, my stomach dipped as I dropped into a sharp dive over the edge of Pistyll waterfalls, feeling the water's cold spray hit my face. I pulled up sharply above the surface of the lake, gliding over to land softly at the rocky water's edge. Althea landed moments later. She tucked in her wings, shaking water droplets from the velvet-soft white fur that adorned the top of her head and spine. Peering in her direction, I laughed gruffly again as I spotted the harsh look she was sending me, her icy blue eyes fierce.

You know, Dracho, you don't need to show off how fast you are at every opportunity? she thought irritably. The draconis' magical ability to communicate with our minds had been bestowed on us by the first mages aeons ago.

My grin was smug as I tilted my horned head. *Come now, Althea, if I don't remind you all who's boss around here now and again, you'd have my head.*

She rolled her eyes—something she did often during our conversations. *That sounds about right, but we've hardly seen you all summer... How is your apprenticeship with your father going?*

Her eyes had softened in concern, the action sending a flash of regret through me. It was true; I had been absent more than usual this summer, and other than passing comments, this was the first opportunity we had had to talk about it alone. My nostrils flared as I let out a long breath, and the rant left my head before I could filter anything.

I don't understand why it's all so sudden. I'm only twenty-six. My father always told me that preparing for my future role would take decades. Now, I feel like a weight has been placed around my neck. The training has been more rigorous over the past year, but I just put that down to precautions. Then out of nowhere, this summer my duties have doubled!

My shoulders relaxed as I talked. I could tell Althea almost anything; we had been close friends since birth, growing and training together. At one point, nearly more than friends... but I didn't like to dwell on that. My studies meant that I couldn't see her much these days, but when we did, it was like nothing had changed. That meant a lot to me.

Training has never been a bother before, I went on. *But with the additional statecraft lessons this summer... I've tried talking to Boone about it, but he just explained that after one of their conversations—a small huff* left my nostrils as I shook my horned head—*he and my father thought it best to start my preparations this year.*

But... I can feel something coming under the surface. It's as if...

My words trailed off and I clenched my jaw as I looked down at the ground, the soil breaking apart under my black claws. The extra schooling didn't concern me much. It was the decisions being made for me when I wasn't even being consulted. It was the gut instinct that things had been hidden from me—and that wasn't something I was willing to share for fear of Althea worrying. She carried enough on her shoulders without sharing any of my burdens.

Althea wouldn't push me. She knew if I wanted to say something, I would.

Perhaps it has to do with these wyvern attacks we've heard about? she suggested.

We had picked up the rumours during combat training, whispers spreading through the guard, and my father had confirmed them when I asked, his face more solemn than usual. 'Wvyerns' was the term we used to encompass all animal wildlife throughout the whole continent, Ruvalon, from the gentle butterfly to the terrifying creatures that roamed the planet's oceans. And over the past couple of years, to the south-east of our border, multiple attacks had been carried out, seemingly at random, on the unsuspecting mortals in their realm by wyverns of all shapes and sizes—and at an increasing rate.

Increasing and alarming, judging by my father's emotional state. I had caught him pacing his study on several occasions. If a thousand-year-old draconi Emperor, one of the most powerful beings in Ruvalon, was worried about something, then I should share that worry. The burden of rule would fall to me one day, and it would be my responsibility to ensure the survival of Tenebris.

No pressure, then.

Anxiously, my magick swirled in response to Althea's suggestion. I shifted my head from side to side, weighing it up.

It is possible, and certainly something I want to help with. The difficulty is that the attacks are moving further south into the human realm. The thought had crossed my mind that we could simply approach the southern rulers and offer our help. But not only were the mortals terrified of us, we weren't supposed to visit their realm. They had no idea that we could shift into human form, and to give that away would be a huge sacrifice to us.

A creeping feeling of being watched settled over me, and I caught Althea studying me closely, her intense eyes practically burning into the side of my face. Her gaze met mine, and my eyes narrowed in amusement. *See something you like, darling?*

Althea softly chuckled. *Most certainly not. I was just thinking... if they need someone to venture south, and you wish to take an extended vacation from your studies, perhaps you should offer to do it yourself?*

My head shot round, and I was shocked at the seriousness in her face. *To venture south?! I can't tell if you're joking or not. Do you honestly believe my father would ever allow that to happen? He would laugh me out of the throne room if I asked.*

Well. Althea stood, craning her neck as she extended her graceful wings, ready to take flight. *You'll never know unless you do ask, Dracho.*

Dust flew up as she took off without a second glance in my direction, and I considered what she had said. The idea of venturing into the human realm did fill me with a surge of adrenaline, my magick churning in excitement.

If I went, I might be able to find the answer to why the wyverns had started these attacks so close to our borders—because if the mortals suspected our people of being the cause, it could start a war. My eyes felt heavy when I thought about continuing my studies, my brain over-stimulated from the monotony of daily hours of reading.

It didn't take long to make up my mind. My dragon form urged me onward as I stood, stretching the muscles in my legs before unfolding my wings, adjusting to the airflow around me. Pushing down hard, I took off towards the palace.

And there it was—the aerial view of all that mattered to me. Beyond the city, lush green and floral lands lay, a beautiful tapestry upon the earth's skin as far as the eye could see. Within the city walls were the various bustling districts, scattered around the river which flowed through the centre. Several tiered waterfalls of different sizes led it over the basalt rocks and met at the bottom where a paradise-blue lake sat, only disturbed by the foam that lathered at the base of the falls and the creatures that swam beneath. The lake was surrounded by weeping cherry trees that swayed in the cool air.

If possible, the city looked even more stunning at night, when the lights glowed like luminous stars that had dropped to earth. To the north stood tall, enchanting spires of stone so white that it captured and reflected all light; even by night you could still make them out clearly, a shining beacon in the darkness. And for each room that the spires contained, a smooth balcony adorned the outside. The royal palace of Tenebris.

Landing on my balcony, I folded in my black wings tightly before shifting into my human form, my dragon internally sighing at our relaxing morning flight. Whilst unable to have a normal conversation with my inner beast, I could feel his emotions—he usually being the more irrational one. When I was growing up, I thought it was strange, knowing that once I turned thirteen, I would have another entity living within me—but after living with him for half my life, it felt as natural as the skin I had been born into.

I took the stone steps down into the main chamber of my room. A slight cough from the corner caused me to jump, surprised to be caught off guard for once. A glance showed me a streak of white through long black hair and sharp amber eyes on me. I laughed.

"If you wanted to see me naked, Ant, you need only have asked."

I grabbed a shirt and some black trousers from my cabinet as he sat, severe as ever.

"Cold out, is it?" my best friend asked.

I shot him a raised brow.

"I've been sent to retrieve you. Your father wishes to see you in the throne room."

"What a coincidence—I want to speak to him. There's something I wish to ask of him." I buttoned my white shirt in front of the mirror, contemplating my reflection and wondering if I would fit in within the human realm. We had been human once, before being blessed by the mages. But sometimes, our draconi forms felt more true than our mortal ones.

The unusual blueness of my eyes might stand out, but since the end of the war, the rest of the continent south of Tenebris had been full of all kinds of fairie folk and creatures, so moving around unnoticed shouldn't be too much of a challenge. Brushing strands of hair back from my face, I turned to face Ant. I could tell my statement had piqued his interest from the subtle narrowing of his eyes. It took everything I had to keep a smirk off my face, waiting for him to take the bait.

"Fine, I'll bite. What's the request?"

There it was. I feigned shock. "What's this—our great seeker of knowledge *doesn't* know something before everyone else? I'm surprised our dear Althea hasn't told you already. It was her idea."

Ant's ability to move around almost undetected, thanks to his silent footsteps and impeccable hearing, made for the ultimate spy. He was usually the only person who could take me by surprise.

His eyes narrowed. "I see how it is—you speak to Althea at a wisp of her wings, but not your closest friend?" He mocked hurt by covering his heart with his hands, poking out his bottom lip. I responded by firing him a rude gesture.

"It's not like that. Althea is beautiful, but... too close to home for me—and anyway, I thought you would enjoy witnessing it for yourself." I headed for the door. "Well, are you coming?"

His smile stretched from ear to ear as he stood up from the corner chair. "Oh, I wouldn't miss this for the world."

2

Those seeking an audience with the emperor could do so in the impressive throne room at the palace's centre. Two large stone braziers, constantly alight, stood on either side of a wide staircase. A jade and silver rug, my father's colours, ran down from the throne and split to encircle the entire hall, whilst banners with gilded silver edges draped from the walls. Between each flag were wall-mounted torches; a few had been lit to illuminate the hall, though they weren't really necessary with the midday sunlight flooding in.

Whilst the rest of Tenebris used advanced electrics, the main throne room maintained the old ways—of flame. Smaller braziers lined the steps, leading up to a radiant throne of marble that was covered in symbolic engravings, a jade dragon carved into each of the slim arms. A large, colourful tapestry hung above the throne, displaying the ancient tales of our people. Four large ivory columns stood behind the throne, holding up the domed ceiling.

There were no walls or windows between the columns, leaving that end of the hall open to the elements, but beyond them was a vast granite balcony where Father stood talking to Boone and my uncle, Thuban. Uncle was slightly broader than my father, and his russet hair just touched his shoulders. His eyes, as black as coal, could seem as cold as the shadows on a starless night, but the fine laughter lines at the corners betrayed their first impression. His crossed arms and worn leathers were scattered with old scars from the many battles he had fought, and his nose was crooked after being broken a few too many times. His smile turned wide as he watched our approach.

Boone couldn't have been more different. His purple robe stood out brightly and he stood taller than the rest of us; although I was over six feet, my head only reached the tip of his chin, where a brilliant white beard grew. The mage wore a golden ring through his left nostril and golden hoops in his ears that caught the sunlight as he turned and bowed his balding head towards us.

"Ah, the prodigal son joins us!" Uncle joked. "Come, come! Help us ease the poor burden your father has upon his shoulders." I felt the weight of his hand as he clapped his arm around my shoulders, pulling me further into the group. From my father's crossed arms and the way he was playing with the ends of his long white hair, he was annoyed.

"Father?" I asked.

He opened his mouth to speak, but Thuban interrupted. "Your dear father is deciding who to send south to review the most recent attacks. They, um... they attacked Mythbrook."

My mouth fell open in shock. I had never been there myself—never even ventured south to the human realm. But everyone in Tenebris knew about the people of Mythbrook. It fell just south-east of the borders of Tenebris, past the Ballaraan mountains. Though it was within the human realm, the people of Tenebris had watched over the small human village for generations, and still did so in secret since the war ended twelve years ago.

No one could remember when the relationship had begun, but our scholars had delivered aid during the war, sent supplies during the harsh winter months, and educated the young children. The people there believed that the scholars lived with us *winged beasts,* never knowing our true secret. Some of them even believed us to be gods, sent to protect them. The thought used to bring a smile to my face.

Mythbrook was very close to the heart of the people of Tenebris. It was full of farming people, with many families but no standing force to protect it. This news was devastating.

"Did anyone survive?" My voice was quiet, but I had to ask. I knew it was practically impossible that anyone had. Wyverns usually stayed clear of the human populations and never gathered in large groups, but lately... The rumours described tracks from feral beasts of all sizes across the far east just before our borders—and now into the south, as if they were intentionally heading towards human regions. Whilst no attacks had taken place within Tenebris, several solitary travellers had been killed just beyond our borders. Now, an entire village had been attacked.

My father's lips thinned as sorrow filled his eyes, and I knew his answer.

Thuban let out a rough breath before speaking. "Your father's worried that the humans may start to accuse us of these attacks. The last thing we want is them turning up on our doorstep—things have always been tense with them as it is. I think we should send someone. Find out what they know."

My stomach clenched at the thought. He was right. If the humans weren't suspicious already, they would be soon.

The human realm was ruled over by two kings: King Teyrnon Cervidae of Meridium, the largest city on the continent, and further south, King Jareth Proditor of Stillmere. Should they become suspicious, they might send out scouts or even mercenaries for answers. If they had any suspicion that the cause of the attacks lay at the doors of Tenebris, it could give them a reason for war.

My father had always ruled in peace, never entertaining the idea of conflict with the mortals. Our kind could wipe out their armies with ease—but it would come at a cost. When we had been blessed by the first mages, we had made a promise to protect the balance and remain impartial wherever possible. To protect life. If we were to break that promise without provocation, the spirits would take our magick.

My pulse thrummed under my skin as it quickened. I could do this. For Tenebris.

For Mythbrook.

A shred of my subconscious self understood that this was also a selfish endeavour. A chance for a break from my royal duties; a chance to see the continent and all it offered. But the thought of helping my father in this endeavour overrode that. I cleared my throat, sensing Ant's questioning look from beside me.

My father huffed. "Thuban, it's not as simple as sending someone South—"

"I will go." In my eagerness, it burst out as a statement rather than a question.

The silence—and varying levels of surprise on their faces—was almost hilarious. Only Boone stood with a knowing look on his face.

"I mean, I would like to request your permission to go, Father."

Uncle's head tilted, considering me, whilst Father started shaking his head. Ant just stood frozen; eyes wide. I'd have to add that to the shortlist of times that had happened.

"Absolutely not, Dracho. You're far too young." Father's firm grip squeezed my shoulders, turning me to face him. "You've never ventured into the human realm and know not of the dangers." His jade eyes flashed with some emotion I couldn't decipher.

But something within me knew this was the right thing to do. I rested a gentle hand upon his arm. "Honestly, I'm not quite sure why—but it's in my gut that I should do this, Father." I had no idea if this was making sense and laughed lightly, but I needed him to understand. "I feel that it's the right thing to do."

He looked sceptical.

"I'll be careful, of course. My training has prepared me well enough to fend for myself and, if it helps protect Tenebris and gets answers for Mythbrook—then it must be done." I raised my head, meeting my father's eyes. "That's all that matters."

His features turned sharp, and I saw something that looked like pride flash across his face before he turned, facing Thuban and Boone to ask for their opinion.

"I think it'll do the boy good, brother. What is it the mortals say—let him sow his wild oats?"

I groaned, my hand covering my face, and heard Ant make a vomiting sound at the mention of my love life.

Father looked to Boone, who gave him a nod of approval. Even with their acceptance, he seemed to take his time considering it.

I held back a gasp as a genius idea came to me. If anything would convince my father to let me go, it would be the idea of a companion going as well. And I knew just the right person.

I rushed the words out. "If it makes you more comfortable, Father, perhaps Antares could accompany me?"

A choking sound came from behind me. Father looked at Ant for a second, an amused smirk playing the edges of his lips, before staring at me intently. I started to shift on my feet. It felt like he was studying my features as if he'd never see them again.

You're sure you want to go? He spoke only to me.

I gave him a soft smile and nodded.

His exhalation was resigned. "Very well... you shall leave at dawn." I couldn't imagine the look of shock on my face, but I almost laughed at the surprise on my uncle's. My father ignored it. "I must stress how imperative it is that no mortal learns of who you are, son. You must control yourselves. Not just for your safety, but the safety of the realm."

It was tough to disguise my excitement—to hide the giant grin that was fighting to make an appearance. This was a serious matter, but at the same time, this was freedom. It was adventure; an opportunity to see the world.

"I understand, Father. You have my word, and—thank you."

"Hmm. Yes, well. Go and prepare. And I mean *prepare!*"

I gave a quick bow to the three elders before turning and walking back through the throne room.

"What were you thinking? Did you not think to consider asking *me* before we entertained your father?" Ant demanded as he caught up.

"It's not something I planned; it just came to me in the moment. I'm sorry, but don't pretend you're not excited at the prospect—exploring the human realm?"

He hissed. "Not like I have a choice now, is it?"

I couldn't help but snigger.

"So, what's your big plan? Do share, considering we're about to enter unknown territory."

My cheeks reddened. I sent him an awkward smile.

"You don't *have* a plan, do you?" His tone rose in alarm. "Well, brilliant. We're only going to be surrounded by a species that would rather see us dead, and you want to go traipsing into their lands with no idea what you're doing."

I raised a brow. "Dead is a bit of an overreaction. They're just scared of our powerful, 'beastly' forms. And remember, we technically belong to the same species as them... or used to, anyway. Everything will be fine, Ant. We'll keep to ourselves, avoid unnecessary contact, find our answers and be back home before the next full moon."

Ant didn't look appeased by this.

"Maybe," I conceded, as my mouth stretched into a crooked grin.

3

The afternoon passed quickly. I spent it saying goodbye to my friends in the Edjer guard, those born into the chosen families with whom I had spent most of my childhood in the training arena. Though Tenebris was a peaceful nation, it was an old tradition that the strongest of us would train our bodies and minds to join the Edjer Guard. Hone into the magick we had been gifted, and keep ourselves strong. The arena had been abuzz with excitement once I'd told them of my journey.

"Be careful out there," Althea had said, punching my arm lightly. I was sure I could see a tear in her eye.

"Crying over me, Althea? It's to be expected. I imagine all the ladies are crying over my departure."

Her next punch wasn't so soft. I might have imagined that tear after all.

I prepared for my departure, putting spare clothing and necessities into a bag, along with an old map I had acquired from Thuban. Boone popped by shortly afterwards to inform me that once I'd finished, Father had requested my presence in his study.

I took a leisurely walk through the palace towards my father's study, steeling myself for the instructions he would likely give me. As I opened the thick door, I found him leaning over his desk, reading old texts and lost in his thoughts. I stepped forward, craning my neck to see emblems of emerald green, and silver stags, and grey and red falcons.

He looked up, finally noticing me. "Dracho, sit." He pointed to one of the rich red armchairs in the corner of the study.

I obeyed and took a deep breath. "Father—"

"Dracho—"

We both chuckled, and an awkward silence fell between us. I indicated for him to continue.

"There isn't much I can tell you about travelling south. The last time I ventured there myself was during a time of war. We are all at peace now, or what appears to be a semblance of peace between all the realms." He sat in an identical chair next to me, a small side table between us, where he placed the book he had been reading.

"It was a very different time, but the end of the war...Well, it left some leaders unsatisfied. They were, for lack of a better word, furious because we didn't pick a side." My mouth opened to object, but he raised a hand. "The main parties were King Cervidae of Meridium and King Morven of the elven kingdom of Stillmere."

"I remember my history lessons, Father!" I interrupted. Not to be rude. But those were some of the most recent histories that I could remember.

"And so you should. The more you know about our past, the better prepared you are for your future." My father's brows rose as he looked at me pointedly, tapping my hand. "The final destruction that led to the end of the war—the destruction of the mage's homeland, Volente—made those of us avoiding the conflict step up. We decided enough was enough. And so, we called a council of leaders to agree on the treaty."

I nodded. The justification behind the war—now usually called the Tain—was mostly unknown, so it was generally assumed kings had kept the provocation quiet; but the devastation was impossible to deny. Towards the end of the war, when the fighting was at its bloodiest, mages from Volente had been divided. Some had sided with the elven king, Jandar Morven and his extreme views—that the land, which had solely belonged to the elves and mages millennia ago, should return to such ownership. A magickal land where no mortals, djinn, or faerie folk lived. But most mages, understandably, believed that all should be able to live in peace, together.

What culminated in the final battle was a mass dispersion of magick which destroyed Volente and desecrated the land forever. Too many had died—from all sides.

Once the council was formed, Morven was outnumbered and so reluctantly agreed to leave Ruvalon and his rulership of Stillmere. Ruvalon would never be rid of humans or other fairy folk, as he so desperately wished. But upon his departure, he vowed to return should the peace treaty ever be broken, to take back the kingdom and continent which he believed was rightfully his. Morven took his subjects, including some mages, across the sea to the south-east continent of Eshmnor, where he started a new elven kingdom, Farcross.

Jareth Proditor, once a very ambitious lord, was elected to rule and now resided as king in Stillmere, meaning there were now two *human* kings ruling over Ruvalon for the first time in recorded history. The draconi families agreed to remain in their realm, Tenebris. King Proditor greatly feared the power that we held and made this an integral part of the treaty. He was not aware of my father's ability to change forms; Boone had conversed on the emperor's behalf, his magick allowing him to communicate with my father in his draconi form.

I knew all this. I had been in my early teenage years when the Tain started, and I would never forget the utter desperation I felt when my father left for that treaty signing just over twelve years ago. Mother and Father had refused me when I had asked to accompany him. My deepest fear during that time had been that my father wouldn't return, that I would lose one of my parents.

Only my father hadn't been the parent I lost. I swallowed; my throat suddenly tight as I willed the memory away.

Father took a deep breath. "But during the war, the mages and elves suffered grave losses—and I know Morven would look for *any* excuse to reclaim a part of Ruvalon or destroy King Cervidae."

My lips pursed. I had never found out the reason for Morven's grudge against King Cervidae, it seemed to go beyond a disdain for humanity in general; my father had always claimed he didn't know it.

"I think there's more than meets the eye to these attacks, and you may well find the answer—but remember, Dracho, a wise ruler does not seek conflict. Always use your head to handle yourself, but your heart to handle others, and you will be guided rightly, for there are evils in the human realm you cannot anticipate." His gaze skipped away from mine, his mouth turning down as regret flashed in his eyes. He blinked it away. "They run to a lesser moral code than us, following their baser emotions and instincts, and they have no qualms about harming each other—and if they discover who you are, son, they may look to use you against us or to gain entry to our long-shielded home."

Understanding dawned on me that, in such a scenario, my father would be forced to choose. Between me, or Tenebris.

My father was a wise ruler and had been for centuries. I watched as he turned his head, looking at the portrait that hung behind his desk. My late mother, Irena.

"I miss her," I let slip, staring up at her face. The image was so realistic and full of beauty, but void of all the life and laughter that had made her *truly* beautiful.

The weight of my father's hand upon my shoulder said more than any words could. "I miss her too—but she is always with us. She now resides in the splendour of the stars, and I know, wherever she is, she is exceptionally proud of you and loves you dearly. As do I."

I clenched my jaw, trying to keep the emotion at bay as I looked at my father, whose eyes held many things he had left unspoken.

"Father?" I rasped.

"Oh, ignore an old fool. It's a poor affliction to have a sentimental heart," he said with a light chuckle. "Besides, shouldn't you be preparing to leave?"

I nodded, my limbs feeling stiff as I stood. "Yes, Father." We grasped each other's arm in a firm hold before I was jerked forward into an embrace.

Releasing me, my father touched his forehead to mine briefly. "Be safe, Dracho."

My chest felt heavy, my stomach full of stones, but shaking it off, I offered a small smile. "Goodbye, Father."

I turned, walking out of the study before I let myself get too emotional, my thoughts scrambled.

"Oh, Dracho?"

I paused, my hand resting upon the door handle.

"Your best bet would be to start in Laugharne. It's a trading town to the west."

I nodded.

"And should you need to head through the Crystalwood to get back to Mythhollow, stick to the eastern border until you come upon a carved tree. There is a wider path hidden beside it that will grant you safe passage through the forest."

My brow arched. I had read about the forest in my studies, but never thought I would venture there.

"Eventually, there is a large clearing you will come upon—and the most amazing lake a bit further. It's the safest place to stay there."

The urge to ask questions rose within me, but I simply nodded again, pulling the door with me as I exited. Before it fully closed behind me, I heard my father give a quiet farewell.

"Goodbye, son. May the light of the stars shine upon you."

4

"Had you told me last week that I'd be venturing south with nothing but you for company, and some human coin from Thuban to rub between my fingers, on some fool's errand... I would have at least spent the week in the Ryu district."

Ant shuffled begrudgingly along behind me as he referenced his favourite drinking haunt in the centre of Tenebris. We'd spent many a night together in the Ryu district, under the stars, discussing life and our studies.

I looked up at the rosy glow of the dawn sky, shaking my head in amusement. He loved the Ryu district—and not for the ale it served. Ant was a mean hustler when it came to cards. He was naturally quiet, never boastful, and could read most people in a room faster than I could read the front cover of a book. Traits I hoped would come in handy along the way.

We had left the palace on foot before most awoke and headed for the entrance to Mythhollow, the cave that would take us through the Ballaaran mountains. These were a vast, dangerous mountain range that extended across the continent, completely separating Tenebris from the southern realm. Some of the mountains stretched so high they pierced the clouds that blanketed them, reaching out to the stars. Legend said that millennia ago, the foremother of us all, the first Empress of Tenebris, foresaw that our kind would need protection. So, she sacrificed her place amongst the stars—her place with her dearly departed emperor—with her dying breaths.

Instead, she chose to lie across the continent, burying herself deep within the earth, forming the Ballaaran mountains. Each peak represented a spike from her back, and the mountain range had been sacred to our kind ever since.

Those not of Tenebris naturally avoided it. Not only because of their fear of what lay beyond, but something that ran much deeper than that. The humans knew very little of the magick that the first mages had gifted us. They believed us all to be trapped within our beast form—obsessed with power, aggressive and forever restless, constantly taking to the skies. The shock they'd get if they ever made it into the city... which was why the magick extended to the mountains. Any mortal that *was* brave enough to attempt the trek found themselves inexplicably turning around, an uncomfortable unease settling into their bones the closer they got to the mountains. Should they venture further despite that, they would come across a magickal barrier that would prevent them from entering Tenebris.

There had been many scholars over the years—usually mages— permitted to enter, of course. Those were sworn to secrecy; their oaths of magick prevented them from divulging our secrets to out- siders. Of course, we could come and go through the mountains as freely as we wanted. And, if we truly wished to, we could escort someone through unharmed.

All I could think about was heading as far away from the moun- tains as possible. My body buzzed with excitement. I had spent my entire life within the comfort of home, never venturing beyond the borders. My adrenaline had been spiking ever since we left, feeling as if a security blanket had been ripped off me. The anticipation of the unknown left me excited, not afraid. I wasn't sure whether that was a bad thing.

"Well, now we can get drunk in a proper human establishment?" I pointed out.

Ant's brows bunched together. "I don't think *that's* advisable."

"What's wrong? Worried I'll get into a fight and transform, trashing towns in the meantime?"

"That's exactly what I'm afraid of."

I laughed. "Lighten up, Ant. It will be a fun, new experience." Pulling out the map my uncle gave me, I examined it closely. "Looks like the nearest major town is Laugharne. A port town—although judging by how old this map is, I dare say things have changed a lot since then." I held the map out away from my body by a corner in distaste. The mouldy old thing offended my nostrils. "But it's still our best bet. If we keep a good pace, with no distractions, then we'll be there by morning tomorrow."

Night came, the skies above allowing the bright crescent moon and stars to shine through passing clouds of muddled grey. We'd been walking non-stop since Tenebris, passing through Mythollow uneventfully.

As soon as we had exited, the great tree of Aion, the mages' homeland, stood out in the distance: a tree so tall it kissed the clouds. Its sister, Volente, had once stood as proudly as Aion did. Before the war and its destruction.

Now, most mages resided in Aion. It was a haven closed off from most, and full of magick. Throughout my studies, I had been very interested in the mages. It was their ancestors that had blessed our kind with magick, and together our people had made an oath. We had promised to protect the balance and the people of Tenebris, whilst the first mages had promised to never betray our secret. The more I had learned about the Aioni, with their different way of life and their own language—some of which I had a basic understanding of—the more I had been enthralled by their culture. Seeing their home in person was awe-inspiring.

We had travelled many miles since leaving the mountain, heading west; far off in the distance, Crystalwood glinted in the starlight. I wasn't surprised we had made it this far already—the pureblood draconis' stamina was much more than that of a mortal man.

It wasn't long past nightfall when we started discussing making camp for the night. We had stopped to assemble the tent Ant was carrying when the sounds of growling and signs of a struggle reached my ears. I looked at him with an enthusiastic smile.

He shook his head fiercely. "No. Nope. Not a chance."

But I was already jogging stealthily towards the sound, crouching low in the long grass. I heard Ant exasperatedly muttering a prayer to the stars for help.

The sounds of the fight became more apparent as I crept closer, shielded by a pile of boulders. I closed my eyes to concentrate, placing my palm on the ground and tapping into my dragon senses; he came forward excitedly. The energy flowed through my fingers, spreading through my body, my senses heightening. Two sets of human feet vibrated through the earth, the distinct heartbeats confirming their number. Without my enhanced hearing, I would never have picked up on the almost silent steps of the creatures surrounding them.

"On your back, Vyn!" one of the humans called out to his comrade, the tone deep and gravelly, slightly breathless. The unmistakable sound of steel slashing through the air reached my ears, the weapon slicing at a smaller enemy that could move with considerable speed. From the yelps I heard, it seemed that, impressively, the pair had already taken care of a couple of the pack, with only a few attackers remaining.

But they were circling close.

The scene played out in my head. Without my interference, at least one of these men would be gravely injured. I rolled my sleeves up, reaching over to find the smooth wooden handle of my glaive, unsheathing it from its place along my spine. I twisted the handle, extending the weapon to its full length until I felt the click of it locking into place.

My arm was suddenly tugged sharply.

"What are you doing?!" Ant hissed—aloud, which showed how annoyed he was.

"I'm not going to sit here and listen to them be slaughtered. Not when I can do something about it." If I could help them, then I would.

"That's exactly what you should do."

I frowned stubbornly, and Ant pinched his nose in frustration. I turned back to the action and stood, preparing myself. A feral snarl ripped through a wyvern's throat, and I heard as it dug its claws into the ground, set to pounce.

"Come on then!" one of the men shouted as the creature's stance shifted.

When I felt a shift in the air, I scrambled swiftly up, launching myself over the boulder with a loud cry, weapon outstretched. Before I'd even landed, my eyes darted around, analysing the situation much faster than a human would.

It was a pack of loscura. Smaller, wolfish creatures like dark shadows taken form—midnight-blue fur, short all over and longer at the neck. Eyes an ethereal, ghostly white, razor-sharp teeth, and elongated ears like a bat, with a long wispy tail. Utterly beautiful animals, but deadly, especially in a pack. There were several in the mountains of Tenebris, but they never usually dared drift inland. One of them had launched itself at the bulkier male's back, whilst he fought off the other two with the one he had called Vyn.

Swinging my glaive around in one swift motion, I bent my

knees, landing smoothly a few feet away from the nearest male. The leaping loscura now lay motionless, its crimson blood seeping into the ground. Glancing up, I met the eyes of the unknown man; axe raised, his thick boot was pressed down upon the throat of another creature, which was thrashing around, as he looked toward me in pure shock. He shook his head, bringing his attention back to the matter at hand, and with a mighty swing, embedded his weapon into the creature's skull. Its movements stilled.

Behind him, the other man crouched low and folded his dagger along his forearm, waiting for the last loscura to strike. The fur on its haunches rose as it pounced—but almost immediately it fell to the ground, the shaft of an arrow vibrating as it stuck out of its eye socket.

Our gazes turned towards the boulder, where Ant stood, his arm still crooked from loosing the arrow. He relaxed and strapped his bow to his back, jumping down to join me.

So much for not getting involved.

Do piss off. His tone was sharp.

I knelt, placing my hand upon the fallen loscura for a second as the larger man walked towards me. His face was peaceful, with deep chocolate eyes and a broad smile on his full lips. He stood slightly taller than me, his dark brown hair twisted into tight, neat rows along his scalp and tied at the nape of his neck. Underneath his open shirt he had a broad, muscled chest and arms, which were covered in lines of black ink, and his fingers were calloused upon my arm as he lifted me. He had an air about him that said he didn't follow orders easily—if anyone was brave enough to give him one.

I reciprocated his shake, and he held my forearm in a firm but friendly grip.

"Dracho. My friend over there with the bow is Antares," I told him, returning my glaive to its shortened length and clipping it back to my leather armour. Before we'd left, Ant and I had discussed using false names, but the risk of slipping up was too great. Fortunately, thanks to my father, my name was not known to texts or the mortals. Not until my coronation as emperor would it be formally announced.

The man eyed my weapon before nodding. "Thanks for the help. Name's Bastion Ekker." With a tilt of his head, he indicated his companion. "And this is Vyn Kaze."

The taller of the two, Vyn, had an effeminate air. His white-blonde hair shone in the moonlight, and his half-moon glasses slightly hid his sharp yellow eyes. There was a pink tint to the skin around his eyes, as if he had rouged them. I knew what he was immediately, and could tell that Ant knew as well. His appearance, along with the hum of energy that hid underneath his pale skin, alerted me that we were in the presence of a djinn.

He spoke, his voice smooth, his eyes shining playfully. "Well, hello. Aren't *you* delicious?"

"Why, thank you. I do think of myself as rather tasty." I shot him a wink and two-fingered salute.

"I was talking to the pretty boy next to you."

My neck cracked from snapping in the direction he indicated—at Ant, who gave me a sidelong glance and shrugged, an amused smile tugging the edges of his mouth. I pursed my lips.

Bastion stood off to the side, shaking his head and rubbing his palm over his sweaty face. "Well, chaps! You got us out of a bind there. How can we thank you?"

I raised a brow in Ant's direction. He shook his head minutely. I rolled my eyes and turned back to our new acquaintances.

"Well, we wouldn't say no to directions... or a spot by your camp for the night, if you have the room spare." The anger rolling off Ant was like tidal waves crashing against an unsuspecting beach. "Just until the morning, when we can gather our bearings?"

Bastion's lips pursed in thought. "We'll have to ask Eli—"

In spite of myself, I winced at the name as memories of my parents resurfaced. Eli had been the nickname Mother used for my father.

"—but I'm sure that wouldn't be a problem. Least we could do for you saving our arses," Bastion finished, rubbing the back of his neck.

"Eli?" asked Ant as I cleared my head. I wondered why their companion hadn't been helping whilst the pair were fighting—and almost losing to—a pack of loscura.

"Yes. Eli—"

A grunt left his mouth as Vyn elbowed him in the ribs, cutting off his words. Bastion glared at him; some silent conversation seemed to go back and forth before Bastion's eyes widened with a look of realisation. He turned back to us, a smirk on his lips. "As I was saying, Eli is our commander, and would definitely like to meet you after your help."

I filed their exchange away for later and clapped my hands together. "Excellent, lead the way!" All that mattered was that we had shelter for the night.

What happened to keeping to ourselves!?

I chose to ignore Ant's anxiety. If he had been able to manifest his thoughts into physical objects, I was sure I'd have a thousand tiny daggers penetrating my body right about now. But it seemed logical to me that these humans could be a help rather than a hindrance.

Bastion retrieved his weapon from the ground, and I fell in step next to him as we all crossed the field towards our new companions' camp.

"So," Bastion started, "what brings you out here? We've already established that you can handle yourselves in a fight. Are you... mercenaries?"

The way his hands twisted around the handle of his axe showed he was nervous, and I wondered why. But Ant and I had discussed our story as we left Tenebris and knew we could tell some truths to the humans. We would, after all, need their help to gather any information we could about the attacks.

"Mercenaries? No. But we've recently travelled here. To be honest, we're trying to find out about some village attacks that have been happening in the northeast."

Bastion's brows shot up. "Really? Hmm. So are we."

Well, what a stroke of fortune. I flashed him a grin. Hopefully, we could gather as much information from them as possible before moving on.

"How strange! Who are you working for?" I asked, noting how Bastion glanced at me quickly before looking away.

"No one, really. I mean, Eli is in charge. But after Mythbrook, we're really only doing it to help people."

I smiled. "So, what have you found so far?"

"Ah, you're better off talking to Eli about that. I'm more of a... grunt, in this endeavour," Bastion said, giving a sly chuckle to himself at some private joke. "So—why are you investigating them?"

"We have our reasons," Ant interjected, his tone final. The less we delved into those reasons, the less we'd have to lie.

Though lying would protect not just us, but our people, being dishonest filled me with immense guilt. I was used to being completely myself—wearing my heart on my sleeve. To try and ease my discomfort, I tried to see it as a role. A chance to play whoever I wanted to be. I supposed that was exciting.

As long as I could keep it up. As long as no complications arose.

Bastion bit his bottom lip, suppressing a grin. "Well, you might be disclosing those reasons sooner than you think."

My mouth opened to ask what he meant, but the scent of rich, earthy smoke reached my nostrils—a campfire. I heard the crackle of the logs as the embers buried deep within them burned, and crisp air from the clearing in the trees ahead brushed against the exposed skin of my arms. Fallen leaves crunched under my feet as we strolled into the making of a camp. It was only small, made up of two decent-sized, raggedy tents patched up from a lot of use, a campfire situated in the middle with a rabbit roasting on a spit above it, and logs placed around it.

"Eli! We've got some people we'd like you to meet!" Bastion called into one of the tents, a sly smile on his face.

I walked around the fire pit, looking for clues as to the travellers' origins. As I came around one of the logs, sidestepping the camp's bucket of water, I heard someone quietly clear their throat.

I suddenly realised that I was only a couple of inches from colliding with someone. Time seemed to slow as my eyes darted down, locking with long-lashed, unamused eyes of vivid emerald. I lost balance as I brought my foot back, trying to stop myself from colliding with her, and felt my foot suddenly go cold as I stepped back into the water bucket, before tripping and landing on my arse.

Water spilt all over the ground.

Looking around, my cheeks flamed in embarrassment. Ant stood stock-still by the entry of the trees, tight-lipped but clearly trying to contain a shit-eating grin, whilst Vyn and Bastion roared with laughter.

"Well, as first impressions go, I'd say that's a new one for me," the woman's silvery voice drawled.

5

I looked to Bastion, warm with irritation and embarrassment.

"I take it this is Eli?" I asked, nodding in the young woman's direction. She was watching me with a sceptical eye. Bastion's teeth flashed in an amused smile as he nodded.

Getting to my feet, I shook my cold leg, where my breeches were sticking unpleasantly to my skin, then I dusted myself off and picked up the bucket.

"I apologise for the water; my name is Dracho," I informed Eli politely, and held out a hand.

Her features made her look so delicate, but the way she held herself showed an unshakeable sense of confidence. She ignored my hand, instead turning to Bastion with hands on her hips, dismissing me entirely.

I frowned at the back of her head, lowering my hand. Who did this woman think she was?

"I take it you ran into some trouble?" she asked, her tone long-suffering. Perhaps trouble had a habit of finding her companions.

Vyn chuckled. "You could say that. Shit-For-Brains here went stomping through the meadow so loud he encouraged the presence of a pack of loscura."

Or maybe just the big one.

Vyn eyed Bastion over the top of his glasses as the latter gave him an obscene gesture. "Luckily, these two were able to jump in with some assistance." He nodded towards Ant, still standing off to the side, and me as I took my place on one of the logs.

I decided to start again, giving Eli the benefit of the doubt. "It was no trouble at all. As I said, my name is Dracho, and my companion here is Antares. We won't infringe upon you for long; we're just looking for a bed for the night whilst we gather our bearings. We're not too familiar with the area."

Eli's eyes narrowed. "Where are you from?" Quick off the mark, this one, suspicion practically dripping from every word. There was a slight southern lilt to her accent. "This is one of the most well-known terrains in all of Ruvalon. You must have travelled *very* far, if you're unfamiliar with it." She crossed her arms.

My dragon stirred at her challenge. "Well, obviously not *too* well-known if your comrade didn't know there were packs of loscura in the area, no?" I joked, and could sense Ant shaking his head, exasperated.

Idiot, he bit into my mind.

Fuck off.

"Oh, I like this one. This should be good." Bastion gave a deep chuckle as he nudged Vyn's arm. Vyn looked away, his eyes widening over his glasses as if astonished at my audacity. Eli stood, unmoved, considering me.

My exhalation was rough. I was right; no getting around this one. "We're from Eshmnor."

All except Ant looked shocked at this declaration.

Our backstory made sense. Travelling the continent with outdated knowledge would be suspicious, so it was logical that we had to come from somewhere else. The elves that shared the continent of Eshmnor with humans always aroused curiosity, so we hoped people would care more about that than our own story.

"You came from the continent? Why are you out here?" Eli asked, her suspicion unwavering—and rightly so. Hardly anyone from Eshmnor travelled to Ruvalon, unless trading.

Bastion chimed in. "Same reason as us, E. They're looking for answers to the attacks."

She looked mildly interested at that. "And why should we trust you enough to provide accommodation for the night?"

"If I wanted to kill you, I could have done that instead of saving their lives. We're not thieves, if that's what you're worried about," I told her bluntly.

Bastion whistled, turning his head. Vyn crossed his arms, seeming amused by the tone of the conversation.

Ant rolled his eyes. *Like I said—idiot.*

Her gaze travelled over me, taking in my appearance before stopping on my face. "I'm not worried about *you*. What about that one?" She tipped her head towards Ant. "Let's not pretend he isn't the most lethal one of you both."

My brain stuttered for a moment. Sure, I always boasted about my agility and strength at home... but it was true. For sheer viciousness and strategy, Ant was a honed weapon, having merged with his draconi form. How this human could tell that, I didn't know. But it explained why the other two hadn't felt the need to explain to her about our skills when we entered the camp. She could already sense we were a threat.

The issue was, I couldn't sense how much of a threat *she* was—which was unheard of.

Astute, this one. Ant didn't react outwardly, though I could sense he was slightly wary. But he was exceptionally good at reading people, and whatever he could tell about Eli was good enough for him. His gaze was piercing as he placed a hand over his chest, then bowed his head. "You have my word, on my honour; we mean no harm and will be gone by first light."

Thought you were against this whole idea?

Well, it would be even more suspicious if we were to change our minds now, wouldn't it? he bit back.

Eli eyed him for a moment before exhaling. It seemed to satisfy her—somewhat. "Very well. You may stay tonight and eat with us in the morning before you go on your way. But I warn you: should you try anything, I'll gladly end you myself."

My gaze roamed over her and I smiled, bowing my own head. "Thank you."

She rolled her eyes before taking the bucket from my side.

Ant muttered something under his breath that sounded suspiciously like, "No distractions." I flashed him a wide smile.

"I'm going to get water, since our *last* lot is all over the floor." Eli looked meaningfully at me.

I jumped up from the bench. "I'll come with you."

"There's no need."

"I insist—just in case there are other loscura out there."

Sitting on one of the logs as he ripped off a leg of rabbit, Bastion snorted.

I'll come with you. Make sure you behave, Ant said.

Me? Misbehave? I started to follow Eli, heading towards the stream. *Best not; she's rather suspicious. See what you can find out from that pair.* I turned just once to see Ant joining Vyn and Bastion, giving me a look of warning first.

It was a silent walk to the stream; Eli was clearly not in a talking mood, and I couldn't for the life of me come up with a subtle way to start a conversation. She was challenging to read. I felt the thrum of my magick as I opened up my senses to see if she was, in fact, mortal. All I got was a scent of blackberries and jasmine.

No magick.

As we slowed, the sound of bubbling water rushing over the rocks in its shallow depths drew my attention. I stayed back as Eli stepped forward, bending over to dip the bucket into the water. Thick mahogany hair fell over her shoulders, almost black in the shadows, the colour reminding me of the rich Tenebrian soils after the spring rains. Two dark braids crowned her hair, wrapping over the top of each ear before being pinned at the back of her head.

An awareness settled within my gut: this woman deeply intrigued me. How did a southern woman become a leader of her own crew? True, they had required our help for a moment, but they were trained, and I'd never heard of women below the mountains leading their own men before. But then again, we knew our information was slightly outdated.

Her brown trousers clung closely to her shapely legs, which were encased in a pair of thigh-high black leather boots, but it was the dagger strapped to her leg that caught my eye. Not a simple blade from any old blacksmith, but an ornate, finely crafted dagger with a green stone embedded into the handle. It wasn't the only weapon she had, either. She wore a ruffled white shirt cinched by a wide leather belt, and I realised that it was adorned with a set of smaller throwing knives. A practical and comfortable outfit for combat— similar to something Althea would wear.

"You know, staring won't give you the power to see through my clothes," Eli said flatly, her back still turned to me, interrupting my train of thought.

My dragon surged, his amusement lifting my lips at the corner. I crossed my arms, squaring my shoulders. "You could always just take them off?"

Mentally, I slapped my dragon upside the head. Flirting with a mortal, especially a suspicious one, was not in my best interests right now.

"Now, why would I do that when I can just allow your imagination to drive you wild, trying to get *all* the details right?"

I sucked in a breath. *Oh.* I was in trouble.

I cleared my throat, changing the subject. "So..." My voice cracked. I didn't have to see her mouth to know she was smiling in amusement. "Eli—what's the name short for?"

"Who says it has to be short for anything?"

"Well, if it isn't, I'd say your parents *really* wanted a boy."

She exhaled sharply. I smiled widely, amused at her irritation.

She finished filling the bucket and walked over to me, shoving it at my chest, where I caught it with both hands. Her eyes were unforgiving as she studied my face with intense interest for a moment.

"You have very unusual eyes," she stated, with an underlying tinge of suspicious curiosity. And they were unusual, the same too-blue eyes that my mother used to have. *She should see them in my other form.*

"Why would two from Eshmnor travel all the way to Ruvalon for information? Are the elves involving themselves in the matter?"

I shook my head, hoping to steer this conversation somewhere else. "I don't involve myself with elves." Her eyes narrowed sceptically. "We're not from Farcross"—the elven stronghold— "and my reasons are my own." It wasn't exactly a lie.

"I just find it strange that you came so far north instead of stopping to make enquiries in Meridium first. Or even Stillmere," she pushed.

"How do you know we didn't?"

Her lips quirked. "I'd know if you had been seeking answers in the cities."

Despite the frustration coursing through me, I trained my face into a mask of indifference. This woman was infuriating! "We figured the closer to danger, the more accurate the information. Before it was diluted down through rumours."

"Hmm—I'm not buying it." Her head tipped to the side as she challenged me, her hands still on the bucket, the only thing separating our bodies. Stars above, it seemed that this woman really disliked me.

"Good thing I'm not trying to sell anything then. As I said, my reasons are my own."

Never in my entire life had anyone pushed me like this. True, I was used to Althea and the back and forth that usually entailed any conversation with her... but this was different. I wasn't entirely sure why it was bothering me so much. The worst part was that she knew she was getting under my skin, and from the smug look on her face, she was enjoying it.

"Well, hey, if you've just come for some good information to take home—"

"I had family in Mythbrook," I blurted out, somewhat angrily. Both at her and myself, for losing some of my control and having to resort to lying. "And I need to know what happened."

I hated liars. I understood that this was for the good of Tenebris and my people. But dishonesty was a necessary pill to swallow about this whole endeavour.

I didn't remove my eyes from hers, for fear of further disbelief. Her face fell, uncertainty showing.

My bones felt cold as a shock ripped through me, my hands itching. I recognised the sensation of claws scratching gently beneath the skin, trying to break through. My true form, agitated at being questioned incessantly and seeking a way out.

I was unnerved that I hadn't noticed how annoyed my dragon had become. I vowed to keep a tight lid on it from this point, especially where this woman was concerned.

Manoeuvring one hand underneath the bucket, I used the other to pinch the bridge of my nose, closing my eyes. I took a deep breath, not only to ease the anger but the guilt settling in my stomach from lying to her. A memory of a mother's lesson about honesty flashed before my eyes. I blinked it away. It wasn't such a big lie; the village did mean a lot to my people and me.

A silence hung between us whilst Eli seemed to process the new information, her lips pursed as she chewed the inside of her cheek.

After a few seconds, and for the first time since our meeting, her face suddenly morphed into a soft, sincere expression. "I'm sorry for your loss—and for pushing you. I have to shield my own. I hope you... understand?"

I nodded, a bit taken aback by the sudden turnaround. Taking the bucket from her hands, I turned, starting to make my way back to the camp.

6

Bastion shared a tent with Vyn; Eli had her own, whilst Ant and I shared ours. Surprisingly, I slept soundly.

I was alone when I awoke. From the light shining in between the tent flaps, it was early morning. I groaned as I stretched, leaving the tent clad only in a long nightshirt, and spotted Bastion fully dressed as he cooked over a new fire. Ant was talking to Vyn on the outskirts of the trees; he looked over and nodded.

I strolled over, filling a horn with water before sitting beside Bastion. "Morning," I said groggily.

Bastion took in my state of dress with an amused expression, and I realised I should have put my clothes on before exiting the tent. Being naked was not something that bothered people in Tenebris—whenever a draconi transformed, we ended up unclothed—but I had no idea how they felt about it here.

"Please! Call me Bas. A beautiful morning it is!"

"And why's that?" Raising my cup to my lips, I took a sip of water.

"Well, firstly we've got sausages," he told me, pulling them out of a cool pack—a crafted metal box that contained a small electrically powered fan to keep food fresh, similar to ones we had in Tenebris. The lifespan of the fan was made infinite by a small amount of magick.

My eyes narrowed, wondering where they came from to have such advanced technology and access to a mage.

"We haven't had them for a while. Picked them up yesterday from this little farmstead," Bastion went on, kissing his fingertips. "Secondly, no one's died this morning. That's always a plus."

I laughed nervously. "Those are the standards for how your day is going? It's barely sunrise."

He tilted his head as if I'd missed an obvious point. "Well, I mean... with E, we've learnt to expect anything. So—yeah! This is a pretty good morning! I'm surprised you came back in one piece from the river."

Clapping a hand to his large back, I stood. "Don't worry, I can take care of myself."

He pulled a face as I walked off that made it clear he didn't believe me at all.

"Morning," I greeted the others. Vyn smiled. His glasses were missing, highlighting the yellowness of his eyes. Ant grunted at me.

"Who pissed in *your* water?" I asked him.

"Besides the fact you try to cop a feel in your sleep? Nothing," he said, wrinkling his nose.

I put my hands on my hips and rocked on my heels. "You should be used to that by now. You know I can't help myself when I find myself next to such an enticing *pretty boy*."

He pushed me. I lost my balance and landed hard on the ground, laughing breathlessly as the shirt rode up.

Ant's hands shot up to cover his eyes. "Put that away, would you!" he spat.

Vyn snickered. "Not the sausage I was expecting this morning. But I won't complain."

Eli came out of her tent, fully dressed, strapping her miniature daggers onto her belt. Her eyes fell on me and widened as my hands covered my nether region. I shot up and tugged at the hem of the shirt to pull it down.

"Once we're packed up, we're heading to the town—Laugharne," Eli told us. I gave Ant a pointed glance. "Rumour has it that there is some information there. Would you like to join us?"

I tried to keep my expression neutral, but I knew I looked surprised. "Yes... that would be fantastic... thank you!"

Eli nodded, giving me a tight smile, and returned to her tent.

Vyn smacked a hand down on my shoulder. "Let's eat, boys."

Wow. We might actually find some answers today. Whilst Ant and I had agreed that we should be as careful and intentional with any human interaction as possible, I had a good feeling about this group. My dragon swirled in agreement.

❧

"So, Vyn..."

Vyn's eyes slid sideways to acknowledge me, his brow raising in a silent question. "You see... I—"

"You want to know about me?" he asked calmly, no hint of irritation in his gaze.

I nodded. Having found myself walking beside the djinn on our journey to Laugharne, I was thankful for the private opportunity to bring it up. Eli and Bas were walking further ahead, Ant scouting from behind.

"Sorry if that's too personal. I've met one of your kind before, a long time ago when I was young, and I'm just curious."

Vyn inclined his head. "I would rather you ask so that you can feel more comfortable around me—and I am an open book when it comes to my past. Bastion says I like to share *too* much." His laugh was dry as he looked ahead, before taking a deep breath. "I am half djinn; my dear, departed mother was a mortal. My father—a pure-breed—raped my mother."

I suppressed a wince, surprised at his candour.

"My mother tried to rid herself of the pregnancy many times, but failed. When I was born, she realised that I had inherited some of my father's traits. She couldn't bear to look at me, so did the only thing she could—besides resorting to killing a child, of course; she left me."

I looked at him, appalled.

"I was taken in by the local church, who took care of me," Vyn continued, "until one day, a brown-haired little waif of a girl punched one of the bigger orphans for picking on me, breaking his nose." He gave Eli a look of adoration as her head turned, and she shot him a small, genuine smile. I frowned; we must have been speaking louder than I'd thought. "She decided then and there that her... family would take me in. I found out years later that my mother passed away."

"And your father?"

Vyn's eyes flashed a brilliant yellow. "The djinn are supernatural beings, some capable of shapeshifting and manipulating the elements. Generally, they mistrust humans. Some actually find delight in punishing mortals for any harm done to them... My father has never been seen since attacking my mother." Vyn glanced over, his eyes glinting. "If it is my fate to come face to face with him one day, I will bless the opportunity to slit his throat myself."

Can't blame him for that. I looked down as old memories resurfaced. "The way you describe a djinn's nature and abilities—it's not how I remember the man I—"

"As with any species, there will always be good and evil. A cycle," Vyn interrupted, raising his hand. "Myself, I harness the ability to manipulate the air." He flicked his fingers outward; a giddy current of wind manifested inside his palm, a swirl of white rotating gently.

"And it has its advantages," he added, his face a conflicting myriad of emotions, before flicking his wrist and glancing over his shoulder. I turned to watch as the breeze glided over to the side of Ant's face and tucked his hair behind his ear.

Ant jerked and smacked at the air, and his eyes shot up to look at us, glaring. I laughed as Vyn sent Ant a coy wave. Ahead, Eli and Bas looked back to see the commotion before shrugging and continuing onwards.

"So," Vyn said. "What about you?"

"M-me?" I stuttered, my laugh dying.

"What's your story? I know you have your reasons for being here; I won't pry—not until you're ready to tell me. But what's home like? And what's *his* story?" he asked, flashing Ant a sidelong glance. I smirked, knowing that my friend was probably listening.

"Honestly, there isn't much to tell... no siblings, unless you count Ant back there. We practically grew up together. I couldn't imagine a better adopted brother, to be honest. He's saved my arse more times than I can count."

Would you like a hug? Ant sniffed.

Piss off.

I hesitated. "This is actually the first time I've left home and explored other places, so... it's a bit of a shock to the system, I suppose." I shrugged.

Vyn nodded in understanding. "I can get that. I remember the first time we left Meridium. Leaving home makes you realise how small your little world is."

Interesting, Ant said.

I tilted my head. "You're all from Meridium?" That was the largest city in Ruvalon.

Vyn's eyes widened, a horrified look of realisation settling across his face. "Um, yes."

This could probably work in our favour. If anyone had heard

anything about the wyvern attacks, it would be people in the cities. Vyn looked uncomfortable at having revealed the information, so I decided not to press him for now.

"And what's Eli's story?"

His eyes shifted to me quickly before looking away. "That's her tale to tell." He smiled apologetically and tapped my shoulder, before jogging to catch up with his companions.

Ant caught up to me. "What was all that about?" he muttered quietly.

"Which part?"

Do you think his nature is a threat?

Not at all, I replied. *I didn't sense any animosity when we talked about it. I got the feeling that he slightly resented that part of him. He was rather... open about his past.*

Ant nodded. *You should know by now, Dracho—oversharing is a trauma response.* He looked at me pointedly, and I clenched my jaw. Ant coughed. *Anyway, he wouldn't discuss any information on the female—*

Eli, I corrected him, heat filling my face.

Yes, Eli. But his heartbeat increased when you asked. They're hiding something. He scanned the trio with narrowed eyes.

I agreed. *But hey, I'm not going to begrudge them for keeping their secrets. We've only just met. Besides—it's not like we aren't keeping any of our own, is it?*

7

We reached the edge of Laugharne just after midday. Fresh sea spray and the tang of salt floated on the breeze as we neared, along with the subtle scent of freshly caught fish; the gulls above cried in their repetitive way. The town was made up of sun-bleached buildings, all huddled closely together. Our group stopped just before the main square, the bright rays of the early afternoon illuminating the cobblestones, and I tilted my head upward, closing my eyes as the warmth kissed my skin.

"I'll send word to our host that we've arrived, but for now let's head to The Griffin." Eli's voice carried over the sounds of the townsfolk around us.

"The Griffin?" I asked.

Bas looked at me, dimples showing as a shit-eating grin spread across his face. "It's the local."

I laughed, rolling my sleeves up. "Love your ale, do you?"

He nodded vigorously. "It's my mission to drink in *all* the pubs in Ruvalon."

I slowly turned to face Ant, who rolled his eyes and exhaled deeply through his nose.

Bas laughed. "Not a fan of ale?"

"Not a fan of this one *on* ale," Ant said matter-of-factly, jerking his thumb in my direction.

"I'm not that bad," I insisted.

"The last time you got drunk, you set my clothes on fire. I had to strip off."

"Yes, but you didn't die."

"That is not the point," Ant said between gritted teeth.

Bas roared. Eli watched on from the side, shaking her head.

"How interesting," Vyn said, eyes sparkling with amusement.

"How in hell did you manage to set him on fire?" Bas asked.

We both froze as I laughed awkwardly. "Can't quite remember."

Actually, I did—I'd taken a few too many bottles of strong ale to the lake at the bottom of Pistyll falls, got far too drunk, transformed, laughed at something Ant had said, and set fire to his breeches.

"But I'm not eager for it to happen again," Ant muttered, and I snorted.

Someone unexpectedly grasped my shoulders from behind, and I jolted, before realising from the small hands that it was Eli.

"What's the tattoo on the back of your neck?" she asked.

She must have noticed the bottom of my mark as it peeked from under my hairline. It wasn't a tattoo at all, but a mark that set me, and others like me, apart from the rest of the people of Tenebris. It represented our blessing from the first mages: the mark of the chosen families, those who had the power of transformation.

"Uh, drunken mistake," I mumbled, Ant glaring.

She snorted and gave me a push. "All right. So we'll keep him away from any fireplaces... and maybe the ale too!"

My dragon sighed in relief as I looked back at Ant and grinned. Vyn led us towards a brightly painted building with an artistic sign hanging outside: The Griffin.

The heavy wooden door of the tavern creaked as it opened, and we were immediately welcomed by the sounds of laughter and merry singing. The place was full of circular tables with curved benches; a long wooden bar was situated upon the back wall, where a stocky barman wiped a glass clean.

When the rowdy men at the centre table saw Eli enter, a loud cheer carried through the inn. One of them rushed forward and dragged her to greet the rest of their table, a lopsided grin plastered on her face. Bas squeezed past me, and another cheer vibrated through the rafters. He threw his hands up in the air and walked over, Vyn joining him. Ant and I took the opportunity to sit at a nearby table.

Their interaction interested me. The men at the tables all wore armour of the same colour: steel, coloured with pastel hints of sea green and terracotta that matched the banners strewn throughout the town. They were all displaying the emblem of Laugharne, a slightly beaked whale.

How had our friends from Meridium become so familiar with the soldiers of Laugharne?

Eli left the table and headed over to speak to the barman. I couldn't hear over the raucousness as they spoke, the barman pouring some drinks and placing them on the bar. He pointed to a back door, through which Eli left. Before I could follow, Bas called Ant over for help with the drinks, delivering one into my hands without a word.

Ant took the empty seat next to me on the bench, pushing away the glass whilst I took a cold mouthful of mine.

"Not a drinker?" Bas asked him.

I swallowed the amber liquid quickly. "Ant likes to keep his mind a temple." I turned to my friend. "Actually, I don't think I've ever seen you drunk?"

Ant looked at me impatiently.

Bas grabbed Ant's discarded pint, pulling it next to his first, which he cradled with both hands. "I've missed you so much," he told it softly, before chugging several mouthfuls. I shot Ant an amused look; he shook his head.

You all right? His discomfort was obvious in the set of his body.

Fine. It's very busy here.

Crowds sometimes bothered Ant; he could quickly become overstimulated and need time to recharge. I didn't make a move to comfort him, not wanting my touch to add to his stress.

A shout echoed from the group of soldiers. "Hey, Bas!" It came from a male who must have been older than us by a few years, his shaggy dark brown hair brushing his shoulders. He had a red scar crossing his nose from one cheek to the other, which didn't take away from the pleasantness of his face. "Who're ya friends?"

"This here is Antares," Bas said, smacking a hand down on his shoulder, "and this is Dracho. Boys, this is my good friend Fabian, captain of the Laugharne guards."

I gave Fabian a friendly nod, and he raised his tankard in return.

"Pleased to be meeting ya, lads!" he said in his sailor's drawl, getting up to join us at our table. "So, how'd you be knowing Eli?" He gave us a conspiratorial smile.

"We only met yesterday. We had common interests, so she kindly invited us to join them on their journey," I answered.

"They're here for the same reason as us, Fabe," Bas explained, his tone serious.

Fabian's brow arched. "Somewhat out of character for Eli, letting strangers join ya."

Oh? Maybe she didn't dislike us—me—as much as I thought.

Captain Fabian stroked the rough stubble along his jawline; his warm brown eyes travelled over my shoulder quickly before returning to look at my face with a sly grin. "What did you do to sweet-talk her into tha' one?"

The atmosphere in the inn changed instantly, the tables around us falling silent as the soldiers waited for my answer. Ant's gaze skipped past me, and he tensed in his seat. *Don't—*

"What can I say? It's hard to resist my charms." I leaned back, elbows resting on the table.

"Oh?" an amused, silvery voice asked, close to the table behind me.

My heart stuttered as I shot back upright and turned. Eli had returned through the front entrance and now stood with her hands on her hips, her lips turned up in a satisfied grin. The crew of Laugharne guards erupted into laughter, the sudden noise making me flinch, and my mouth opened and shut. Eventually I rubbed the back of my neck and forced out a laugh.

"H-hello there, Eli."

Ant turned into the table, pulling my pint in front of him like a shield from the attention on us. "Tried to warn you. You've done it now," he muttered.

"Oh dear," Eli flourished her arms out to the company, making a show of my humiliation, "it seems the proverbial cat has certainly got our poor boy's tongue!" The tavern descended into further noise on my behalf.

"Stop teasin', E! Not all o' us are as versed in the language o' love as you are," Fabian joked.

From the ferocious look Eli sent his way as he held his hands up in the air, there was an underlying story there. The scowl, however, fell from her face as she turned to face me again, her eyebrow raised.

"Now, come on," she drawled, sauntering around the table towards where I sat, a sway in her hips. My stomach started to flutter nervously.

She perched herself on the bench next to me, my eyes clocking the way her curvaceous legs straddled it as she leaned towards me. She was close enough that I could feel her body heat and smell the scent of blackberries. I looked up, reaching her bright eyes, seeing their pupils dilate.

She was enjoying this game. Like catching prey on a snare.

"A pretty boy like you..." Her eyes roamed over my face, and my breath hitched. Her face drew closer. "I bet you had your choice of the women where you come from?"

She drew a fingertip along my bare forearm, the soft touch almost unbearable. Goosebumps erupted as she went. I took a deep, shaky breath, willing my dragon to stay suppressed, and swallowed hard. I was aware of the deafening silence, of the devilish grins on the men's faces around the tables. I focused on that. I could sense Ant behind me, still as a statue—partly prepared for anything that might happen, but mostly amused by my embarrassment.

"What?" Eli asked, her doe eyes widening innocently, and her warm, sweet breath brushed across my face.

Heat flooded my cheeks at our proximity... and started to spread to other parts of my body. My dragon, who had been churning within, suddenly stilled, curiously waiting and assessing the creature before me as a shiver ran down my spine, causing the hairs on the back of my neck to stand on end. A vision of gripping her thighs as I turned, pinning her underneath me on the table, flashed to the forefront of my brain, and I gritted my teeth to chase the dragon's urges from my mind.

My back stiffened as I heard Ant snort, no doubt sensing the shift in my body language, and I internally cursed myself, adjusting my position on the bench just a fraction. Eli glanced down for a second before looking into my eyes, smirking as she leaned in even further. This close, I could see the freckles that scattered across her nose, and to my surprise, a thin streak of yellow around her green irises.

"Don't tell me you've not even shared a kiss with a fair lady?" Her voice was soft, but loud enough for the quiet room to hear whilst brushing her lip against the shell of my ear. She had raised that damn fingertip and was trailing it over the apple of my cheek.

A small, nervous laugh left my throat as a current, as sharp as electricity, ran through me, all manner of inappropriate thoughts consuming me as my magick churned in my stomach. The crew broke into raucous guffaws.

Ant snorted again, this time into his—my—drink. *Smooth.*

I coughed and shook my head.

"O-of course, I've kissed my fair share of women."

The men only laughed harder as Ant dragged a hand over his face. Eli had a sideways grin on her face as she drew back, removing herself from the bench. I took the opportunity to breathe freely. Evil woman.

My dragon seemed to disagree, seemingly pulling towards her as it purred.

Ant's thoughts brushed my mind. *You're in trouble.*

Didn't I bloody know it? My face felt like it could melt off with embarrassment.

At that moment, a tall, neatly dressed woman entered the tavern and the merriment ceased, my humiliation forgotten as all the guards stood to attention. I focused on taking deep breaths of fresh air and clearing my head of indecent images.

"Eli!" The woman smiled widely and walked over, pulling her swiftly into a hug before holding her at arm's reach. "It's been too long!" Her aqua-blue eyes shone as she looked down on Eli. She had flawless skin, high cheekbones, and pink lips that reminded me of a rosebud.

She looked towards the soldiers, tucking her short, golden hair behind one ear. "At ease, men."

They gave her another cheer and went back to their drinking. I was slightly taken aback. She must have been someone of importance within the guard. And Eli was positively beaming at the woman—an expression which lit up her eyes and spread into every part of her. My breath caught at the difference in her. It was the first time I'd seen her genuinely smile.

"Demetria, it's so good to see you," Eli said, still holding the woman's hands as she led her towards our table. "These are the people I mentioned in my message."

Ant quickly stood and I followed, offering my hand, Eli's eyes following my action.

"Pleasure to meet you; my name is Dracho. My companion here is Antares."

"The pleasure is all mine. I look forward to receiving you all at the castle this evening," Demetria said, shaking my hand.

"The castle?" I asked, eyes shifting between the two women.

"Yes," Demetria told me as if it was obvious, her eyes skipping to Eli, "we'll be dining there together this evening, and that's where you'll be staying."

I looked to Eli in shock, and she held a hand up.

"The misunderstanding is entirely my fault, Demetria. I hadn't explained it to them yet. Demetria here is the Lady of Laugharne."

Ant's face remained as emotionless as ever, but for a split second I stared at her in astonishment. I started to bow at the waist, Ant following suit, but Demetria waved her hand, dismissing the formality as Eli watched us closely.

"Please, there is no need," Demetria said with a smile. "I shall expect you all this evening, and we'll discuss matters then." She swept out the front door. Eli turned to face us and crossed her arms.

"Thanks for the warning," I said gratingly.

She tipped her head to the side and flashed a sly smile. "You're welcome."

8

The castle was situated a stone's throw from the main town. It rested upon a hill between a fork of the river Taf, perfectly protected and only accessible from one side. And from its location, you could see everything: the port, the town square, traders, and anyone approaching from most directions. The castle itself and its walls were the strongest things for miles around, every grey stone differently shaped but carefully put together, as if made by loving hands. It had two robust round towers with domed roofs, ramparts travelling between them, and a great hall in the middle. The wooden drawbridge was lowered over the river that flowed around the castle's front, leading us to a lush green that filled the castle grounds.

As we entered the great hall, my mouth salivated at the multitude of aromas that hit me: fresh river trout baked in clay and roasted pig turning on the spit; tables lined with meat pies, a thick soup which looked to be made from barley, crusty hot breads, and further down the table, kegs of ale—enough to get the whole town drunk. Bas was evidently delighted.

An earthy feast for the heart and soul, I thought as we followed Bas, Vyn and Eli. There were three long wooden tables running the length of the hall, with a top table at the very end where Lady Demetria sat, talking into the ear of a short, dark-haired woman who sat between her and Fabian. She caught sight of us and turned to stand, opening her arms in welcome.

"My friends!" She smiled widely, showing her perfectly white teeth. "Welcome to Laugharne Castle! This is my partner, Adrie." She indicated the woman next to her and took hold of her hand.

Adrie's straight hair was shaved at the sides, the rest pulled over the top of her head and tied at the back. Her ears were pierced with multiple hoops, with another through her eyebrow, and an intricate vine was tattooed into the side of her head. It wasn't the only aspect which drew the eye to her face; upon her cheek was a scar. It was now a thick thread of silver that shone in the light, but had once obviously been a nasty wound.

She gave us a bold look, as if challenging us to make a comment. On what, I wasn't sure.

"Please join us." Demetria held her other hand out to the empty seats at the top table. We took our place, Eli greeting her and Adrie with an embrace, as servers brought us an array of different dishes and tankards of ale.

It wasn't much different to the banquets we used to have back home, which sent a pang of longing through me. I couldn't remember the last time we'd had a feast like this in the palace—not since my mother had died.

The delicious ale warmed my stomach, and as we ate, I listened to everyone exchanging stories—Bas was the loudest of all—and allowed my gaze to roam the hall. Two soldiers in a far corner were arm-wrestling, the company around them laughing and cheering on their champions. Elsewhere, a pretty girl sat on a soldier's knee, the latter whispering in her ear. Throughout the hall there was joyful conversation, and the atmosphere was incredibly relaxing.

A creeping sensation suddenly shot down my spine. A warning from my magick.

I scanned the crowd, finding nothing out of the ordinary until a flash of white caught my eye. A scholar?

The figure was shrouded in shadows, standing in an alcove beside the entrance. His robes were bright white with a gold trim, a matching chain tied around the waist, and the hood pulled up to mask most of his face. The only detail discernible was the stubble that covered the chin. Even with my heightened eyesight, his face was difficult to make out.

He looked like a regular scholar in those robes, though the colour was a little ostentatious. Scholars usually wore differing shades of blue, depending on what order they came from. I'd never seen one in white before. My stomach flipped in apprehension as my magick swirled; though I couldn't see his eyes, I could have sworn they were fixed upon me. I pushed up from the table and stood, intending to make my way over.

"Dracho!"

My head automatically swung around; Demetria was waving me over. I turned, looking back towards the alcove.

It was empty.

What is it? Ant asked. He was frowning.

Did you not feel...? Never mind. Come on. I grabbed a stool to sit opposite Demetria, Eli and Adrie. "Thank you for having us, Lady Demetria."

"Please! It's my pleasure, Dracho. And call me Demer. Gents, you've met Adrie," she said fondly, her thumb gently rubbing Adrie's fingers where their hands were clasped on the table. "She was running errands for me out east near Morcroft when she stumbled upon some... information."

Fabian chuckled and muttered *errands* under his breath, earning himself a middle finger from Adrie's free hand. "You mean she 'eard some drunk gossiping in the pub and brought that to your attention?"

"Yes," Adrie stated.

"No," Demer said at the same time, and pursed her lips. "Anyway —the source doesn't matter. It's all we have to go on at this present moment."

"What was the information?" I asked eagerly, leaning forward.

"The man, some young lad called Derwin, claims to have seen the devastation of Mythbrook first-hand—says he's the only survivor," Demetria said.

I looked at Ant as my heartbeat sped. *If this is true, he's the perfect witness.*

If *being the key word*, Ant stressed.

"What did he see?" I demanded, turning back to Adrie.

Her eyes turned on me, narrowing as she leaned back in her chair, picking up an apple off the table. "He claimed to have seen hulking monsters, and kept mumbling to himself about strings. I couldn't get anything else out of him myself. Bit of a wreck, if you ask me."

Fabian scratched the beard along the edge of his rough jawline. "It's not much to go on."

"It's nothing to go on," Bas snorted into his pint. Vyn rolled his eyes.

"It's all we have after weeks of investigation. He's the only person claiming to have seen an attack." Eli rubbed her forehead, visibly frustrated.

I eyed Adrie curiously. "Did you believe his story?"

She stared at me thoughtfully. "Whether I believe his actual story about monsters and shadows... he said he lost his entire family that night. Something certainly happened that terrified him. Terrified him enough to keep quiet about the whole thing."

The table fell silent.

I tilted my head slightly to Ant. *He must be talking about the wyverns. It's worth checking out.*

His brow was furrowed in thought. *Monsters? Most likely. But what about these strings? We should go to Morcroft and speak to him.*

I agree, but we'd need a guide to ensure we take the quickest path. We can't risk him having moved on.

Ant scowled. *They don't seem confident it's a lead worth following up.*

We need that lead. If we convince them to come with us, we won't waste time following an outdated map.

Hmm, Ant reluctantly agreed.

He turned, lowering his voice as the table talk resumed. "Hey, Bastion. Didn't you say you wanted to try *all* the ales in Ruvalon? I've heard eastern ale is some of the best. Maybe something worth checking out if we can gather the story first-hand at the same time?"

The way Bas' eyes lit up reminded me of when I'd received my first training weapon. "Hey, E! Why don't we just head to Morcroft and speak to him ourselves? We'll interrogate him and see if there's any truth to his story."

Genius.

Naturally, Ant responded smugly.

I noticed that Eli was staring at me, apparently deep in thought as she chewed on a piece of bread. When she caught my eye, she turned the other way. "What do you think, Demer?"

"I agree with Bas. It's the only solid lead we have at the moment."

Bas' mouth fell open. "Wait—you're agreeing with me on something?"

Adrie threw her half-eaten apple down the table at him. "Ugh. If being an idiot was a currency, you'd be king."

"And that would make you all my subjects!" Bas threw his arms out.

"Being subjected to your idiocy is quite enough without the thought of being ruled by you," Vyn said, the corner of his mouth twitching. Bas lowered his thick arms to his lap, pouting.

"You two—what do you think?" Eli asked me and Ant.

The rest of the table went quiet, awaiting our answer. I paused for a moment, surprised to have been included in the decision. Gut instinct told me she knew we would go to Morcroft, no matter what her choice, so I decided to be truthful.

"We'd like to check it out," I told her. "We would go ourselves, but, as you know, we're not familiar with the area, so we'd likely get there faster with your assistance. We're also likely to get answers quicker if we work together."

Eli's lips tightened as she nodded. "That's settled then. We'll head to Morcroft once we're finished here. Now, if you'll excuse me," she got up from the table, "my cup is empty, and there's ale calling my name." She gave me a mocking bow before walking away.

My eyes followed her as I blew a big puff of air out my cheeks. *She's a funny one, that one.*

Laughter erupted around me, making me jump. I had, apparently, spoken out loud. Bas appeared beside me, pulling up an extra stool before smacking a heavy, muscled arm across my shoulders and pulling me in closer.

"That's our E. But don't worry, you'll get to know her. She just likes to keep her cards close to her chest. She may not be showing it well, but she likes you both. It's just—trust is an issue for her."

"Why is—?"

"Ahh." Bas waved his hands in the air, his ale sloshing out of his cup. "Not my story to tell, sorry, brother. I can tell you're a good one, but—you know," he finished sheepishly, offering me his tankard.

"I understand completely," I assured him, clinking my tankard against his.

❧

Morcroft was a few days' journey to the east, so we spent some time preparing for our trip. Ant took up Vyn's offer of a tour of the town, much to my surprise; I guessed it was his way of establishing whether there was any real threat from the djinn. Or perhaps Ant was indulging in some human flirting himself.

Whilst gathering food supplies from the market, I did some exploring on my own. It was a beautiful town, full of stone and whitewashed buildings. Despite how busy it was, folk going constantly about their business, there was peace here. You could hear the slap of the sea waves against the wood pilings, the artisans selling handmade wares from their stalls. In the centre of the busy, cobblestoned town square, an elaborately carved wooden monument of a whale was displayed.

As I scanned the area, my eye was caught by strands of mahogany hair carried upon the breeze from the top of the port wall. Eli was watching the waves as they brushed up against the town walls, chewing her cheek, seemingly deep in thought and oblivious to all around her. My feet had already moved a few feet in her direction of their own accord when I heard my name being called from behind.

"Lady Demetria." I bowed.

Her smile was bright, one that drew you in. "No titles necessary, Dracho, just call me Demer." I nodded, a small smile upon my lips. "So, you come from Eshmnor. Had family in Mythbrook."

It wasn't a question, which meant that Eli had told her. Anger disturbed my peace as I turned to look back in Eli's direction.

"Oh, don't look so indignant. Eli didn't betray your trust—Bastion did."

My neck cricked as I swung back round to Demer, sharply inhaling through my nostrils.

She started laughing. "You should see your face." But her own became serious, as if a mask had slipped into place. "Listen. Bastion did not tell me anything of your story, and it's not something I will pry into. He merely informed me where you are from and why you are here, and that's because *I* insisted. My reason for doing so is

because you travel with Eli... and I will do *anything* to protect her."
She tilted her head, giving me a pointed look. "*Anything*. Do we have
an understanding?"

The dragon within pushed forward slightly, growling faintly as
an instinctual response to the veiled threat. I resisted his urge to
flash a warning to the lady. She was only protecting her friend—and
sometimes the beast within could be... irrational.

Everyone was so protective over this woman. It only made me
more curious.

I swallowed tightly, plastering a smile upon my face. "We do." I
placed my hand over my chest, feeling the steady beat there. "Trust
me; I'll be doing everything in my power to help Eli—so that we can
all find answers."

She raised her chi. "Excellent."

"Out of curiosity, my lady—" Her brow rose. "Uh, Demer. Why
is Eli looking into the attacks?"

The smile fell from her lips, and she glanced away, taking a
moment to answer. "Eli... she may come across as brash, but she
loves people, and people love her. You'll come to find out, Dracho.
Anything that would put those she loves at risk—well, she couldn't
just sit back and let that happen."

I didn't fully comprehend what she said, but I knew that was as
much as I would get from her. I turned to look in Eli's direction, and
found her looking straight back. Demer tapped me on the arm, and
I heard her footsteps retreat. Letting out a small breath, I strolled
up the sloping path to join Eli, who had turned to look back over
the calm waters. We stood together silently for a few moments.

"So, what were you talking to Demer about?"

"Nosy little thing, aren't you?" I teased, turning to face her, my
eyes travelling over the soft curve of the nose. She pursed her lips,
and I grinned as she turned to face me.

"Little?" she asked sharply.

"Well, you are rather short." It wasn't a lie.

I bit my lip to stop myself from laughing, and her eyes followed the action before lifting to mine. They were a fierce emerald fire that blazed right through me.

"You look angry. Shall we put all that energy to good use?" I winked, and the corners of her mouth pulled up—just a little. "Ah, there it is! I knew there was some humour in there, deep down."

She pushed me away, grinning begrudgingly. "But really. What were you talking about?"

I wondered why this concerned her, but for the sake of our journey ahead, it was best to trust each other as much as we could. "I asked her why finding out about these attacks was important to you."

She stiffened.

"Demetria said you care about people and want to protect them."

"That's it?"

I nodded. "Why, is there more?"

She took a deep breath. "When I heard about what happened to Mythbrook, it broke my heart. True, it's only a small town... but all those families." Her heartbeat was steady. She was telling the truth. She clasped her hands together on the wall in front of her, a crease appearing between her brows. "I don't need a reason to save people. If you see something bad happening, and you have the ability to help stop it—the real power to make change—shouldn't you?"

She turned to look at me, her eyes every green hue of the springtime.

A pang of guilt struck me. Here I was trying to protect my kingdom from potential war, should these attacks continue—but aside from the people of Mythbrook, I had never stopped to truly consider those involved. If an average citizen like Eli could go out of her way to help save her fellow people, then it was the least I could do to help. Not just for Tenebris, but for all of Ruvalon.

"Yes," I told her. "You absolutely should."

9

I felt that Eli and I were in a place of mutual understanding following our conversation. We hadn't really spoken since—only small exchanges since leaving Laugharne.

Demetria had met us at the castle's drawbridge to wish us luck the morning we left. "Take care of each other," she had whispered in my ear as she embraced me. I guessed there was a particular person she had in mind. I released her, nodding, and whatever she saw in my face must have satisfied her.

It was the second night we'd set up camp, still another day's walk from Morcroft. After a wide-eyed Vyn had watched a tiring sparring session between me and Ant, something stirred me from my sleep.

I shot up, woken from dreams of golden waves and green pines, feeling like a voice had whispered across my skin, calling my name. Ant still slept soundly, undisturbed. Whatever I'd heard must have been in my sleep, but I stood, stretching whilst I exited the tent. It was early, and the sun was blooming on the horizon. Its golden rays stretched ever outwards, penetrating the richness of the clear sky and igniting the birds into choruses of melodies as warmth caressed the land.

A whimper sounded.

I froze, arms still in the air, listening closely. There it was again—

sobbing. It was coming from Eli's tent. I was surprised that Ant hadn't woken at the sound. I stepped forwards and halted a few paces before the entrance, my hand outstretched.

What was I doing? I couldn't just walk into her tent. *But she's upset...*

My dragon pushed my hand forward, reaching for the canvas. I didn't allow myself time to overthink it, pulling back the tent flap and entering.

She was... asleep? A thin sheen of sweat was visible on her brow as she tossed and turned beneath a thin fur, strands of hair sticking to her face. I stepped in, letting the canvas fall back into place. Eli's breath came in pants as her head slowly turned from side to side. She was muttering quietly, but now and again a loud whimper would escape as her hands balled into fists, clawing at the blanket or the flimsy scrap of fabric she wore.

I knelt beside her, wary but hopeful that I might carefully rouse her from whatever nightmare disturbed her slumber. She gave a sharp cry when I placed my hand on her shoulder and bolted up-right. Her eyes were wide and unfocused. I felt a pressure on my thigh and looked down.

In her white-knuckled hand was her emerald dagger, the tip of it pressed against me. Any sudden movement and my blood would be spilt over the floor. I'd be dead within minutes. How had she managed to move that quickly without me noticing?

I slowly removed my hand from her shoulder.

"Eli?"

She turned her head slowly to look at me, eyes devoid of any emotion.

"It's fine. It was just a bad dream."

She blinked a few times before shaking her head, light returning to her grassy irises.

"Dracho?" Her voice sounded lost.

The shock of how fast she'd moved paled in comparison to the shiver that ran down my spine when she spoke, and I froze for a second, caught up on the fact that it was the first time I'd ever heard her say my name.

"Are you all right? You were—"

"Leave." The word was a quiet whisper.

"What?"

"I said. Get. Out." She stared at me, eyes still blank and cold, the dagger unmoving.

I stood slowly, avoiding the blade, not feeling my feet as I walked backwards to leave the tent. She held perfectly still the entire time; before I closed the tent behind me, I whispered an apology.

As I turned into the fresh air, devoid of her scent of jasmine, I noted Bas walking in our direction. He reeled as he spotted me.

"Is she all right?" There was no hesitation in his voice, as if this was a regular occurrence for him.

"I—I don't know. I heard her...but I don't know if I made it worse.' I sucked in a breath, holding my head in my hands. "Does she always have nightmares?"

His eyes shifted away from mine, uncomfortable. Not his conversation to have. "Not *always*. I'd best go check on her." He gave me a light punch on the shoulder as he walked past.

"Bas, tell her... tell her I'm sorry."

His head tipped. "You were just trying to help. I'm glad you tried. There's nothing to be sorry for, brother."

❧

We left shortly after breakfast—I ate in my tent—and the journey was understandably quiet and awkward. It seemed that Eli was hell-bent on ignoring the situation entirely. I decided to do the same and save embarrassing either of us.

Ant privately asked me what was wrong a few times, but I told him to leave it. Not because I knew he would rage at the fact I'd been close enough for her to hold a dagger to my nether regions, but because it felt like I was betraying her privacy.

Even though they lay further to the east, the air grew warmer as we travelled closer to the Vildspire Dunes: a sandy, vast, and coarse pan of emptiness where every ounce of terrain was covered in barbs or thorns, looking to snare any form of life that dared go near it. It was an erratic contradiction of hot and cold, where once there had been life.

Where Volente had once stood, before the end of the Tain.

Volente, the famous erstwhile home of the mages: a great city within a proud tree that stood so tall it kissed the sky, rivalled only by its sister tree, Aion, where the mages now lived. The people had been, and still were, revered by all as powerful and wise, protecting the balance of energy that flowed through the planet.

Only a small minority had tainted their magick by siding with the elf king, Morven, during the war, and declaring magickal supremacy throughout the land—be it celestral magick or elf magick. Nevertheless, the friction had caused a rift between the mages, brother taking up arms against sister. The battle had raged until the pure magick of the Volente mages collided with the corrupt magick, causing a violent explosion. A vicious and unforgiving blemish now stretched for miles across the land wherever the magickal dispersion had touched.

Thick mud from a nearby riverbed clung to our boots as we entered Morcroft, a human territory that was nearly as old as the continent itself. It was clear from the rundown houses and suspicious glances from the locals that Morcroft had fallen on hard times. The sight made my stomach twist; I wasn't used to seeing people live in such conditions. Eli's face hardened as we walked.

We found the tavern—illegible sign hanging precariously, one of the door hinges broken—and as we entered, the gloom fell over me like a blanket. It seemed mostly abandoned; the few people inside were silent and kept to themselves. Wooden beams supported the old rafters where electric lights hung broken. Candles were lit in their place, dotted around the various surfaces. The walls were utterly void, except for a layer of heavy grime. The bartender was reading a newspaper in a chair behind a small wooden bar and made no attempt to acknowledge our presence.

A few sets of eyes skipped to us as we made our way in, interested in the unusual company; several lingered on Eli for far too long. I was heading to the barkeep when a firm hand grabbed my arm. I didn't need to look to know it was her, but my head shot round to meet Eli's eyes anyway. A spark of primitive anger bolted through me; my dragon infuriated that she would dare touch us after ignoring us all day. I pushed his irrationality out of my mind, focusing on the woman before me.

"What are you doing?" she hissed.

"If anyone is going to know this 'Derwin', it will be him." I shook her off and turned away, walking over to the bar.

The man raised his eyes from his paper, eyeing me suspiciously.

"Fine evening." I flashed him a charming smile. The man didn't respond.

Great start, Ant offered, and I sent him a mental image of my middle finger.

"We're looking for someone, and we were hoping you could be of some assistance?"

The man got to his feet, placing his paper down before putting his hands flat upon the bar. "Depen's on how well you're goin' to *assist* this 'ere establishment."

The surge of anger that travelled along my veins from the beast was a slight overreaction. *Humans with their greed!* I didn't look away, seeing a flash of fear cross the man's face.

Reel it in, Dracho! Are you trying to give him a heart attack? Ant growled into my mind.

Clearing my own, I shook my head.

What is up with you? Ant demanded.

I wanted to know that myself.

Eli came forward, placing a few gold drams, the currency used in the south, in front of him. "Any information would be most appreciated," she said, flashing a bright smile. The barman seemed stunned for a moment, staring at her, but he nodded, sliding the gold pieces off the bar and into his pocket.

"'Ow can I 'elp?"

"We're looking for a man called Derwin."

The barman sneered. "Should've just called out 'is name, this 'ere is practically 'is 'ome." He pointed to a dark corner. "Tha's 'im over there."

We all turned to see a reasonably young man sprawled over a table in the far corner. He looked drunk, drool dripping from the corner of his mouth as he slept. I made to walk over as Bas complained from behind me that he hadn't bought an ale yet, but Eli's hand slapped against my chest as she stepped in front of me.

"Let me take the lead on this one," she said confidently. It wasn't a request.

The breath that left me was only slightly fuelled by irritation, my brain scrambling between annoyance and the current running through my chest at her touch.

"And why's that?" I asked. Bas and Vyn were snickering to each other off to the side.

She smirked. "Just trust me."

"Why should I do that?"

Her eyes narrowed in amusement. "Let's just say it's my feminine charm."

I swallowed, feeling my cheeks heat as I was taken back to that day in the Griffin. "Funny, I've yet to *witness* said charm."

Her grin was knowing.

"Hey, Vyn—do you think these two should just bone and get the tension out the way?" Bas mused.

"Ew. I cannot believe you just said that," Vyn muttered, covering his eyes with his hand. Ant stood beside him, arms crossed impatiently.

Eli looked at Bas with fury in her eyes, then spun on her heel. "Move. And if anyone says anything unnecessarily, I'll cut out your tongue myself."

I followed right on her tail, amused even as my dragon raged at being told what to do. "Got quite the mouth on you, haven't you? Perhaps someone should teach you how to use it."

Fuck's sake, Dracho! Ant fumed.

Eli whirled on me, causing me to back up a step. Her eyes glinted in the dim light. "Oh, I don't need teaching. I've had plenty of experience using it."

"Oh?" I scoffed.

"Yes," she said, her tongue moistening her bottom lip as she leaned in conspiratorially. "Just ask Bastion."

Wait, what?

She flashed me a wink, her hair whipping my face as she turned.

I started after her. "You can't—"

She spun back to me, her fingers reaching up to gently brush her lips. "Oh, and it was..." Her eyes rolled upwards, fluttering as if in the throes of pleasure before snapping down to mine. "So delicious."

I turned slowly, feeling uncomfortable and confused. Bas was frozen in place, a blush rising on his cheeks.

"What?" I blurted out. Since meeting Bas and Eli, there hadn't been any hint of anything more than a friendship between them.

No overly affectionate gestures. They certainly didn't seem like a couple...

"Fucking distractions. I told you. Come on, move!" Ant practically snarled at me as he pressed past Bas, grabbing my arm and pulling me towards the back corner.

Vyn, chewing his bottom lip to suppress a shit-eating grin, nudged Bas forward.

10

Eli sat in the chair directly opposite Derwin and indicated for Bas to wake the sleeping boy as Ant and I settled into the space behind her. Bas, his embarrassment momentarily forgotten, slammed his hand onto the table next to the boy's head, rudely waking him from his slumber.

His head shot up, eyes wide but hazy. His baby face showed how young he was to be addicted to the tavern's poison. His hair was sandy blonde, a shaggy mess atop his head. His clothes bore far too many stains to be anywhere near decent. And from the smell, he hadn't bathed in a while.

Ant's nose wrinkled in disgust. He didn't have time for drunks or addicts. He had seen how it changed a person, how it could take a hold of someone and claim their entire life.

"Hello there." Eli sent the boy a feline grin.

Derwin stared at her for a moment, looking her up and down, before eyeing the rest of us.

"I didn't steal anything." His voice was thick and slurred from sleep, or the drink.

Bas snorted loudly.

Eli shook her head. "We're not here for that." She leaned closer and lowered her voice, bringing her hands together on the table. "I was wondering if you could help me with something?"

The boy's hooded eyes squinted slightly as he subconsciously leaned in, and I smirked to myself. *Feminine charms indeed.*

"I heard that you have been through an awful tragedy recently, Derwin. One I'd very much like to discuss with you."

The boy's face suddenly seemed to age in front of me. His eyes stretched unnaturally wide, mouth opening and closing soundlessly like one of the great golden carp that swam under the Pistyll falls. His heart was thundering in his chest. If the boy didn't calm down, he might pass out.

It seemed Eli had the same idea. She snapped her fingers in front of his face, and his eyes seemed to focus back on her. He shook his head.

"I-I can't help you. I'm sorry." His shoulders slumped, and he buried his face in his hands. "I've done *everything* to try and forget that night."

Getting to her feet and walking around the table, she knelt next to him, placing a hand on his knee. He jumped slightly at the contact.

"Listen." The boy looked at her face, his eyes glassy. "We need that information, Derwin. I understand that it's difficult for you to share. You went through something traumatic." Her eyes dropped. "Something like that has happened to me in the past too."

I froze, my eyes skipping to Bas. He nodded a tiny fraction up and down. Was this the cause of her nightmares?

"But we're here to put an end to these attacks—and we can't do that without *you*, Derwin. You can help us save everyone. You'd be a hero."

I knew she had him by the balls with that. This kid was young, and drinking himself to death in some run-down shack in the middle of nowhere. Offering him the chance for glory, a chance to make a name for himself, must be an opportunity many around these parts were never given.

"I also have something I can gift you... but only if you can give us the information. It will provide you with security, pay and maybe even more."

I had to admit it: she was good. The way she spoke made it appear that all the power of the decision lay with Derwin, but it was obvious who was really in control of the situation. The gift was news to me, though. We hadn't brought anything with us to offer, to my knowledge. What power did Eli carry that she could promise such things?

The boy's eyes shimmered with curiosity. He sat up straighter, running his hands through his greasy hair. "I don't even know where to start," he mumbled nervously.

"Just start with why you were there," Vyn suggested.

Derwin blushed. "I, uh... I was meeting up with a girl—Isa—in the barns."

Bas whistled. Eli glared at him, shaking her head.

"Her, um, parents didn't know about us yet. So she rushed home straight after... she's gone now—anyway—" The boy coughed to clear his throat, and a twinge of sympathy hit me. The girl must have been killed in the attack. "I fell asleep in the corner of the barn and woke up to—to the smell of smoke and the... screaming."

Bas shifted uncomfortably, stuffing his hands into his pockets. Eli stood and sat back in her seat, but she rested her hand atop Derwin's, encouraging him to continue with a light squeeze.

He swallowed thickly. "I-I didn't leave the barn." He looked down at his shoes underneath the table. "I, um, peeked through the doors. People were running into the streets—on *fire*. No one made it very far. They were cut down by—by creatures. They looked like wyverns, but their bodies were... *wrong*. As if they were diseased, deformed. And they moved strangely—as if being controlled. Like a puppet? I know that doesn't make sense." He dropped his head into his hands, frustrated.

What do you think he means? I asked Ant.

I'm not sure... puppets? Does it sound like they might be controlled by magick?

Magick? It was an idea. But if any mages within Ruvalon were causing this, it meant that someone was betraying the balance. Using dark magick.

Hmmm. Perhaps.

"Derwin, did anything happen to provoke the attack? Any strange visitors to the town before it happened?" Eli pressed.

His head shook. "No. It had been a totally normal day. We've had the odd creature venture into the town before, but it's usually something some of the villagers could handle. There were just... so many."

"What kind of wyverns?" Antares asked, earning a scolding look from Eli.

"Um. All sorts. There were hounds, and mountain cats, but...there were worse. Wendigos and some I've never seen before in my entire life."

That's not normal. Ant pointed out.

I agreed. *For so many different wyverns to be in the same proximity of each other—no. It's—*

Unnatural. Ant finished.

Vyn stepped forward, placing a hand on the boy's shoulder. "You're doing so well, mate. I know it must have been terrifying."

The boy's head shot up so quickly that Vyn stepped back. Derwin's eyes were wild. "You don't understand! My family was in one of those houses! I stood by and *watched* as they were all cut down or burned by those—those things! And..." Tears fell steadily now. He seemed shocked by his confession, as if he was finally voicing the dark thoughts that had been living inside his head. "And I did nothing... I didn't have any weapons. I-I was a coward. I stayed there till they left, and when I found everyone dead... I ran as far as I could in the opposite direction." His shoulders sagged at the release of his burden.

I couldn't agree with his assessment of his actions. One of the first things we were taught during our training in Tenebris was how to analyse a situation and choose the best course of action. Sometimes that just meant surviving.

"Derwin."

He didn't move.

Eli reached her hand up, gripping his chin and tilting his head to face her. I watched closely, wondering what she was about to do. "Derwin... you are human. Feeling fear doesn't make you a coward. It's a part of *being* human." He squeezed his eyes shut, as if fighting more tears. "There was nothing that you could have done, and had you run for help, you would have died—we would never have found out what happened to your family. You told their story."

My chest swelled at her words. Derwin's eyes scanned our group, and Bas nodded as I sent him a small smile.

Eli released Derwin's face but continued, "Now... to continue down the route you're going," she motioned to the empty tankards on the following table, "would be to dishonour your family and be a coward in truth. Or, as I mentioned earlier, you could accept my gift of a new life."

He nodded furiously, a glimmer of hope within the depths of his eyes. A chance to escape the current squalor he dwelled in—an opportunity for freedom from his demons. Who wouldn't accept that?

Ant and I knew that offering someone that one chance was all it took to pull someone from the abyss of despair. We shared a knowing glance.

"Very well. Pack your things. You'll leave first thing to head to the Griffin in Laugharne. Ask for Fabian. He's Captain of the Laugharne Guards. There you will find purpose and perhaps family. Not by blood—but chosen nonetheless. This offer has come from Lady Demetria herself. You may recognise her partner, depending on how drunk you were at the time."

Derwin's eyes widened, and he launched himself out of his chair, landing on his knees in front of Eli, gripping her hands between his. As if a queen herself had just knighted him.

"Thank you, my lady."

Vyn guffawed and Bas' mouth twitched, but Ant's forehead had puckered.

What's up? I asked him.

Nothing... just a strange feeling.

"I can't ever repay you for this," Derwin said.

"You have. By telling us the truth. And you can, by serving Lady Demetria well." He nodded, releasing her hand and getting to his feet. "Go and pack; meet us on the outskirts of town to camp for the night. Sober up before you leave in the morning," Eli added pointedly, and his cheeks reddened. He bowed at the waist, sending a quick nod to the rest of us, and made a swift exit.

"Well, that was... interesting," Vyn said, sitting down opposite Eli.

"You're telling me." Bas blew out a puff of air, shaking his head as he walked away.

Eli sat quietly, her lips pursed as she chewed on the inside of her cheek.

"What are you thinking?" Vyn asked her.

She paused, her eyes skipping to Ant. "You." She jutted her chin in his direction. "What do you think?"

I frowned and followed her gaze. Ant had his arms crossed, the sleeves of his shirt rolled up to his elbows as he tipped his head back to observe her.

Clever of her to know I'm the smart one, he drawled. I scoffed, playing it off as a clearing of my throat.

"I have my suspicions. Could be poison—not one I've ever seen, though. Could be magick. But I wouldn't be quick to place blame upon the mages."

"No... it certainly wouldn't be wise." Eli blinked, her eyes returning to the djinn sitting across from her.

Vyn gave a lopsided grin. "Are you thinking what I'm thinking?"

Eli leaned her elbow on the table, scowling as she rested her head upon her open palm.

I looked between them. "What?" I asked as Bas returned, carrying a pint in his hand.

"Well, the best course of action, considering we are way out of our depth, would be to speak to someone with knowledge of magick." She looked to the ceiling, running her tongue along her top teeth before inhaling deeply.

I scoffed again. "And where do you suppose we'd find someone with *that* kind of knowledge without venturing to Aion? Without an invitation, I might add." Since the Tain, only invited guests were granted entrance to the new mage homeland, and those were few and far between. The mages themselves rarely left their home.

"Meridium," Bas stated, taking a sip of the ale and grimacing. "This tastes like shit!" He glared at Ant, whose lips were curling at the edges.

The capital? I thought, looking at Bas quizzically.

He looked at Eli, then said, "Someone lives—teaches—there."

Ant squinted at them both. *There's something more to this.*

I agreed. *Yes. But at the moment... we don't have many options.*

I don't like it. But I follow your lead on this, he conceded.

"So... Meridium?" I asked, clapping my hands together.

Eli looked as if she'd rather come face to face with a huskound, one of the mythological beasts that guarded the entrance of Purdue.

The continent believed that was where unfulfilled souls went after death. A slight shudder ran along my back at the thought.

Eli exhaled roughly, then got to her feet. "We'd better get going then."

Meridium was to the southwest of Morcroft, about a day's journey from our current location. I'd only ever studied its image from tactical maps or seen it in books in the library at home, but from what I remembered, it was huge: the largest city on the continent, besides Tenebris, and historically the seat of Ruvalon's royalty. It was situated strategically beside the Bay of Solva, a body of water that led to the sea; entry into the bay was so narrow, it would be impossible to sail a hostile fleet through. The city itself had never been infiltrated, thanks to high walls and a large standing army. It was currently the home of King Cervidae, and my stomach twisted at the thought of being so close to danger. Any slip-up wouldn't just expose me, but Ant too. We risked revealing Tenebris' biggest secret just by going there.

We spent the rest of the evening camped outside Morcroft with Derwin. He was much more open to conversation now that he'd sobered up. I could sense that he was a good lad—just young, and he'd been through a trauma. I guessed he'd been starved of good company for too long. He chattered, involving himself in every conversation he could in a way that said he was desperate for connection.

His mood did dip for a short time when he asked us what we would do with the information he'd provided us with.

"Well, we now think there may be some outside influence going on. We just need to figure out where it's coming from," Eli told him, tension in her eyes.

A silence fell over the group, and I watched them with confusion.

Bas was the one to break it, throwing his arms up. "Come on, E, do we *really* think Tenebris would bother to do something like this?"

Dread blossomed in the pit of my stomach, though Bas was looking at her as though the thought was ludicrous—which it was. Ant was utterly still, his hand hovering close to his sheathed weapon. His golden eyes met mine, holding the promise of protection, should the need arise. I shook my head minutely.

"It's the land of *dragons*! If they wanted to destroy Ruvalon or start a war, they could simply fly over the mountains and do so," Bas continued. A sliver of anger jolted through me.

"Maybe that's it," murmured Vyn.

"That's what?" Eli asked.

"Mythbrook lies just under the shadow of the mountains. Besides the random attacks on travellers, Mythbrook is the first village to be completely decimated. Perhaps the creatures *came* from the Ballaaran Mountains."

Another silence.

They were wrong. High above the treacherous mountains, protected by magick, only draconi could fly. And no evidence had been found of any within the mountains. No attacks had taken place within Tenebris itself...

"You know," I chimed in, "legend says that an ancient dragon chose to lie across the entire continent, burying herself deep within the earth to form those mountains."

White-hot rage slammed into me from my left; I focused hard on ignoring the spiel of curses and threats streaming into my mind. I looked anywhere but at Ant, worried that if I did, I wouldn't be able to keep a sly grin from my face. That would surely tip him over the edge.

Vyn stared at me, confused. "How is that something you know? And why is that relevant?"

Clearing my throat didn't help; my voice hitched. "I like to read.

I thought that was common knowledge?" I winced internally as they shook their heads. I knew full well it wasn't. "And as for your second question, those mountains are too dangerous for anything to survive on them. No land wyverns, anyway."

"Well, that rules that *brilliant* idea out." Sarcasm dripped from Bas' tone.

"I never believed those rumours anyway," Eli commented.

I felt some relief at that, but made a mental note to find out what exactly the rumours were. Her eye caught mine, and I nodded towards Derwin, who had been quiet during the whole exchange as if musing to himself. She pressed her lips tightly together, as if suddenly remembering he was there.

"So, Derwin," she said with a warm smile, leaning forward. His eyes snapped to hers, apparently surprised she was talking to him. "Would you like to hear more about Laugharne?"

His answering smile made him look his age.

The conversation branched out, everyone doing their own thing, and for a moment all seemed good. I stared into the golden flames of the campfire lighting each face; contented smiles, warm food and stories were shared. Even Ant, despite his suspicions, sat comfortably conversing with Bas and Vyn about his favourite card game, papst. Eli sat cross-legged beside the fire, speaking animatedly to Derwin about Demetria and the Laugharne Guards. He watched her in awe. The glow of the flames danced across her tanned skin, drawing attention to the light which had now returned to her eyes—a light which had been missing since the night before.

As if she felt my gaze, our eyes suddenly connected.

Something in me felt fixed and broken at the same time. The beast within shuddered and whispered a warning as her eyes held me there, my heart racing. I swallowed hard, a slight vibration moving though my body. It had been days since my last transformation. I was used to transforming almost every day, and my dragon was feeling the effects of that. There was no physical need to, but it took an emotional toll. The longer I went without transforming, the harder it would be to control his urges.

Derwin said something to Eli and she broke the connection, turning away to answer him. I breathed deeply, clearing my head.

What was that? Ant asked icily.

I have no idea what you're talking about.

No? he said, projecting a fuzzy image of Eli and me looking like we were in the middle of an intense staring contest. *Don't think I can't see you making googly eyes at each other.*

Googly... eyes?

He rolled his eyes. *You know what I mean. It's a complication we don't need.*

A muscle twitched in my cheek as I turned my head, returning my gaze to the fire. *That 'it' has a name.*

Ant was quiet for a moment.

I don't like this, he finally said.

Like what? I asked, my shoulders stiffening as I focused my attention on the ground.

Heading to Meridium. It's too much of a risk.

I caught his eye for a second. *It is a risk, but if we're going to find any valuable information, it's going to be in the biggest city on the continent. Besides, it's not like we're going to stroll up to the king's doorstep and announce our arrival.*

Ant's jaw clenched, but he didn't respond.

As I settled into my tent that night, sleep seemed to evade me. All my senses were on alert for the slightest sound. But nothing was so much as whispered.

II

When morning came, our farewell to Derwin was short; his spirits had lifted, and he was very much looking forward to his journey
to Laugharne. He left with the sun rising, and we began our journey
not long afterwards to make the most of the day.

The forest grew thinner as we walked further away from the
town; firmer ground gave way to moist soil full of tall reeds. Land
that had once been a marsh. In the warmth of the sun, dragonflies
danced playfully, brushing the tops of the grass.

I increased my pace to catch up to Eli, who was leading our party
alone. "So, Eli, is it nice to be going home?"

She tensed, and it took her a moment to relax. "It'll be nice to
see the people again. I haven't seen them in a long time." She smiled,
but there was a helpless look in her eyes.

It didn't elude me that her answer avoided my question, and it
made me wonder if the cause of her nightmares was in Meridium.
Ant was also paying attention; he sent me an image of Vyn and Bas'
shared glance.

I put it aside for now. "Tell me about them."

"The people?"

"Yes. What can I expect from the people of Meridium?"

She squinted at me, but then looked away as her face brightened, clearly taken back to memories of carefree and happy times. Times that made her forget whatever bad thing had happened.

"They're a proud people, and most are loyal to a fault," she started. "The Tain was tough on the kingdom. There were a lot of orphaned children after that... I used to spend a lot of time with them on the streets. We soon formed our own little gang."

I could see it now. "Used to terrorise the elders of the city, did you?"

She laughed. The sound was pleasant, like the soft tap of rain on a window. "Something like that. It was an escape."

I frowned at that, my dragon encouraging me to ask further, but I didn't want to pry.

"Anyway, I grew up with those children. They became my adopted brothers and sisters." She turned to look at Vyn, who flashed her a wicked smile. And then her expression turned full of sorrow. "I had a real brother once."

I processed that. "Really?"

She nodded. A few moments passed in silence.

"His name was Morgwn," she told me. "He was older than me by a few years. We were quite close."

It was an unusual name for this continent, but I didn't comment on it. "How... did he pass away?"

"The Tain. He went with my mother and father to battle."

"Your mother fought in battle?" I asked thoughtlessly. From my schooling, I had gained the impression that southern women were quite... subservient. But then again, most of our teachings dated back to Morven's time. No one ventured out of Tenebris to the human realm anymore, so it was understandable that things would have changed. Besides, the women I had met along the way so far had proven our texts to be incredibly incorrect. Maybe the rest of the continent was more like Tenebris than we'd always thought.

Eli's eyes were wide as they regarded me. "Yes, my mother was incredibly fearsome. There would have been no stopping her from joining the fight."

"She must be an amazing warrior."

"She was," she said carefully. "I lost her during the same battle as my brother."

I watched her silently, my heart clenching for the huge loss she had suffered.

She turned her head to give me a questioning look and caught me staring. My mouth flapped open and shut a couple of times whilst my brain caught up, and an amused look crossed her features.

"What?" she asked.

I huffed out, "You... you just kind of amaze me."

A pink tinge spread over the apple of her cheeks. "Shut the fuck up." She turned and started to walk off.

I chuckled and caught up. "I mean it. You've been through a tremendous amount, and I'm amazed by how strong you are. You'd be surprised at how many people allow trauma to eat away at them. They become the very thing that tried to destroy them in the first place."

"You sound like you know from experience."

I gritted my teeth. "I'm quite lucky... I can't say I've been through such a *large* amount of trauma as you. But I did—I mean... I lost my mother just after the Tain."

"I'm sorry. Trauma is trauma. No one's is more important than another's."

I waved it off. "My mother was sick. We... we knew it was coming, you know. But what I meant was—Ant and I, we both know from a mutual friend who's had to suffer through it." My mind flashed back to memories of carrying someone home who had drunk far too much, had suffered too much.

Eli nodded. "You can't ever undo the trauma that's been done... only try to overcome and adapt to it."

I smiled at her. "Exactly."

&

We reached the outskirts of Meridium in the late afternoon, and Bas full-on belly-laughed at my reaction coming over the hill.

I was simply stunned. I had never thought I would see a city as beautiful as Tenebris in my lifetime, but Meridium *almost* rivalled it. It was breath-taking—a city of light, all pale grey walls and sparkling blue waters.

The high outer rise of the city reached all the way around in a perfect circle, with a smaller inner ring further inside. There were intermittent gates now and then, which Eli explained separated the different areas of the city. The residential sections were situated next to each other, then there was the trading district, the soldiers' training grounds, and finally the palace grounds. Outside the walls were large stables and a training corral for the horses.

We headed for the western entrance, which was exclusively for trade and connected to the Silent Road: the main highway which travelled directly from Meridium along the continent to the other kingdom of Stillmere. From what I could see, gates segmented the city like an orange, with small canals running to a magnificent light grey castle which glowed in the light of the late summer's day. The front of the building had an enormous green stained-glass window, depicting a stag's head; multiple spires rose upwards, reaching into that stretching blue, like a proud temple of old.

As Eli led us around to the western gate, the sounds of traders and travellers grew louder. I spotted a circular area halfway into the segment where a statue stood; from my vantage point, it looked like a deity of some sort.

The closer we got, our pace slowing amidst the crowd waiting to enter, the more nervous Eli became. Her fingers tapped a haphazard rhythm against her leg as she chewed the inside of her cheek. Nerves tickled along my spine as an idea struck—possibly a stupid one. Loosing a breath, I scratched the back of my neck and then grabbed her hand softly.

Immediately, as if she'd been burned, she yanked it free, shooting me a glare.

I sighed and caught her eye. "Hey. It's going to be all right." I held my hand out again in offering.

Her eyes widened and then softened, understanding. She placed her hand in mine, accepting the comfort I offered. My dragon purred.

What. Are. You. Doing? Ant's voice was like ice.

There it was. *Chill out, bro. I'm just helping her relax.* I rolled my eyes.

Did you just call me 'bro'?

I smirked, knowing that would piss him off more. *We need her. If she's freaking out, she isn't going to be much help. It's my duty to do everything I can.*

Uh-huh. Just focus on the mission, Dracho.

That's precisely what I'm doing, I bit back, annoyed he would even suggest otherwise, though a trickle of guilt settled in my stomach.

Sure you are.

We joined the busy road.

"Hey, why's it called the Silent Road anyway?" I asked the group.

"It was renamed after the Tain," Bas said. 'During the war, it was so empty—so quiet..."

"Well, that's not morbid at all." Ant caught up to me as he grumbled under his breath, earning himself a laugh from the company.

I clapped him on the back with my free hand. "Who knew you could be funny?"

"I don't know—he always has funny things to say about you." Vyn clicked his tongue at me as he passed.

I frowned, looking between them. "Traitor."

Ant threw me a foul gesture without so much as a glance back.

The large wooden gates set into the stone walls were open with a guard stationed to either side, wearing the Meridium colours of green and silver, the city's emblem stitched ostentatiously into their uniform. As we approached, it took everything within me to keep the astonishment from my face. I had never seen such a diverse crowd in person before. Aside from the humans who were most common in Ruvalon, I saw pixies, gryphons and trolls. They shuffled forward, talking amongst themselves, the sounds of laughter and creatures' calls reaching my ears. We drifted near a couple of trolls—traders—their conversation floating over to us.

"Yeah, disgusting, it was. Bleeding all o'er the place 'e was. Said someone attacked 'im. Poor lad was just holding on when we got to 'im," one grunted.

"Never! Round these parts?" the smaller companion, his face covered in warts, gasped.

The troll nodded, pulling the strap of his bag higher onto his shoulder. "Only a young'un. Alone, too. Delirious when we saw 'im. Tried getting up, said 'e 'ad to get to Laugharne. Well, the poor lad didn't realise 'ow bad 'is injuries were. Only 'ad moments left when we found 'im."

Eli's grip on my hand was a vice. Vyn and Ant moved closer, Bas' mouth dropping open. I released my senses so that I could monitor the man's heartbeat, searching for the truth to his statements.

It couldn't be him.

"Laugharne? Bit of a trek on your own."

"Yeah. 'E said something weirder, though."

"What was that, Rolf?"

"Said 'e was from Mythbrook... Well, you know what happened there. No survivors." The troll sniffled, his too-large eyes lowering. "I asked if 'e had any last words. Poor lad—name was Darwin or

Derwin, if I 'member correctly. Just said to tell the nice lady 'e did his best."

12

My stomach twisted.

A choked sound made its way out of Eli's mouth. I threw my free arm out, my other hand losing sensation under Eli's grasp as I clenched the troll's shirt between my fingers.

"Excuse me, sir... Rolf, is it?"

He nodded, alarm written all over his face. His companion looked at me in outrage, his snout flaring.

"Where did you find this boy?"

"L-less than 'alf a day's ride, due northwest from 'ere. You can't miss it. It's a couple miles from Miss Margerie's stead. Caused a 'uge fuss, it did."

I thanked him, releasing him from my hold. Rolf hurried off with his companion, clearly slightly shaken by the exchange.

My gaze found Vyn. "Miss Margerie?"

"One of the farms that supply crops to the city. I'll go," he said.

"Antares. You'll go too," I commanded.

"What?" Ant rounded on me as I felt Eli's grip relax.

"Derwin was our only source of information on these attacks! And now he's been attacked."

"Possibly."

"You'll go." I was in no mood to be challenged. *Plus, I know you'll bring me the truth of any other information found.*

His jaw clenched, but he nodded in agreement. He turned, pushing back through the crowd with Vyn.

An assassination on our only point of contact to these seemingly random attacks could only mean one thing: they weren't random; they were coordinated. Someone was doing this intentionally, and Derwin had scuppered their plans by surviving.

But did they know he had informed us of that night's events? Did that now make us a target? In which case, there was no real danger to Ant and me—but...

I turned, suddenly realising my hand was free of Eli's. I found her on the grassy bank to the left of us, under cover of some trees, Bas rubbing her back as her chest heaved up and down.

I rushed over, kneeling to place my hand gently on her shoulder. Her knees were brought up to her chest, hands clasped to her neck as she curled up as tightly as she could.

"What's wrong with her?" I demanded of Bas.

"Panic attack. She used to get them when we were younger. But she hasn't had one in years." Sincere concern softened his face.

"It-t's all-all my f-fault," Eli stuttered out through laboured breaths, her eyes clenched shut.

Her words were like a slap to the face. She blamed herself for Derwin's possible demise; she was the one who'd offered him a place in Laugharne.

I scanned her face, blowing out a breath, then took hold of her hands, pulling them away from her chest, which proved difficult. Bas fired me a look, moving to stop me.

"It's all right," I assured him. He seemed sceptical, but desperate enough to try anything as he looked between Eli and me. "I promise it'll be fine."

He dropped his hand, moving back to give us space.

I held her hands firmly, pulling them away from her body as she muttered words under her breath, fast and sharp. "Eli. You're having a panic attack. I know it's tough, but I want you to focus on the sound of my voice."

Her hands tightened on mine as if in recognition.

"That's it. We're going to get through this together." I started to release her hands, but her breathing picked up as if my hold on her was the only thing keeping her grounded. "Hey, hey, hey!" I grabbed her hands and placed them on the sides of my face. Her eyes shot open to meet mine.

"That's it. Focus on that. What you can touch," I told her, tapping her soft fingers on my face. They curled against my cheeks, sending that familiar current under my skin. "Now, I want you to keep your head still but look around, take deep breaths, and find *two* different things that you can see. Can you do that for me?"

She blinked in confusion a few times before nodding. I didn't take my eyes off her as she took a deep breath, her eyes darting to our surroundings before returning to me.

"Um, t-the guards standing at the—the main gate. The flag flying from the rise."

"Good. Now tell me three things you can hear."

Her brows creased in confusion for a moment before relaxing in concentration. Her eyes unfocused. Her breathing was starting to go back to normal, and the tension had mostly left her body. Her fingers were relaxed against my cheeks, her palms now lying flat.

"Um..." Her tongue darted out to lick the dryness from her lips, her voice hoarse. "I c-can hear the sound of the horses' hooves, traders chatting on their way into the city... and the thorntails singing in the trees."

I smiled. "Birds, huh?"

"What?"

"Well, honestly, I would have pipped you for a horse girl." Her eyes narrowed. "You know—strength, beauty, and grace, but you can use them to trample all over someone if you need to?" I laughed as she tried to move a hand to smack my face, holding it firmly where it was, a grin fighting to break out. "How are you feeling?"

Realisation hit her, and I allowed her hands to fall away as she pulled them back, resting them in her lap.

"You don't have anything to feel shame about, Eli," I told her seriously.

"He's right, E," Bas chimed in. Eli jumped as if she had only just realised he was kneeling off to the side, her mouth setting in a hard line.

"It wasn't anyone's fault," I said softly. "And I'll share my reasoning on why I think so later. For now, I care about *you*. Are you feeling better?"

She nodded, her eyes drifting to the ground. "How... how did you know what to do?"

I hesitated. "My friend back home, Althea. She used to suffer from attacks just like that."

She said nothing, but her eyes lifted, thoughts swimming about in her spring-green irises.

"Can you get up?" I asked. She gave me a small smile, and I reached out, helping her to her feet. "Do you want to take some time, or join the road again?"

"I'm fine. Let's just get into the city."

I nodded, taking a deep breath.

A sudden unease settled over me, and I looked around as Bas gave Eli his flask to drink from. Scanning the busy crowd heading towards the gate, I felt a familiar creeping sensation across my spine, and my eyes shot towards the hulking gates. A flash of white robes —the same ones I had seen in the castle hall back in Laugharne— caught my eye.

My hands clenched at my side. This was no coincidence, and I trusted my magick.

I was taking a step forward when Bas pulled me into a quick one-armed embrace, thanking me.

"No worries," I muttered quickly, but when I looked back, the mysterious figure had disappeared from the gates. My dragon growled in frustration at losing him again. Was he a figment of my imagination?

I offered my hand to Eli again as we re-joined the crowd, and she surprised me by accepting it. It got a bit close for comfort as everyone pushed together to get through the gate, traders showing any documentation they needed. Eli ducked her head as if trying to hide her face, and I pulled her closer.

"All good?"

She nodded, her eyes tight.

As we were passing, I noticed a guard glance over us and then double-take, his eyes scanning over me and then roaming lower to the petite woman at my side. He pulled down a cord from the wall next to him and held a strange cone-shaped metal device to his mouth, speaking into it, then bringing it to his ear. A communication method?

I leaned down, speaking closely into Eli's ear. "I'm not sure if I'm being paranoid... but it looks as if our arrival has garnered some attention," I told her, nodding to the guard.

As Eli looked in his direction, the guard froze, his eyes widening. I definitely wasn't wrong.

She groaned loudly. "You're not being paranoid. Come on!" She tugged on my hand, pulling me further into the crowds as she pushed Bas forward.

"What's going on?" I called, hearing the guard shout after us.

"I'd rather make my own way there instead of having an escort."

Confusion and suspicion filled me, but all I said was, "All right..."

The pathway from the main gate to the inner wall was a narrower tunnel for a few hundred yards. I could make out where it opened into the main street, and I surged forward, pulling Eli behind me, then glancing over and catching sight of Bas' head not far ahead. We squeezed past a trader's cart, hiding from another set of guards, and were finally in the city.

The streets were immaculately clean. I had the distinct sensation that it would be easy to get lost in this city—but that the people who lived here knew every inch of it. To either side of me was a row of shops, two levels high. They were beautiful structures of stone and glass with a balcony on each building, fauna growing from every single one.

People, human and fairie folk alike, stood on many of the balconies, dealing wares. Some leaned over the railing to catch a better look once they spotted us, whispering as we walked along the street.

"She's back!"

"Bless my soul!"

"It's her!"

The words reached my sensitive ears as we moved through a large, sunny courtyard. Some people would double-take, as if they couldn't believe their eyes. Others would run up to our group to greet Bas as a friend or tenderly touch a hand of Eli's before walking away. They seemed to treat her like the very ground she walked on was spun from gold. An elderly woman emerged from the front door of a nearby shop and saw Eli, falling to her knees as she started sobbing like a newborn. Eli went straight to her, comforting her like a close friend, stroking her hair.

I couldn't help watching, thoughts full of curiosity and confusion. More and more stopped and reached for her, touching her arms as she passed, hugging her or speaking soft words. A wide smile graced her features as she spoke to every one of them, but the slight flush to her cheeks revealed her discomfort. The event at the gate seemed to be forgotten.

Bas spoke from my side. "The people of the city love her. The streets were our playground when we were kids—she mother-henned practically every kid our age. Took them all into her little group." He smiled to himself, lost in his memories. "That old woman—a few years ago, her son was gravely injured at one of the gates... Eli gave him mercy."

My insides suddenly felt empty. That was no easy decision to make. *May the stars shine upon him.*

"It was Eli's suggestion to implement the gates. To segment the city, with different purposes for the entrances into Meridium. The residential sections are together, meaning that the people can travel between them easily enough. It also limits the risks of what comes into the city at which gate. Or what could happen at them."

My eyes narrowed. "And how did she have the resources to do that?"

"Well, what do we have here?" A gravelly voice interrupted from across the courtyard.

A man with muddy brown hair, rather displeasing to look at, sat outside a popular-looking tavern—The Grey Fallow—his feet resting upon a table. He pushed himself up to approach Eli. I noticed her shoulders square, an impatient breath leaving her lips as she craned her neck to look up at the man.

"Leander."

He flashed a broad smile, showing several missing teeth. Judging by the mediocre armour he was wearing, the coin purse and weapon at his side, he was a mercenary.

"Surprised to see you back here so soon," he announced smugly.

"Thought you'd run off to find fame and fortune after your father *forbade* you from joining the hunt."

I saw the quick tensing of her jaw and flash of fire settle into her eyes before she plastered on a smile I could tell was disingenuous. "Oh, no need to seek my fame or fortune, Leander." She leaned in closer with a mock whisper. "People already know my name."

Bas guffawed, and several other patrons laughed along.

The smile dropped, a dark shadow falling across the mercenary's face. "You know, Princess, King Cervidae has placed a very handsome bounty upon your safe return."

"Princess?" The word left my lips before I could stop it. I swung round to Bas, ignoring the situation developing in front of us. Dread was seeping into the very marrow of my bones as I waited for his answer.

Bas winced.

This—*this* was the secret that they'd been hiding. The information that Ant and I had known they were keeping from us. Princess. Cervidae. King Cervidae of Meridium.

He nodded apologetically. "Eli avoided going by her family name whilst we were away—too much notoriety." He shrugged as if it was no big deal. But to them, it wasn't.

"You don't say." I didn't bother to hide my sarcasm. "So we were always headed towards—?"

"The palace." Bas nodded, and my heart dropped into my stomach.

The princess. The future queen. And, possibly, my enemy. Should my identity be revealed—and it be revealed that I was breaking the treaty—it would be her father who would enforce punishment. My chest tightened as the gravity of it settled into the pit of my stomach.

If we had believed that we were the wolves dressed as sheep, sneaking through the flock... we had unknowingly walked right into the den of a rival pack.

"Maybe I'll drag you before your father—find the cause of these attacks myself—and claim the reward?"

I snapped out of my daze. The mercenary had stepped forward and taken a grip on Eli's arm just above her elbow.

She gazed at his hand intently for a moment, her eyes glazing over—going somewhere else—before returning to Leander's face. My dragon, which seemingly didn't care about the reveal of her identity, snarled as he tried to take control of my body to step forward, but a hand stopped me, pulling me back. I looked to Bas for an explanation.

"Just watch, brother. His first mistake was outing her name before she could tell you herself."

Eli opened her doe eyes wide, sending the man a seductive smile and tilting her head. It seemed to stun the man for a moment, but the subtle flex of her fingers at her thigh didn't escape my notice.

At almost inhuman speed, her free palm shifted upwards, striking Leander's face, smashing into his nose. Blood spurted outwards, tiny droplets splashing onto her cheek. A cruel but satisfied smirk graced her lips; the crowd gathered around us let out various noises of shock or amusement, and a muffled but agonised howl left the mercenary's mouth as he covered his face with his hand.

But Eli's flexing fingers had already unsheathed her emerald dagger from its place on her thigh. As she stepped back to shatter the brute's nose, her other hand flew up in a graceful arc to slice through tendon and hard bone.

And remove the hand that had grabbed her.

Bas scratched the side of his head. "His second mistake was touching her."

The hand that had *dared* to touch her without her permission.

How could this human move at such speeds? It amazed me how

outdated my schooling about the South had been. Everything I had learned said it was highly unusual for a woman, let alone a princess, to be trained in the ways of a soldier.

Bas chuckled. I gave a strained laugh, making a mental note never to piss her off—more than I already had. Even if a small thrill shot through me at the idea.

The mercenary fell to the floor, clasping his now handless arm. He screamed in inconsolable pain as blood soaked his shirt and the ground below him. Eli walked calmly to him, crouching and lifting his chin with her blood-soaked dagger. The hate in his eyes was palpable.

It only made Eli smile wider, her teeth flashing unnervingly. "Don't let me find you in Meridium again, Leander. Next time I'll take an appendage you value much more than a hand."

He blanched, eyes flashing with fear, his breath coming out in pants through his clenched teeth.

She wiped her blade in his shirt before getting to her feet, stepping over him and turning to face us. "Well, are you coming?"

Bas' mouth twisted in amusement as he shook his head and joined her. I followed his lead as we pushed through the town square, continuing on our way to the palace.

"So... is this a regular thing?" I asked him.

Bas laughed. "I told you, a morning without bloodshed is a *glorious* day."

13

I was pretty sure I was in shock.

It had been a rather stressful morning. Derwin, Eli's panic attack, and finding out her true identity... my head had started to ache. Now I kept switching between guilt and pure rage. On the one hand, I was fuming that she—that *all* of them—had hidden her identity from us, when it could affect my home.

But then, I couldn't tell them that. We were hiding our identities too, and for the same reasons—I thought.

My head whirling, I kept quiet as we made our way to the palace. Oh, by the stars. The palace. I was going to meet her father: King Cervidae. It took everything in me not to hyperventilate or come up with some excuse not to keep walking. If Ant were here, he'd be blowing smoke about now. But he was out of range of my ability to communicate with him, so he must have been a few hours away at least from our location. The distance for our ability to mind-speak varied; those closer in bond were able to do so at greater distances. Ant and I could maintain contact for a couple miles or so, which was higher than the average draconi. I wished I could speak to him now.

We had reached the statue I had noticed from outside the city. It wasn't a deity; it was a woman, and the most beautifully crafted statue I had ever seen. It was as tall as five fully grown men and carved out of pure white marble. She stood on a plinth in a flowing long-sleeved gown, one hand gracefully outstretched as if offering it to the person standing beneath her. An intricately carved veil covered her face; even made of stone, you would almost swear that a breeze could shift it off her face. Her features were still distinguishable, a peaceful look in her large eyes and a sharp cupid's bow to her upper lip as a small smile played upon her face.

Eli stepped forward, placing one hand upon the foot of the statue and her other upon her chest.

"Who is she?" I asked, turning to Bas.

"Don't you see?" he replied, quiet.

I turned away, looking back to the stone face. I studied it further, squinting up at the alluring eyes, sharp at the corners—noticing the delicate shape of the nose and cheekbones. And the neat plaits arranged around her head, covering the tops of her ears.

"Hello, Mammy," Eli whispered.

"Princess Eliana," a stiff voice interrupted from the other side of the statue. I peered around curiously whilst my companions huffed in obvious annoyance, Eli throwing her head back, her dark locks falling from her shoulders.

"Eliana?" The last syllable rolled smoothly from my mouth. "So *that's* what Eli is short for." She shot me a look as she stormed past me. "What? I like it."

The royal guard stood to attention, staring straight ahead once Eli came into view. He wore full Meridium colours with a deep green cape draped over one shoulder. The captain of the guard.

"At ease, Connaught," Eli said, a hint of sarcasm in her tone as she pulled up just a few feet in front of him. The height difference between was almost laughable, especially as she ordered him about.

"I shall escort you to the palace, Your Highness." I could see the softness in his eyes as he looked down upon her, and could hear it in the tone of his deep voice. The dragon within stilled, watching the exchange with interest.

"Did my father send you, Connaught? A bounty for my return—*really*?"

"Come now, Eliana—"

She scowled.

He said nothing but gave her a pointed look in response, which caused her to huff again. She turned to us, her gaze lingering on me for a second. "This is Dracho. He and his companion, who will be arriving with Vyn shortly, are our *guests* and to be treated as such."

Connaught's brown eyes travelled to where I stood, considering, before snapping back to Eli. He bowed his head, pulling a handkerchief from his pocket to hold out before her. "Of course, Your Highness."

Eli tutted, snatching the fabric and pushing past him to storm down the path towards the palace. "Enough of that 'Your Highness' shit, Connaught, before I throw up." She wiped the specks of Leander's blood from her cheek.

The captain's head lowered as he smiled to himself, before Bas strolled past me, chuckling; he and the captain clasped hands, pulling each other in for a one-armed embrace.

"Nice to see you, brother. It's been too long!" Bas clapped Connaught on the back.

"Well, if you hadn't taken her and run off, it wouldn't have been such a while." The words were light, but a glimmer of rage lingered in his eyes.

"Hey! Do you really think it was *my* idea?"

Connaught sighed. "No. I know her well enough to know she likely dragged you both into it. Still, I'm glad you were with her. So...who's the new guy?"

Bas smiled in my direction. "This here is Dracho. He's on the same mission as us. Been a huge help—even saved my arse. Manages to challenge Eli too."

"Really?" Connaught asked, one brow raised and curiosity burning in his gaze.

I had no idea what that meant, but I shot him a close-lipped smile. "So," I started, looking around, "are there other guards for the escort?"

He grinned as if I was missing a joke. "No more are needed."

"Oh."

Bas shook his head, wrapping his trunk-sized arm around my shoulders and dragging me forward. "Come on, kid, let's go show you the palace!"

Everything in the central courtyard before the palace was so open, so light. Golden elm trees lined the pathway, which branched off to various water fountains, each with a differing statue atop them. I couldn't help but stare, in awe of the beauty as we walked past.

"Your father has arranged for you to meet him in his study," Connaught informed Eli as we made our way up the steps.

"Us," she corrected him.

"Excuse me?"

"My father will meet with *us* in his study."

"I'm afraid that—"

"Listen, Connaught." Eli stopped halfway up the staircase, holding a hand in the air, and caused us to awkwardly stumble to a halt behind her. "I haven't seen my father for nearly two years."

Holy shit. Two years? I couldn't imagine it. I'd never even been away from home before now.

"We've returned for a specific reason. Otherwise, I wouldn't be here at all." Connaught's eyes hardened at that. "Now," Eli's hands found her hips, "my companions have been incredibly instrumental in helping me gather information. I will *only* provide this information on the basis that they are present when I give it. Understood?"

I watched, thoroughly amused, as several emotions flickered through the red-headed guard's eyes. A muscle twitched in his jaw before his shoulders sagged in defeat. "Fine, Eliana."

"That's more like it." She grinned, tapping him lightly on the arm before heading back up the stairs.

"Keeps you on your toes, doesn't she?" I mused. Bas guffawed as the guard looked at me, pained.

"You have no idea."

"You'll have to ask him about that time with the gullfaxi, Dracho," Bas said.

What? Gullfaxi were incredibly rare; considered the lords of all horses, having mastered land and sea, they were equally fast and strong, and hardly ever seen by humans.

Connaught groaned. "Sweet goddess, save me that embarrassment for some other day, please. For now, I'll just say it involves Eliana—of course, the harbour, and a moonlight swim I didn't think I'd be having."

I grinned. "Now, this I need to hear."

"Another time, over a drink—or three." Connaught climbed the steps to the palace doors, where Eli was waiting. He held his hand out, indicating that we should follow.

A sense of trepidation settled within me the closer I got towards those tall doors. As soon as I stepped foot within the palace, there would be no turning back. If I was found out as a draconi, I'd be arrested for treason—for breaking the treaty that had been in place since the Tain. If they discovered who my father was, it could start a war. But if I didn't continue... it would mean we might never find the answers to what was happening in Ruvalon.

Steely resolve strengthened me as I made a silent promise not to expose myself. My father would have been furious if he'd known this was happening, but it was worth the risk to protect Tenebris.

As future emperor, I truly believed that putting myself in danger was outweighed by the greater good.

I drew a shallow breath. Though I hadn't had a plan for our journey, I had known we'd probably interact with mortals... but I had never expected Eli.

I couldn't even think about going our separate ways. And I wasn't sure if that would be my downfall.

❧

"The king will be along shortly. He has just been notified of your arrival," Connaught informed us as he opened the double doors of a simply decorated study. A large oak desk sat towards the back; a decanter filled with amber liquid resting upon it accompanied by a single glass.

"Thank you, Connaught." Eli strode over and planted herself on the desk, before pouring a generous portion of the alcohol and downing it in one. She hissed at the after-burn and then glared at us. "What? I'm going to need it for this next conversation."

I held back a smile as Connaught looked to the ceiling, as if in prayer, before returning her gaze. "Just *try* to behave, or be nice. For once. Please?"

Her mouth opened to bite back, but she visibly stopped herself before saying, "Yes, *sir*."

His eyes flashed and his jaw clenched. "You know, for a grown woman, sometimes you can act like a spoiled brat."

He slammed the study doors as he left, and I caught Bas' eye as we both looked anywhere but at the woman between us. I could hear the tapping of her fingernails on the wood.

At last she huffed out a breath. "I'm sorry. I'm just..."

"Anxious?" Bas offered with a smirk, which she ignored.

"What's the actual plan?" I asked no one in particular.

Bas hesitated. "I'll direct that to the spoiled brat."

"Piss off," she hissed. "We need to speak to Sizwe. She'll have knowledge about magick and whether it could be used to control wyverns in this kind of manner."

"Sizwe?" I asked.

Eli nodded. "She lives here in the castle, as both a teacher and trainer. She taught me from a young age."

I hummed. "That's who taught you to fight."

"Her—amongst others."

My eyes skipped to Bas, who nodded. That explained how she was so well-trained in combat; multiple warriors had instructed her. The idea of finding out exactly how much she knew, possibly through training with her myself, made a thrill of excitement shoot through me. I shook away those inappropriate thoughts for another time.

"All right. How would she have this kind of knowledge?"

"She's a mage," Eli told me.

Well, shit. That was what they hadn't been saying back in Morcroft. I pushed down the irritation that flooded me, crossing my arms. "There's a mage... living here?"

"Yes," she answered, as if it wasn't an issue at all.

But to me—to Ant...

Magick knew magick. It recognised its own and bore its mark, like my own mark upon the back of my neck. It was different from that of others, like Vyn. The djinn, elves, and others like them, blessed with a long life or the ability to manipulate the elements; their magick had its limits. But *celestral* magick—the kind that flowed through the planet, the kind that the first mages had gifted my people—was limitless. Power could be increased and, should the spirits choose to, taken away, which was why those blessed with it respected it so much. All magick was only borrowed, and when we returned to the stars, it returned to the ancestors.

Someone of that same magick, with heightened powers, might recognise another born of it.

"Um, all right. Great! What about your father?"

A rich voice sounded behind me. "What about her father?"

The hairs on the back of my neck stood. My arms dropped, and I spun on my heel.

A finely crafted silver crown lay upon his head, the crown a criss-cross of sharp points—not points; antlers. They all came together to make an intricate circlet that held back his blue-grey hair, revealing a strong, charming face. Light stubble adorned his smooth skin and brought out the colour of his eyes. Deep, emerald-green eyes.

A rush of dread washed over me as I stared at the man now standing between the open doors, arms held behind his back, one brow raised as he glanced over us all. His gaze faltered on Eli, the corners of his eyes crumpling as a mixture of emotions crossed his face.

"Eliana." He took a breath, as if he'd been starved of oxygen and had taken his first saving gasp of air for a long time.

She pushed herself off the desk, stepping forward slightly, unsure. "Dad."

The king exhaled roughly, then strode forward to pull her into his arms. Eli stiffened, her arms hanging loosely at her sides, until she slowly brought them up and embraced him back.

This was a private moment, and I felt like I should leave—but I also didn't want to interrupt by moving. Bas was finding the blank wall fascinating; I turned to face the window, keeping them in my peripheral vision.

The tension seemed to leave the king's body as soon as he held his daughter. A smile played on my lips as I watched them from the corner of my eye, unable to imagine how it felt for him at that moment to see Eli safe and sound after so much time.

After a long moment, he pulled back, holding her at arm's length, taking in every inch of her. He raised one hand, touching her cheek tenderly before running it gently over one of the braids at the side of her head. "Look at you." His voice was rough, his eyes glassy. "How is it possible that you are more beautiful than the last time I saw you?"

"Father," Eli said, shifting uncomfortably from foot to foot. "We have guests."

"Ah, yes." He coughed and reluctantly let her go. I turned around as the king did, facing Bas with a wide smile on his face and stretching out his arms. "Bastion!"

He embraced him like family, Bas returning the hug, clapping him on the back. The king released him, his smile suddenly disappearing, and clasped a hand on the back of his neck. "Next time you run off with my daughter, I'll feed you to my hounds."

Bas grimaced. "Yes, sir... but you should know better than anyone that there's no telling her."

Eli scoffed as the king's lips twitched. "Well, I can't argue with you there. She is her mother's daughter."

"I'm standing right here," Eli said, irritation dripping from her tone.

I chuckled, and the king's eyes skipped to me, his mouth parting slightly as his head tilted. He released Bas, clasping his hands together behind his back as he stepped closer.

"And, ah, who do we have here?" Amusement seemed to roll off his tongue.

I inhaled slowly, calming my racing heart as I bowed. "Your Majesty. My name is Dracho. My companion Antares and I met Eli—" His brows rose. "Um, Eliana and her crew on the road to Laugharne." It seemed best not to add specific details unless asked directly.

He turned his head, catching Eli's eye. "Laugharne? Demetria has been helping you on your little quest, has she? I think I'll have to have a few words."

"No, you shall not," Eli stated loudly, causing the king's eyes to narrow. "Father... I have returned to inform you of what information we have gathered on the attacks. I felt it best to update you."

"And?"

"And?" she echoed.

"Eliana, playing coy doesn't suit you. You may have run off for over a year, but you are still *my* daughter. You did not come all this way just to provide me with information that any mercenary could have gathered. You're not giving up this hunt—despite my explicit instructions to stay out of it. You're here for something else. Now tell me what it is, or you'll never leave this castle again."

Eli's eyes widened in fear and surprise, and I picked up the stuttering of her heart. The comments from Demetria and the mercenary were starting to make sense. Here she was, willing to do anything to help her people—to solve the riddle of these attacks happening near her kingdom. And her father had tried to stop her. Understandably; I couldn't blame him at all. He was trying to keep his only daughter safe, after already losing his wife *and* son.

But deeper than that, I realised that this was what she was scared of. Being kept in a cage.

It must be why she had run away. I wondered what I would have done in that scenario—if my father had said no to my request. I probably would have shaken it off and gone about my day. But here was this woman, potentially risking her life and her relationship with her father to find out the answers. She put me to shame.

I stepped forward, hoping to deescalate the situation between them as Eli's nostrils flared with barely contained panic. "Your Majesty. We wish to speak with the mage that resides here."

Eli's glare was fury incarnate as the king's eyes narrowed. "Sizwe?"

I looked to Bas; he nodded. "Yes," I went on. "We believe that magick may be involved in this matter, so we'd like to speak to her. See if there's any information she could give us. With your blessing. And all information will be relayed back to yourself, of course."

The king mulled over the words, rubbing the stubble along his jaw. His eyes softened as he studied my face. "You have my permission."

I exhaled deeply.

"But..."

I froze. *There's always a but.*

"You may speak with Sizwe, and afterwards, Eliana shall meet with me to discuss *all* the information you have gathered. Then we may talk about the best way forward. There is, however, a condition, Eliana."

Eli looked up, but said nothing.

"You shall have dinner here—tonight. Just an informal meal."

That didn't sound too bad. A dinner with her father—

"All of you. And Sir Connaught."

A close family dinner with the King of Meridium and his captain of the guards.

Great.

14

When Eli had begrudgingly agreed to her father's conditions, Bas went off to his private quarters and she offered to show me to a guest room in the east wing, informing me that, when he returned, Ant would be staying in the room next door. She also advised me that there were plenty of capable guards around to take me down if I tried anything. That is, if *she* didn't get to me first.

Anyone would think she didn't trust me yet. After everything I'd done already. *Give a guy a break!*

As two staff members opened the ornate double doors, Eli surprised me by entering the room, walking silently over to the window. I followed, the doors shutting behind me, and watched her closely as she twirled a strand of hair around her finger, staring through the glass.

It must be bizarre to be away from home for that long, away from all the airs and graces of being a princess, out in the open world. Her room probably had a dozen maids waiting for her, ready to groom her for tonight's dinner.

I could see why she would hide her identity, but why leave it all behind? I had seen a snippet of the struggles of the commoners in Ruvalon in Morcroft, a shock to someone from Tenebris, where all lived equally, none in squalor. Those people must dream of a life with riches inside a palace, believing it to be all freedom and luxury.

Something else must have drawn her out of her cage. Something additional must have caused her to run away. I wouldn't push. But for some reason, I found myself hoping she'd eventually trust me enough to open up a little, and not just because her secret had unknowingly put me and my friend in danger.

My dragon was still a little sore over that.

"That's why you didn't pry," he forced me to blurt out, the day's events catching up to us.

"Excuse me?" She was still staring out the window.

Thanks, I said to him. I didn't particularly want to have this conversation.

"It's why you didn't pry more into our story." She looked at me as I spoke faster, trying to get it all out before I lost my temper. But I couldn't help it. My dragon thrashed about, reminding me that I'd unknowingly been led to the one place that was the most dangerous location for me to be. "Or why we're here—you didn't want us looking into your background. Finding out who *you* were."

Her cheeks started to darken as she turned away. "It's not that I was actively trying to hide it. It's just, well, I didn't know you... and people tend to treat you differently when they know you're royalty."

I couldn't disagree with her there. Guilt filled me, like a sickness in my stomach. I couldn't be annoyed. I was hiding secrets of my own.

Then why, deep down, did I feel... well, I wasn't completely sure how I felt.

A muscle in her cheek twitched. She turned to face me again. "And don't try to act so self-righteous. It doesn't suit you." I recoiled as if she'd struck me. "Don't think I'm that dim-witted. I noticed."

"N-noticed what, exactly?" My brain ran a mile a minute. I couldn't think of a single thing that would have given me away.

"You introduced yourself to Demetria before Antares—using the correct protocols. No commoner would offer their hand to a lady, unless they were from a similar station."

Shit.

"And then outside the gate, I heard how you spoke to Ant. You gave him an *order*. He isn't here with you as your equal—he's your protector."

My stomach churned. *Shit, shit, shit.* This woman would surely be the death of me. I turned, looking towards the door as if for an escape.

She continued smugly, taking a seat in the wingback chair by the window, "Or is he here as your servant?"

My head snapped in her direction. "He is no servant!" I almost snarled the words, the beast within furious that our brother had been deemed so inferior. Servants didn't exist in Tenebris; those working in the palace were happy to do so and paid handsomely for their work. Our people loathed that people suffered such servitude below the mountains. It simply wasn't right that someone would be treated as lesser because of their station.

Eli froze, narrowing her eyes at me. "A protector, then. All of that meaning, of course, that... you're what, a lord? Tell me. Why are you really here? To gain access to Meridium?"

"No! Everything..." I exhaled roughly, closing my eyes as I ran a hand through my hair. "Everything I told you was the truth. Our mission is the same as yours." I hated the half-truths. But it wasn't just myself I was protecting.

She looked at me sceptically, resting her head on her index finger and thumb.

I threw my head back, hating what I had to do next. "But you're right... I am nobility. I'm a lord back home, and... Antares is here as my personal guard."

Like *I* needed protection.

She looked genuinely bored with the conversation. "And why should I believe anything you say? Why do you care about what's happening here?"

My teeth creaked as they clenched. The beast within surged us forward and slammed my hands on the arms of her chair, careful not to touch her as my face rested inches from hers. Eli remained still; her eyes unflinching.

"You once told me that if you saw something bad happening and you could do anything to stop it, you would. There were *many* children in that village. Innocent generations of farmers that had never done anything other than provide for those who needed it the most. You, stuck here in your ivory tower, may not have known of them. I did. So, whilst I may not have ever ventured out here to the oh-so-mighty kingdoms of Meridium or Stillmere, I still knew of that tiny village of Mythbrook. Could you say the same before it was destroyed?"

She had the decency to turn away from my gaze.

"In the end, does it matter where I come from or who I'm fighting for?" I growled, frustrated at having lost my temper, and her eyes snapped to mine. Nervous energy coursed through me as the air tensed between us. The silence was deafening as she held my gaze for a few moments.

"It doesn't," she said.

I blinked. And blinked some more. All the anger and frustration left my body. "I'm sorry, what?"

"I said it doesn't matter."

"Are you feeling well?"

She scoffed, pushing me up as she stood. "It doesn't matter because if I get so much as a whiff of anything untoward... well, we both know what'll happen." Her finger pressed into my chest, her smile innocent.

I gulped as I felt the swell of my magick under the surface.

The irritation came from my true form as it rumbled against the fingertip digging against the skin underneath my shirt. This woman seemed to sense no indication of any threat at all, but I could. My hand started to itch.

She closed her eyes, taking a deep breath in through her nose, and removed her hand.

"But..." She opened her eyes, the fire within them dimming. "You haven't done anything but help my crew so far on this journey. Including saving my men's lives, and... *helping* me when I was vulnerable. And I haven't forgotten the time you *tried* to help me. Even if I did kick you out of my tent."

Her lips pursed as if she was ashamed to admit it. I started to speak, but her hand shot up, preventing me from doing so. "It's not something I will forget anytime soon, and it's something I'll always be grateful for, which is why I'm giving you the benefit of the doubt. I know in my bones there's more to your story. But it's *your* story. And I believe you'll tell me when you're ready."

My jaw dropped open slightly. "Th-thank you, Eliana." She was truly remarkable.

She rolled her eyes, grimacing. "Please, call me Eli."

I grinned at her. "Not a chance."

❧

I found it almost impossible to shake the nerves that consumed me as I waited for the dreaded dinner. I'd nearly choked on my relief when Ant's voice had sounded in my head, close enough to communicate with me. We hadn't spoken about his discovery, deciding to talk about it in person later that evening.

I blew out a long breath. Soon I was to sit down to sup with the king of Meridium. If I slipped up, it could cause a war between his people and mine.

No pressure.

The suit Bas had secured for me from Vyn's room didn't exactly ease my anxiety. It was a little snug, but suitable, I supposed. It would have been better fitted to Ant's wardrobe, him being a similar build.

I stared at my reflection, feeling strange, somehow. I had been born into royalty and wore formal attire often, but I never grew used to it. Styles in Meridium were definitely different; Tenebrian nobility tended to wear long robes of magnificent colours. The suit I currently wore was more tailored, all sharp lines and no flashy embroidery. Out of my comfort zone. When I was younger, I used to hate the older lords who strolled around in their official robes, ordering me about. Loitering about in the streets with Ant and Althea had appealed more to me—spending time with the people I would eventually rule.

I had been watching Meridium from my balcony. From what I could tell, it was quite similar to Tenebris. The gates were for safety, but there was no segregation of the people. Everyone worked together for the good of the city.

As early evening struck, a pretty young woman knocked on my door to inform me that I could head to dinner. She blushed as she caught my eye, looking to the floor before rushing out of the room. I checked my reflection one last time and tried to brush the silver strands of hair back out of my face, hoping I looked the part for a fancy dinner with a king of the human realm.

15

As I made my way downstairs, a portrait in the middle of the staircase stopped me in my tracks.

She was standing, facing straight forward, with her hand gently touching the other in front of her. If possible, the portrait was even more stunning than the statue. The statue may have caught the shape and physicality of the late queen, but this portrait captured her vitality, her emotion. Especially the life in her eyes.

In Eli's eyes.

They weren't the same colour; they were a hypnotising powder blue, like the tropical waters of a far-off paradise you only heard about in legendary stories. But they were precisely the same shape—large, round eyes with long, dark lashes. Her hair was shorter but the same rich brown as her daughter's, with the same braids on either side of her face.

"Ah, Queen Laurellen," said Connaught. I'd been so lost in the portrait that he managed to surprise me from a few steps behind.

"She was radiant," I commented quietly.

Connaught hummed in agreement. "I was only a couple of years into my training when she sadly passed away. But she was the kindest and most gracious woman."

"A trait that skipped Eliana?" I joked lightly.

His face fell, his eyes shadowed. "*Princess* Eliana has been through a lot."

"I gathered that," I bit back, a trickle of guilt settling into my gut. "I imagine that's why she's as strong as she is." I said it to myself more than to him.

He flinched for some reason, his eyes shifting away from my face. "Eliana is the strongest person I know. And she seems to trust you." He ignored my surprised look. "For that reason, I'll allow you a warning." He stepped closer so that I had to look up at him. "You may be her guest and companion at the moment, but if you hurt her in any way—you'll have me to answer to."

I smiled at him, the magick within purring at the challenge. "Not a problem."

His eyes flashed with uncertainty for a moment, but he shook it away. "Good. Let's head to dinner."

I took another glance at the portrait of Laurellen before following him down the stairs.

As we entered a small dining room, my breath caught. The walls seemed carved from spun silver, so bright I felt like I was lying on the clifftops of Tenebris under the midnight stars. Half-a-dozen crystal chandeliers hung from the ceilings, the light capturing every facet, sending a lovely, diffused radiance over every surface. A grand table was laid out in front of me, set for seven, and even though it had been described as an informal dinner, there were staff everywhere, hurrying about with trays of various things within their arms.

I sighed with relief as I saw that Ant and Vyn were already sitting at the table, Bas opposite them; I wouldn't be waiting alone with Connaught. Ant must have sensed me enter. His eyes checked me from head to toe.

Are you all right? he demanded.

Fine. You?

All good. Well, it seems we have much to talk about. What in the actual fuck? His mind was skittish, a complete contradiction to the calm that showed on his face.

Calm down. Not here. I glanced sideways, indicating Vyn, who was squinting between the two of us.

"Finished eye-fucking, have you?" he quipped.

Connaught rolled his eyes. "I see you haven't changed at all, Vyn."

Vyn eyed him lazily. "And I see you haven't removed that stick from your arse."

I suppressed a laugh at the captain's expense. Connaught ignored him and walked off, taking his seat next to Ant, beside the head of the table. The king's seat.

I greeted a smiling Vyn and joined Bas at the table, leaving a seat next to me for Eli—who had yet to arrive.

"No sign of Eliana?"

He smirked knowingly. "I imagine she'll be the last to arrive after what the king gifted her."

"What do you—?"

An elderly man—clearly the head of staff—interrupted us. "Gentlemen. His Majesty, King Cervidae."

We all stood for the entrance of the king as he swept into the room, wearing a glorious suit of basil silk. The crown of thorns had now gone, but a brooch was pinned to the front of his suit. Emerald eyes set into a silver stag—Meridium's sigil—shone brightly there.

He strode to the table, his steward pulling his chair out for him. The king gave us all a quick glance, his eyes lingering on Eli's empty chair for a second longer, before saying, "Sit, sit! Thank you, Farley."

He began a conversation with Connaught, but his eyes kept skipping to Eli's seat.

After a few moments, I leaned over and asked Bas, "Should I go and check on her?"

"Honestly, brother, she'll be fine. If I know E—and I do—she'll be—"

And then the chatter stopped. Someone at the table choked on their drink; a silence fell over the room. The only sound was a soft click of shoes behind me. Wide-eyed gazes peered at something over my shoulder. As Connaught swallowed, I turned in my seat, and realised what the king had gifted Eli.

Because there she was, and the air had left the room.

The dress, as deep as the forest green of her eyes, was draped off her shoulders, swooping respectfully to the swell of her breasts and pulling in at her waist. Flaring skirts contrasted the fitted bodice, and it was all outlined with black lace and flowing to the floor.

Eli's hair was down and braided as always—I could just imagine her threatening to cut anyone who tried to do anything else with it. Her eyes, however, were lined with black, making them stand out even more than they already had, her lips a cherry red. Atop her head, in black with tiny green stones, was a smaller version of her father's crown.

Fuck. She looked like a dream.

She stood, glaring every single one of us down as her hands clenched the skirts tightly. She may have looked the part of a princess, but the way she stormed to the seat between Bas and me was all Eli.

Royalty usually would sit at the head of the table—especially the daughter of the king, taking her rightful place beside her father. But part of Eli's conditions for attending tonight had been that she sit beside us, as we were her guests. The king shook his head as he watched his daughter; Connaught, beside him, covered his mouth in amusement.

Eli exhaled as she finally settled into her seat, and talk resumed as staff started fussing about with various decanters around the table. I leaned towards her, smelling fresh jasmine.

"Don't you dare," she warned.

"What?" I fought hard to keep the grin off my face. "I was merely going to say how horrible you look."

"You're incorrigible."

"Ooh, I love big words. Say it again."

"It's because your vocabulary is so limited," she retorted, but a small smile now tugged at the edge of her mouth.

I chuckled. "But all jokes aside, Princess... you look exquisite."

Her sultry eyes slid to the side as she glanced at me. "Thank you. You don't look so bad yourself."

I ran my hands down the front of Vyn's jacket. "Scrub up rather well, don't I?" I waggled my eyebrows at her and she shook her head in amusement.

"Maybe. But if you call me Princess once more, I'll remove your tongue myself."

Anticipation ran through me. "You've threatened that before, Prin—"

The flames in her eyes cut me off.

I leaned in as close as possible, inches away from the side of her face, ensuring no one else could hear—apart from Ant, if he wanted to. I was hoping he didn't. The smell of her was stronger this close and I swallowed, heat flooding me.

"I'm starting to think you have a thing about my tongue. But if you want it that badly..." I bit my lip, my eyes roaming the expanse of her neck. "All you have to do is ask nicely."

I couldn't get a read on her expression as I pulled back, but I could see the faint trace of goosebumps that trailed along her arm and shoulder. *Interesting.*

The magick stirred in my veins as I patiently awaited what would no doubt be her biting retort. She swallowed, and her lips parted.

"I—"

The clearing of a throat brought silence to the hall, our attention snapping to the steward at the head of the table. Eli shook her head, turning back in her chair, and I clenched my jaw.

He bowed his head in thanks. "Good evening, ladies and gentlemen. His Majesty thanks you for your presence tonight and would like to say a few words before we begin." He indicated the king, who stood, a small glass held in his hand. I sensed Eli stiffen in her chair.

"Good evening. Well, this is an unexpected dinner." With my advanced hearing, I could hear the slight tremor in his voice. "It's been some time since we dined in this room, and to be rather honest, I wasn't sure when we next would. To new company, welcome." He raised a glass to me and Ant, and we nodded in return. "To company we haven't had for a while—welcome back. And to my darling daughter Eliana... please forgive an old, protective fool."

Eli looked up from the table towards her father, alarm written across her face.

"I've had the pleasure of watching you grow into the most incredible woman, even if I missed the last two years. But it's so wonderful to have you home. Bastion, Vyn... thank you for accompanying her. I couldn't ask for better adopted sons."

"No need for thanks, Your Majesty. She took us in when no one else would." Vyn smiled warmly at Eli, and a pink tinge flooded her cheeks. I imagined a stubborn little princess sneaking all the young orphans into the castle.

The king tilted his head in agreement. "And to our new guests, Dracho and Antares, we offer thanks for all the help you have provided to our kingdom thus far." It sounded like Eli had already updated her father about who we were and why we were here. "And we bid you welcome. To Ruvalon!"

He offered up his glass, and everyone joined in the toast. "To Ruvalon!"

Eli coughed, clearing her throat before announcing, "To Derwin."

I smiled at her as everyone joined in solemnly, before casting my eyes to the king, and finding that his still rested upon me.

16

My tastebuds rejoiced in the foods that were brought before us: the most succulent roasted lamb, reared right here on the outskirts of Meridium; a piping hot leek soup that kept burning my tongue because it was too good to wait for it to cool. But the best dish had to be the little flat cakes. I'd never seen them before; they were browned on both sides, with little currants running through them, and sprinkled with sugar. After swiping Bas', it took everything in me not to return for thirds. I sincerely gave my compliments to the chef once I had tried everything on offer, along with a few different flavours of Meridium wine.

I was just eyeing the remaining cake on Vyn's plate, wondering what he would do if I swiped it, when a royal guard entered the room during dessert, whispering into Connaught's ear. I watched curiously as his eyes widened in alarm. He leant over to give whispered counsel to the king, who closed his eyes, sorrow crumpling his face. Anxiety knotted in my gut.

He raised a hand, and the table fell silent once more. "I have some grave news."

I held my breath; my dragon stilled, poised and ready for action, even though he sensed no immediate threat. This was it. Our identities had been revealed, and all hell was about to break loose.

"We have just received word that Chaepstow has—has been destroyed. Most of it is burnt to the ground."

Gasps sounded in the dining hall. Ant's eyes and mine met across the table before returning to the king. Chaepstow was a small settlement to the south-west of Mythbrook. It was also a farming town with no military force to protect it.

It seemed the attacks were coming closer to Meridium.

"There were no survivors."

Eli's mouth closed, horror darkening her features.

The king looked at us all, his eyes lingering on Eli for a moment. "I understand that this tragic news will make you want to hasten your investigation into these strange happenings. And you all have my full support."

Eli's head snapped up. "We do?"

King Cervidae nodded solemnly. "Chaepstow lies closer to us than Mythbrook. It seems your prediction from last year of this blight spreading is coming true. You may speak with Sizwe in the morning. Sending my only daughter on this mission is not something I want. But I know when there's no stopping you. Still... I *will* be kept up to date with your findings."

Eli nodded, a small smile playing on her lips. "Thank you, Father."

He returned her a tight smile. "Now, please finish. I anticipate busy times ahead. And a toast: to those we have lost." He lifted his glass once more as we joined him. "To the people of Chaepstow."

The toast was less upbeat than the first. As I lowered my glass, a firm hand grasped my thigh under the table; my leg jerked. Eli suppressed laughter as she saw my face, but she merely said, "We must speak tomorrow."

I nodded, still feeling the shiver up my leg for minutes after she removed her hand.

Returning to my room later, I sighed when something shifted in the corner. My dragon and I were both exhausted by the day's events.

"For fuck's sake, Ant, how did you get in here?"

"The fact you didn't sense me before you even entered proves you're getting soft." I shot him a look of fury. "I scaled the wall between our room windows," he told me calmly.

I groaned, dropping myself into a chair opposite him. "So, what happened?"

"It *was* the boy from Morcroft."

"Derwin," I said, sorrow rushing through me.

He nodded. "It wasn't pretty, Dracho. Whoever silenced the boy had skill with a weapon. The wounds were made with careful precision so he would not survive. It shook Vyn up a bit."

I wasn't the only one who had concluded that the attacks were coordinated. "Are you sure it wasn't a coincidence?"

He gave me a pointed look. "You know I don't believe in coincidences."

I rubbed a hand over my face. "Great. Well, it's a good thing we're speaking to this mage in the morning. Hopefully, we can gather some more information from her."

"Hopefully." He switched to speaking with his thoughts. *But you know the mage is a risk.*

He was right. *But even if she does realise who we are, she can't expose us. She'll risk losing her magick.*

If she's so loyal to Meridium, that may be a risk she's willing to take to protect them, he pointed out.

Then I'll just have to show her that I'm not a threat.

The breath he released was long. *I hope you know what you're doing. Just get the information, then we can get the fuck out of this city.*

I smirked. *It's not that bad.*

It's not bad at all. The city is rather pleasant. You know why I worry.

I did. He was here as my companion, as well as my friend. Being this close to danger left him on edge. But there was also something comforting about the city; it might have been the love of the people we'd met along the way. It was evident that Eli and her father cared deeply for the people and went to extreme lengths to protect them. Strategic and compassionate. They had surprised me.

My mind drifted back to the white-robed man from the gates. I didn't bring it up just yet, not wanting to add more stress to Ant's shoulders.

"Ant, do me a favour tomorrow whilst I speak to the mage. Scout the outer wall." His brows lowered, seemingly baffled by why I would ask such a thing. I waved a hand. "Please. Trust me. If we'll be moving on soon, and this assassin was less than a half-day's ride away... I want to make sure there are no surprises when we leave."

He gave me an expression that suggested he didn't quite believe me, but I schooled my face into a look of indifference, and he nodded. I exhaled. This journey had brought about so many unexpected turns, and I wondered how many more waited in store.

17

After a glorious bath and breakfast in my room the next morning, Ant went to scout the castle walls and I met Eli in the foyer.

"Good morning, Eli."

Her eyes narrowed, her head turning slightly. "You're in a good mood."

"I had the most amazing bath."

She rolled her eyes. "Got one of the maids to give you a sponge bath, did you?"

My mouth fell open. "You can do that?"

She stared at me incredulously for a moment. "No... they probably would, though, the way they were going on about you." She mumbled it more to herself, her face pinched in annoyance.

"What was that?" I leaned down, grinning.

She scowled at me. "You just made an impression on poor Milly, is all."

"Milly?"

"One of the maids."

I remembered the girl who'd escorted me from my room for dinner. "Ah. Well, I can't help my dashing good looks."

"Or your humble opinion of yourself either, apparently."

I gave her a wicked smile as I brought my head down further, hearing her take a breath. Her silent, churning eyes held mine as my dragon purred, magick vibrating lightly underneath my skin.

"There's only one person I would hope to make an impression on, *Princess*."

As if a switch had been flipped, her eyes held that fire I'd started to crave. She shoved me back before stalking off down one of the hallways. I laughed heartily as I caught up, offering her my hand once more—which she pushed away, making me laugh harder.

"So," I said, a smile still playing on my lips, "what did you want to talk to me about?"

She came to a stop, spinning. "Yes—right," she said, as if she'd only just remembered our exchange the night before. She glanced around nervously before pulling me over to a darkened alcove. "I know you've probably spoken to Ant already about... about Derwin."

I nodded, my mood sobering.

Eli took a deep breath. "And I think we've both concluded now that there's more to these attacks than meets the eye?" she asked pointedly.

"Attacks on random travellers were easy to pass off as accidents. But with everything that's happened since, it's obvious someone is behind it all," I agreed.

Her sigh was full of relief. I realised it took some weight off her shoulders. If someone was behind this, then as soon as they found out Derwin had survived, they wouldn't have stopped until they had silenced him. This gave Eli some closure. Some assurance that she wasn't at fault for his death.

"We'll find out the truth," I promised. "But first, we need to speak to your mage."

She nodded quickly, stepping around me to lead me there.

"This mage. She's the one who trained you?"

"After my mother died, she schooled me and trained me in combat, yes."

"Why?"

"What?"

"Why would a mage decide to leave Aion behind to help raise a princess?" It was odd. The matter must have been of extreme importance to leave her people. Judging from the look on Eli's face, I was on track to uncover some of Eli's past.

"My mother."

"Queen Laurellen?"

Her jaw clenched. "The mage—Sizwe—was my mother's most trusted advisor."

"I see." It was common for royalty to have an advisor, sometimes several. It was very rare, almost unheard of, for them to be a mage. My father had Boone, but I'd always considered him the exception. This Sizwe must have been extremely close to the late queen to leave Aion. To stay behind, and take care of the motherless child.

Nervousness prickled at the back of my neck. If anyone could reveal my secret, it was this Sizwe. I hoped that she would sense my good intentions. But if she was this close to the Cervidae family, I couldn't be sure. Either way, due to the oath between our people, I didn't think she would dare anger the ancestors by outing me.

Eli was quiet as we continued our walk, but the tension in her shoulders said enough. These little crumbs of her that I was picking up taught me so much of her character—and I wanted to know more. I'd be quiet when I needed to, ask questions when I could get away with it, push her buttons when the occasion struck... and when I felt like I wouldn't get stabbed for it... and hope she'd come to trust me with whatever other burdens she was carrying. Because if we couldn't trust each other, even just a little bit, we risked failing everyone.

Of course, this was all because Eli was an important political figure. Nothing else, despite whatever Ant might think.

It all made my dragon nervous. Should the mage disclose who

I was, I would either escape or be caught, and that would almost certainly make Eli hate me. I wasn't sure why the idea of that made me feel sick to my stomach.

The library almost rivalled Tenebris for the knowledge it held. The tall mahogany shelves looming over me, full of ancient volumes, reached the ceilings; scholars pottered about in the dim lighting, reading or climbing the ladders scattered about the room in search of books. The smell of old parchment, leather and candle wax brought a smile to my face as I scanned the vast room. Memories of lessons held in the Tenebris library with my mother flashed before me as I followed Eli down a small set of steps to a large recess set into the floor. A woman stood there, watching us.

"Dracho, this is Sizwe."

The mage's chestnut eyes did not leave my face as she held her hand out, offering it to me.

It was a test, of course.

Not a single wrinkle marred her smooth skin, but I could sense that she had seen hundreds of years; magick and wisdom swirled beneath her skin, buried within her very veins. There was no point trying to hide my magick. I couldn't even if I tried.

But she wanted to see if I *would* try. To see if I was trustworthy.

With surprising calm from my dragon and a steely resolve, I took her hand, shaking it firmly and feeling a positive charge from the magick flow through her calloused fingers. Her face remained emotionless, but I caught the dilation of her pupils as she felt the similar energy flow between us. To my surprise, my dragon was rather subdued. It made me worry a little.

The corner of her full lips twitched. "Pleasure to meet you, Dracho. Eli has told me much about you."

That was… unnerving. "The pleasure is all mine, Sizwe. I'm afraid the courtesy hasn't been reciprocated. I haven't been told anything about you." My gaze sharpened on the woman as I opened up my senses. There was a knowing glint to her eyes; her lips parted in a small smile.

There was no hint of distrust or threat. In fact, all I felt was a comforting warmth coming from the mage. When my eyes widened, she laughed slightly, the sound throaty.

"Well, that doesn't surprise me at all." Eli shrugged as Sizwe looked at her pointedly. The mage leaned in closer, lowering her voice. "Likes to keep me secret, that one."

My body instantly relaxed, along with my dragon, as I realised she would protect my secret.

Eli shook her head. "Sizwe. Tell him what you started to tell me."

The mage gave her a sour look of impatience. "Oh, hush, child. Permit me my playtime." I looked playfully at Eli. "Your witness, before he was assassinated. He told you the wyverns looked deformed, or diseased?"

I nodded. "He did. He also mentioned something about strings and puppets, but I took that to mean as if they were under the control of something."

"They're the same thing," Sizwe said.

"What?" I didn't follow.

Sizwe's smile was grim. "That deformity he described is proof that some maleficence has befallen those creatures. Someone is controlling them… and using them to do their bidding."

My instincts had been right. Eli and I shared a look.

"So it is magick?" I asked for clarification.

Sizwe stroked her chin. "I believe it is ancient; I heard about it when I was but a girl. However, I'm afraid I don't know much about it myself. I couldn't be sure without seeing it up close. It is a corrupt magick—not a kind that Aioni mages would ever use. It's a desecration of the celestral ancestors and their gift. To control not just one but many wyverns at the same time, and have them carry out such merciless acts... that would require incredibly powerful magick and a deeply malevolent will. Tales of such things were told to me as scary stories when I was a girl."

"Dammit," I exclaimed. Eli shrugged at me, pursing her lips as if this was the reaction she had also had at Sizwe's news.

"There is... someone who may be able to give you more assistance," Sizwe said quietly.

Eli stared at her. "Who?"

The mage closed her eyes, pain etched into her face. "My sister. Bisa, chief mage of Aion."

Surprise flickered through me.

"Your... *sister*?" Eli asked incredulously, her cheeks flushed with anger. "All—all this time, you told me you had no family left. You practically raised me, and you never thought to mention this until *now*? I'm assuming Father knows?"

All the mage did was smile gently. Well... at least I wasn't the only one who had been kept in the dark about something.

"We never told you because I didn't want you to grow up carrying any guilt about my decision to stay in Meridium."

"That's bullshit!"

"Watch your language with me, child." Sizwe's eyes glowed as they narrowed.

Eli huffed, turning away. Why *would* the mage keep something that big from her? Whatever her reasoning, it worked out in our favour and gave us a new direction to head in. Without permission from one of the Aioni, we couldn't enter their homeland.

"Put your misguided tantrum aside, Princess," I said. Eli glared at me as Sizwe tried—and failed miserably—to keep a straight face. "This is good news. Sizwe, would you assist us in visiting your sister?"

She took a moment, studying me intently, before nodding. "I will. I shall write to Bisa, but you will need to ride. The journey is far, about five days' riding, and too dangerous to travel by foot. There are, of course, other ways to travel." Her eyes strayed to mine mischievously, and my spine straightened. This was where she would expose me.

Eli, confused, opened her mouth to speak, but Sizwe interrupted her.

"By boat, of course, if you don't like to ride. But it does take longer." The mage grinned.

I flattened my lips together, amused in spite of myself. She was playing with me.

"...All right?" Eli drawled.

I coughed and bowed my head. "I give you my thanks, Sizwe."

Eli made a noise of disgust before stomping her way out of the library.

Shaking my head, I made to follow before feeling a soft touch upon my arm. Sizwe's grip tightened, the magickal current charging through my veins from the contact between us.

"Take care of her. And when the time comes, Dracho, remember... some people hide the best of themselves," she looked at me pointedly, "but some people should be allowed to hide what they believe to be the *worst* of themselves."

I blinked a few times in confusion and unease. It seemed clear that she was referring to me, but I was also sure that she was talking about something else.

Before I could ask what she meant, one of the scholars pulled her attention away from me. Letting go of my arm, Sizwe nodded at me before turning back and disappearing into the stacks, leaving me alone.

18

Surprisingly, and in keeping with his word, the king granted us permission to head on to the great tree, Aion, without even a show of reluctance. Some of the mages might be able to sense my magick especially those with heightened powers, but in spite of that I was excited about seeing the place for myself. Since the end of the war, hardly anyone had ventured into the mages' home.

Unfortunately, despite my eagerness, our preparations for the journey ahead meant we didn't have time to explore Meridium, other than a quick visit to the training grounds after breakfast one morning. For some reason, it drew quite the crowd.

Ant and I hadn't sparred in a few days. I teased him about looking a little plump—which was of course completely untrue—and he demanded a session in the royal grounds just after dawn. Neither of us wore armour, which astounded the two soldiers present. They stood watching us, chattering excitedly, upon the erected platform around the outside of the training circle as we prepared. One of them, a soldier with dirty blonde hair, rushed out, and I smirked to myself, guessing what was about to happen.

Are you ready? I asked Ant as he finished strapping his wrist.

His eyes shifted up to mine, the corner of his mouth lifting slightly. *Ready to lose early, are you? Before our audience has arrived?*

Right on cue, the doors were thrust open. The blonde soldier had returned, accompanied by around a dozen others. I rolled my eyes at Ant.

Best get started then, I said, pulling my glaive from the ground beside me.

Don't worry—I'll take it easy on you. Ant unsheathed his short sword from his side, resting it upon a forearm as he pointed it at me.

To the soldiers above, we might have seemed entirely unmatched, Ant using a much smaller weapon than mine. But it was his skills that made him the most formidable opponent I knew.

Keep it hard for your boyfriend later. I winked, flashing him an image of Vyn; his eyes narrowed.

I advanced quickly, Ant slowly. When I was only feet away, I slid sideways and jabbed my glaive forward, but he batted it away faster than I could follow, leaving his side exposed. I swung my glaive, trying to catch it. Snake-quick, his sword flicked back and parried my blade, the metals screaming as they collided. We danced like that for several minutes, neither of us gaining ground. I jumped back, putting some space between us before advancing again and trying to knock him off balance. He anticipated the move, leaping into a back-flip.

He was showing off. Not enough to make the mortals question our humanity, but enough to demonstrate our skill. The shocked gasps from our audience would have been distracting, if they weren't something we were used to. Ant and I trained like this daily in Tenebris.

He landed, sweeping his sword out in one clean motion, and I arched backwards, the cold steel narrowly missing my chest. Reaching out, I caught his wrist before I fell. Ant smirked, tossing his blade to his other hand. I righted myself as I dropped my glaive, kicking out at his leg; he cursed as he dropped to one knee. As he struck again with his blade, I released him to yank my dagger from the sheath at the back of my trousers. The sound of them colliding echoed across the pit.

Ant panted as he grinned wickedly at me, inches from my face. *I think that's game over for you, my friend.* He glanced down.

I followed his line of sight; he had pulled a second sword out of nowhere and currently had it pressed against my abdomen.

I met his eyes and raised a brow. *Funny, I was about to say the same to you.*

I tapped him on the leg twice. His eyes widened just a fraction as he took in the second dagger I'd pulled from my boot, which I was currently holding close to his crotch. He let out a huff, rolling his eyes, but relented, sheathing his short sword and helping me up as excited chatter broke out around the podium.

Loud clapping silenced the soldiers, and we looked to the platform to see them part—and the king come forward. Ant and I bowed as he leaned forward, his hands resting upon the wooden railing.

"Excellent show, boys. I'm glad that my daughter has two extremely skilled warriors in her company. Calms a father's nerves. Dracho, I was wondering if I could have a word?"

I nodded, my stomach dipping. Had Sizwe given me up? I handed Ant my glaive. *Stay calm. I'll catch you later.*

I'll be listening, Ant promised.

Grabbing my shirt from a bench, I ascended the steps, the wood creaking underneath my feet. The king waited patiently at the top as the soldiers flowed back into the training pit, readying themselves for the day.

He gave me a genuine smile as I reached him, his eyes crinkling. "Walk with me."

He strolled out into the palace grounds without a look back; I followed, slightly behind. After several feet, I heard footsteps behind me and realised that Connaught was accompanying us. That didn't unnerve me much—it was unusual for royalty to be seen without an armed escort.

We moved through the training grounds, and I was impressed by the apparatus scattered around. Large targets for archery sat at one end of the area, whilst a bigger arena was fenced off in the middle, an array of weapons racked up at its side. The king and I walked in silence until we reached one of the smaller rises overlooking the city. Connaught stayed some distance behind, giving us privacy. From here, it was easier to see the way the city was sectioned and defended. It would be almost impossible for an enemy to attack one particular area specifically. The gates at either end of the segment would lock them in, ensuring no way forward or back. Really, it was strategic genius. Even Ant would be impressed.

"It's magnificent, isn't it?" King Cervidae's voice pierced the silence.

"Yes. I was told it was Eli's—" His gaze tore from the city to look at me from the corner of his eye. "Um, Eliana's idea?"

He hummed in acknowledgement, then paused. "I wanted to know your thoughts on this blight that is currently sweeping the North. Do you agree with Eliana's thoughts?"

I nodded. "Yes, Your Majesty. Based on what information—albeit scarce—we have managed to gather so far, I believe there is some magickal element involved. Derwin did not lie. He was scared beyond all measure. It was only thanks to your daughter we got the information to begin with."

His lips pursed the way Eli's did when she was thinking. "And... do *you* think there's any merit to the rumours?"

"Rumours, sire?"

He scrutinised me. My stomach churned. "That those who lie beyond the mountains may be involved?"

The question rolled over me like a cold shower. This, ultimately, was what he wanted to know. If those in Tenebris—*my people*—

were a threat, or plotting some takeover. I willed calm into the magick that was roiling through my body in a potent mixture of fury and fear.

"If you don't mind me asking, Your Majesty, how did those rumours come about?"

He gave me a small smile. "It was brought up during a conversation with King Proditor when he visited last year. I updated him on the situation, and it was an idea he suggested. Suffice it to say, it somehow made its way around the citizens. With the attacks being so close to the mountains at the moment, it seems to *some* people that they must have come from there. Do you not think so?"

"No, sire."

"No?" Oddly, he didn't seem surprised by my answer, merely awaiting clarification.

Clearing my throat, I said, "Your Majesty, all my learning has shown me that Tenebris is a land where they value honour greatly. I do not believe they would want to manipulate or control wyverns, nor would they resort to such underhand methods, even if they even wanted to attack." My pulse quickened. "If anything, after what Sizwe told us, I would suggest that someone is trying to make it look like Tenebris is involved."

A small smile tugged at the corner of his mouth. "Interesting. Thank you, Dracho, for your honesty. I can see why Eliana likes you."

I tried to school the shock from my face.

"She wouldn't have allowed you to accompany her all this way if she didn't." He gave me a sidelong glance.

Well, that was a... relief to hear? A pleasant warmth filled me at the thought that Eli did now consider me at least an ally. It would make our mission a hell of a lot easier.

Even if I did like her feisty side.

"She is definitely unlike any other woman I've met before," I dared to tell the king.

He chuckled deeply. "She's very much like her mother was." A nostalgic smile came over his face, before fading. "You know, when we lost Laurellen, I wasn't sure how on earth I could raise a young girl—a future queen—on my own. Her mother was an extraordinary woman, an even better ruler than me. I had no idea how to teach Eliana everything about being heir to such a vast kingdom. It turns out I didn't have to do much. She's a complete natural. The people love her." He swallowed hard. "But... I worry about the wolves that will surely circle when she takes her place on the throne."

"Then it is a good thing, Father, that even though I am not a lion, I have a lion's heart." Eli's silvery voice rang out from behind as she joined us on the rise.

The stag's head brooch pinned to the front of the king's robe flashed in the sunlight as he turned with a gruff laugh. "Of course, my dear daughter." He clasped her arms, placing a gentle kiss on her forehead. "I, as always, have every faith in you." He glanced at me once more, giving a slight incline of his head. I bowed in return before he left us.

Eli offered a tight smile as she came to stand beside me. "My father worries too much."

"I think he worries the right amount for a father," I told her, and she rolled her eyes. "Then Aion it is?"

"I think your performance earlier in the arena solidified my father's decision." She smirked. "If he didn't feel that I'd be safe before, he certainly does now, according to the talk from the guards."

I held back a grin. "What can I say? I'm an impressive specimen."

She scoffed. "Someone's got a big ego."

"That's not all that's—"

She waved her hands in the air. "All right, I walked right into that one!"

I laughed, enjoying the back-and-forth that seemed to come so easily with her, then studied her face as she looked out over the city. The city she helped protect.

"Do you miss the city?"

She turned to me as if it was the last question she'd expected to hear. Her eyes lowered. "Yes... and no, sometimes. I miss the people, mostly. Helping and taking care of them. But there are... shades here that haunt me."

Ah. The nightmares.

"Is that why you left?"

Her tongue darted out across her bottom lip. "Partly. Some memories are difficult to chase away."

I nodded in understanding. I'd seen a glimpse of the torment those memories gave her that night in her tent. But I wouldn't pry—not until she was ready.

"That's the only reason I don't miss it here sometimes," Eli went on. "But it wouldn't stop me from coming back. Even if I wasn't heir to the throne. I always planned to, but when I was ready. The people need me, and I—I need them. They remind me that there is some *good* here. Some good in the world."

I lightly touched her elbow with mine. "I think I just learnt something about you," I told her warmly.

"Oh?" A flash of teeth as she smiled.

"You're incredibly selfless."

The smile faded, and it occurred to me that, outside her close circle, she wasn't used to receiving many compliments about her character. She shook her head as if to clear away a thought and coughed. "Well, thank you. But, um, are you sure I'm not just a—*distraction*?"

I looked at her in confusion, and she laughed.

"Antares?" she reminded me.

My eyes widened, remembering Ant muttering it back in Morcroft. "You, er, you heard that, did you?"

Fucking Ant.

"Well, I suppose I should take it as a compliment."

"You should," I said, too quickly. I was just rambling under her intense gaze. "But er, yes, all of that. Um, all of you. Well, it could be distracting."

She was silent, her eyes locked with mine for a moment, before letting out a small, silvery laugh. "Well, I'll try my best not to *distract* you."

I let out a relieved breath, thanking the stars she had just brushed over everything I said. *Not my finest moment.* Why was I so clumsy with words around her? It was as if she made *me* nervous, something which didn't usually happen to me around women.

"So, when are we planning on leaving?" I asked, changing the subject to safer topics.

"Tomorrow. Everything is mostly packed and ready to go. There's just one more thing I need to get..." Her eyes travelled over to where the port was.

"What's that?"

She smiled to herself—a secret smile, full of anticipation. "You'll see."

19

"Quiet!" Vyn barked.

Apparently, whatever Eli needed was from the freezing cold bay in the dead of night. After dinner, we'd accompanied her down to the port. We now stood not too far from the jetty, awaiting this big surprise.

"What the hell are we doing here?" Ant asked, as baffled as I was.

Vyn frowned and placed a finger to his lips and I suppressed a laugh.

I have absolutely no idea. I told Ant.

"I thought you'd want to see this," Vyn chuckled. "Eli said I could invite you."

My eyes widened as Eli stepped into the bay, the water reaching up to her knees; her black skirt floated on the surface around her.

Well, that's her dress ruined.

I smirked at Ant's inner monologue.

Eli squared her shoulders, taking a deep breath, before bringing her fingers to her mouth and making a piercing, whistling noise that travelled across the water and hurt my sensitive ears.

Silence.

I frowned. "What—?"

Vyn shushed me at the same time I sensed a disturbance under the water's surface. Whatever it was, it was fast, and it was coming straight for us. Instinctively, I adjusted my stance, and then realised that Eli was still in the water. Ant was looking from her to Vyn in bewilderment.

Just before I could rush forward, something breached the surface of the bay, sending a wave of cold water over us all.

Once I had wiped the moisture from my face, my breath caught at the sight before me. Towering over Eli was the most handsome horse I had ever seen—if you could even call him a horse. His coat was a subtle chestnut dapple, but it was his mane that drew the eye: a luminous golden white that stood on end, as though electricity had charged right through it. His eyes glowed with the same colour. As he walked gracefully forward, his mane settled against his neck and dimmed to a dark blonde. The horse's eyes were now a red-brown that watched Eli intently.

Not just a horse. A gullfaxi, lord of all horses.

Eli reached a dripping hand outward. The great creature loosed a breath as he swatted it away with his nose, stepping closer to nibble her wet hair affectionately.

The droplets of water making their way down my body weren't the only thing making me feel cold. Gullfaxi were rarely seen and known to stay away from mortals. So how could this woman summon one?

"Guys, meet Engel." Vyn motioned towards the horse.

"He's an old friend," Eli explained, moving round to scratch behind the creature's ear.

Ant steepled his fingers over his mouth. "And how did *you* happen to come upon a gullfaxi?" His suspicion was evident.

Eli's eyes flashed to him, the line of her jaw hardening. She took a moment before answering. "He saved my life when I was a girl."

My heart thumped. "How?"

She glanced at me. "I sneaked out of the palace one night—

just for a walk along the dock. Fell into the bay. I wasn't a strong swimmer... and he saved me." A small smile appeared as she looked fondly up at the gullfaxi, and he looked back with fierce intensity and intelligence. Eli's smile faded, and I guessed it had to do with why she had been out that night rather than her near-drowning.

Memories that haunted her.

"I couldn't tell you how he knew I was there, only that he helped me and brought me to this exact spot... where Connaught was waiting."

"Soaking wet from where he'd dived in looking for you," Vyn added, smirking. One side of Eli's mouth turned up as she walked beside Engel out of the water.

This was the tale Connaught had been talking about. When it he'd mentioned it, it had seemed like a happy memory, but the despair that had flashed across Eli's face showed me there was more to it. I wouldn't ask tonight, but I wanted to find out the reason for that sorrow.

"So, Engel is... yours?" I cringed, realising the stupidity of my words as soon as they left my mouth.

Eli's hand stilled on the horse's side. "Engel belongs to no one. I can't explain it—ever since that day, we've had a connection. He permits me to ride him, but I do so rarely and only with his blessing. I wouldn't trust any other beast with my life... which is why he's coming with us." She nuzzled his nose affectionately.

I swallowed and nodded, lifting my head and catching Engel staring at me intensely. I wondered if the lord of all horses could sense other magickal beasts. From the way his warm eyes considered me, he was aware of something, but I didn't think he believed me to be a threat. His eyes travelled over to Ant, widening slightly.

He just seemed—curious. As if seeing something new for the first time.

I took a tentative step forward and dipped my head. "Pleasure to meet you, Engel."

His eyes bounced between Ant and me before he threw his head back, nickering slightly. I took it as approval and laughed.

In a dazed silence, we started walking back towards the castle, Engel following of his own accord. Amusement washed through me as I pondered the strange events of the night.

"What are you smiling at?" Eli asked, peering under Engel's regal head.

"I knew you were a horse girl," I said, and she scoffed. "No, I was just thinking... this is not what I had in mind when you said you had to pick up one last thing." I laughed, and she grinned. "You're forever an enigma, Princess."

Her gaze flicked to me, the creases at the corners of her eyes deepening, but she said nothing.

"So, tomorrow we head for Aion," I said.

She nodded.

"Nervous?"

She snorted, then a slight blush darkened her cheeks. "Not nervous, no. Actually, kind of excited."

I smiled. "Of course you are."

Her eyes narrowed. "What?"

"You were born for this kind of stuff. Bravery seems to be in your blood."

She looked to the ground, mulling over the words, before giving me a small smile. "If there is no fear, there is no being brave," she said softly, and left me to ponder that.

20

The tree of Aion was visible from most of Ruvalon, its vastness seeming to touch the clouds, and it dominated the scenery as we drew closer to it. A charge seemed to flow through the air, setting magick coursing through my veins and energising me as we set up camp. It had been a long four days, and my back was sore from all the riding. I had often found my eyes drawn to Engel. It had been an honour to witness a gullfaxi on land; Engel was exceptionally graceful, and never showed any signs of tiring as he led our party.

Our final morning of travel found us sitting around a fire, just outside the forest that surrounded the tree. Its branches reached out over us, leaves swaying in the pleasant breeze. Ant had managed to capture a few hares; he sat off in a copse of trees preparing them for our final breakfast before reaching Aion. Engel roamed freely, whilst our other steeds were tied nearby; they seemed at home in his presence, as if he evoked gentleness in them.

Bas held his hands up. "I'm just saying... just because Sizwe speaks to me in a different language sometimes doesn't mean I don't know that she's cussing me out."

Eli and I, sitting on a log opposite him, laughed heartily as Vyn shook his head at the gentle giant. I relished the back and forth between the group. I often found that I didn't have to participate at all, even though I wanted to. I could simply relax and enjoy their company.

It was similar to what I had with Ant and Althea—which was rare. Many of those I called friends back in Tenebris would often get caught up on *what* I was, not who I was. Being the son of the emperor had its perks, but also plenty of downsides. Here, I felt like I could be completely myself—well, almost completely—because they had no idea of my destiny. This day, under the leafy canopy, I was just Dracho.

"Well, you obviously make an impression on her." I tipped my cup towards him; his white teeth stood out against his warm skin as he chuckled. "So, Bas, how did *you* end up living with Princess here?"

"I swear I'll cut you," Eli threatened, but she was smiling.

"Promises, promises..." I gave her a sultry look as she shook her head. I'd been making sure to call her Princess at least twice a day, just to see her get worked up.

Bas smiled. "My father used to be captain of the guard. I'd train with him in the palace training grounds. When he went off to fight in the Tain with Eli's father, the king graciously allowed me to continue training with the remaining guards."

"That's not the only thing you did, though, is it?" Vyn asked, his yellow eyes flashing mischievously.

He nodded. "I ended up practically living in the palace. Eli had dragged this one in," he jerked his thumb towards Vyn, "and I followed shortly after. Whilst the parents were away, the staff stood no chance." He chuckled deeply.

"Remember when we set pigs loose in the kitchens?" Vyn asked, a grin lighting up his face.

Eli dragged a hand down her face. "I genuinely thought Farley was going to leave and never come back."

The three burst into a fit of laughter and I smiled at their easy companionship, a sudden pang of longing for Althea's company running through me.

I turned to face Bas again, noticing from the corner of my eye that Engel had paused in the meadow, staring in our direction. "So, your father...?" If Connaught was captain now...

Bas' smile widened. "My old man's retired now. He lives in Meridium with me mam. Next time we're there, I'll introduce you."

I smiled at him, flattered he would even think about doing such a thing. "That would—"

"Silence." Ant's quiet voice cut across me.

My dragon was as frozen as the rest of me, astounded at Ant's command. He was staring intently at the thick bush of trees behind us; a muscle ticked in his jaw as his nostrils flared.

"Something's coming." His voice was a sharp whisper that crept over us like a cold mist. In seconds, his small dagger appeared. "No one move."

What is it? I asked him.

Nothing we've encountered before. But...

But what?

I'm not sure.

A bolt of shock went through me at his admission. If *he* couldn't get a read on this presence approaching, then we would have to prepare for anything.

Ant slipped further into the shadows of the tree canopy, his footfalls as silent as the thing that neared us, and lowered himself to the ground in the thick bushes. He crawled towards the jungle, graceful and supple, like a predator before it pounced.

Vyn's eyes were wide. Bas barely parted his lips. "What's going on?" he whispered without moving his mouth.

I held up a finger, staring intently at a tiny gap between the bushes. I could have sworn I had seen a flicker of colour there.

"There's something beyond the thicket," Eli breathed against my arm. She had inched so close that I could feel her body heat.

I nodded, slowly unsheathing my dagger as Ant crept closer. Engel stepped silently beside us, his muzzle sniffing low to the ground.

A low growl rumbled through the bush, stopping Ant in his tracks. I opened my senses, inhaling deeply, but no scent could be found. There was an earthy charge in the air, but as we were on Aioni soil, I couldn't differentiate between it and anything else magickal. Engel huffed, shaking out his mane.

To my astonishment, I heard Ant chuckle in amusement. He sat down, crossed his legs underneath him—and placed his dagger upon the ground.

Ant!

It's all right.

What—?

The thicket rustled and shook. Two gem-like blue eyes were now visible between the branches, making their way towards us. No one moved as it stalked forward.

I'd never seen a creature like it. The cat's muscles rippled along its back as it came forward, its paws big as saucers, padding silently until it stopped a few feet in front of Ant. A faint, ethereal blue glow surrounded the indigo fur, highlighting the green tufts that ran down its spine. The tail—*tails*—were like the feathers of some exotic bird, in shades of blue, purple and green. The end of each looked razor-sharp. The creature's movements were a fluid grace that no person could match.

Well, perhaps Ant.

"He's a spirit guide," Ant said calmly.

"What? How can you tell?" I demanded. A spirit guide was powerful, usually taking the shape of an animal. They were rare, usually only accompanying a mage of great importance. No one knew why, but that was the way of the ancestors. I scanned the area behind it. If the guide was here, it meant that a mage was close behind.

"The glow," Ant said aloud. *I can sense the magick,* he added in my head.

The charge in the air, I agreed.

The cat just stared, breathing steadily. Ant held out a hand, offering it to the animal, leaving it hanging in mid-air a few inches from its face. We watched, mesmerised, as its large, clairvoyant eyes scanned the party, before it padded forward the extra step, touching its nose to Ant's hand. A collective sigh of relief seemed to leave the group, but another movement in the trees startled us. I stood and stepped forward so that Eli was blocked from view.

The person who stepped out was one of the most captivating women I had ever laid eyes upon. Her hair was a mass of shiny black spirals that highlighted the sharpness of her features. There was a deep richness to her skin that also shone in her light brown eyes.

She stood before us all, barefoot, intrigue upon her face. "Well done, Cubra, you found our visitors." She smiled at the beast, then turned to us. "Who are you?"

Eli manoeuvred herself around me; the woman's brows rose in response.

"Hey, I'm Eli. Are you from Aion?"

The woman hesitated and looked to the feline again. It was currently sitting directly in front of Ant, nudging his hands with its nose. I gaped at him; I'd never seen Ant so relaxed or at peace with anything in his life. A smile tugged at the corner of the woman's mouth as she looked at them, before her eyes snapped to mine. She held my stare as she answered Eli's question.

"I am. But you didn't answer me. Who are *you?*"

Ah. She could sense my magick, but that didn't mean she knew what I was.

I stepped forward again. "My name is Dracho. My friend with your... guide"—her eyes flashed— "is Antares."

Ant didn't take his focus off the cat, but waved a hand.

"Eli, you've already been introduced to."

Bas stepped forward to Vyn's side so suddenly that he almost tripped over. He gave a short bow. "I'm Bastion, ma'am."

Vyn whispered "Ma'am" back to him, and Bas tried to subtly elbow him in the ribs, causing a loud "Oomph!" to sound through the camp. "And this here is Vyn."

I faced the mage again, shaking my head. "And before we tell you our reasons for being here, it'd be nice to know *your* name."

I could feel Eli's scowl burning into the side of my face, but the mage simply smirked. "The name is Roux. Roux Xolani," she told us.

"Wait—like Sizwe Xolani?" Eli asked.

"You know Aunt Sizwe?" Roux blinked, taken aback. "May I know your full name?"

Eli's mouth opened, then snapped shut.

"She's Princess Eliana Cervidae of Meridium," Ant said.

My back went rigid as Eli's head snapped to him, fury written in her expression. Roux looked surprised. I ran my hand over my face, my dragon thinking about punching Ant in the face.

Better I say it than anyone else. It isn't like she'd threaten me *anyway.* Ant's cruel cunning knew no bounds sometimes.

At least give her a chance, Antares.

"*You're* Princess Eliana?" Roux's voice was a few octaves higher.

Eli flinched. "I am... but it's Eli."

"Then why are you here?" No malice in Roux's question, just pure curiosity.

"You are the daughter of Chief Bisa?" Vyn asked.

"I am."

Eli walked to her satchel, handing Sizwe's letter wordlessly to the mage. Roux's head tipped down as her fingers reached out, brushing over the magickal seal.

She looked uncomfortable as she looked back up at us, mild regret bleeding into her tone. "I'm sorry. I can't allow you all to enter Aion so heavily armed. Two may enter."

Bas opened his mouth to object, but Vyn nudged his arm.

"Dracho and I will come," Eli told the young mage. "The others will stay here until we return."

Roux seemed to be considering something. She looked at Cubra before nodding towards Ant. "Actually, that one will come too."

Ant, caught by surprise for once, got to his feet as the creature walked over to the woman. "Nice cat." He flashed his teeth at the mage.

"His name is Cubra. He likes you." She scratched Cubra's ear as he pressed himself into her side, his eyes venturing past Roux to watch Engel curiously.

"The feeling is mutual." Ant tipped his head forward an inch.

Of course, a man who naturally shied away from most people would get on better with such a dangerous beast.

"Well then, Roux. Lead the way." I held a hand towards the forest.

We said our goodbyes to Vyn and Bas—who weren't exactly pleased about being left behind—then set off into the jungle.

21

The sunshine wove through the trees, a chorus of vibrant greens, as we headed deeper into the embrace of the forest. I inhaled deeply, hyper-aware of the energies surrounding us the closer we got to Aion. I looked at Ant, whose hands were clenched at his side, knuckles white. I followed his gaze up to the towering branches of Aion and stared, awestruck.

"It's gorgeous," Eli said. "I've never seen so much life in one place."

"It's the ancestors," Roux answered her, a broad smile showing perfect teeth, "and the magick they give us. It lives within all of the lands of Ruvalon. But more so around Aion." She stopped, her cheeks darkening as she started fidgeting with the skirt of her long dress, whose colours matched the vibrancy of the forest around us. "It's just ahead, through these trees. Um, we haven't had guests in... a long while. There may be a bit of excitement. I apologise in advance."

I gave her an encouraging smile; she was doing us a favour, after all. "No need to apologise, Roux. We're happy to be here." Her returning grin lit up her face.

Ant scoffed. *Speak for yourself, suck-up.*

Fuck off.

We followed the mage through some enormous leaves, emerging

into a clearing. We had reached Aion: a giant, hollowed-out, rich red tree that touched the sky and beyond. Before us, there was a gap in the trunk big enough to walk inside. Big enough for *fifty* men to walk inside.

Inside, several columns reached high to a curving ramp that followed around the entirety of the core to the very top. Coming off the ramp were carved walkways that connected the columns. Platforms allowed people to create their homes, stalls, communities.

Aion, the sister tree to Volente—before the Tain. Now all that was left of Volente was the marked ground and the spirits of the people who'd died there. Mages, elves and humans. No life remained of the great tree, and no one dared go there for fear of angering the ancestors.

"Welcome to Home Tree," said Roux.

As we stepped into Aion, electricity pulsed through me with a sensation of pinpricks to my very fingertips. I looked at my hands, expecting to see something, but found no difference there. From the corner of my eye, I saw Ant's jaw clench.

All good? I asked him.

He sent a quick nod in my direction, folding his arms tightly across his chest. I made a mental note to speak to him about it later.

We moved inwards, and delicious aromas assaulted my senses; my magick was heightened upon Aioni soil. Tables held steaming bowls of different dishes as mages tended huge frying pans, heating them with fire magick. Further up, several women sat upon the ground, crafting beautiful necklaces of colourful beads.

People along the path noticed our arrival and froze where they stood, excited chatter following us the further we went. Several children were suddenly upon me, running around my legs and pulling me by the hands. Eli laughed as she, too, was pulled forward. I looked over my shoulder, noting Ant's pale face as he shrank back towards Cubra.

Roux chuckled. "I warned you. Come, Mamona will be this way."

I knew the word *mamona* meant mother in their language; suddenly I felt grateful for all my lessons.

We made our way up the spiral walkway, more Aioni people exiting their homes along the way, stopping to watch our arrival. Everyone was welcoming, giving smiles and greetings. There seemed to be no distrust or malice—surprising, for a people that had kept themselves secluded from outsiders for over a decade. But I understood why they did. The Chief Mage wanted to prevent anyone like the elf king Morven from poisoning the minds of the mages again. Only a minority of them had been sucked in by his promises, but the power they'd held had been devastating. If something like that were to happen again, it could destroy the mages once and for all.

The journey through the centre of the tree took a few hours; my legs were soon as tired as my back. The crowd following us grew larger and louder. As we neared the top, we approached the largest of the crafted homes, which I guessed to be the chief's residence. The chattering group now at our backs waited on the sloping pathway, but word of our arrival had evidently reached the chief before us, with several children running in and out of the home. As we stopped a few feet from the front door, the curtain was pushed aside and a small girl, no older than thirteen, stepped out.

She glanced over us all; a shining smile lit up her face. "Hello. I'm Azande."

Roux walked over, wrapping an arm around the young girl's slender shoulders. "Eli, Dracho, Antares. This is my sister."

That sweet smile rested upon the young girl's face as she watched us, wisdom and awareness in her eyes. The resemblance between the sisters was uncanny, the younger's hair just a shade lighter. I smiled as she caught my eye, and a slight blush darkened her cheeks.

The curtain moved once more and an older mage stepped through, her salt-and-pepper locks tied in rows away from her face.

A silence fell behind us as the woman looked us over, a twinkle in her eye.

"Well." The woman's voice rang out. "The great city of Meridium has come to Aion—finally. I did wonder how long it would take."

The three of us exchanged a glance; Eli turned to the elder. "Chief Bisa?" she asked.

The woman nodded.

"My name is—"

"Eliana Cervidae," Bisa interrupted.

Eli blinked in shock.

"You look so much like Laurellen; I would recognise you any-where."

Cubra stepped out from behind Ant, drawing the mage's eyes towards us.

"And who do we have here? Travellers from *beyond* the realm." Gold specks in her brown eyes flashed brightly.

I froze. My dragon reared his head to pay attention, but remained perfectly calm—as he had done with Sizwe—whilst Ant tensed at my side, his nerves already on edge.

Easy, I told him.

I flashed her what I hoped was a charming smile. "Greetings, Chief Bisa. My companion Antares and I are travelling with Eli and her crew." My body wasn't nearly as relaxed as my casual tone sounded. I stepped closer to Eli, removing Sizwe's letter from her satchel. "Your sister sent us."

Bisa's brows moved a smidge, betraying the surprise she tried to hide as she walked forward to take the scroll, evaluating it as Roux had. She stared at us for a long moment before speaking. "Come. We have much to talk about."

She entered the home, Roux waiting for us to follow. I nudged Eli forward.

The space inside could easily fit us all; there was a small desk along the far wall, scattered with various texts and sketches, and a bed in the corner. Azande sat on a colourful rug, playing with a small kitten as Roux stood by the entrance curtain.

"So, my sister has sent you all this way. It must be for good reason." Bisa half-smiled as she tapped her fingers along the seal on the scroll.

Eli stepped forward, opening her mouth to speak but closing it immediately.

"You're wondering how I knew your mother?" Bisa spoke softly.

Eli nodded.

"We fought side by side during the Tain." I saw Eli's eyes fill with pain. "But before that, Laurellen was my greatest friend."

Eli's mouth popped open audibly. Whatever she'd expected to hear, that wasn't it. Momentary panic flashed across her face as Bisa looked at her intently. "I-I can't remem—"

"You wouldn't, dear child." Bisa's eyes crinkled at the edges, filled with an emotion I could tell she dared not speak. "You were much too young to recall, but tensions throughout the continent were high for a long time. It was too dangerous for either of us to risk seeing each other—your mother as the queen, or myself as chief. This is why Sizwe opted to stay with your family. We had our own ways of communicating. It was only when the final battle started that we all saw each other for the first time in many years..." She trailed off, looking at the ground as everyone fell silent. We all knew Laurellen's fate that day.

I could tell that Eli wanted to ask more, but she only cleared her throat, her voice as rough as sand. "Sizwe explains everything in her letter."

Bisa remained where she stood, scroll in hand, waiting for Eli to continue.

Eli stepped forward. "Over the past year, there have been attacks to the north. Strange attacks involving wyverns. They were sporadic at first, with no survivors. But now, two entire villages have been destroyed. A boy named Derwin survived—briefly."

Eli's eyes ventured elsewhere for a moment. I reached out and gently brushed the back of her hand with my fingers, causing her to shake her head and continue. "He told us the wyverns looked deformed. That they were being controlled, like puppets..."

Bisa's eyes glowed unnaturally as she concentrated intently on every piece of information Eli provided. Finally, the mage waved her hand. A flash of blue broke open the seal upon the scroll, which she unravelled and started to read.

Eli exhaled roughly. "We didn't understand it, but from what he said, they looked like they were being manipulated... by magick."

Bisa huffed out a small, humourless laugh. She rolled the scroll back up, placing it on her desk before turning to lean against it, suddenly looking exhausted. I shared a look with Eli, worried but hopeful.

"The creatures are not being controlled by magick. Well, not by magick the likes of which you have ever seen," the chief told us.

"What do you mean?" Ant demanded, obviously fed up with being given more questions than answers at this point.

"It's an extremely old power," Bisa told us. "One which hasn't been seen in thousands of years. That means not many are around to have encountered it before."

Her eyes shot to mine, and a shiver made its way up my spine. It was quite obvious at this point that she knew of our magick. Maybe she had an inkling as to our lifespan as well.

Bisa sighed. "I have only heard of it because of my great-grandmother."

"Grandmother Yelena, Mamona?" Azande asked from where she sat, her head tilted up in interest.

"That's right, *ma chemiel.*" Bisa smiled down at her. "My great-grandmother was one of the first."

"The—the first mages?" I blurted out in astonishment, catching the mini mage's blush.

The first? Those who had blessed my ancestors with long life that matched their own and the magick that allowed them to transform? Magick that now ran through my veins... through Ant's veins.

Well, that certainly makes things more interesting, Ant noted.

Hopefully not.

A coy grin illuminated the chief's face. "The very same. She was here the last time someone sought to use it, when we mages lived in Volente."

A pregnant pause rolled between us all like an errant wave.

"Use it? It's not a person?"

"Yes"—she nodded, before shaking her head— "and no. They called it the Hollow. Knowledge of it has been lost to time, unless you're as old as I am."

My eyes turned to Ant. Ant, who consumed as much knowledge as he possibly could in his spare time. Who loved to educate himself on any and every type of magick the world had to offer.

He simply shrugged, his brows dipping in confusion. How had we not heard of such a thing, if it could be used in such a way?

"Before the Tain, and the creation of the Vildspire, people didn't venture near, terrified that it was a benevolent god or an ancient evil. But the Hollow itself is neither good nor evil. No one alive knows where it came from, or how long it's been here. It has always been. It has no beginning, and it will have no end. It just *is*." Bisa waved a hand. "It's like the very air you breathe. But..." She turned, plucking something from a pot on the desk, before walking to Eli and clasping her hand. "It is *man* where evil can sow a seed. Where greed, control and power have blinded and corrupted the hearts of those who are lesser." She opened her palms to reveal the seed she had dropped into the centre of Eli's hand.

Eli looked up at the elder's face. "So, the Hollow itself is being controlled?"

Bisa smiled. "The Hollow is energy. Not like our celestral energy" —her eyes rolled over me— "but something far older, and lesser known. It rests in the north-east. It cannot be controlled... but its essence can be taken and manipulated to infect a chosen, if you have the knowledge and power to do so. It's a dark and ancient magick, frowned upon by the magickal community. The chosen must have been upon the brink of death—and unwilling... it is not pleasant. This Hollow being will be in a constant state between living and dead, unable to prevent themselves from doing their master's bidding."

My mind went to Derwin and the tale told by the traders outside the gates of Meridium. The precise and violent wounds Ant had spoken of. The thing that must have killed Derwin whilst he travelled to Laugharne. Was this the chosen of the Hollow?

"But why would anyone want to do such a thing?" Eli breathed

Ant gave her a dry look, his arms crossed. "Isn't it obvious?"

The awkward silence only seemed to worsen the tension; we all knew the answer. To obtain power.

War.

"So that's it? This essence is—being transferred to the wyverns? Is that how this *chosen* is controlling them?" Ant directed the question to Bisa.

She pursed her lips. "Possibly. I'm sorry, I can't say for certain. I'm no expert. Your best course of action would be to visit the temple and scholars that live near the Hollow itself."

I inhaled sharply. "People *live* there?"

"Yes. The Hollow itself isn't dangerous, only those who seek to use it. Those who seek to control what cannot be contained or controlled... and that is what we should be frightened of. For it could be the end of us all."

My stomach lurched as I turned to Eli. I didn't need to hear her thoughts to see that she had the same idea as me; I could see it in the depths of her grassy eyes. I looked to Ant, who tilted his head in agreement.

"Then we shall visit this temple. Any further help you can provide us, Chief Bisa, will be much appreciated. But we won't trespass upon your company for too long."

"Nonsense! We will help as much as we can. But for now, no more talk of dark, dreary things that cloud our hearts. I understand you have more companions at your camp?" She asked us but looked at Roux, who nodded. "They shall join us here tonight, and we will celebrate your visit upon the beach."

Azande jumped up, excitement lighting up her youthful face. I jerked and nearly tripped as she grabbed my hand, pulling me towards the curtain and out of the hut. "You'll love the beach!"

I shouted a quick thanks to Bisa as I was dragged away; her laughter reached my ears as I followed the youngling along the sloping pathway.

22

A smile never left my face as Azande pulled me down the slope and to the back of the great tree, where there was another opening, exiting to a long wooden ramp. My feet halted of their accord once we reached it. This side of Aion was a completely different world from the one we had entered. The tree was so large that this side grew beside the ocean, the very air different to the jungle side we had left behind.

The branches were sun-kissed even in the early hours of the evening, the air a salty brine. Marram grass scattered the ground on either side of the walkway. The sand was a beautiful, soft gold. And before me, a steady procession of waves gently kissed the shore. The water was an exquisite shade of sapphire as the sun's rays reflected off it. My breathing steadied just looking at it; a blanket of peace calmed me from my head to my toes.

My dragon sighed contently, and I felt his urge to spread our wings and take to the skies, the sensation like pins and needles across my skin. A thread of longing filled me.

Azande looked up at me quizzically. "Are you all right?"

I shook my head. "Um, yes. It's just, um, pretty amazing here."

She flashed me a toothy smile. "Praise the ancestors."

I smiled back. The Aioni people believed, as the draconi did, that all our magick was gifted from the ancestors—the celestral spirits and energy that lived within the planet itself. It resided in those who were blessed until we died.

There, our beliefs differed. The Aioni believed that the magick, along with the souls of their people. returned to the planet together, adding to the ancestors. In Tenebris, the draconi believed that, whilst our celestral magick returned to the ancestors—the ones who had gifted us our powers—our souls journeyed to the stars to be with those who had passed before us.

"Mamona says we're lucky to have Aion," Azande told me. "After what happened to Volente. We must *always* count our blessings. People outside aren't so lucky."

"Your Mamona sounds like a very wise woman."

She nodded smugly. "Now come on, Master Dracho, you should see how clear you can see the fish by the coral!"

I laughed at her enthusiasm and followed her down towards the water, marvelling at the beauty that surrounded me. The people along the beach smiled or acknowledged me as we passed, speaking excitedly. My cheeks bloomed with nervous heat; I waved back bashfully. Azande was right: the water was so clear when I stepped around the coral that I could see the fish distinctly as they swam fearlessly about our feet.

Everything about this place was remarkable. When I'd left home, I had truly believed I would never venture to a place as beautiful as Tenebris—that nothing below the mountains could hold a candle to the magnificence of home. How naive I'd been! The welcome we had received was heart-warming and like nothing I could have imagined, considering they had been closed off from the outside world for over a decade.

Much like my people...

The mages embraced us with open arms and warm smiles as we helped them prepare for a celebration upon the beach in our honour. Some used their magick to carry great logs for the bonfires. A couple had graciously offered their homes for us to stay in for the night, refusing to take no for an answer and clearly considering it a tremendous honour to take us in. How could we say no to that?

Whilst I waited with Ant, Eli and Roux ventured back together to fetch Bas and Vyn shortly before sunset, leaving the horses outside the entrance. When they returned, Eli brought Engel to the shoreline, watching as he galloped into the water with elation, disappearing beneath the gentle waves.

Bas' face as he took in the scene was a picture. "Holy sh—"

Vyn cut him off with a sharp heel to the shin. Unfortunately, the next obscenity wasn't so quiet, earning a laugh from the chief's younger daughter.

We were all quite taken with the young mage. She spoke with knowledge that made her seem wise beyond her years, showing that Bisa spent a lot of time educating her daughters about the way of the world.

Once the pinks and purples of the sunset started to merge into the early navy of the night, and the stars started to take their places in the clear sky, the Aioni used their magick to light the bonfires, the flames reaching upwards and lighting the many faces spread out along the beach. Bisa had invited us to sit with her family at the largest bonfire in the middle of the beach, where they passed around bowls of cooked meats and various delicious fruits. I could feel the steady beat of the drums in my chest; the people hummed or sang in the language of Aion, their souls becoming one as they celebrated our visit together.

Azande, who sat beside me, patiently answered any questions I had—and asked many of her own. "Mama said that there are mountains that grow as tall as our Home Tree to the north! Is that true?"

I opened my mouth, but it was Eli who answered. "They are

enormous. But I think Aion may *just* win that competition." She winked.

Azande grinned. "I've never seen mountains. I think I'd like to see them someday. I heard that beyond them is the realm of *dragons!*"

I gave her a wide grin and glanced at Ant, who rolled his eyes.

Bas was creeping up behind Azande. "That's right, mini mage, and one day," he scooped her up, throwing her over his shoulders as she let out a squeal, "you'll see them too!" He spun as her scream turned into laughter, those around us looking on in amusement.

"Put me down, you giant oaf!" she called out between giggles, smacking his back.

Vyn smirked. "I like her."

A tugging sensation pulled at my chest as I watched.

Stop it.

I glanced up to find Ant scowling at me from a few seats away. *Stop what?*

Getting all broody.

Fuck off.

His chuckle vibrated through my head as I mentally flipped him off. *I was... just wondering how Althea is.*

He sighed. *I'm sure she's perfectly fine, putting the trainees through their paces and looking forward to our return.*

Only because she can't wait for us to take Jeshwa off her hands. Thinking of the over-enthusiastic recruit who followed Althea around like a puppy brought a nostalgic smile to my face.

Ant suppressed a grin. *You can't fault him for trying.*

With Althea? He'd have more luck with my uncle.

A rare laugh burst from Ant's lips, causing people around us to look curiously in his direction. Ant morphed it into a cough, looking towards the water.

Roux turned to Eli. "These attacks—do you think they'll spread to more villages if they go unchecked?" Concern echoed in her tone.

My smile fell.

Eli was tight-lipped, her brows pinched together. "I do. At first it was just sporadic. But the attacks on Mythbrook and Chaepstow were controlled destruction. Like..."

"Like someone planned it," Ant finished.

Roux looked at him, pursing her lips. "Then it must be this Hollow," she muttered, more to herself.

"What do you know about it?" I asked her.

She blew out a breath. "I asked my Mamona after you headed for the beach. Not much is known about it. She believes that tales of what happened the last time it was used have been scrubbed from our histories, to prevent others from using it once more."

Ant scoffed. "Doesn't seem to have worked out so well."

Eli shot him a glare before turning back to Roux. "I'm sure we'll get to the bottom of it."

Roux nodded. "I hope so. If it's a mage responsible, we'd like to help however we can."

Eli ducked her head, trying to catch her eye. "You could always come with us, you know?"

Roux's visible surprise matched my own. "Come with you? Leave Aion?"

"Well, I mean... if that would be all right with your mother?" Eli glanced to where Bisa stood, further down the beach.

"I am of age, so any travel is of my own decision-making. I just— have never had any reason to before. I may not be as powerful as my mamona, but I suppose the prospect of protecting my home would be the best reason of any."

"Well, whatever your decision, it would be a pleasure to have you with us, Roux." Vyn tipped his head towards her, and she smiled at him, then met my gaze.

Nervousness seeped through me. I had no idea if she knew what I was, but I could tell she knew something was going on. If she came along with us, it would be a lot harder to prevent her from confirming her suspicions.

 ❧

Later that night, my head rested upon my hand, my eyes on Eli, who stood by the water. The slight breeze picked up stray strands of her hair as she stared at the horizon.

"Got a bit of drool there, buddy." Bas' voice wrenched me from my perusal. He smiled slyly.

"All right, mister *ma'am*."

Vyn roared with laughter at my reference to Bas' awkward introduction to Roux. Bas' cheeks darkened in embarrassment.

"But whilst we're on the topic... what *is* the deal with Eli?" I asked them, glancing around. Most of the Aioni had fallen away from the beach, heading back to their homes. Only small pockets of people remained, talking in muted whispers as they enjoyed the lingering flames of the bonfires.

Bisa had taken Azande home, removing the latter's sleeping form gently from my side as she mumbled dreamily. Roux had stayed with our group, indulging in her curiosity about Ruvalon and how it had changed over the years; she had never left the safety of Aion. Eli had dived right into answering every question, her smile reminding me of the one she'd bestowed upon Demetria. It washed over me like a loving caress.

At some point, Ant had exhausted his social energy and taken a walk along the beach, Cubra following close behind. The feline spirit guide—one of many we had spotted within Aion, in all manner of animal shapes and sizes—had watched all our exchanges intently from where he lay beside Ant. The intelligence in his eyes was evident, and it seemed Ant had found another creature he felt at home with.

Bas' head turned to me at Eli's name. "What do you mean?"

"Well, it doesn't seem like you two are still a thing." I was just asking to get more information about Eli, I told myself. Purely for the sake of the mission.

His cheeks darkened further. "It was never really a *thing* at all," he mumbled.

"All right, but... is there a man around? Or a woman?" I queried.

Bas looked at me as if my wings had just sprouted out of my back unannounced.

"What?"

"Um... I'm not sure how it works in Eshmnor, but unfortunately... *that* is still not something that is openly, um, exhibited by most? Or even spoken about." Bas looked over at Vyn, shooting him a wistful smile. Vyn just shrugged.

"Oh." Peculiar... and tragic. "So, er, Vyn—?"

He smiled knowingly at me. "Yes, I enjoy the company of other men. No, I haven't found anyone of my own. Yet, anyway. And though I live my life truthfully, it is something I have experienced backlash for. Remember the bully I told you about when I lived in the church?" I nodded. "He bullied me because I was slightly more... feminine than the other boys."

I folded my hands against my legs. "That's... awful. That in this age, you can't be embraced by your entire community. Love is love. Vyn—it's courageous to be you, especially in a place where they tell you to be somebody you're not."

Vyn said nothing, but his eyes swam with gratitude.

Bas sniffed, mock-wiping his eyes. "You're gonna make me cry, man."

I laughed, shaking my head.

"And no. With Eli, no one around... at least"—he caught Vyn's eye, a warning there— "not anymore."

"Ahh, so there is someone." From the way Eli and Bas interacted,

I assumed they had been fairly short-lived—that the relationship perhaps had been more physical than emotional. I wasn't sure if that made me feel better.

Vyn's lips formed a tight line. "There *was*. But don't go bringing it up unless she does first!"

I winced. "That bad, eh?"

Vyn gave me a pointed look, and I surmised that the relationship had most definitely had a messy end. That made me curious, but I wouldn't push it.

"So," Bas started, "I gather that it's very different to Ruvalon, where you're from?" His eyes flicked to Vyn and back.

I snorted, picking my cup from the ground. "Oh. Yes, it's definitely more, um—*relaxed*. You should come and visit some time."

"That sounds like a solid plan, brother, but um..." Bas trailed off as Roux started to walk towards us. "I'm definitely a one-woman man."

I smirked. "Uh-huh."

He continued watching as Roux wandered past, his head turning to trail the movement of her hips as she walked away.

Something invisible smacked him upside the head.

"Hey! What was that for?" Bas rubbed the back of his head, glaring at Vyn.

"Stop ogling, pervert."

"Don't act all morally superior. Not when you ogle Antares and Dracho every chance you get!"

My cup paused on its way to my lips. "Wait, what?"

Bas clasped his hands together, planting a dreamy look upon his face as he raised his voice a few octaves. "Bas, they're training again. Look at those abs. Man, I'd love to lick the swe—"

This time the invisible hand clapped itself over his mouth.

"Mother-fuc—!" he shouted, the sound muffled, and my entire body shook with mirth.

Vyn's smile was positively devilish. "What can I say? That's a manwich I would not refuse in a heartbeat."

I grinned, setting the cup down as I got up. "Believe me, Vyn, you're not missing out... it's a *manwich* I've already been a part of."

Bas froze, his cup falling from his hand as Vyn's mouth dropped open. With a wink, I headed down to the water.

"Excuse me?"

I didn't glance back.

"Y-you can't just drop that bombshell and walk away! Dracho. DRACHO!"

I was still grinning at Bas' hysterical laughter when I caught up with Eli, who was dipping her toes in the sand as the shallow waves lapped at her feet.

"What was *that* all about?" she asked.

"Oh, just winding Vyn up about his sexual fantasies."

She nodded. "Ah. Of which there are many."

"You'd know about them, would you?"

She hummed, a soft smile on her face. "Who d'you think is the first to hear about them?"

I winced, clicking my tongue against the roof of my mouth. "That's... great. Well, prepare for some interesting ones coming your way."

She lowered her eyebrows, regarding me suspiciously. "Why, what have you done?"

"Nope. Nothing," I pronounced, lips pursing.

"Something tells me that's not true."

"I'm sure you'll find out soon," I reassured her, waggling my eyebrows. She smirked, and a beat of silence passed between us. "It truly is stunning here."

She nodded. "It is."

"Must have been hard for Sizwe to leave all this behind."

Eli's eyes narrowed as she brushed a strand of hair from her shoulder. "You don't have to spell it out. I know."

"So," I drawled, "you'll forgive her for not telling you about being Bisa's sister?"

She sighed. "There isn't anything to forgive. I could never comprehend the sacrifice she made to stay with me, but I'll always be grateful to her for doing so. She's done so much for me."

I smiled. "Well, it's thanks to her we're here now. And hey!" I nudged her arm with mine. "Now we have a direction to go in. This temple for the Hollow sounds promising. We should find more answers there."

"True. But I doubt what we're looking for is there."

"Why do you think that?"

She looked disturbed. "I'm not sure. I just have this weird feeling."

"Well... it is important to trust your instincts. We'll speak to the others in the morning and then decide?"

She considered that for a second before nodding. "What if—? Never mind."

I faced her. "No, go on."

"What if we *don't* find any answers there?"

"Then we'll hunt down the son-of-a-bitch doing all this and deal with it ourselves."

My answer seemed to please her; a smile tugged at the corners of her lips.

I brushed her hand with my fingertips. "I'm not going anywhere. Not until I have the same answers as you. I'm in this for the long haul. For Ruvalon."

She smiled wider now, warmth in her eyes as she exhaled through her nose. Realisation dawned on me: she had been worried that at any point, Ant and I might return home and leave them to deal with everything alone. "Thanks, Dracho."

"Anytime, Eli."

23

Bisa gave us a detailed map to take on the rest of our journey. It was a much-appreciated gift, being far more up-to-date than the old one my uncle had given me. The temple of the Hollow lay to the northeast, situated in the Vildspire dunes. It was a fair trek; the quickest route led us back to Meridium to take a boat from the port there. It was decided over breakfast that this was our best course of action, as we could update King Cervidae on the information we had found here.

I couldn't shake the weird tingles that had settled over me since waking up. My magick itched under my skin, leaving me with a strange uneasiness. I put it down to the intense magick in the area, sensing that Ant was on edge too and looking forward to heading off.

I would miss this place.

Bisa, Roux and Azande walked us to the entrance to Aion, the youngest mage having stayed by my side the entire time. I knelt, facing her.

"It has been a pleasure to get to know you, Azande. Perhaps one day, when you are old enough, we will brave those mountains to see the dragons beyond?" I smiled a secret smile to myself. This was a promise I would keep one day.

Her eyes lit up as she bounced on the balls of her feet. "That would be amazing! Bas can come too?"

I laughed, looking over her shoulder at Bas, who was saddling up the horses. "I'm sure he would love that."

She flung her arms around my neck and hugged me tightly. I froze in shock for a moment, then returned the embrace. I had always enjoyed the excitement of the children of Tenebris whenever I'd ventured outside of the palace. Once, when I'd been younger, some children had found me as I relaxed in my dragon form next to the Pistyll waterfalls. They had watched me, daring each other to get as close as they could. Before they knew what was happening, I had taken a mouthful of the water and soaked them all. They'd run away laughing.

I enjoyed seeing their innocence and sense of wonder. But I had never been embraced by a child, probably because of my position there.

Azande pulled away. "It was nice to meet you. Goodbye, Dracho."

I nodded, getting to my feet. Roux caught my eye, a sweet smile on her face at our exchange.

"You know, you are always welcome to join us, Roux," Eli said as she came to stand at my side.

My back stiffened, my magick extra aware of that very same energy that ran through Roux's veins. It would be a lot easier to expose me should she choose to join us...

But then a jolt of realisation hit me. I had just spent twenty-four hours with this amazing community, and I felt completely safe. It was obvious that Bisa could sense my magick, and perhaps some of the other elder mages. But everyone had been welcoming, with no malicious intentions evident.

I wasn't worried about everyone finding out who I was. I was worried about *Eli* finding out—and how she might react.

Roux's teeth flashed in a wide grin. "Thank you for your kind offer, but my place is with my people." She gave her mother a warm look.

I saw Bas pout in disappointment as Eli nodded, stepping forward to embrace Roux. When she pulled away, she turned to Bisa, who grasped her in a firm hug.

"It's taken us a long time to get here, Eliana. But I'm so glad you finally found your way to Aion. Your mother would be so proud of the woman you've become. Give Teyrnon my best." She twirled a strand of Eli's chocolate hair around her finger. "Never forget who you are. You have kings, queens, magick and dreams flowing through your veins. Don't forget it."

Eli's shoulders had tensed through Bisa's goodbye, but she nodded at the chief before turning to walk towards Engel.

Bisa exhaled deeply, her eyes turning from Eli to rest on me. "It has been a true pleasure to meet you, my dear boy. I thank you for bringing Eliana to me."

I shook my head, feeling peaceful. "It was nothing. It has been incredible to meet you all and be embraced amongst your people."

She placed her hand over her heart. "Well, thank you, Dracho." Her face sobered. "I sense you have a rough journey ahead, and I wish you all the best. Take care of them, and take care of yourself."

She pulled me into a bone-crushing hug—my second embrace in a matter of minutes—and I tensed, slightly anxious over the surge of energy I felt from her magick. She stayed silent, so I allowed myself to relax into it. Before coming here, it had been a long time since I'd been embraced like this. My chest constricted as I realised I had missed it.

Over Bisa's shoulder, I saw Eli watching us, an unfamiliar softness settling on her face. Releasing the mage, I tipped my head to Roux, turning towards the others. Ant was off to the side, scratching behind Cubra's ea.

"See you, Cubra!" I called, tying a bag of supplies to my horse's saddle. The cat growled affectionately.

"We'll ride until sunset, then set up camp," Vyn called out to the group. I looked to the sky; sunset was only a few hours off, since we'd spent the morning getting ready and being given various supplies by the Aioni. But we could make a reasonable distance in that time. Everyone mounted their horses, Engel giving Eli's hair a nibble before she swung her leg over the saddle.

I nudged my horse towards her at the front. "Ready?"

"Never been more ready."

The horses walked steadily on, that feeling of peace ebbing as we rode away, waving to the mages.

Our pace was relaxed as we ventured away from Home Tree; by the time we stopped to set up camp, we hadn't travelled that far. An unspoken reluctance had fallen over the group. All of us were sad to be leaving behind the beautiful Aion and its people—and nervous about where our next journey would take us.

Eli asked me to grab some kindling. As I walked away from the camp, I heard Vyn sigh behind me.

"I can't wait to have a proper bath again," he groaned.

Bas snorted. "*I* can't wait for you to have a proper bath again."

I chuckled at them just as a strange awareness ran along my spine, like a whispered warning in my ear. My magick reaching out to me? I shook it off.

"It won't be long before we'll reach Meridium. Then both of you can take a much-needed bath," Eli called out.

"Like you smell of roses!"

I glanced over my shoulder as Eli scoffed at the notion, flipping her hair and looking very much the princess she was.

"Damn heightened senses. You all stink of shit," Ant muttered to himself with a sniff, his nose wrinkling. I laughed aloud.

"What?" asked Vyn, turning with a smirk on his lips.

Before I could answer, Ant's hand clenched on a tent peg, his knuckles turning white. *Can you feel that?* he hissed.

The smile on my face faltered as that awareness transformed into a chill. It worked its way through my body, my magick tingling. Something was nearby.

"Dracho!" shouted Vyn.

That something stood several feet away from the camp, stopping close to the tree line, where it must have come from. Fear lanced through me. How had it sneaked up on us?

It was a humanoid figure, armoured from head to toe. Its gauntleted hands held a long-winged spear, leaning on it as if for support. My eyes were drawn to the weapon.

The blade itself was unadorned; no decoration or engraving marred its steel. Its very aura suggested it was used to being hidden, kept secret—in the shadows. Dual-edged and razor-sharp, it was perfectly crafted for blocking incoming attacks and piercing enemies as easily as a hot knife through butter. The wing lugs at the base of the blade curled like the talons of a great bird, ready to embed themselves in flesh once the blade had made its first mark.

The hilt was tightly wrapped in smooth dark leather, with a shimmering dark green stone set into a titanium bolt at the end. It wasn't an especially luxurious or even attractive weapon—but it didn't need to be. A creeping evil surrounded this spear, a stench of death and despair. This blade was death incarnate.

What did that make the wielder?

I scanned the creature, surprised by how unimposing it appeared. Its light grey armour, almost white in the evening sun, was worn and battle-scarred. No face was visible under its visor, though I could feel eyes studying us through the thin slits, and it was oddly still.

I took a deep breath, focusing my senses, reaching out. A faint hissing could be heard coming from beneath the chin guard where its mouth was. Or should be.

There was also something puzzling in its posture—as if it had fallen a long time ago, then been picked up and held upright against its own will. I would have sworn—if it weren't wearing gauntlets— I'd have been able to see its knuckles turn white, as it gripped onto the hilt of the spear it used for leverage. The way it was leaning, I was surprised it could control anything, let alone wild wyverns. Reaching out with my senses, there was a faint trace of unfamiliar magick, but its aura felt... weak.

My gut told me that this was the assassin that had ended Derwin's life back in Meridium. The horrifying entity that had been reaping havoc to the North, destroying villages as it went.

The Hollow.

Hot anger crept up on me, like a snake in tall grass moments before it struck. This was the horrifying thing that had ended whole villages—had destroyed Mythbrook, had murdered Derwin in cold blood.

Whatever its reason was for turning up now, I didn't anticipate it being friendly. But it wasn't making the first move. Breathing harshly through my nose in a bid to calm my dragon, I took a cautious step forward.

Eli was suddenly next to me, grabbing my arm; the creature's head snapped to her. Eli didn't seem to notice, but I did, and so did my dragon. We didn't like it. I had to grasp the reins of my anger before it went galloping onwards in the compulsion to bare my teeth, drawing its attention back to me.

"Don't. Can't you see there's something wrong with it? Can't you feel the energy around it?" Eli's posture was stiff. She glanced quickly at the Hollow before returning her gaze to me.

The entity's head tilted, still looking in her direction as if captivated by her every word. Removing my eyes from it for a brief moment, I turned to study Eli. Worry and fear were etched into every line of her face. I had never seen her display such emotion. What could she possibly see in the creature that scared her so much? There was something unnatural about the weapon it wielded, but the thing before us looked as though it could do with a good night's sleep instead of a fight.

My dragon, taking control before I could comprehend what was happening, brought my hand up, brushing the back of a finger over the soft apple of her cheek. My gaze roved over her face, greedily taking her in as her eyes stretched open in shock.

I cleared my throat, wrenching control away from the beast, and my hand dropped to my side. "I'm sure it's nothing I can't handle."

I tapped her hand before removing it from my arm and turned back towards the being before me, its head rotating slowly to look at me. Eli backed away a step as I reached over my shoulder to remove my weapon before extending it fully, twisting it to lock into place. The whole time, the creature just stood, statue-still—watching.

Holding my weapon out with one hand, far from my body, intentionally showing that I had no plans to use it—or at least, not unprovoked—I took one step forward.

Its stance suddenly shifted.

The shaft of the spear left the floor inhumanly fast to meet the wielder's other hand, the sound of the steel gauntlet ringing out across the field. It stood straight now, the spear now held across its body. Instinctively, I echoed the movement, bending my knees into a defensive position and hearing the party behind me preparing themselves for attack.

I tapped into my power, my breathing increasing as my dragon surged, and the Hollow's head tipped. I reached out again towards the assassin, and sensed...

Nothing.

No aura, no emotion, just—endless emptiness.

The adrenaline started my heart pounding in my chest so fast that I hoped the creature couldn't hear it. There would be no reasoning with this being. No negotiation. This would only end one way: with its death.

Do we fight? Ant asked, a growl in his mental voice.

We fight. We have no choice.

I shifted my stance again, swinging the glaive around onto my hip to hold it with one hand. In response, the creature rolled its shoulders.

Eli spotted it too.

"No!" she shouted as we both shot forward. "*No!*" I guessed that someone else had drawn their weapon – probably Bas.

Ant loosed a blackened arrow from his bow; the creature easily knocked it away with the spearhead. Another bounced off the creature's armour.

Shit! I won't be able to get through that steel.

My jaw clenched. Ant's arrow-tips had been forged in dragon-fire and should have been able to pierce anything.

The assassin's entire demeanour changed, the power of its aura lashing out before I could brace myself. The evil that had crept around the blade seeped into its wielder, who seemed to grow taller before my eyes, as if its spine had been stretched out and straightened. The exhausted air was gone, the faint hissing from before replaced with a chilling clicking noise as its neck twitched. It lunged forward, sweeping its weapon in a bid to bring it down on top of my head.

Almost a split second too late, I dodged, a shock of unfamiliar emotion running through me. I swung the hilt of my weapon smoothly around to catch my opponent in the stomach—but the assassin caught it.

We stood closely together now, our faces just inches apart, the beast inside staring at me from behind the slits. That shock of strange emotion settled in my gut. Rashly, I released a hand to yank my dagger free from the sheath at my hip. Quick as thought, I brought it down hard into the thin gap between the plates in the armour at the creature's knee, then twisted.

There was... nothing. No cry of pain or reaction to steel slicing through its sinew and bone. The creature merely tilted its head, and though I couldn't see its face, I could sense the baring of its teeth in a wicked smile at me.

That emotion scuttled along my spine like a spider chasing its meal. How could I fight something that could neither feel nor fear pain—or death?

And then realisation dawned over me, the shock like a pail of ice water. Intimidation. *Fear.* This creature... intimidated me. I could lose this fight.

That had never happened before.

Blinding light burst behind my eyes as pain erupted in my forehead. The assassin had thrust its head forward in one impossibly quick movement. My dragon let out a snarl in shock, my hand itching as I stumbled back gracelessly several steps before falling to the ground. My dagger had come loose; my glaive fell to the floor. My now free hand flew up to my face, feeling warm wetness above my brow.

"Dracho!" Ant shouted aloud in shock as he rushed forward to reach me.

The creature sent a snarl in his direction as it pulled its spear from the ground, stalking towards me: its prey.

24

Eli was closer than Ant. As my vision cleared and I stared at the crimson liquid on my hand, I was vaguely aware of her throwing herself in front of me.

No one had ever made me bleed before. Not even in training... not even the masters.

Eli's hands were outstretched. The assassin's steps faltered, seemingly unsure of how to proceed.

"Please."

I heard the quiver in her voice, and I gritted my teeth, unnerved at the hint of a fang brushing the edge of my tongue. In my shock, I had failed to notice my dragon thrashing, fighting to tear through my seams—my control was barely holding. Glad that Eli wasn't looking at me right now, I felt Ant's eyes burning into the side of my skull as I closed my eyes to get a handle on it. But *I* wouldn't beg for mercy from this—this thing.

The thought of transforming briefly entered my mind. I would be able to rid us of this creature in a second if I was in my true form. But it would mean giving up my identity, and possibly hurting Eli with her so close.

I pushed the temptation, and my dragon, down.

Easy, brother. Ant's unease whispered across my mind, his concern a cool balm to my hot rage.

As a shaky breath left me, a strange ball of golden light with threads of black slammed into the creature, sending it flying across the field. Relief hit me as everyone looked to the source of the magick: Roux, the white of her cape billowing behind her, her hands outstretched like the claws of a jungle cat. Cubra stood by her side, the green fur along his back standing on end as his tail feathers coiled and stretched out like a venomous snake. The mage's dark eyes glowed, volcanic fury burning across her glorious face as she stared down the enemy.

The corrupted being of the Hollow wrenched itself to its feet, spinning around to stare her down.

"These are MY lands, and you do not belong here, forsaken one! Nor shall you stay. Leave and harm no one further!" she directed across the field, her authority not to be questioned. The impatient energy that rolled off her was palpable.

We were still on Aioni soil.

No one spoke, awaiting the response. I could see every inch of the creature shaking with rage. A small crack flared in its aura, a taste of bitter regret coating my tongue as it moved its head minutely to glance at Eli and me, causing my lips to peel back over my teeth.

It looked back to Roux and expanded its chest to let out the most ear-piercing, rage-filled screech from its steel-covered mouth; all of us covered our ears at the punishing sound. Its scream ended, an eerie silence blanketing the field, before it stabbed the butt of its spear into the ground, kicked off, and jumped unnaturally high into the air, taking the weapon with it and disappearing behind the tree line.

The rage from that scream stayed with us a long time after it had left, settling into our very bones.

Eli swung round, starting towards me as if her feet were on fire, and I offered her a small smile as I got to my feet. "I'm—"

"*Are you completely mad?!*"

Her cheeks blazed with rage, but I was so shaken by the previous altercation that I didn't see it coming. A stinging pain caught me squarely in the jaw, hard enough to rattle my brain. I stumbled over my own feet and fell to the ground once more.

"You could have got one of us killed!" From the corner of my eye, I saw her dart forward with her hand clenched, ready to strike again, before pulling up short as a black blur appeared before her.

The knife at her throat lifted her head.

The sharp tip slid up the delicate skin of her slender neck, tilting her chin further upwards. Vyn rushed forward, his hands flexing and a fierce wind swirling within them, his eyes a myriad of conflicted emotions. I heard leather twisting as Bas tightened his grip on his axe, his thick black brows pulling together.

"Antares—*not* necessary," I bit out as I pushed myself to my feet, rubbing the side of my face. I could feel a bruise forming on my jaw, as warm wetness dripped from my brow onto my cheek.

Ant cocked his head, his face emotionless as his amber eyes roamed over Eli, her breath hitching. He took a slow step closer; Eli's jaw snapped shut, eyes aflame. Once he was satisfied with whatever he found in the depths of her stare, a chilling grin split his face.

"If you strike him again... I will rip out your spine." He flashed his teeth once more, a full, wide smile, before he made to walk away.

His smile vanished. Wrapped around his legs was a silent, swirling torrent of air, keeping him from moving. Ant's stunned gaze snapped to Vyn as mine did; the djinn bared his teeth.

"Release me," Ant commanded, his deep voice like the promise of thunder.

The corners of Vyn's lips turned up. "Ask *nicely.*"

Ant's eyes widened, but with a flourish of Vyn's hand, the

wind-like binding subsided, allowing Ant to move. He stormed towards Vyn, stopping inches before him, his stare furious.

"Do that again..." Ant trailed off, his jaw clenching.

The smirk on Vyn's face was mischievous as he leaned closer. "And you'll do what?"

The flaring of Ant's nostrils was almost comical, but he only huffed and walked away, muttering to himself. I was almost choked by the awkwardness that seemed to grow in the silence that followed.

Well, that could have been worse, I suppose, I thought, shaking my head as I strolled towards Eli.

You're fucking welcome, Ant snapped.

I stopped before her. "There would have been no avoiding a fight, Eli."

She started to argue, "You don't know that—"

"I do," I told her in a tone that reminded me of my father, something that made me feel pride in spite of everything.

"He's right," Roux said.

Eli turned on her incredulously.

Roux continued, "That monstrosity was here for a reason. We may not know what it is—but we were lucky we were here to stop it. There would have been no treating with it, Eli. Dracho is right."

I nodded in thanks, and she smiled at me. I couldn't let them know that it was no assumption; that my abilities told me the creature would not rest until it had destroyed us all. Underneath the physical armour, there appeared to be no soul—no semblance of humanity—left at all.

❧

"What made you come and find us, Roux?" Vyn asked whilst we made camp.

Things had settled down a bit. Bas finished setting up an area around the fire as Ant stood before me, cleaning the cut I had sustained to my head. Various curse words and acid remarks streamed through his thoughts as he wiped it softly, to my amusement.

When he was done, I walked away from the group, noting Eli sitting on her own and looking steadily to the horizon, her face aglow with the last tangerine rays before twilight beckoned the first stars of the night. I watched her closely as she tilted her chin upwards and closed her eyes, soaking up the dying sunlight as it lit up her pale skin. In the tall grass on the outskirts of the trees, Cubra pranced about, attempting to catch the grasshoppers that were trying to escape his claws.

A heavy quiet had fallen between us since the confrontation. All of us were on edge.

"I spoke with my mamona... we both felt that my journey with you had not finished. She sensed I would be able to help you." Roux spoke over her shoulder as she joined me where I stood solitary on the border of the campsite, far enough that no one would hear a private conversation.

She took a deep breath. "Seems she was right, and I arrived at *just* the right time."

I winced, turning from Eli to smile sheepishly at her. It didn't feel natural to be suspicious of her decision to join us, but I couldn't help it. I had no idea if she knew about Ant and I. The same magick that ran through her veins ran through mine. I could feel it, so it only made sense that she could too—even if she wasn't entirely sure exactly what we were yet.

"I can see the gears running in your mind without me speaking mine." Roux was straight to the point. I huffed slightly, shooting her a close-lipped smile, and nodded for her to continue. "I don't need to know what you are. It's not my business." Her voice was hushed, but she remained cool and calm.

I extended my powers, trying to evaluate the truth in her words.

The smile she gave me was sly as she placed her hands on her hips. "I can feel that, you know."

I withdrew the magick. "I apologise—that was rude of me."

"It's all right," she laughed, "it feels familiar." She lifted her face to the sky, eyes closed, at peace. "Like my own, but not like my own. Like a sibling..."

Her expression softened as she turned to look at me, and my chest clenched with emotion. I'd never thought of it like that before. I had never had a sibling; being an only child was often lonely. To know that the magick within me was shared with many others made me feel less alone.

She continued, "Our magicks know each other. I imagine it's rare—to be apart for so long and then come across each other again. The same energies that have wandered the planet for aeons. They just want to say hello. Didn't you feel it when you entered Aion?"

"Is that what it was?"

Her smile was radiant, the edges of her eyes crinkling. "Yes. Your friend—Ant? I could tell he could feel it too. I imagine he's one who likes to maintain control over his emotions at all times?"

I rolled my eyes. "You don't know the half of it."

Roux chuckled. "Give me your hand, *nboku*." She extended her own. I eyed her suspiciously.

"*Nboku?*"

"It means 'friend' in our native tongue." She tilted her head. "And don't worry, the others won't notice a thing. Now give it."

"Bossy," I muttered under my breath, holding out a nervous hand. She took hold of it, turning it palm up. Placing her own just above mine, she left a small space between them. My dragon awoke, rearing his sleepy head to watch curiously.

"Extend your magick a little, concentrating it into your hand.

Trust me—they want to say hello." She spoke quietly, and I nodded, taking a deep breath.

Feeling the familiar electrical energy flow through my body, I focused it down my arm and into my hand. Unlike Roux, who could manifest physical magick, my gift was transformation—but that didn't mean the magick didn't exist within my human form. I could feel the energy focusing atop the skin of my palm as my dragon peered closer in wonder.

Roux manifested a magnificent golden wave, with black tendrils floating along the edges. I audibly gasped, and for a moment worried about our companions—and Ant's reaction. But my magick was invisible. To them, it should just look like I was holding the flow of Roux's magick between our hands.

The feeling was incredible as I flexed my fingers; a pleasant warmth spread along each of them and along my palm, as the power extended past it and into the space between our hands. Roux mirrored the movement, awe in her eyes, the wave ebbing along with the flow of her hand. I could feel it as the magicks twisted around each other as if embracing—greeting one other as a long-lost friend.

It wasn't long before they returned to their respective owner, and the feeling eased. We shared a look, laughing, before retracting our hands. I looked down, rubbing mine together, and then pulled Roux in for an embrace, which she reciprocated enthusiastically. It felt good to have another friend.

25

When we pulled apart, Roux and I turned towards the camp to see two sets of eyes watching us: one molten gold and one emerald green.

We ate food in relative silence, as Ant's glare burned a hole in the side of my face, and everyone retired to their tents quite early, eager to sleep off the awful taste left behind by the Hollow's presence.

What were you thinking?! Ant demanded once we were within the safety of our shelter for the night.

I flung an arm across my face, wincing as I caught the wound on my forehead, and let out a rough breath. "You know what, Ant, I wasn't. I'm just kind of winging it at this point."

It was the truth. Every new bit of information revealed potential new enemies, more questions than answers, and the realisation that this quest was so much bigger than I ever could have imagined. This issue was more significant than just Tenebris. This threat endangered all of Ruvalon—perhaps even the realms beyond, if it continued to spread. We needed to find out what it wanted, which meant venturing to where it came from.

And today had taught me that I was in no way prepared for it. *We* weren't prepared for it. Not if we couldn't work together.

Today... today, my pride had been stung. Not only had I been bested and made to bleed in front of my peers—but it had happened so quickly, as if I were a youngling in my first days of training. I was the son of an Emperor! It was unheard of.

It made me wonder how many times my friends had allowed me to win.

Ant's exhale was an impatient puff of air. "I know what you're thinking... and *no*."

Removing my arm, I turned, looking at my oldest friend as he lay in his sleeping sack beside me.

"No one could have anticipated what happened today, Dracho. That adversary was unlike anything we've ever seen. It wasn't some stray wyvern or mortal. Nor, to be honest, are we trained for such a being." He sounded frustrated. "You're too hard on yourself. I can read your doubt all over your face."

Don't think for one second that outcome had anything to do with your training. He switched to conversing mentally, in case anyone was close enough to hear.

Just because you're the son of Tenebris doesn't mean anyone in the Ejder Guard would dream of going easy on you. If anything, it encourages them more to try and best you. Do you honestly believe Althea would pull her punches when sparring with you?

He could read me too easily. My upper lip curled. *Althea would knock me on my arse if I even suggested it.*

She knocks you on your arse anyway.

I laughed. "Roux said she could tell you felt the... energy?"

He hummed, not offering anything further.

"Well? What did it feel like to you?"

His eyes seemed to shift uncomfortably around the dark tent. Odd.

My nerves were on edge from the past few hours, and it wasn't like him to stay his words with me. "Out with it, Ant."

His eyes blazed as he rounded on me. "Don't take your shame

and bad mood out on me. Some of us need time to process exactly what's going on. We're not *all* afforded the luxury of being able to freely speak our minds when we want."

An awkward silence elbowed its way between us for a few moments.

Ant rubbed his hand over his face. "I felt—jittery? I don't know how else to describe it. As soon as we entered that place, it felt like a warmth had erupted through my entire body. Like static." He seemed positively irritated by that. "I knew it was the magick, but it annoyed me that I couldn't subdue it. It was like sensory overload."

I smiled to myself. Stars forbid Ant experience an emotion he couldn't get under control! "That's why you seemed so on edge?"

He nodded. "And everyone was so—friendly—so open. It made the magick... respond, which felt confining. You know I'm not a people person. I'd rather keep to myself."

I suddenly felt guilty for pushing him. Ant had always kept to himself a lot, analysing every situation, and would disappear as soon as his social energy ran out. Sure, he could let go, but only in the company of his closest friends and those he trusted.

"If it's any consolation, I felt the same. My magick was all over the place. I genuinely had no idea what was going on with my own body." I chuckled.

He smiled dryly. "You know—that's not what a real apology sounds like?"

"But it's the best you're gonna get." I exhaled, putting my arms behind my head.

He laughed gruffly. "Prick."

I set my head down for the night, satisfied that he and I were good, but I couldn't fight a sense that, in some ways, Eli was right. Had my actions today with the assassin set us on a course there was no turning back from?

❧

"Dracho!"

I roused from sleep, bringing my dagger up from beneath the furs.

Bas stared at me from between the tent flaps, his expression unusually worried. "Er, I come in peace? You need to get out here —now."

His head disappeared. I stretched my tired body and quickly made myself decent to head outside. *What on earth could have happened now?*

The urgency became apparent as I rubbed the blurriness from my eyes. A tang of iron shifted upon the breeze; cold foreboding struck my gut. To the south... billowing red smoke and pink clouds wrapped the sky around the great tree.

Shock moved my feet forward. "What the fuck?"

I whirled on Vyn and Bas, who stood close to the horses, talking under their breath. "Has she seen it?"

Vyn shook his head. "We thought it best to wake you first."

"Where's Antares?" I asked.

"As soon as he saw it, he went to scout the area in our travelling direction."

"Son of a bitch!" *Ant!* I called uselessly; he wasn't close enough to hear me.

"Who's a son of a bitch?" Roux asked, smiling as she exited Eli's tent, Eli behind her.

Everyone froze.

Anguish twisted the mage's face as soon as she saw the clouds blossoming pink behind me. A mere split second passed before she bolted. I swung around, catching her by the waist.

"LET ME GO! RELEASE ME!" she screamed. Engel reared, but I held on, channelling my strength into my arms. Roux kicked as I lifted her into the air, trying to calm her, and then a sudden burning sensation travelled through my arms. I pulled her close, confused, and looked over her shoulder to see her hands upon my arms.

She was burning me.

The heat increased. I gritted my teeth as magick surged, my dragon snapping his teeth and encouraging the change. But I knew if she wanted to *really* hurt me, she could.

"Let. Me. Go," Roux said, eerily calm. Terrifying.

"No. Roux, think about this, we need to—"

She threw her head back into my nose, and my arms dropped.

My hand flew up to cover my face. "Mother-f—!" I was surprised I wasn't bleeding again.

Bas had already sauntered forward, blocking her path, standing rooted like a tree with his arms crossed. He smirked. "Not on my watch, little mage."

Roux gave him a cocksure grin, rushing at him without faltering. A few feet in front of him, she dropped to the floor, gliding under and through his legs, flipping him off as she went, before gracefully jumping back upright and taking off again.

Bas' face fell. "Hardly fair."

All of a sudden, she came to a stop, as if an invisible lasso had taken hold of her and tightly wrapped itself around her arms.

Roux fell to her knees. "Let me go!"

I looked around, spotting Vyn stood off to the side, frowning in concentration.

"LET ME GO!" Her magick shook the nearby trees.

Vyn was shaking with the effort to keep hold of her. I didn't notice Eli move until she had passed me, patted Vyn on the shoulder and walked to stand in front of Roux.

Roux looked up at her. "P-please?" Her voice broke on a choked sob before her head fell, her shoulders sagging in defeat.

Eli lowered herself to her knees, placing her hands upon Roux's shoulders. "We'll go with you."

Roux's head jerked up; she looked at Eli with disbelief in her glassy eyes. "You will?"

"But you need to trust us, Roux. Running off could put your own life in danger. Let us *help* you." She offered the mage a hand.

Vyn relaxed, Bas catching him as his legs gave way, and Roux exhaled in defeat. She took Eli's hand, rising to her feet.

"Where's Ant?" Eli asked. I shook my head, her eyes narrowing. "Vyn, Bas. Stay here for when Ant gets back. Then meet us in Aion."

"Are you sure that's a good idea?" Vyn queried breathlessly.

Eli nodded firmly. "Stay at camp." Her eyes bored into their faces as they looked at her with twin expressions of concern. "And if that thing shows up—run."

She glanced at me and I nodded, fetching my armour and weapons from my tent. No more words were exchanged as we made our way towards Home Tree, unease swirling around my stomach.

26

We could hear the moans before we entered Home Tree.

My feet skidded to a halt as we entered, unfinished questions leaving my mouth as the sight hit me. It was too much. Even the late afternoon clouds seemed morose, despite the blue sky that backdropped them. Such mindless, brutal destruction.

The ground was scattered with slain bodies of the Aioni; the earth was baptised with poppy-red blood, the air permeated with residual magic and the bitter perfume of death and grief. Sounds pierced my ears as we advanced further into Aion: the violent, suffocating sounds of anguish and loss.

Gone were the children who'd played around my legs, full of laughter. Gone were the stalls with their tantalising delicacies and mystical, magical totems. Now everything was laid to waste or strewn about the ground. Survivors rushed about, searching for more and gathering what supplies they had left. People barged past us, bumping my shoulders, searching erratically and then uncontrollably falling to their knees when they found their loved ones—withered elders standing in desolate silence at the loss of their future leaders and legacies. A woman trudged past catatonically, a small knitted blanket hanging from her fingers. Surviving children sought refuge in any broken shack still standing.

It looked like the work of an army—so much destruction in such a short time—but the precise, familiar wounds that adorned the dead made it obvious that the creature we had named the Hollow had joined in with the destruction. A being with a power we must have only seen a snippet of.

It was too much.

I watched in silent shock as Roux begged an elder where Bisa and Azande had last been seen. Cubra nudged the foot of a fallen mage and mewled. I looked away, feeling as though I was intruding on a private moment. Eli was standing silently to the side, hugging her arms, her shoulders drooping. She was always very adept at keeping herself together, but right now her eyes were glazed with tears as she bit her bottom lip tightly in a bid to prevent any sound from escaping her lips. My heart sank. She was feeling guilty. She thought that this was our fault.

My fault.

"She was seen by the beach." Roux's words summoned us from our thoughts.

Eli looked at me with heavy eyes, and I motioned for her to go on before me. We rushed down the previously peaceful path to the sloping walkway to the beach. Along the way, we encountered more bodies, more grief, and several injured mages, some too far along for help. Their cries did nothing for the heaviness in my chest.

There was a crowd further down by the water, and a familiar braided, black-and-grey head of hair broke away from it, standing from a kneeling position. Bisa was alive. Relief flooded me, and I released a breath as Roux broke into a run to her mother. Eli and I fell into step beside each other as we continued to walk slowly towards the crowd, watching Roux hug Bisa desperately. Bisa's face was torn in anguish, tears running down her face as we neared. She took a tight hold of Roux's arms and held her just out of reach as we watched her say something. Roux recoiled, dropping her arms as if she had been stung, looking towards the water.

My eyes narrowed. I tried to use my advanced hearing, but the sounds of grief were everywhere. Eli, perceptive as always, had noticed something amiss too. Roux pushed through several people towards the water like a woman dying of thirst, stumbling in the sand. People moved in behind her so that we could no longer see her...

But the sound that ripped from her throat stopped me where I stood.

It wasn't a sound that belonged in life. I had heard screams before; of fear, where someone encountered a wild wyvern, or when they were startled by an unexpected noise. This was something else. A scream of visceral pain that echoed in my bones. The sound of a wounded animal.

Eli staggered forward as I shook myself from my reverie and ran along with her. We pushed through the gathered crowd and found bodies scattered across the beach. Roux was in the middle of them, on her knees, rocking back and forth whilst wailing to the sky. Her knees were sandy, and cradled in her arms...

Was Azande.

Her head hung limply from the crook of Roux's elbow, her once proud curls now slick with blood and the lapping waves. My senses didn't need to reach out to confirm what I knew; I could see the greying of her skin already taking hold as her eyes stared lifelessly at the sky above us.

Something felt broken inside me. An endless turmoil settled in my stomach, full of wasted youth and promises that could never be kept.

She was just a child.

"It removed her tongue."

I could tell it took a lot of effort, but Bisa cleared her throat to whisper from behind us. The gut-wrenching gasp that left Eli's mouth plucked at my already cracked heart, her hands flying up to cover her mouth.

I caught the woman's gaze, my voice barely a whisper. "What?"

"Along with several others. They won't be able to perform the rites." Her teeth clenched. "She—she cannot move onward with the ancestors." Agony dulled her eyes as she looked at Roux, who continued to rock, sobbing in desolation.

Despair threatened to swallow me whole. I had never felt such sorrow and guilt. Never felt pain in my chest this intense over such an injustice, even when my mother had died. I lifted my hand to place my palm over where I knew my heart to be, wondering how it was still beating.

"There must be something we can do," I choked out as I stared down at Roux.

Bisa shook her head slowly. "There are only the ancestors. Everything is done with their permission, and what is permitted is their wishes."

"What fairness is there in that?!" I turned on her and demanded like a petulant child; my dragon rumbled in my chest.

Her head tipped up, strong chin defiant, and she looked at me with resolve in her hazel eyes. I turned away, choking on the guilt. The poor woman had just lost her daughter. She didn't need me snapping at her.

Roux had stopped wailing now; she stared longingly at her young sister's face, stroking her soaking wet hair away from her features. "I need to... prepare her, Mama." She sniffled quietly. "I would like to prepare her for the Uhane ceremony, please, Mamona?"

It seemed, despite Bisa's warning that some of the dead would be unable to undergo their rites, Roux still wanted to try.

"Of course, ma chemiel." Bisa nodded at her solemnly, unshed tears in her eyes.

Without thinking, I stepped forward and knelt on one knee beside Roux. "May I... help, in any way at all?" I held out my hand.

Roux didn't take it, but looked up at my face with deep gratitude. "Thank you, but no, *nboku*. This is something I must do on my own."

I got to my feet, bowing my head as I took a step back, and watched in surprise as Roux got to her feet with ease with Azande still in her arms, as if the girl were as light as the air itself. She took one shuddering breath and started towards Home Tree with her sister and mother. Eli and I glanced at each other, unsure of what to do for a second, but with a nod of her head Eli began to walk in the same direction, and we fell into a steady rhythm side by side.

The walk back up the sloping pathway, through Home Tree to the chief's home, showed that only the lower levels had been decimated by the Hollow. The walk up was a silent one, and felt much longer than our previous trips along it. The quiet was broken only by sobs as people moved out of the way; as we passed more of the Aioni people, they started to kneel along the sides of the spiralling slope out of respect, both for their elder and their fallen. I watched from behind as Roux lifted her chin and walked with determination, shoulders back, the ends of Azande's hair fluttering over her arm in the breeze. I could tell from the way she was breathing that she was crying, but she didn't stop.

As we finally approached the homestead, Roux's legs started to shake with either exhaustion or the emotional toll. Eli rushed forward and supported her arm as Roux's legs finally gave out, her arms tightening on her sister. She looked up with wide eyes, terrified.

"Help me, please? I-I can't do this... I can't do this alone." Her head shook, as if ashamed she had ended up asking for help—she sounded so insecure, so small, despite being so strong. It left me feeling helpless.

"Of course I will." Eli smiled gently at her, helping her stand fully upright before walking her into the hut.

I turned to Bisa. "Bisa. I apologise... for snapping before. I'm going to take a look around, see if anyone needs my help. Would you like me to do anything?" It was all I could do at this point.

She took hold of my hand and gave it a gentle squeeze.

"No apology necessary. You're very kind, young Dracho; many thanks, but no. I need to tend to my people before retiring to help my daughter. The preparations will not take too long; it is our custom to complete the Uhane ceremony within three days of—of a loss.' She smiled a sad smile that didn't reach her eyes and started heading back down the tree.

27

I stayed in Aion for three days, doing what I could to help. Even with my draconi strength, my body ached from our efforts to rebuild. Twenty-six mages, out of the ninety-four that lived in Aion, had been killed during the attack—twelve of which had had their tongues removed. I had learned that the atrocity had indeed been carried out by the armoured being we had met. Using its spear and a dagger, with a ferocity and quickness they had never seen, it had cut through those who had tried to stand against it whilst children ran and hid—a few slain before they could find a safe place. The creature had only fled when Bisa and a few of the elder mages, using their advanced magick, managed to keep it at bay.

It made me wonder why it had fled from our small group after Roux had attacked it. Maybe, with Aion so close, it had chosen to attack it out of revenge for that encounter.

Rest had eluded me most nights as I tried to quell the worry I felt about Ant and having not seen Eli or Roux at all since leaving them at the chief's home. Not had there been word from Vyn and Bas. I had not ventured to see them, unable to bear leaving the people of Aion. The guilt ate at me.

It was a foreign concept to me, preparing a loved one on your own. When members of the royal family were prepared for the pyre in Tenebris, it was a colossal affair. Many respected scholars came to clean and dress the body—to bring gifts from far-away lands to be burned with the deceased. The idea of doing it yourself to someone as close as a sibling... Such an intimate act humbled me.

The Uhane ceremony was to be performed in the early evening of the third day, and a silent calm had settled over Home Tree. The Aioni people prayed before heading to the water's edge, so the winding path heading up through the boughs was practically silent. I would only see someone when I came across family members carrying the deceased, placed in beautifully woven wooden caskets adorned in rose-pink lilies.

Bisa had explained the ceremony to me. On the day of the ceremony, the dead in their woven caskets were carried to rest on the beach. At twilight, they were lovingly pushed into the water, where the *wansembe*—priestess—began the Uhane ritual. The Aioni believed that their soul resided in the body until this calling on the spirits accepted the deceased's final rites and allowed them to move on into their last journey with the ancestors. Bisa explained that, similar to my beliefs, all energy was only borrowed; when they passed, it must be returned. It was a tremendous honour to have been allowed to borrow the magicks and to return them for future generations.

What had happened to Azande and some of the other mages—to potentially be unable to undergo the rites in death and return their magicks—was a great dishonour. But since it was not the fault of the Aioni, Bisa and Roux still wanted to try.

After the Uhane ceremony, the bodies would be cremated on a great pyre and their ashes released from the top of the great tree. The ceremony represented the Aioni people's symbiotic relationship with the elements: the final rest on the beach for earth, the placing in the water, cremation upon the pyre, and the release of ashes upon the wind. It was all a balance.

Azande's casket was the last to be brought onto the beach, carried by Roux and Bisa. Eli followed closely behind, her white dress—borrowed from Roux, I guessed—flowing in the breeze and her hair in a tight coronet that wrapped over her ears and was pinned at the back of her head. The Aioni, all dressed in white, united in their grief, whispered prayers of adoration and longing over each casket before gently gifting them to the shallows, each one gently rising and falling upon the flow of water.

Roux stepped forward between the caskets, the skirts of her dress sitting atop the water. She spoke beautifully in the language of the Aioni as they sang out with her, performing the ceremony with a grace in sorrow I had never witnessed. Roux's words rang clearly, hoping to pierce the veil between the living and celestial.

From most of the caskets, some of them too small, brilliant orbs of light appeared, floating above the surface of the water. But no more, and none from Azande's casket as Roux's prayer came to an end, the people's voices diminishing to silence.

Raw anguish tightened my chest as I bowed my head, hearing a sob erupt from the mage in the water. I had wished upon all the stars, ancestors and deities that the ancestors would permit the Aioni people to move on. This was a huge blow to the clan—the worst since the Tain—and I felt lost, knowing I could do nothing to help.

Nothing marred the silence, other than the breaking of soft waves upon the shore and the muted crying of people around the beach. Everyone stood in solidarity, together in their grief.

Until I heard it.

A lone voice which rose above the whimpers—the cries. A voice which rolled over everyone like a balm, bringing grace and along with it, the haunting knowledge that only tragedy had brought out her song. It was a voice that pierced my draconi soul, my magick easing in comfort. Turning my head slowly, as if the movement would wake me from a dream and end the soothing song too soon, I spotted her.

I had been so lost in my sorrow that I had not noticed Eli wade into the shallow waters. She stood waist deep, surrounded by the rose-pink flowers and wooden caskets, with arms spread outwards, palms towards the sky. Her eyes fluttered closed as she sang a wordless melody, her brow slightly furrowed as she turned her face up to the first stars of the early evening. There was nothing but her song.

Looking around, I worried that someone would stop her, but no one interfered. The Aioni people watched, transfixed, and Roux stood in the water a few feet away from Eli with her head resting on her hands in prayer, mouthing words I could not hear, tears flowing down her cheeks. They knew this was a plea. A calling to the spirits to carry the wayward souls across the peaceful water and lead them onward—lead them home.

Almost as if woken by her siren song, pulsing from within each of the caskets was a bright, flickering sphere of changing colours. My fist clenched by my side. This wasn't supposed to happen... was it?

I looked back to Eli, shocked to see the same colourful light rolling from her palms into the water like a fine mist, as if her hands were creating it.

The orbs of light rose out of the caskets to dance across the water, twirling without a care, so free, forming a wave of beauty and light. One gracefully swirled around Roux's still form, following the ebb and flow of the water. Looking out, I saw ribbons of pink and lavender transfigure the sky as the last rays of sunlight sank below the horizon, leaving behind a morsel of dark orange. My spirit soared at the sight, the emotion of it all causing my chest to tighten as I swallowed hard. But as I watched the magicks dance majestically across the water, I couldn't help but form a semblance of a smile.

I glanced back and stared in wonder at the side of Eli's face. Her eyes were wide now, staring at the sky, and she continued to sing. Her chest heaved with emotion that she struggled to keep contained, her voice breathy and tears slowly trailing down her ashen cheeks.

I suddenly realised I had been holding my breath and inhaled deeply, shuddering. My chest ached, and I coughed quietly to try and clear it, earning a sideways glance from an elderly mage beside me. As I looked abashedly at him, I noticed Bisa a few steps along the beach, giving me a knowing look. I stared into the chief's eyes, wondering what she saw in the depths of my own, and the corner of her lips turned up in an amused grin, as if she knew a secret I didn't.

The orb that had danced around Roux glided along the shore, swooping around Bisa, who placed her hand over her heart, silent tears travelling down her cheeks as the Aioni women around her placed their outstretched hands upon each other's shoulders. It then moved to stop before me, glowing so brightly that the colours were almost translucent. I stared at the beautiful sphere of light, my brows pinching as its aura washed over me. I contained the choking feeling that started to overcome me and forced out a smile.

"It was nice to meet you. Goodbye, Azande," I whispered.

Almost as suddenly as it had begun, Eli's prayer came to an end. Upon the final note, she raised her hands and placed them on top of each other on her chest.

The crowd gasped as the brilliant spheres burst into millions of specks of light, causing a blinding wave of illumination to flow over everyone as if the sky had ignited with a thousand tiny stars. Eli's head bowed with a trembling breath. The people moved closer, comforting each other and chatting loudly in elation. Roux moved to embrace Eli, sobbing into her shoulder.

"Go to her, *Inyoka*."

Panic lanced through me like an exposed nerve as I reeled, heart hammering, staring at Bisa. I knew the magickal term for my people. The mages' word for *dragon*.

"Do not fret—your secret is safe with me, Dracho." Her smile was genuine, so I trusted in her words. It was a relief, knowing there were those here who accepted me. It gave me hope that perhaps one day, Eli and the others would too.

Bisa's smile faded slightly. "Go; she will need you now." My eyes skipped to look at Eli, heading towards the shore, hugging Roux close to her side. "The spirits accepted her prayer and allowed our people to move on—but at a price. That will have taken much of her energy, and she will need rest, perhaps healing."

"I don't understand. How—?"

"Whilst Eli may not have celestral magick of her own, her wish for our people was pure of heart. It's not for us to understand why the ancestors do what they do. But in this case, I thank the stars that they did." I felt like the chief knew more than she was letting on, but before I could ask, she tapped my arm affectionately before moving on to speak with her people.

Conflict and confusion rose within me, but I put them away for another time. I wasn't sure whether Eli would even accept help from me, but my feet moved of their own accord towards her across the beach, my dragon pulling me forward. As I neared her, my sharp eyes could see the shake in her legs and her bleary-eyed expression, despite her soft smiles to the people thanking her.

She had only taken two steps onto the beach when I reached her, and she looked up into my eyes with what looked like relief. Her breath seemed to stutter in her chest before she let it out, tension leaving her body. Her hand reached out for mine, her eyes fluttering shut as her knees buckled and she surrendered herself to my arms.

28

Dipping the cool cloth into the bowl of water once more, I pressed it to Eli's warm neck before moving it to her head. Worry had locked me in place for the past two days as I guarded her bedside, only taking breaks to take care of my essential needs as I waited for her to wake up. I told her stories, skipping out the major details; whispered compliments to try and bring out that blush that occasionally graced her cheeks; and occasionally told inappropriate jokes that would make even Bas blush, hoping it would trigger her fury. No reaction followed.

But I stayed. So proud of what she had accomplished on her own for Aion, but unable to squash the fear that balled in my gut. *What if she didn't wake?* I pushed the thought away. She *would* wake—and berate or stab me for sponging her head whilst unconscious.

Only Bisa came and went, her eyes tight but constantly reassuring me that Eli would come to. She informed me that word had been sent to Vyn and Bas about Eli's condition, and though they wanted to join us here in Aion, they would follow her last orders.

That meant Ant had not returned. My chest tightened with conflicting emotions. On one hand, my dragon and I wanted to flee this place and find Ant, knowing I could not rest until I did. But Eli's body lay weakly beside me. I couldn't leave her.

Once, I dared to ask Bisa how she dealt with caring for so many. How was she coping so well with the responsibility of so many people placed on her shoulders? My insides and thoughts were trying to consume me.

She gave me a smile so motherly I had to turn away. "The burden of leadership is heavy, Dracho. We must wear many hats. We are the calm breeze that helps the honey-bee along its way, pollinating the fauna for its next cycle. But when forced, we are also the hurricane—the beautiful, violent destruction that shows no signs of stopping... until it does. Because it *chooses* to," she told me with a shaky exhale that made me grit my teeth. When I looked at her, I could see the truth.

She knew exactly who I was. Had always known that I was destined to lead Tenebris.

"What if I can't?" A whispered secret. A sacred admission.

Her hand pressed lightly upon my shoulder as I stared at Eliana on the bed. "You must choose to. Those of us born into greatness... we all have our time, until we pass on our light to another. Just remember, a leader is a servant."

That was all she said before she left us. I clasped Eli's hand to still the trembling in my own. I couldn't allow my worrisome thoughts to consume me right now, not whilst I cared for her. Her body was so drained that a sickness had overcome her; she shivered with fever, a harsh, scratchy cough ripping its way out of her throat every now and then. Her eyes flickered under her darkened eyelids whilst she slumbered, between dreams and reality, and I longed to see the green of her eyes.

On the third day, when I roused from sleep, I spotted a visitor. I'd fallen asleep sitting by Eli's bedside; at some point I must have rested my head beside her arm. I squinted over at Roux, taking in the gauntness of her face. The same white dress from the Uhane ceremony hung off one shoulder as she fiddled with her hands.

"Roux?"

She shot me an unreadable look, a crooked smile forming on her lips. "I, um, just wanted to see how she was doing."

I almost jerked at the difference in her voice, the sound grating my ears. I didn't lift my head from the bed but watched her, cautiously, as my dragon's ears perked, his teeth baring slightly. Roux must have sensed the change; her hands dropped to her lap, her brow furrowing.

That's when I saw the blackened fingertips. The thin black threads, like tree roots, spreading up through her fingers and hands.

"Roux, what's—?"

"I'm just waiting for her to wake so we can leave."

"Leave?" I asked carefully.

Roux's head twitched, an eerie smile spreading across her face. "To go and find the Hollow, of course. I *need* to find it."

My eyes widened. "Roux, I thi—"

I gasped as a soft touch, the barest of strokes, brushed over the skin of my neck before running through the strands of my hair.

"Dracho?" a voice asked weakly from the bed.

I didn't notice Roux fleeing; Eli held my whole attention. *There you are,* my dragon purred.

Those springtime eyes rendered me speechless. If it had been anyone else, I would have been able to turn away—but with her I was always drawn in, always wanting more. A shaky exhalation shuddered through me as I touched my head to her arm, clasping her hand like a lifeline.

"You're all right."

Her tongue darted out to lick her cracked lips, her voice hoarse. "H-how long have I been out?"

"Two days."

Eyes widening, she tried to sit up. "Two days?!" She winced, clasping her throat. "We have to leave."

Clasping her shoulders, I gently lowered her back down against her pillow. "Leaving is the *last* thing we'll be doing. Not until you're better."

"I'm fine—"

"You still have a fever." Her skin felt warm to the touch but, thankfully, not as heated as it was. "Bless the stars, it's broken."

"What have I missed?"

"I don't know." I chuckled at the confusion on her face. "I, um, haven't left long enough to find out."

Her fingers lifted, brushing over the cut I had sustained from the Hollow. It had almost faded, thanks to my quick healing.

"You—stayed with me..." A whispered statement, her eyes roaming my face. Heavy tension filled the air between us, like thick mist cascading over still mountains.

The dragon within pulled towards her as my heart hammered in my chest. I blinked in the dim light, keeping her intense gaze, and wondered why that surprised her. "Of course I stayed."

For a long moment we just looked at each other, and I thought I could get lost in her gaze—like roaming through the densest forest.

She coughed, breaking our connection as she looked away. In the beat of a bird's wings, the tension evaporated, creating a distance between us that made my dragon pout.

"Um." I cleared my throat. "We should probably discuss Roux."

"What's wrong with Roux?"

❧

"Roux is succumbing to her grief and anger. If she does not face it, it will consume her," Bisa told us.

"What does that mean?" Eli asked.

I was standing in Bisa's home; Eli sat upon a chair in the corner, her legs curled under her. Bisa was on her feet too, a colourful dress swaying about her ankles as she took a deep breath. "The magick gifted to us by the ancestors is used within the balance. Roux is so focused on seeking out the Hollow for revenge, it's corrupting her magick. If it continues... she'll start to lose herself completely."

"You mean—"

"She'll go insane?" The words were like ash coming from my mouth. I knew what Bisa was insinuating. But there wasn't only anger and grief; Roux was consumed by guilt. She had attacked the Hollow to save my life. She must have reached the same conclusion I had: that its attack on Aion had been retribution.

"Dracho!" Eli exclaimed.

Bisa went to the chair, kneeling beside it as she clasped Eli's hand. "No, he's right, Eliana."

Eli's mouth fell open, her eyes darting about the chief's home before resting on her face. "What can we do?"

Relief showed on Bisa's face. Her mind seemed to wander for a moment before she looked at us, a flash of fear in her eyes. "You need to take her to the Vildspire. To Volente."

"What?" Eli's shock echoed my own. "That's not possible— Volente is ash. It was—"

The chief mage interrupted her. "Volente—some of our great old tree still stands."

"Excuse me?"

"It is no longer living. It is essentially a graveyard. The land does not thrive, and the energy there is filled with the angry spirits of our lost ones."

"Sounds like a *great* place to visit." My sarcasm earned me exasperated glares from both of them. "That's why you allowed the world to believe it was decimated. A land full of unsafe magickal energy."

Silence fell.

I rubbed my forehead. "If people knew the once great tree still stood, it—"

"It would become a spectacle." Bisa looked up at us. "Our tragedy would become a display for all." She pursed her lips and shook her head. "I would never allow that to happen."

"But now—?"

"But now... it is the only hope Roux has."

"Why? Why there?" Eli quizzed her.

"The ancestors... the magickal energy there is unsafe. They are angry and lost, like she is. But Volente has become a haven for mages who find themselves full of rage now." Bisa stared off through the window as if seeing something else before her. "If you take her before them, they will offer her a trial. A judgement of her soul, if you will. If she passes, they may grant her powers greater than she has ever known—powers that could help you on your journey going forward. Especially with the Hollow. The trial will help ease her from this pain. But whatever the outcome, try your best not to linger in those lands."

"Well, that sounds fantastic. Let's go." I clapped my hands together, though frustration marred my thoughts. I wanted Eli to heal and I wanted to help Roux, but I itched to find out more about the Hollow. For all we knew, it was tearing through all the villages of Ruvalon at this very moment.

But I would stay, and I would help Roux: because, deep down, I felt some burden of guilt, wondering if it had been *my* actions that had driven the creature here.

Eli's eyes narrowed as she stared at the woman; the chief's face was torn. "'Whatever the outcome'? What if she fails?"

The mage swallowed hard, breathing through whatever emotion she held back as she looked out to the fading sunlight. It was a moment before she faced us again. "If she fails..."

She didn't need to finish. Her tormented eyes said everything her lips wouldn't. If Roux failed her trial...

She'd die.

29

Eli had requested a moment of my time after Bisa's revelation, and hadn't said a word since. She walked, or rather stormed—somewhat unsteadily—in complete silence all the way down Home Tree until we reached the soft sand, then halted halfway down the beach. I stopped a short distance behind her.

She took a deep breath before spinning, her eyes wildly aflame. "There's no fucking way!"

I reared back, eyes widening. "W-what do you mean *no* way?"

"You heard what she said! Roux could die, Dracho."

"*Or* she could go insane and go on some magickal rampage in her vengeful bloodlust!"

"We don't know that's a certainty."

"We don't? I only saw her once, but it was scary, Eli. She's not... coping. What happens if she comes across the Hollow like that? Near a crowd of people?"

Eli's mouth opened before snapping shut, her thoughtless retort lost as she considered my words. "We're not discussing this, Dracho. There must be another way. She can't do this."

"Then it's a good thing it's not your choice." Roux's voice rang out from behind me. She stood with arms crossed, hands fisted tightly to hide the decay of her magick.

Eli walked past me; my hand darted out to grab her wrist.

"Roux—" she began.

"It's my decision, Eli. I truly appreciate what both of you are saying. I know it's because you care." Roux smiled weakly at us, seeming more lucid than when I had seen her earlier. "But it's my best chance of helping my people... and finding the Hollow. My magick has already started to corrode." Her eyes darkened as her fingers twitched outwards, the black tendrils in her hands moving under her skin as if alive. I stepped forward, blocking Eli slightly, and saw Roux note the movement. A shuddering breath left her as she squeezed her eyes shut. She took a deep breath before opening them again. "I need peace. Whether that's from healing or with my death, it doesn't matter. To stop anything like this from happening again, I need to do that trial."

Eli exhaled shakily and I turned to place a comforting arm around her, hoping she wouldn't shove me off. I was taken aback when she sagged into me, defeated—or exhausted from draining herself.

"We respect your decision, Roux," I told her. "And you won't be going alone." I gritted my teeth as soon as the words came out of my mouth. I needed to find Ant.

But I couldn't leave Roux to fend for herself. Not whilst the guilt of what happened to Aion festered in my gut. I looked down at Eli, who nodded in agreement.

Roux sighed. "I'd like that a lot. Eli"—Eli lifted her head— "I didn't get to say it before, but... Um, what you did, for my people. F-for Azande. Thank you."

Eli held her hand out, my dragon watching warily as Roux stepped forward to clasp it firmly. "No thanks needed—*ever*. It was my honour to be able to do that. For you all."

Roux smiled, a genuine smile now, before she came forward and wrapped her arms around the small brunette. I curled myself around them both, placing my free arm around Roux, squeezing them tightly.

"This is nice."

"Don't make this weird, blondie." Roux's voice shook with amusement.

"Wouldn't dream of it." I added, smirking, "Wouldn't wanna make Bas jealous." I didn't have to see Roux roll her eyes to know that she had.

Eli pulled out of the embrace. "Shit—the others!"

"Don't panic," I told her. "They will have waited back at camp. We really should get back and find Antares..." Why hadn't the others come to Aion? Had he not returned to camp yet?

"Ant hasn't returned yet?" Eli scanned me in apparent surprise.

Roux shook her head. "Don't worry," she said, "Mamona sent them a message. They're clued up on what's going on. Well, they were told you were sick. We haven't told them..."

My eyes skipped to Roux.

"...everything else yet."

Eli ran a tired hand over her face, blowing out a puff of air. "All right. We'll deal with that when we get back."

"Get back?" I asked.

"From Volente."

"Are they not coming with us?"

"Ant hasn't returned. So no. They can stay where they are until he's back safely." Her words sounded harsh but were belied by the concern that shimmered in her eyes. My dragon whined, missing our brother. I opened my mouth, but she continued. "They will be fine."

Roux nodded in agreement. "Mamona has sent some mages with supplies to accompany them, for their own protection."

That was a slight reassurance.

Eli's fingers brushed against the back of my hand and I jumped slightly, looking at her.

"We won't leave Antares," she promised. My throat tightened. "But Roux needs us for now, and we need to go. Sooner rather than later."

I suppressed the anxiety and made myself smile. "Whatever you say, Princess."

An impatient frown graced her face as her cheeks flushed, and I thought that if she were her usual self, she would definitely be physically reprimanding me.

I turned to Roux. "Are you ready for this?"

"It's now or never," she declared, giving us an obviously forced smile.

I took a firm hold of both their hands, giving them a reassuring squeeze. "Whatever happens, you have us."

⁊

If you walked east along the beach of Aion and carried on walking for a day, you would eventually reach the marshes that bordered Volente. The Aioni didn't stray too close; most never travelled through the marshes. But we would sail through them until we reached the old tree.

Many of the Aioni people had approached me and Eli to say goodbye as we prepared to leave. Meeting these beautiful people over the last few days had been an amazing experience, and I loved that they had embraced us so fully in their community, through the happiness and despair. I truly felt sorrow at leaving Home Tree. All I could hope was that my efforts of the last few days had brought them comfort in some way.

Roux sat silently upon the beach, Cubra resting his head upon her knee. "I'll miss you, boy. Do me a favour—promise you'll be good? The next part of my journey is dangerous, so I can't lose you too. I need you to look after Mamona, all right?" Tears filled Roux's eyes, but my soul soared at her request as she wrapped her arms around Cubra's neck. She had felt it best to leave him behind, as he was a spirit guide and we were heading to a place full of angry souls; she didn't know how he would react to such a place, and she also didn't want to leave her mother alone—in case the worst happened.

Engel had shown up on the beach, as if he knew Eli was heading off into danger. He would stay behind too, but his head shook restlessly as Eli stroked his muzzle, whispering soothing words to him. She sent him off back to camp, promising to return soon. Reluctantly, he trotted off in the direction of the forest whilst Eli watched, a solemn look upon her face.

My mind couldn't help but contemplate death as we stood, about to take those first steps. I had seen death that wasn't pretty—some of it extremely recent—but most of us in life, especially those who were born warriors, hoped for a good or clean death, even if it wasn't peaceful. As Bisa said a tearful goodbye to her surviving daughter, it was as though she was sending her off to their maker with a clear conscience, knowing that whatever happened, death came to us all, in the end. That was what the mages knew better than anyone else.

In the end, we all returned to the celestral. To what gave us life.

Bisa knew that there was no choice in this matter. Roux's pure magick would wither and turn dark as her anger and grief festered and corrupted her. Her mother trusted that Roux had the strength to overcome it, to face whatever the ancestors gave her... and come out stronger.

Despite my determination to see Roux through her trial, I admired her for choosing her path instead of giving in to her emotions. Her strength became my own as I pushed myself forward. Continued that path along the beach, knowing that only two of us might return.

We had commandeered a boat from one of the fishermen—he had given it willingly, pressing his many blessings upon us and our journey. The silence was painful as I loaded it with our tent bags and supplies and pushed it into the muddier waters of the eastern coastline; I picked up the paddles as we took our seats and started to row. Memories of paddling through some of the calmer waters in Tenebris flashed before my eyes. Though we favoured flying in our draconi forms, Althea and I had always enjoyed exploring the more human activities.

Life thrived on the edges of the coastline; thick patches of bulrushes sprang from the embankments as damselflies of all colours flicked across the water. Each creature and organism interacted with each other in a harmonious balance, keeping the land healthy. It was the same energy that thrived in the forest around Aion, an energy that made magick thrum in my veins. Made me feel alive. My thoughts drifted for a few hours, going over the events of the past few days. Eli and Roux sat quietly as we skimmed across the water, seeming to enjoy our surroundings, the former dipping her fingers into the clear water.

Until we edged closer.

The smell of the marshes reached us before any sight of it: a rotten, sulphurous scent that stung my eyes. Life started to disappear as we approached the Vildspire. I could no longer see those damselflies skipping about, and where bulrushes had once been abundant here, there were only broken stalks and dry, cracked banks.

The oars were coarse against my palms as I pulled harder through the water, thick with ash, and I knew exactly when we came upon Volente. Eli's gasp cut sharply through the silent air and I turned, taking in the view of the once-magnificent tree. The trunk, its edges jagged as if the tree had snapped, was aged and decayed. It no longer stood tall like Aion; its cracked edges reached no higher than the spires of the palace at Meridium, its bark withered and peeling. No branches reached out proudly from it; no foliage was to be seen anywhere. The ground around it for miles, spreading out to the dunes of the Vildspire and to the edges of the marshes, was darkened and dull. Only sporadic patches of thorny bushes grew here, sharp and menacing.

Roux stared up at the remainder of the tree, seemingly void of emotion. It was Eli whose reaction stunned me. Her knuckles were white as she clasped the edge of the boat, her teeth clenched tightly together.

I had forgotten. What this place meant to her; what she had lost here. She'd believed this land had been decimated, so she had never visited the site where her mother and brother, Morgwn, had fallen. Now, seeing the true extent of the event with her own eyes, I guessed it must bring back some of that wrenching pain for her.

I released the oars, reaching over to pull her towards me. There was no fight; her body moulded to mine as I placed her in my lap, careful not to tip the boat.

"I'm sorry," I whispered as she buried her head in my neck, small sniffs escaping.

Roux's blackened hands picked up the oars, her lips set into a thin line as her anguished eyes—the only place she allowed herself to show pain—met mine. I nodded in thanks, my hand continuing to stroke Eli's arm. We stayed like that until we met the shore.

The boat creaked as we pulled it over the cracked ground, leaving it for when we returned—hopefully, all three of us. The contrast between Volente and Aion was as harsh as night and day. Aion felt like a safe haven, the magickal energies raising life within me as easily as the rising of the morning sun. But this place... Energies surrounded and pressed down upon me like the steel bars of a cage, threatening to strangle me, the thickness of the air choking me the closer we got to the ruined tree. I imagined the scales along my dragon's back flexing as he urged me to fly away.

This place felt like a scar. No... a wound. It still bled profusely, into the land and the hearts of all those around.

Eli and Roux could feel it too, Roux staggering under the weight of it. Hooking my arm under her, I held her up as we continued forwards, together.

For a few hours we walked, Volente growing ever closer, until we travelled the sloping path into the once-great tree; I felt a muscle twitch in my temple as I tried to ignore the magicks that whispered along my neck. My dragon swung its head, snapping back and forth as if shaking off the spirits. We stopped just past the entrance, noticing a great chasm dipping into the centre of the tree, the darkness swallowing whatever was down there.

"I'm guessing as near to the top as we can get?" Eli murmured, glancing to a narrow path that travelled up what remained.

As if in answer, an indistinct figure of crackling blackness appeared before us, startling us so much that Eli let out a squeak of fright. I looked at her, raising a brow, and she flashed me a middle finger.

The shade said nothing, made no sound as it hovered in the space, but it seemed to beckon us forward as it moved towards that chasm.

"Guess we're going down instead... is this really a good idea?" Eli asked.

I swallowed the lump in my throat. "It's not like we have any other choice."

Well, that's hopeful, my dragon seemed to snort internally.

"I can do this on my own," Roux said, her voice weak.

I grasped her tighter. "We're not going anywhere."

Roux looked to Eli, who nodded.

I helped the mage along the broken ground towards the cavern that had opened up below the tree, following that shade as an ethereal glow appeared around it, lighting the way. Eli clung to the back of my shirt, her hand grounding me and reminding me—and my dragon—to be strong for both of them.

The spirit led us to a vast chamber blocked by debris, and I let go of Roux, who sank to the floor. The air was even thicker here, as if the grief and anguish of the spirits that surrounded us had polluted it. The shade moved before Roux, shifting into a form more closely resembling a human. It crouched down, its featureless face inches from hers.

"Why are you here?"

Shivers crept like ice along my body. The shade spoke with not one voice, but many. A united voice full of anger, loss and pain.

Roux gritted her teeth before clambering to her feet, swaying slightly. She inhaled, tipping her chin up defiantly. "You *know* why I'm here."

The shade tilted its head—and a loud, mighty wind burst through the chamber as it transformed again, forcing me to my knees and Eli to cover her ears with her hands.

The magick that manifested before us did not take the form of the Hollow... but of Roux. Not the woman we knew: this poor imitation of her had blackened, empty eyes with a cruel smile. This was Roux, should she give in to her grief—her anger.

The false Roux moved its head like a fox, looking at us and then staring at the mage like a meal, a sly grin on its face. From where I knelt, I could see Roux trembling as she faced down the mirror version of herself.

Her shoulders shook as a sob broke through.

"It's not real, Roux!" The harsh wind muffled my shout as it cruelly whipped my face. "It's your fear—fight it!"

The shade twisted in my direction, unnatural eyes bearing down on me as I suppressed the shiver my magick felt under its gaze. It raised its head high into the air and took a long sniff in my direction, smelling me. Those dark, ethereal eyes widened as it lowered its face slowly, still staring intently at me. My dragon purred, submitting to its raw celestral power, and my chest thrummed with the energy coursing through my veins.

"You'd know all about *fear*, wouldn't you, Son of the Ancients?" it asked with its many voices.

My blood ran cold. Of course the spirits would know me. The same magick that conjured the shade ran through my blood. The power of the transformation.

But due to the oath, it would not reveal me and betray it, and neither would I. I could not interfere—not even upon Roux's death. The consequences would fall upon the people of Tenebris as well as myself, and cost all of us our magick.

I gritted my teeth, my heart in agony, but I knew I had no choice. Without taking my eyes from the shade, I nodded subtly as an acknowledgement to the agreement made millennia ago with my ancestors.

Eli turned to me, confused, and called out over the noise, "Dracho?"

I shook my head. "You know she needs to fight this herself!"

"Dracho!"

"Eli!" I rounded on her, praying to all the stars that Roux was listening to me, knowing I was toeing the line with the spirit before me. "It's a manifestation of herself. Don't you see? She can only help herself. We can't do it for her."

"But—"

"She has nothing to be afraid of, not even herself! Only *she* can control her fear."

The shade stared at me, calculating. Eli clenched her jaw, tears in her eyes. Her chest heaved.

"Roux!"

"Eli, don't—"

"Roux, I have spent most of my life terrified! Of things that have happened and things that might happen! But you need to realise it's that fear... it's *fear* that's the real enemy!" Eli's hands still covered her ears, protecting them from the wind as her hair whipped around her face. "So kick its arse! Let's get out of here and live the life *we* want to live!"

The shade smirked down at Eli as she faced the ground. My heart started pounding in my chest, so hard I hoped they couldn't hear it over the wind. It screamed and rampaged now, becoming so angry that I had to crouch to avoid being swept away. Through the roaring in my ears, I could sense that all the magickal energy was focused with terrifying precision on Roux, waiting for her response as she fought within herself. My hands covered my ears as the overwhelming pressure caused them to pop, Eli groaning.

"You're right."

Roux's whisper cut through the wind, which abruptly died down. Silence settled in the chamber.

"What?" the shade demanded.

"I can only control my *own* fear."

The shade's eyes flashed. "And what is it you fear?"

Roux inhaled deeply. "Giving in completely to the anger. To my grief. Becoming like those who were banished from these lands. Who destroyed Volente all those years ago."

"So why should we permit you more power instead of taking it away?" the eerie voices asked.

"Because I am *not* them. They neglected the ancestors, abused the balance." Roux stilled, her eyes meeting her mirror self with fierce self-assurance. "I will restore it," she promised.

The shade reached her too fast for even my eyes, but Roux merely lifted her chin. It smiled. "Very well, Daughter of the Firsts." The shade backed up, reaching out. "Heed our warning; this gift does not come without consequences. Should you misuse it... we shall remove it entirely."

Roux stepped forward. "I understand."

"And—should you survive—this will not be pleasant."

Roux hesitated for only a second before clasping the spirit's hand.

The blackness drained from her fingers, gold vein-like threads instead spreading up her arm. She threw her head back, her mouth opening up in a silent scream as her other hand gripped her head under some unseen force.

"Roux!" Eli sprang forward, but I grabbed her around the waist.

"Wait!"

I held on tight as Eli clawed at my arms, watching as Roux's knees started to bend, her back arching. The shade was dimming, fading; its eerie eyes met mine before it disappeared completely.

A pulse of magick energy thrummed under our feet, spreading outwards as Roux's hand fell back to her side. I had a split second to dart forward, catching her before she hit the ground, her body limp in my arms.

"*Roux!*" I ran my hand along her clammy cheek to the back of her neck, supporting her head.

She didn't move.

"No—no! Don't do this." I shook her body gently. "Come on, wake up!"

A sharp breath left me as her eyes fluttered open and she gasped.

Eli choked on a relieved sob. "Don't ever do that to me again! Or I'll kill you myself!"

"Sure," Roux muttered breathlessly, a slight smile softening her face.

30

We left the tree as soon as Roux was able to stand. We were able to make it a few hours towards the marshes—my nose now becoming attuned to the smell—when Roux needed to stop. Reluctantly we decided to camp for the night; I set up a tent for them to rest in, Eli comforting Roux, whose head was aching horribly.

I did not sleep, guarding their tent throughout the night as the oppressive spirits suffocated the air around me.

I wished Roux had been strong enough to make it to the boat so I could row us back to Aion, but she hadn't been able to continue. It seemed that her every movement made the agony in her head worse. I had thought the trial would give her more power, but now I wasn't so sure.

I needed to get back to Ant.

In the morning, to my shock, Bisa and a male mage appeared. The chief mage wrenched Roux from her perch on a stump to pull her into her arms.

"What are you doing here?!" Roux hadn't long woken up; she said she had slept poorly, but she looked much better than she had the night before.

"I had to know. I felt a great change within the energies. I *felt* it happen. I had to know." Bisa flashed us a quick smile before scanning her daughter from head to toe, hands clasped, brow furrowed. "How do you feel?"

A weary sigh escaped Roux's lips. "I feel... fine. Tired—with an ache in my head the size of Home Tree—but fine, surprisingly."

Bisa exhaled in relief, before a stern expression settled in place. "There will be a price?"

Roux nodded solemnly.

"You know there's always a balance. Be careful, *ma chemiel.*"

"I will, Mamona."

I turned, walking several feet away to give the two a private moment. As I stood watching the first golden rays of the sunrise over the horizon, hearing the wind rustle the stripped branches of the trees around us, I felt Eli's presence beside me.

"What's wrong?" she asked cautiously.

I closed my eyes. So much had happened to bring us here—my heart hurt thinking about it. So many had lost their lives, including all the souls in Mythbrook and Chaepstow. And now people of Aion had perished.

I opened my eyes, looking to Eli, who was patiently waiting for me to work through my thoughts.

"It's my fault."

Her face changed, as if she hadn't expected those words. Her hand curled delicately around mine, comforting me, despite the trepidation I sensed in her. "What's your fault?"

My heart beat faster as my throat tightened, a knot of emotion growing, clogging my chest. I swallowed, looking away to the cracked shorelines. I couldn't help but feel that I was at least partly to blame for what had happened in Aion. My decision to confront the monstrosity behind this and keep my identity a secret meant that I wasn't using my true power to help people.

"All of this." I spat the words out. "Aion. Roux having to suffer for increasing her power—"

Eli stepped forward, placing her free hand on my cheek. The current that sparked through my skin made me jerk slightly. "Dracho, no... no, no. *None* of this is your fault." A comforting squeeze to my hand. "None of us could have anticipated this would happen. Listen..." Her tongue flicked over her bottom lip. "I know I gave you shit for it, but—you were right about the Hollow."

I frowned in surprise; she sounded like the admission had been unexpected to her too. A worried crease formed between her brows as she looked up at me. Her green eyes, every hue of a new spring season, looked at me with a softness I had never seen.

Staring into her face only made me feel guiltier.

"Dracho... the Hollow would never have stopped. Not until it had killed you and perhaps all of us. I *know* that now. Its foul disease is spreading, and unless we do something to stop it, Ruvalon will be lost."

I looked down, releasing her hold on my face—looking away from her pure eyes.

I couldn't deny her logic; there had been no course of action that could have swayed the Hollow from its path. It was too powerful. That was clear from the way it had easily beaten me. For now, we just had to find more information.

But that didn't assuage the hollowness inside my gut. It worsened the more I thought about everything that had happened. I had, in my own way, contributed to the sorrow that now filled this part of the land.

"Do not allow your heart to bear such a heavy burden, young Dracho," Bisa called to me as the mages made their way over to us. "The emotions that weigh upon you are not just your own. They belong to this land. I warned you not to linger here too long, for the tragedy that happened here left a smear no magick can remove. It affects all, heightening our own feelings." She indicated the land around us which had wasted away, leaving no trace of wholesome life. "The magicks are trapped here, and eat away at anything good that ventures close enough. Stay too long, and you would succumb to madness."

"That's..." I wasn't sure how to finish my sentence. It was a relief to know that this suffocating cloud of emotion wasn't entirely mine; I didn't think I could move forward feeling this way. But the thought of all those spirits lost and wandering here with no way to move on themselves was awful.

Roux offered me a small smile which I returned, exhaling shakily. "How are you feeling?"

"Small headache. But much better." She nodded, looking brighter than she had last night. "I want to thank you," she added, shyness darkening her cheeks all of a sudden, "for what you did back there."

I stepped forward and engulfed her in an embrace. Although she was taller than Eli, I still had to bend slightly—but she reciprocated enthusiastically, a ragged breath escaping as she relaxed. When I released her, she hugged Eli, who had stood silently waiting.

"There was another reason for my visit," Bisa told us, sounding hesitant.

I eyed her. *Ant?* Dread blossomed in my stomach.

"Sizwe had another letter delivered. She found out after you left, Eli, that your father met with a dignitary from Stillmere."

Eli didn't look surprised by the information, merely nodded. "Yes, he does so yearly, I believe. It's all to help the public perception of peace between the kingdoms." She rolled her eyes, and my ears perked up. Was there some friction between Meridium and Stillmere that I didn't know about?

"Well, this new emissary of King Proditor—he once had an interest in ancient and dark magick... such as the Hollow."

That was not what I had expected. I pondered the potential implications of this man working for King Proditor and meeting with King Cervidae. "How do you know this?"

"He is... *known* to my sister and I," Bisa replied.

Eli voiced my question. "How is that possible?"

"He is a mage." Another royal family with a mage for an advisor. "His name is Kanu."

The colour drained from Roux's face as she stared at her mother.

"He was one of the mages banished after the Tain," Bisa went on slowly.

This was strange. A few dozen mages had been banished from Ruvalon after the war—those that had sided with the elf king, Morven. How had this one been allowed to return?

Bisa sighed. "I know this to be true—because he is also my brother."

What the fuck?

&

Exhausted, I rubbed my eyes with my palms whilst Roux and Eli discussed our next course of action. Bisa had filled us in on the history concerning her brother as we left Volente. Every step away from the forsaken land was like a weight removed from my chest.

Kanu, the youngest of the three siblings, in his youth had grown close to King Morven, who'd ruled Stillmere before King Proditor, and had been drawn in by his elitist ideologies. When the war had started, he'd chosen to abandon his family and instead fight against them, believing Morven would usher in an age of magick where elves and mages would live harmoniously, expelling mortals and other magickal creatures from the land they deemed rightfully theirs.

Kanu had not perished at Volente; the cowards had lingered back from the heart of the battle. So, along with those who had betrayed their fellow Aioni people, he had been banished from Ruvalon and sent across the ocean to the nearby continent of Eshmnor.

"The question is, how is he here now? As an emissary to a king, no less! And why return?" Roux's magick prickled with anger, her fingers rising to rub her temple.

Eli paced; her arms crossed as she chewed her cheek in that furious way she did when she was thinking. "Surely my father knew who he was?" she asked, her voice taut.

"He most certainly would have. Your family and mine were very well acquainted, thanks to my friendship with your mother. I imagine it came as a shock to Sizwe too."

Eli shifted uncomfortably. "Then... perhaps I should return home? Question my father over this development?"

Bisa's mouth curved into a smile. "I have a better solution. One where you can kill two birds with one stone—so to speak."

I looked at Roux, who shrugged.

"Sizwe also mentioned that your father would be going on a trip soon. He's been invited to a ball, along with all the lords and ladies of Ruvalon."

Eli raised an eyebrow. "And where is this ball to be held?"

"Stillmere. In five days' time. King Proditor himself is hosting."

"What's the ball in honour of?" Eli asked.

The Chief of Aion actually flinched; my eyes narrowed. "The prince's royal engagement."

Eli tensed. There was a moment of silence.

"Is that a bad thing?" I asked, looking between them. "Surely that's a stroke of luck?"

Since Eli, as Princess of Meridium, would surely be invited, we had a way into the ball. We'd be able to speak to Eli's father and Kanu in one night. It was a perfect opportunity.

Roux was the first to speak. "So that's the plan? We head to Stillmere, Eli can talk to her father, and what... I can catch up with Uncle Kanu for old times' sake?" Her voice sounded strained.

"Not at all, *ma chemiel*. We remember and recover. Not forgive and forget." Bisa studied me from over Roux's shoulder. "Though I think it best that Dracho speaks with my brother."

Roux reared back, staring at her mother, but it was Eli who spoke. "I agree, Roux. You've just been through a huge ordeal and obtained an incredible amount of magick. You need to take it easy—we don't want to see you get hurt."

We don't want to see you lose your shit is what she meant. Recognition and a flash of determination dawned on Roux's face before she nodded.

"All right," I concluded. "I think it's best we head to Stillmere." The decision felt hollow, my dragon and I longing to find our brother, guilt shaming me for putting other matters before finding him. If he wasn't with Bas and Vyn...

"You know, maybe we should catch my father on the Still Road before he reaches the city? That way, we could continue on our journey to the Temple of the Hollow with the information he provides," Eli suggested quickly, pressing her lips together in a hard line.

I shook my head. "No, I think it best to speak to this mage ourselves. That he has returned to Ruvalon *and* has knowledge of such ancient magick is suspicious. I know we talked about heading to the Temple of the Hollow itself, but what if the creature has returned there? We're not prepared to face it yet. We need to gather as much information as possible at this point." There was no way I would underestimate it again. "And we need to find out how Kanu seems to have been granted a reprieve from his banishment, and once again become close to one of the continent's leaders..."

It would be so much easier to get a read on him if Ant was with us. He was far better at reading people than me. I rubbed my forehead, frustrated.

Eli chewed her cheek. "True."

Bisa breathed out slowly. "I haven't seen Kanu in a long time, so I can't say how much of my brother still remains. If his magick is corrupt, you should be able to sense it. It may not be helpful. But logically, it seems like the best thing to do."

"That's sorted then." I clapped my hands together. "Let's meet back up with the others, and we should just about make it in time. I'm sure Antares will find us." The words were like ash in my mouth.

Nervous energy seemed to roll off Eli as she nodded.

Bisa placed a gentle hand upon my arm. "All your friends are camped just past the Gwdhŵ rapids. Travel across the sands, and you'll find them not too far past the waters."

"Ant is with them?" I asked eagerly.

Bisa nodded, a calming smile on her face, and relief that swept through me. I sighed, running my hands through my hair. I hadn't realised how worried I'd been about him. What if the Hollow had killed him, and I'd never found out? I'd been so selfish, relying on him having my back and helping me this entire time, that I had never stopped to consider I might need to have his.

But now, anger started to crowd out the worry. My dragon encouraged it as I thought back over him just disappearing like that. I couldn't comprehend what he had been thinking, to not even wait for me to wake or speak to me before leaving. He'd never done anything like it.

Eagerness to get to him and demand what the hell he'd been thinking suddenly filled me. I spun around. "Right, let's get moving."

Bisa clamped a hand on my shoulder, and I looked down at her. She looked sternly at me. "Remember the true enemy."

Her hand was warm; it quelled my anger. I inhaled deeply before giving her a smile. "Thank you, Bisa. For everything."

"No, thank you, Dracho. You and Eli were beacons of light to those whose lives were thrust into darkness." She reached out for Eli, who took her hand. "I fear that still more troubled times lie ahead. But I want you all to remember that sometimes things aren't what they appear to be... and sometimes they are."

Eli and I shared a confused glance, and I couldn't help giving her a small smirk. A sharp slap stung the back of my hand.

"Ow!"

"Wipe that smile from your face, boy—it's no joke!"

Heat filled my cheeks. "Sorry, Bisa."

She tried to hide a grin. "My magick senses that you found each other for a reason. Hold on to that."

Eli and I shared a thoughtful look, and I nodded.

"I shall, of course, miss you all. If you get the chance, you are always welcome at Home Tree. Roux, take care of these young fools for me." Bisa eyed Roux, noting the slight sway in her stance. "And Eli, Dracho, take care of my Roux. I wish she would come home to learn to master her new powers with the elders, but I know this quest is time-sensitive, and I trust you'll help her."

Eli spoke for both of us as she reached forward to lean her forehead against Roux's. "We'll be there for her, however she needs us."

31

One whole day it took us to leave those dry, vicious desert plains and cross the calmer waters at the bottom of the rapids—and walking through that desert was no picnic at night. Though the blistering heat could bring a grown man to his knees in the day, the temperature plummeted at night; even I had to wrap a fur tightly around myself. My eyes kept drifting to Roux, noting how her weakened body swayed and her shaky hands kept rubbing her temples. Eli and I took turns in watching her, ensuring she drank and ate enough.

As morning arrived, the coarse ground gave way to luscious greens, warmer air kissing our skin as we approached the rapids. Roux stunned us by using her newfound powers to quell the torrent of water so we could cross at one of the shallower points, collapsing into me once we landed on the other side. I carried her as she muttered about having a headache, and suggested we settle for the rest of the day. It was better that she took it slow rather than push herself too much.

Eli and I went to fetch water and wood for the night; the churning in my stomach reminded me we were due a decent meal.

"So," Eli began, "we should catch up with the others soon."

I dropped my satchel by a large group of rocks and didn't meet her eyes, unsure of what to reply.

"What do you think you'll say to Ant?"

I snorted. "Honestly, I'm trying not to think about that until I need to."

"And when will you need to?"

"When I see him."

She snickered. "Well, I'm sure there's a reasonable explanation for his vanishing act."

"There'd better be," I muttered under my breath, a spark of anger lighting within me. "Enough about Antares. What can we expect from Stillmere? Is it like Meridium?"

"Most definitely not. Stillmere is...well, you'll see as soon as you're there. There are *some* good people, though. And this amazing boutique we'll have to stop in. A friend of mine works there."

"Why on earth would I need to go to a boutique?"

She looked at me like it was obvious, which it wasn't. "We're going to a ball. We'll need clothes, you arse."

Oh. "Good point."

"It's not like you could just stroll into the palace wearing your leathers."

"I don't know. I think I'd look rather dashing."

"Rather idiotic."

Though I felt and ignored a tingle of magick run up my spine, I struck my chest in mock pain, struggling to keep a smirk off my face. "*Ouch.* Could have sugar-coated it."

"But the truth is much more interesting," she teased.

The smirk fell from my face as I spotted movement and a flash of grey over her left shoulder, behind the rock formations. The dragon within flared its head, my eyes widening as I realised our predicament. My hand instinctively dropped to my sheathed dagger.

It wasn't there.

I cursed myself. I had left my dagger *and* my glaive back at camp, my concern for Roux overriding my common sense. *Has my time here dulled my instincts?* I glanced up at Eli, realising she had done the same; the only weapons she wore were throwing knives at her waist—which right now would be as useful as throwing needles at a fully armoured draconi. A sudden terror spread through me, rooting me to the spot. My eyes darted in a panic between Eli and the creature that stepped out of the border of the trees, my dragon telling me what I already knew.

This was no simple-minded land wyvern, but one of the most cunning and dangerous in Ruvalon: a wendigo.

It was a creature I had only seen in books. Its ash-grey skin, the colour of death, was pulled tight across its body, bones pushing out against it. The skin, deceptively tough to penetrate, was so thin that it shone in the morning light around the creature's gaunt eye sockets, where its eyes glowed red through the light mist from the rapids. Its lips pulled back over yellowed fangs as it sniffed the air, its hot breath blowing across the open space. It hadn't spotted us yet, but it crept slowly closer towards us, dragging its long, gangly arms along the floor. Razor-sharp claws glinted on each bony finger.

"Eli. I, er, need you to stay still for me." My whisper was a quiet breath on the breeze.

She rolled her eyes, crossed her arms, and opened her mouth.

"Do as I say, Eliana!" The harshness of my voice nearly made *me* flinch as every ounce of authority within me and my dragon was pushed into that quiet command, my eyes flashing furiously to her.

Her back straightened, alarm settling upon her face. Her chest heaved with each breath as she lifted a shaky hand, pointing at my face. "Dracho, your ey—"

"Please. *Trust* me. There's a wendigo behind you."

My stomach lurched, realising that she now looked upon the vertical slits of my dragon's eyes. I shifted them back to the wendigo, knowing it was too late to hide them as I watched it sniff the land some way back. Eli maintained her stiff stance, but I saw her nod slightly from the corner of my vision. She turned her head slowly, looking over her shoulder to get a view of the animal.

If it continued on its current trajectory, it would end up directly on her path. My nostrils flared as my senses went into overdrive. My heart pounded; palms clammy as confusion flooded me.

Eli turned slightly, and a twig snapped underneath her foot, drawing the wendigo's attention. Its vile head shot up, drool dripping from its yellowed teeth, eyes wide as it focused on her. Telling Eli to run wasn't an option; a wendigo's speed was almost unmatched once it locked on to its prey. It could reach her and tear out her throat by the time she turned around.

My chest heaved. We were both unarmed, and every instinct in my body knew what I had to do to save Eli. But it meant exposing myself completely—and that would change everything.

I didn't get an opportunity to decide. Eli started to shift into a combative stance, and I realised she would actually try to fight it. The wendigo's head turned in her direction as it let out a feral snarl.

"NO!"

I heard the shout as I closed my eyes, the kindling falling from my arms, and only then realised the cry came from my own mouth. Warmth gathered within me, spreading until it filled my entire body. The heat of my magick. The sensation of changing into my true form.

It was like returning home.

The mark on the back of my neck tingled as my bones and tendons stretched, manipulating the muscles as they rolled through my body. My scaly wings sprang from my back and extended. I felt my power grow and my senses heighten as my entire body rose towards the sky, and vaguely heard a thud, along with a sharp intake of breath. Adrenaline surged through my veins as my transformation came to an end. I took one deep breath through my nostrils before opening my eyes to stare down the wendigo.

It stood transfixed by my dragon form, not daring to move. My shifting had achieved the desired effect; dragons were lords over most beasts, and their presence demanded respect. According to my studies, the mages believed it to be the nature of the magick bestowed upon us—some deep-rooted rule of nature within the celestral energy itself.

The wendigo dared to glance quickly at Eli, a forlorn look upon its face for the meal it had lost, but I took that opportunity to bare my sharpened fangs and let out a low rumble of warning. The wendigo dropped to its knees, bowing low to the ground, before crawling backwards several feet, scrambling to its feet hastily and running towards the forest without looking back.

By the stars, it felt so good to be back in this form. The draconi in me roared in elation as my chest swelled, nudging me to take flight. My eyes went to the sky and I stretched my wings longingly. But, as the adrenaline started to wear off, my heart palpitated with nerves, and I turned my head slowly to the left.

Eli sat on the ground, her back against the rocks, as if she had fallen in shock. Her mouth was agape as she stared up at me, the colour drained from her face as her emerald eyes shimmered with a trickle of fear.

Ah, shit.

The dragon, still its own entity within, snickered.

Keeping my eyes trained on her, I tucked in my wings and slowly lowered my head to the ground, placing it on the grass in front of her. She sat as still as possible, staring at me.

Understanding dawned. She couldn't see *me* in the eyes of this form.

I tested delicately, using my mind, hoping to all the stars that it wouldn't send her screaming. *Hey, Princess.*

Eli gasped audibly, then clapped a hand to her mouth.

I kept quiet, patiently waiting for her to work through whatever she needed to... if such a thing was possible. She was frozen for a while, staring, but eventually she got slowly to her feet, taking care with every step, as if any sudden movement would cause me to lunge for her.

I had some explaining to do. A *lot* of explaining to do. And Ant was going to be furious. But that was something I'd have to deal with later. All that mattered right now was that I somehow explained all this to her. That she didn't leave. My heart continued to pound as my thoughts hit me one after the other. I didn't *care* if she outed me to her father or anyone else. I just didn't want to lose her.

My breath hitched as Eli looked at me intently, taking a tentative step forward. She lifted a hand, surprise flickering through me, then pulled back slightly, hesitating.

It's all right, I reassured her. *I would never hurt you.*

Her eyes caught mine as I exhaled, keeping as still as I possibly could. Seeming to take an age, she moved along my side and lightly touched one of the horns on my head.

That familiar jolt of static that usually accompanied her touch erupted across my scales. Her touch was light at first, as if she had been expecting to feel something different. Or as if she expected me to bite...

My eyes closed of their own accord as she explored the sensitive, scaly skin along my head and neck. Every touch stretched my nerves taut, but I stayed still, my dragon trying to purr as I held both our reactions at bay, not wanting to startle her.

I hoped against all odds that this meant she wouldn't push me away. Wouldn't turn against me. But I wouldn't blame her if she did. I remembered how I'd felt when I had found out who she was. I'd been shocked and annoyed... but there had been nothing to forgive her for.

As for me...

Now she knew what *I* was—well, roles reversed, I would see that as a much bigger betrayal. Our fathers were practically enemies. Did that mean we were enemies too? It certainly didn't feel like we were. Not to me anyway. But with everything that had happened along the way...

Aion. She knew I felt like Aion was my fault, but for different reasons. Maybe she would think now as I did—that I could have prevented it if I had shifted in the initial battle with the Hollow.

Would she blame me, like I blamed myself? Would she be able to forgive me?

Eli's hand changed direction as she made her way back towards my face. Her fingers touched a spot between my eyes and I sighed, rumbling low in my throat. Her hand paused, and I froze, my eyes opening. She was standing at my side, looking into my eye. It frustrated me to no end that I couldn't tell what she was thinking or feeling.

We stood like that for a few more seconds, but then she made her way to stand directly in front of me. She ran her hand down between my nostrils, the feeling eliciting shivers along my spine. My body had finally started to relax when her brows pinched, her breathing picking up.

Without warning, she struck, punching me as hard as she could. The pain was only equivalent to a bee sting, but my head reared up in shock, and I twitched my nose to shake off my surprise and anger. Eli turned, stalking away, shaking her bruised hand.

I was quicker.

I had already shifted back, my dragon taking control of me in his rage so he could get my hands on her. Grabbing her by the arms, I spun Eli where she stood, pinning her against the rock where she had sat mere moments before. A gasp escaped her, and I noticed the tears that flowed down her cheeks. Panic lanced through me and I removed my hands as if she had burnt me, my anger draining from me as she met my gaze. I knew my pupils would be the last features to truly change as I wrestled control from the beast—the thin black slits were probably still visible—but I scanned her anyway, checking to see if she'd injured her hand.

"Eliana?"

"You're—you... A *dragon*. I just p-punched a dragon." Her eyes squeezed shut as her hands grasped my arms. She shook her head. "I can't—can't breathe. I can't— W-who *are* you?"

I realised her breath was coming in harsh pants. Her knees buckled as panic overwhelmed her body, and I caught her arms gently to support her weight. Her breath was laboured as I helped her to the ground and tilted her face up, finding her eyes unfocused.

"Eliana. It's all right, I'm here."

Her head shook again as her hands tried pushing me away, wheezing with each breath.

"G-get away—from me."

Her heart was beating way too fast. If she didn't calm down soon, she'd pass out.

I held her soft cheeks between my hands. "Eliana, *look* at me."

Her eyes skittered over my face, unseeing.

"You are going to be fine. I need you to concentrate on my voice."

Her hands were shaking. I needed to do something more drastic. An image of me hitting her flowed from my dragon. I stared into her glassy eyes and suddenly knew what would snap her out of her panicked state.

"Princess. I'm so sorry about this, but..."

I pulled her face towards mine, bringing my lips to hers.

She froze.

I couldn't appreciate the sensation of her soft lips pressed to mine. I knew that this was a violation, but I didn't care as long as it saved her and brought her out of her panic.

Our gazes met. My shoulders sagged in relief as I watched emotions flash through her blinking eyes. Her panting had slowed considerably; her attack was passing. I pulled back, leaving my hands on her face as she calmed down.

It didn't last long.

My neck cracked as she slapped me across the cheek, and I hissed between my teeth at the pain. "That's the second time you've struck me today." I wasn't as angry as I sounded; relief flooded me that she was all right. "You think it's been *easy* to keep a secret this big for all this time?"

"I think a lot of people know how hard it is to keep a part of them secret for a long time," she hissed. "This is slightly more than a secret, don't you think?" She shoved my hands off, her voice rising. "And you *kissed* me! I'm so confused right now!"

"Believe me, Princess," I told her dryly, "that wasn't a kiss."

She started to bury her head in her hands, then threw it back so fast she caught it on the rock.

"What the *fuck*? You're naked!" she yelled, rubbing the tender spot.

"You were having a panic attack. A bad one. I couldn't get you to focus—it was either kiss you or slap you. I wasn't sure which you'd rather." My laugh was rough. "And obviously I'm naked—my clothes don't grow with me." I indicated the scraps left about the ground, trying to suppress the indecent thoughts that had surfaced at her use of the curse—especially as I stood before her naked. There was probably something very wrong with me.

Eli's eyebrows shot up, a faint blush creeping over her neck and cheeks. "Oh. That makes complete sense, I suppose." She spoke too quickly. "Well, um... would you mind covering up so we can continue this conversation?" She raised her eyes, trying to look any-where but at me.

Oh. Was she...? It seemed wasn't nearly as unaffected by me as I'd thought she was.

Interesting.

"Are you sure that's what you want?" I teased, hoping the panic attach had faded completely.

Her eyes didn't falter now; they narrowed with irritation. "I'm going to grab your bag. Unless you want to lose your favourite appendage, I suggest you put your clothes back on. Quickly."

Panicked, no. Pissed off, yes. My stomach swooped at the intensity of her stare as she pushed herself to her feet. *Definitely something wrong with me.*

She stormed off, disappearing behind the boulders to head back to camp. In the ten minutes she was gone, panic made me nauseous as I thought about the possibility of her telling Roux. Of them leaving me.

Before the thoughts could escalate, Eli returned with my satchel, bringing it to me with her eyes pointedly looking over my shoulder. I took it from her, murmuring my thanks.

"Roux all right?" I pulled some spare clothes out.

She nodded, still looking away from me. "Sleeping."

She walked away from me, stopping at the water's edge as I changed. I didn't even know where to start with this—hadn't thought I'd ever be having this conversation with anyone. I rubbed my face in frustration, looking up to the first evening stars.

What do you guys suggest?

32

"**So**... Tenebris?"

"Yes."

We'd sat facing each other, several feet from the glistening river, as I told her everything. Well, everything I could. I had told her why we were here, about Mythbrook, that we weren't all humongous flying beasts locked behind some mountain. That was the part that shocked her the most, I thought. The blanket of night had already taken over the sky by the time I finished and she finally started asking questions.

"*The* Tenebris? Which is apparently not inhabited by dragons, but those with the magick to transform *into* them—AND, just in case I've missed anything important," she went on with only the slightest hint of sarcasm, "your father is Emperor Eltanin?"

"Yes."

"*The* Emperor Eltanin, 'The Wise', believed to have lived over a thousand years?"

"Well, it's actually closer to two thousand years—which is a lot younger than it sounds—but yes. Can we move on to another question?"

"And you can communicate... using your minds? Wait, so how does that work? Is it only when you're a dragon? Cause I have to say, there've been a few times between you and Ant that have left me questioning."

The speed at which she talked made me laugh. I wasn't surprised she had picked up on that.

"Wait... how old are you?" Her brows pinched.

I chuckled softly. "Firstly, yes, we can communicate in our human form—but only with other draconi. I can apparently do it with everyone in my dragon form, because you heard me. But I wasn't actually sure if that would work. You're the first human I've tried it with." Her eyes widened at that. "And I'm still young in draconi *and* human years. I've only seen twenty-six summers."

"Does that mean you're... immortal?" she whispered.

"Stars, no. I mean, we are immune to the usual methods you mortals resort to when killing each other."

She rolled her eyes impatiently.

"Magickal weapons can harm us, of course." My mind drifted to the creature of the Hollow. "But the magick given to us allows us to live much longer, as long as we keep transforming. My father hasn't transformed in years, and it's catching up to him now. If a draconi never transformed, they could practically live a human lifespan."

"Why would one do such a thing?"

"Stop transforming?"

She nodded.

"Heartbreak, I suppose," I muttered.

She winced, touching my hand. "I'm sorry, that was insensitive. I didn't think."

"It's all right. My parents were estelars."

"Estelars?"

"It's just an old, silly term my people have for two that have been bound to each other."

"Ah, like soulmates."

I nodded. "Sort of. But in Tenebris, there's an actual ceremony held under the stars which binds the couple together."

"Wow. That's... intense." She cleared her throat.

Resting my chin on my hand, I glanced sideways at her. "You know, you're taking this very well. Are you *sure* you're all right?"

Her smile was tight-lipped as she nodded. "Don't get me wrong, I'm still processing. And..." She breathed out. "I'm still pretty pissed. But... everyone has their secrets. If you haven't forgotten, I was also hiding things from you."

"Ah, yes. Stars above, *that* was a hell of a shock, Princess."

Her glare cut right through me. "What's with the adoration for the stars, anyway?"

I smiled widely, looking skywards to the ancestors' eyes that shone so bright. "There's a legend, or I suppose a belief, amongst my people... that when we die and make our way through the Netherworld—if we have led a fulfilled life and earned our place, whatever that's supposed to mean—then our souls will join our ancestors amongst the stars."

"That's a—beautiful belief to hold."

I laughed quietly, tipping my head towards her. "You know, I never used to place much faith in it." My smile faded. "Until my mother died. Now, more than anything, I hope she's up there just so I might get the chance to see her again."

Eli was quiet for a while. "She will be," she said at last. "I'm sure her journey through the Netherworld was peaceful, and she now watches you and your father from up there."

I smiled, hoping that was true, and prayed that her journey *had* been peaceful. I nudged Eli's arm with mine. "I'm sure your mammy is too."

I didn't know if I'd said too much. A strange mix of emotions crossed her face as her gaze met mine, a chill running over me at her beauty. She turned away, breaking the connection.

I wasn't sure what Eli believed happened after mortals died, but everyone in Ruvalon knew of the Netherworld. It was a valley all souls travelled to after death, making their way through to their final resting place. But it was believed that souls who clung on to anything unfinished in life would slip away into Purdue, a limbo where they lingered, lost and unable to move on.

I swallowed hard, forcing my brain away from *that* train of thought. "The people of Tenebris tell stories of how an ancient draconi created the Netherworld." Eli looked up at me, listening. "Eons ago, an evil entity tried to harness energy from wayward souls, nearly destroying the continent in the process."

"That hardly sounds like an appropriate story to tell children at bedtime."

My laugh came out of nowhere and I bit my lip to quiet myself, noticing that Eli's eyes flashed to my mouth. "It's just an old legend. But one of our ancients created the Netherworld—and sacrificed his place amongst the stars by promising to guard it for all eternity."

She nodded. "Similar to the legend you told us before of the mountains." I was surprised that she'd remembered it. "I'm starting to notice a running theme."

"Oh?" I grinned at her.

"The draconi have a tragic history of sacrificing themselves for the greater good."

I opened my mouth, then closed it. Then opened it again, trying to find words.

She laughed out loud, catching me off guard—a genuine, rare laugh. "I don't think I've ever seen you speechless."

I huffed, looking at the ground. I had found myself speechless around her quite a few times, but I was glad she was none the wiser about that. What she had said about my ancestors... I had never thought about it that way before, but she had a point. I couldn't think of many legends where draconi *weren't* doing something reckless to sacrifice themselves for the good of Tenebris or their people.

"So, the mark?"

I jerked my head up as she pulled me from my thoughts. "What?"

She arched a brow as she leaned forward, reaching behind my neck to tap a finger on the mark that crept out from my hairline. Her touch caused a tingling sensation to sweep over my skin, the sweet scent of blackberries filling the air as I inhaled. My dragon leaned towards it, sending a sultry heat through me. I held my breath, willing it away.

"I feel like I've seen it somewhere before, but I'm guessing it's not a tattoo after all?"

Ant had been right when he said she was intuitive. They actually had a lot in common. Between them, they'd probably be the death of me... Was this something I should really divulge? Instinct told me I could trust her.

"Ant has one too, but I doubt you've seen his. It's a mark the leading draconi families carry. It indicates that they—*we*—are the Chosen. If you ever see it, you're looking at someone who carries the magick."

"The *Chosen*?" Eli repeated.

I nodded. "Those chosen by the first mages. By Roux's ancestors. Graced with transformation magick and long life."

"Oh," she whispered. "How many leading families are there?"

"Nine. We age to incomprehensible years to you humans, of course. Closer to what an elf's life span would be." I winked and she frowned. "But, um, children were rare. So now they marry outside of the families to continue the line of the draconi. Some of the families have even died out. I'm technically the last of my mother's line. The last child born of two leading families."

"Wait. The mark is *only* carried by those who can transform. The 'leading families'?"

"It is. See them as a sort of... council of elders—except they're dragons."

"But if there are only nine leading families, and children amongst them are rare, then everyone else in Tenebris is..." Her mouth fell open as she thought it over.

I held back a chuckle. "Mortal?" I offered.

Her back straightened, mouth snapping shut, and I laughed lightly.

"Now who's speechless?" I leaned forward, tugging on a strand of her hair, avoiding her hand as she tried to swat me away. "Yes. The majority of those in Tenebris are human."

"You're telling me that an entire realm of *humans* has been living beyond the mountains this entire time?"

The smile on my face grew as I arched a brow, looking at her pointedly.

"W-why?" she asked, perplexed. "Why not move south and join with the other kingdoms?"

I watched her brow furrow. "I can't speak for everyone, but, from our histories, I've learnt that we were granted our powers to protect the people of Tenebris. Especially since the Tain, our people feel safe. I suppose having grown up for generations under the magick of Tenebris, they don't feel human enough for the southern realms."

Air hissed sharply through her teeth. "That's easy to say for a realm that *didn't* fight during the Tain." Eli shot to her feet, startling me, and walked a few feet to the water's edge, her arms crossed.

Did I say something wrong?

The dragon within seemed to shrug in response, confounded by her reaction. I stood nervously, making my way over to stand next to her. "Everything all right?"

"It's..." She ran her tongue across her teeth, shaking her head, then inhaled deeply before continuing. "They don't feel *human* enough for the southern realms? You mean they see themselves as superior to the rest of us? Purely because they've lived with *dragons*." She spat the words out. "The realms have never been more diverse since the Tain. We accepted all, no matter what their background, after Morven left. After his disgusting views had been cleansed from these lands."

I realised how royally I had fucked up. "I-I didn't mean—"

She held her hand up. "No, wait. You've described such a thriving, advanced and *united* community. Meanwhile, you've seen downtrodden towns like Morcroft, and how—fractured we are. We aren't one nation, living under one banner. You isolate yourselves with your resources when you could help those here, or even just those nearer to you, like Morcroft. You already helped Mythbrook. Would it really be that much of a stretch to help other villages?"

I didn't know what to say. We *had* holed ourselves away behind our mountain, cut off from the rest of the continent. And for what reason? For some treaty signed by wartime rulers who believed they knew best even now in times of peace?

"I know what you're going to say—"

"You're right."

"—that the... what?" She blinked a few times, before studying me suspiciously, as if she thought she'd imagined my words.

"I said, you're right."

"So maybe I *don't* know what you're going to say."

"Listen, Eli, I'm new to all this *leadership* stuff. My father has only been training me properly for rule for the last couple of years, and I've probably learned more since I've been travelling with you than during that time."

Her eyes widened at that, a flush filling her cheeks.

"But I agree with you. It was our fathers who signed the treaty after the Tain. I understand why—I understand the fear that kept the kings of Ruvalon wanting the borders of Tenebris closed. And I understand the fear of my father, who didn't want those same kings finding out that we weren't savage flying beasts all hours of the day. Can you?"

Eli nodded silently.

I stepped closer, daring to touch her hand lightly. "But if we are the *next* rulers, do you think we could work with each other? It won't be a change overnight... but I think we could help improve people's lives. Together."

She gave me a small smile and opened her palm, accepting my hand. "I think—that sounds like an outstanding idea."

I beamed and, unable to stop myself, brought her hand to my lips, planting a kiss on the soft skin there. "Fantastic! So, plan. Let's meet up with the others and head to Tenebris."

Her mouth fell open again. "I'm—I'm sorry, what?" She looked as if I'd just proposed, not just offered a trip to my home.

"After Stillmere, of course. But it seems only logical. I can update my father on everything so far and see if he can give us any information on this Hollow before we encounter it again. After all, he is *ancient*. He might know something which could prepare us."

Eli looked like she'd rather face the Hollow in single combat right now.

"You all right?"

She shook her head. "Well, I mean—are you *sure* I should go?"

"What do you mean? Since when have you ever rejected a chance to get information?"

Her lips pursed, and she started chewing her cheek in that familiar way. I frowned, taking hold of her hands. "Hey, don't close yourself off. What is it?"

She took a deep breath. "Who my father is. Who *I* am. Won't your father hate me?"

My face softened. She had no idea. There was no way anyone could ever hate her. "He'll love you."

"But how can you—"

"Just trust me on this. My father may be the emperor, but he's a softie. First and foremost, he'll be pissed off at me, of course, but he will listen to what we have to say. I promise. He's not called the *wise* for no reason."

She eyed me sceptically, still chewing on the inside of her cheek, before letting out a shaky breath. "Stranger things have happened—perhaps our fathers will get along."

"Now, wait a minute. That's taking it a bit far." I winked.

"Oh, well—you never know." She nudged my arm, looking towards the sky and the bright souls that clung to the black velvet night. "*We* get along pretty well."

My heart stuttered as I stared at the side of her face, a small smile playing on my lips. "Yes. Yes, we do."

33

We fell into relaxed conversation as we walked back to camp, our arms full of kindling and firewood, and failed to notice the dark outline sitting outside one of the tents.

"Why are you wearing different clothes?"

We both froze, spotting Roux, apparently now awake.

"Heh, this—" I dropped the wood, hastily pointing between my new outfit and Eli. "This isn't what it looks like."

Eli arched a dark brow in amusement.

I moved closer to the mage. "Roux, there's something I need to talk to you about." My magick seemed to lean towards her as she smirked knowingly.

"I'm assuming you've finally told Eli what you are?"

I stared, unsure whether I was shocked or more relieved at this point. Eli just shrugged; a smile full of humour playing on her lips.

I could hear the smug grin in Roux's voice. "I mean, I always had an inkling there was something different. I obviously *knew* you had magick. My mamona would never tell me... But I knew for sure who you were once I had my new powers."

"All right then?" I sounded even more baffled than I felt.

Eli dropped her wood beside mine, nudging past me and laughing as she went to sit beside Roux, updating her on what had occurred. I spent a few quiet moments to myself whilst Roux used a small spark of black and gold to light the fire I had built.

We laughed, sharing stories and memories as we ate some sweet bread and fruit provided by Bisa, my stomach rejoicing in the nourishment. They both had so many questions now that my identity had been revealed. And honestly, it was lifting all the tension I'd been carrying in my shoulders. Being able to talk about that side of me, my true self, filled me with a warmth I hadn't experienced often. Not unless Ant and Althea were with me. I was able to be *me*, my authentic self.

And they didn't judge me for it.

I looked over, catching Eli smile at something Roux said, the firelight bringing out the subtle red tones in her hair. I relished this feeling. It gave me hope for the future. Hope for us working together—magickal and mortal communities alike.

Roux caught me staring and gave me a knowing grin, and I shook my head. "Roux. I think I have an idea that may help with your new powers."

Her eyes widened, flicking to Eli and back. "Well, of course, anything you think might help. I keep getting these aches in my head."

I nodded. "I was thinking it over. You've been given a huge boost in power, and, as we know, there's always a balance. The shade said there would be consequences."

"Yes, but I didn't think it would be anything like this. I can feel the magick increasing. The worse it gets, the more pressure I can feel in my head."

She sighed. "I wish Cubra was here."

I winced in sympathy. I couldn't imagine what it was like to have a spirit guide, or to be separated from them.

"You'll see him again." I promised. "In the meantime, you've got us."

I returned the smile she sent me, before continuing. "Thinking about your new powers, I think we need to build up your tolerance. The magick needs draining, but you can't use too much at the moment because your power is so new. So we take baby steps." I gave her a hopeful look as her eyes narrowed in thought.

Realisation dawned in her expression. "Like that day we met the Hollow?"

I grinned enthusiastically. "Yes. I think that's our baby step. You can use my magick as a barrier. Let *me* be your anchor."

For the first time in days, hope filled her eyes. "Let's try it."

"Right now?" Eli asked uncertainly.

"I mean, I feel all right. My hands hurt a little from the pent-up magick, but I'd like to try."

Excited but nervous, I shuffled onto my knees before Roux, holding my palm outwards. With a deep breath, she placed her palm a few inches above mine, as we had done before.

I caught her determined look in the space between our hands. "Ready?"

Her heartbeat increased, but she nodded.

"Hey." Eli touched her knee gently. "You can do this. Just focus."

Roux smiled, squaring her shoulders as her eyes closed. I willed some magick into my palm, holding it there as warmth filled every nerve of my hand.

I felt her magick before I saw it. A sensation similar to pins and needles, tickling the top of my palm, stronger than before—reaching out, investigating my magick. Once it had determined they were brethren, that gold and black wave manifested, spreading a pulse of light between the three of us.

Roux's eyes remained shut, her brow pinched in the effort as the wave grew and shrank under her control. A bead of sweat trailed down her forehead; I could sense how much more powerful her magick was and how hard it was to keep her grip on it. I used my own to bolster her strength, allowing her to practice the movement without fully draining herself.

"You've got it, Roux. You're doing it!"

Her eyes snapped open, gold dancing across her irises as she watched the wave swirl between our hands. A choked sound of happy relief burst from her lips as she looked at us with a wide smile. Eli clasped her knee, leaning her head upon Roux's shoulder.

We allowed the magick to pass back and forth for a few more moments. Eventually Roux pulled her hand back, flexing her fingers as she stared at her palm. "I did it."

|You did. And I'll be here to do this with you every day until you no longer need it."

Her lips pressed together as she held in her emotion. "Thank you," she whispered.

A shivery wave of anticipation hit me when I woke and remembered I would see Ant again today. It manifested into jittery energy as we packed up and left, heading in the direction Bisa had given us. If her information accurate, it would only take a few hours.

The conversation was light, wondering how the others were. I had to admit, I was eager to see both Vyn and Bas again. We'd grown close during our time together, and I'd missed them. But I also thought over the events of the past few days and the relief I had felt at having that barrier—that need to hide myself—removed. The idea of having to go back to that once we re-joined Bas and Vyn made me uneasy. Lying wasn't something that usually came naturally to me. And I didn't *want* to lie anymore.

Deep down in my gut, I knew Ant was who I had to worry about the most. Anything that potentially put Tenebris, or me, in danger, he would view as a threat. He had already been highly forgiving on this trip with many things. I just wondered how he'd take this revelation...

I didn't have long to wait.

After only a couple of hours, I saw a head of familiar black hair. Relief and anger almost split my chest in two. He really was all right.

They had set up camp, clearly waiting for us to arrive, the horses tethered nearby whilst Engel grazed further away. Eli's smile lit up her face when she spotted her four-legged friend.

They spotted us and stood, Ant giving us a casual wave. My jaw clenched. My dragon reared irrationally and filled me with a wave of anger that spread through me, crowding out anything else and burning my hands as I broke into a jog. *That bastard.*

As I got closer, Ant tilted his head, confused by my evident fury. I clenched my fists.

"Oh shit." He started backing up to prepare his footing, but I was already too close.

I swung, connecting with below his left eye. A sickening crunch sounded between us as his head snapped back and pain lanced through my knuckles. Bas and Vyn took a step forward, shocked but ready to intercede if needed. My dragon snapped in excitement, eager for more action.

"Shit!" Ant grabbed at his cheek, his amber eyes turning deadly.

"Where the *fuck* did you go?" I snarled.

Eli caught up, grabbing my arms. The charge that ran through me calmed the fury threatening to burst through. Roux kept a safe distance beside us, concern lining her face as she ran her fingers through her hair.

"Dracho, you need to calm down," Eli told me.

Ant looked at her hand on my arm, and his molten eyes turned to my face.

You told her.

It wasn't a question, and the quiet rage was worse than any shout. Eli winced at his expression. Vyn looked at Bas, who shrugged.

"I didn't have much of a choice," I said dryly.

Ant's nostrils flared as his back stiffened. "Explain that to me?"

"We were attacked by a wendigo. Unarmed."

"A wendigo wouldn't have left so much as a scratch on you."

Vyn's yellow eyes narrowed, flicking between Ant and me.

"We were *unarmed*," I repeated. "And I wasn't alone—it would have killed Eliana."

"Then you should have let that play out." Frankness was always Ant's strong suit. He would never avoid saying something to spare someone's feelings—which had made for some awkward dinners throughout the years.

"What the fuck?"

"Hey!"

"Antares."

Various condemnations of his remark sounded around the camp. Only Eli and I seemed unsurprised; Ant would do almost anything to keep our secret. Anything necessary to protect Tenebris.

To protect me.

He glowered at me before turning his glare on Eli, his eyes roaming over her slowly, violence in his eyes. She stiffened beside me, her hand releasing my arm to drift towards the dagger strapped to her thigh. A rumble of warning sounded from Ant's chest. Seeing that resolve in his eyes, I stepped to the side, blocking her more from his view.

Not her.

His eyes returned to mine, widening as I stared him down. As he understood the meaning behind my words.

No? he challenged, raising a dark brow.

Easy, I warned him, anticipation peeling back and exposing all my nerves. I never wanted to fight my best friend—my brother. But for this, I would.

The unspoken words hung in the air. I wouldn't allow Eli to be hurt. I would rather expose our secret than allow this woman to be harmed.

I'd gone too far.

"You made a vow."

"And I broke it." He wasn't saying anything I didn't already know. The thing was... I had already accepted it.

"Is there something we're missing?" Vyn motioned between Bas and himself, exasperated. No one responded.

"I will deal with the consequences upon my return," I announced.

Ant clenched his fist and sucked his teeth. "See, that's the thing. If this continues, something might happen to you, and you won't be *able* to return! Or worse! You're found out and captured, and this—*issue*—is dragged back home. That's not why I'm here."

His resolve had snapped. He stepped up, inches from my face, teeth gritted, raw power emitting from every inch of his body. Silver claws slowly crept their way out of his hand, his draconi form vying for command.

Ant was usually impeccably in control over his form. Since his merge, I had only ever seen him lose control once. I knew not to rise to it now.

Vyn spied the magick affecting Ant and grasped Bas' arm sharply, tugging him back. Bas looked to Eli and reached out, his eyes darting between the three of us. She was so close to me and Ant, and he wanted to remove her from what he perceived to be a threat.

She refused to move, taking a fistful of the back of my shirt. I could feel her eyes burning into the back of my head, willing me to keep calm. I kept mine trained on Ant, a bored look fixed on my face, not giving in.

He saw my steely determination and took a deep breath. "I swear,

Dracho. You get a handle on this, and focus on our mission... or I'll knock you out and drag you back home myself."

"Where exactly *is* home?" Vyn asked loudly.

My resolve broke. I was sick of hiding. Sick of not trusting good people.

Ant's eyes widened a fraction as he saw me make the decision. *"Don't—"*

"Tenebris," I said.

Eli inhaled sharply through her nose. My eyes slid from Ant to Vyn and Bas behind him. Roux stood silently, looking anywhere but at us as she chewed on a nail.

It was Bas who spoke, his brows high on his forehead. *"Tenebris?"*

34

The row continued as we sat around the campfire, just inside the shelter of some trees.

"Where did *I* go?!" The vein in Ant's neck was throbbing. "After what I saw that morning, I went to scout for any sign of that creature and find out where it was heading. *You*, on the other hand, head off, stars know where, for days on end but sure—where did *I* go!"

"There was an assassin on the loose, Ant! One we had only just encountered! Why didn't you wake me?!"

"Because I knew the first place you'd run off to would be the one place it had just massacred!"

"So?"

"*So?*" His eyes were wild. "So?! My job is to protect *you!*"

Bas' eyes narrowed at the same time Eli's widened.

"You may have forgotten how important you are—and your vow." A flash in Eli's direction. "But *I* certainly haven't. If you keep insisting on running off into the path of danger, then I *will* end this mission."

An eerie silence blanketed us. Roux fidgeted with her hands anxiously, staring at her feet.

Ant rubbed his temple, his jaw tightening; he exhaled impatiently. "I apologise, Roux. I didn't mean that to sound so insensitive." There was genuine remorse on his face as he looked towards the mage, who only glanced up and gave him a slight nod.

"Thank you, Antares."

A hint of shame and guilt darkened his features. He rubbed his eyes with a hand. "Listen, we both know I'm the better scout, Dracho. If you'd come with me, you'd have been at risk if we'd come across that thing again. It doesn't matter what happens to me, but you... you're the future of our home."

Fury eroded every other emotion as I hissed, "I don't ever want to hear that *bullshit* come out of your mouth again, do you hear me? Of course you *matter*."

Ant shifted slightly, and the others suddenly found the fire, the ground or the surrounding woodland more interesting than our conversation.

Bas leaned forward after a beat of silence, clasping his hands.

"So, not to interrupt your makeup session or anything, but let me get this right... you two are from Tenebris and can transform into dragons. I mean actual, flying dragons, with wings and shit?"

Vyn looked over his tankard as he casually swirled the red liquid around. I wished I'd had some, but I had decided that sobriety was essential for this conversation.

"Is that why you've been fidgety for the last few minutes? You've been waiting to ask your inane questions?" the djinn asked.

Bas scoffed. "Obviously. And I don't know what that word means."

"Of course." Vyn rolled his eyes.

Bas just looked at us, waiting, as if it was the most important question he had ever asked.

I sighed. "Yes, Bas."

"And what, you're some kind of royalty?"

"Bas." Eli's tone was impatient. Vyn's hand had frozen on his drink, his eyes flicking from Bas to me.

Bas' grin turned smug. "You think I didn't notice Ant mention he's here to protect you? Or the few times he's said how important you are? I know I come across as a bit thick sometimes, but I'm really not stupid."

"Huh. Maybe he isn't such a dumb grunt after all, Eli." Vyn sounded amused, and Eli's lips curled into a small smile.

I shook my head. "Bas, I don't think you're stupid. The opportunity just hadn't arrived to tell you yet. But yes. You are correct." Everything would be out in the open after this. Everyone would know, and there would be no more burden to carry my secret. "My father is Emperor Eltanin. My name is Dracho Celesta, heir to the throne of Tenebris. And Ant isn't here to *protect* me. He's here as my companion. He's just... taken it upon himself to feel responsible for me." I shrugged as Ant started sending curses into my mind. "I, er, appreciate that this may come as a shock. And I completely understand if my deception has pissed you off."

To my surprise, however, I was greeted by twin smiles from Vyn and Bas.

"Explains quite a bit, actually. And who are we to judge? It's not like we weren't keeping secrets of our own. They might have been on behalf of someone else"—Vyn pointed at Eli— "and they may not have been as big as yours. But secrets nonetheless." He looked at his drink; his swirling continued.

"So can we see?" Bas demanded, his voice high with childish excitement.

"See what?"

Using both hands, Bas pointed at me and Ant. "You," he started flapping his hands, "as dragons."

Eli said, "He's huge, Bas."

I snorted loudly.

She glared at me before returning her attention back to Bas. "We can't risk him transforming again, just in case a random traveller sees him. Where d'you expect us to hide a dragon?"

"*You've* seen him?" His mouth opened wide in astonishment as Eli rolled her eyes. "Not fair." He pouted.

"Anyway, as I was saying"—Vyn scowled at Bas— "we've been through too much, all of us, together now to lose faith. To lose *trust*." He gave Ant a pointed look.

A muscle in Ant's jaw twitched. This wasn't the kind of conversation he liked, nor was used to having as part of a group. He usually kept to himself. He was known as a fierce warrior amongst the Edjer guard, but he didn't socialise with many outside of training beside me and Althea. And that was just the way he liked it.

"It's... it's not about *trust*," he mumbled. "I'll admit at first it was, but I believe you've proven yourselves over our time together."

"Wow, thanks," was Eli's dry response.

He shot her a withering look. "This wasn't a mission I wanted. It was thrust upon me." He frowned at me, and I flashed him a wide smile. "Please understand that I'm trying to protect not only the emperor's son, but my closest friend. Whether he believes he needs my protection or not."

Guilt hit my gut like a war hammer. For the first time, I considered the pressure he had been under. Should I have really expected him to relax for once and take this journey as an extended holiday? That just wasn't Ant. I had taken this trip as a break away from my responsibilities, with the added quest of finding those responsible for the tragedies happening to the human villages. Neither of us could have anticipated where this path would take us. But Ant had remained on high alert for the majority of it.

I swallowed. "I'm sorry, Ant. I've been selfish, expecting you to follow me around whilst I do whatever I want."

Leaning over, he grasped the back of my neck. "Nothing I'm

not used to, brother. You've always acted with your heart over your head."

I chuckled, putting a hand to his shoulder before touching my forehead affectionately to his.

There was a beat of silence. "So," Bas drawled, the word dripping with confusion. "What now?" He took a sip of wine.

Roux caught my gaze and shook her head minutely. Eli and I had discussed our Tenebris plan with her. She thought it was a good idea, but after the emotions of this afternoon, it was probably best not to bring it up now. I'd tell Ant about it later. Stars knew his reaction to that wouldn't be the best.

I sighed. "Now... now we go to Stillmere."

"Why the hell would we go there? If I wanted to surround my-self with stuck-up arses, I'd spend an evening with Connaught," Bas joked, elbowing Vyn, who rubbed his forehead impatiently.

Fortunately, Bisa had updated them on what had happened in Aion and where we had gone with Roux—and why. They listened silently as we told them about our time in Volente and explained what had occurred between Roux and the spirits. Bas' eyes filled with sorrow, returning to her over and over again during our story. Roux sat quietly, pulling at a loose thread in her shirt.

Once we had finished, Bas stood, walking silently over to pull her into a tight embrace. She seemed to melt into it, as if she had been waiting forever for someone to just hug her.

"I'm glad you're still here, little mage," I heard him whisper into her thick tresses. Roux closed her eyes, a small smile playing on her lips as she placed her hands over his, and didn't move back. I glanced at Eli, Volente still fresh on my mind.

We told them next about the mage—Proditor's dignitary, who had visited Eli's father—and explained why going to Stillmere seemed like the best course of action.

"I don't understand. Why would this mage be granted a reprieve from his banishment?" Vyn asked.

"We don't know, but that's exactly what we're going to find out."

"So, we're gate-crashing a ball?" Bas grinned delightedly at Eli.

"Yes. Roux will remain behind."

Tension crept into Ant's face as Vyn and Bas looked incredulous. Roux, still being hugged by Bas, held her hands up to try and halt their protestations.

"Are you sure that's a good idea?" Vyn blurted out. Eli silenced him with a look.

"Now, listen. Roux is still learning to control her new powers. She doesn't want to risk coming up against her uncle and... well, for lack of a better term—"

"Losing control," Roux finished. Eli winced. Vyn reached over to touch Roux's shoulder softly.

"Well in that case, I'll stay behind with her," Bas told us. She smiled into his big arms.

"Count me out too," Vyn said. "I'd rather not have to spend my night within a mile of Proditor's presence."

Eli nodded at him, and I wondered what was so bad about the king. He had apparently been very popular at the time of his election.

I cleared my throat. "All right. In the meantime, I'm going to help Roux strengthen her magick." She and I had already agreed that our little exercise was an excellent way to test out her new powers, and that we'd start doing it daily, just to build her strength up. Roux's answering smile was grateful.

There was silence as they all digested that.

"Well, this journey gets more and more interesting every day," Bas muttered.

35

We retreated to our tents shortly after my evening exercise with Roux, as she sensed rain in the air. It wasn't long before it came— flashing sheets of cold droplets drumming upon the canvas. The campfire was extinguished by the sheer volume of it. The horses stood sheltered under the trees nearby as Engel trotted about playfully in the open, enjoying the water.

As Ant lay down for the night, I pushed our tent flap aside and peered out, noting that Eli had pinned the entrance of her own tent back. She was sitting close to the opening, looking out.

"You like the rain?" I shouted over through the rhythmic pattering.

Her answering smile was a burst of sunlight in the grey ambience. I found myself stunned, my breath catching in my throat.

"I *love* rain!" she called.

Will you keep it down? Trying to sleep, the grump behind me growled.

I smirked and, eyeing the distance between the tents, darted through the rain, catching Eli's look of surprise as I sat down next to her.

I grinned at her. "Why?"

"Hmm?" she asked, her eyes lingering on the wet hair which hung over my eyes.

I chuckled, brushing it out of my face. "Why do you love the rain?"

"That's why you got your precious hair wet? To ask me why I like rain?" I felt myself blush, and she laughed. "Well, I've always loved the smell after a storm. The air smells fresh—it smells like... nature. And without rain, there would be no life. Rain is the promise of new beginnings."

I'd never really thought about it. I sat and enjoyed the sound of the rain, but I'd never appreciated its importance to the earth around us. I supposed it was because my true nature was practically forged by fire—naturally, I felt an affinity to that.

"It's not just that," Eli rushed out. "The rhythm of the drops." She looked at me shyly, as if telling a secret. "It's always helped me sleep—even if my sleep doesn't end up peaceful, it has always helped me drift off. I find peace in the rain."

I smiled indulgently at her, enjoying the way her lips curled up at the edges as she stared back out at the raindrops. Reaching out, I took her hand, rubbing my thumb over the calluses from her dagger. Her green eyes turned to find mine again, momentary shock showing within them before a satisfied smile graced her mouth.

"Don't you like it?" she asked.

Nodding, I said, "I've always enjoyed the sound. But I have to admit, flying in it isn't the best."

She chuckled.

"If I had to choose, I prefer clear skies. There's this... special place in Tenebris where I'd go to find my own peace. You can sit under the shelter of the cherry willows there, along the edge of the lake— more like a huge pond, really. But I'd go there when I was younger, after my..." Swallowing, I found myself surprisingly at ease for the first time ever when almost mentioning my mother. It was a little disconcerting.

Eli squeezed my hand in comfort, and I shook my head.

"Anyway, I used to go there a lot, but especially when there were clear skies. Some nights I started to find that I preferred the company of the stars to people. I haven't had a chance to go as often lately, but… well, I'll show you when we get there."

Her smile was carefree. "I'd really like that, Dracho."

My breath caught again as I gazed at her, tension seeming to fill the space between us. Eli swallowed, and her lips parted slightly. My hand tightened in my lap as the dragon within set my nerves alight, urging me to claim her soft mouth. When I glanced back up to her eyes, as green as the new spring, I realised her pupils had dilated. Her tongue darted out to moisten her lips.

I *needed* to know what she was thinking. It wasn't a desire, but a bone-deep necessity. Did she want me as much as I wanted her?

Her eyes dropped to my mouth as her chin subconsciously tipped up a fraction. Heat filled my chest as my breathing increased. I brought my free hand up, clasping her chin and gently rubbing my thumb over her bottom lip.

Eli's breathing hitched, her cheeks turning darker as she squeezed my hand once more. As I lowering my head to her, her eyes fluttered closed. Our lips touched, just a brush against each other…

Bas' ill-timed laughter boomed from his tent. We whipped apart as if we'd been burnt.

Eli fidgeted, averting her gaze, coughing to clear her throat. "Um, I'm going to head to bed. Busy day tomorrow and all." The tension was well and truly broken, awkwardness seeping between us.

I never wanted her to be uncomfortable around me.

I let go of her hand, smiling gently. "All right, me too." I leaned forward quickly, planting a chaste kiss to her cheek, before ducking out into the rain. I took in in her flushed cheeks and wide eyes. "Goodnight, Princess."

The soft crunching of leaves beneath feet awoke me from my slumber a few hours later. I rolled over, noticing that Ant was awake, sitting upright and frowning as he listened.

It's Eli.

Confusion settled within me as I tilted my head to listen. He was right. The footsteps clearly belonged to Eli. When another, heavier pair joined in, I eyed Ant.

And that's Bas.

He nodded in agreement.

A creeping suspicion filled my veins. I silently removed myself from my furs, grabbed my dagger from under my pillow and walked to the entrance. My confusion deepened as I pulled the canvas back, seeing the duo creep away from the tents and deeper into the wood... where a small orb of golden light was shining a mere foot from the ground.

Shit! I started shoving my boots on.

What is it? Ant asked, alarm crossing his face.

They're about to attack a sujin.

Oh, for fuck's sake.

I grabbed some gold drams—the currency of Ruvalon—from my satchel before exiting the tent, Ant hot on my tail, moving barefoot through the clearing. From my peripheral vision, I spotted Vyn flanking the creature from its other side.

Shit, shit, shit.

I tried to catch up with Eli and Bas silently as Ant branched off in Vyn's direction. Several feet away from Eli, I was able to get a good look at the creature ahead.

Its golden orb hung from the dark antenna sprouting from the top of its mossy green head. It shuffled slowly through the wood, its small brown cloak wrapped around itself—its razor-sharp claws just visible through the opening.

I tried to silently rush forward, but Eli was too close, her dagger in hand. Her grip on the handle changed, ready to strike.

"Wait!"

Eli and Bas froze, their heartbeats increasing as the sujin turned, its large, round, yellow eyes taking in the threat that had been sneaking up on it. I jogged the extra couple of feet to place myself in front of Eli as Ant dragged Vyn from the other side of the trees.

"What are you doing?" Eli furiously whispered.

"Dracho, you know that thing will slit our throats in our sleep if we don't kill it!" Bas hissed.

I shook my head at Bas in exasperation. "You mortals...why is your answer always to kill first, ask questions later?" I stepped forward, the sujin observing me as I knelt on the ground before it.

"Dracho, this isn't time for games. *You* may not be able to die, but, um, we can," Vyn called.

The sujin just watched, its eyes suspicious, until I placed my hand in my trouser pocket. It heard the jingle of the coins, and its abnormally large eyes seemed to widen further. It dropped, crawling to the floor until it came before me, resting its clawed paws gently upon my knee. A gasp rang out behind me.

A smile tugged at the corner of my lips. "That's all you wanted, isn't it?" I pulled three of the drams out, holding them flat in my palm. The creature eyed my companions for a moment before tipping its head to me, swiping the drams into its cloak and then scurrying away through the forest.

"What the fuck just happened?" Bas said, incredulous.

I stood, turning back to the group. "Sujin are water sprites. They only come out to find trinkets, coins—anything shiny they can take and place in their horde. Usually at the bottom of a nearby body of water."

"Lake Lorelai," Eli stated.

I nodded. I knew from the map Bisa had given me that Lake Lorelai lay just to the south of our position. "There's probably a family of them living there."

"They kill people," Bas argued.

I rolled my eyes at his ignorance. "They retaliate. Yes, they are lethal... but after your way of introduction, can you blame them? Mortals' first response is to attack." Bas pouted; Vyn studied the ground. "You saw what just happened. Just give them a bit of coin, and they go on their way."

I wasn't sure who was more shocked, Bas or Eli—the latter speechless for a change. My eyes met hers as I raised a brow, and another blush darkened cheeks as she looked away from me. "I'm... sorry. I never knew."

"Yeah, sorry," Bas mumbled.

"It's all good. We all need to learn a few things if we're gonna change the world." I could tell their apologies were genuine; that meant a lot to me. But Eli noted the double meaning in my statement and gave a small smile that lit up her eyes, just for me.

Roux's curly head popped out from her shared tent as we returned, looking dazed. "What did I miss?" She rubbed the sleep from her eyes.

"These idiots were about to attack a sujin," Ant called out, strolling into our tent and missing Vyn flipping him off behind his back.

She pouted. "Aww, I missed a sujin?! They're so cute."

Bas scoffed, brows furrowed. "*I'm* cute. That thing was terrifying."

Roux laughed. "Whatever you say, big man."

Eli chuckled, following the mage. A hand grasped my shoulder, and I turned to find the ethereal yellow eyes of Vyn.

"Thanks for that, back there, Dracho. I don't enjoy taking life—so I'm glad you prevented an unnecessary loss."

I placed my own hand over his, noting that Eli lingered to listen. "No thanks needed, brother. If there's ever an opportunity to prevent a death, you can guarantee I'll try to take it."

His smile was warm.

In our tent, Ant huffed. "Can we get some bloody sleep now before we continue this shit-show?"

I laughed gruffly, settling myself back on my bed for the night. Sleep found me quickly.

36

Eli certainly hadn't lied when she said Stillmere was... different.

We entered via the western gate; a cold breeze moved past us, rustling the russet leaves of the acer trees beyond the city walls. The colours, warm and inviting and reminding me of Fall feast back home, were vastly different once we entered the city. The roofs of the buildings were all red, which blended well with the surrounding forest, but the stonework was all white, leaving the place feeling very cold—clinical. Where we had received welcoming smiles in Aion and Meridium, now cold and suspicious glances from finely dressed citizens scanned us as we manoeuvred our way through the city. Most seemed to be aimed towards Eli. Everyone was dressed impeccably, not an imperfection in their hairstyles or perfectly cut clothes.

"Say, Eli." I leaned over. "Didn't you say you'd been here before?"

She glanced at me, then noticed a couple staring in our direction and rolled her eyes. The woman wore a beautifully tailored white dress that fell below her knees and covered her arms. Her hair was carefully coiffed, and her cherry-red lipstick stood out on her thin face as she glared at Eli—specifically, at her trousers. The man beside her stood straight in a pinstriped black suit as he glared at Bas and

Roux. Not a loose thread to be seen between the two of them. The whole ensemble made me feel uncomfortable.

"The people of Stillmere are more *traditional* and set in their ways. They are rather judgemental," Eli informed me loudly. The man reared backwards in outrage, ushering the woman away. Even Engel made a disgruntled noise in their direction.

I gave Eli a questioning look. She huffed, flourishing a hand over herself. "Leathers, weapons... not sitting side-saddle. Not behaviour becoming of a *lady*, I'm afraid," she announced, throwing a middle finger in the direction of the retreating couple.

I threw my head back and laughed, my horse starting at the noise. I leaned forward, tapping his neck to ease his fright.

"Personally, I prefer a lady who'll ride astride," Bas said, his lips curling in amusement as he shot Eli a wink. She scoffed at him, and Vyn shook his head as I chuckled, trying to ignore the flash of jealousy that hit me. More Stillmereans passed us stiffly as we moved further into the city, staring at us openly.

The residential area we passed through was too neat. The streets, with unlit lanterns at intervals and no litter in sight, were quiet. Perfectly white houses with crimson rooftops were laid out in neat rows. Each one had the same square patch of turf in front of it, immaculately tended to. Occasionally there would be some glimpse —an ornament, a vase of flowers in a window—of personality, but they were rare.

"Why is the residential area so near a city gate? Not very strategic, should the city be attacked."

Ant rolled his eyes as Eli snorted.

"You'll find it *is* strategic. Jareth's strategy, anyway. All the businesses are further towards the centre. They pay the most taxes... so why place them near an entrance?"

She kept riding, ignoring my astonished expression. As I

continued to look around, it became obvious that an obsession with 'tradition' was not the city's only issue.

"Um, I notice I haven't seen any—"

"People of faerie or colour?" Bas put in. "You'd have to search far to find anyone that looks like me or Roux. Or even like Vyn and Eli."

My eyes travelled over Eli's gorgeous bronzed skin, and I wondered how anyone could be treated differently for something out of their control. I caught Ant's eye, remembering my father's warning about how mortals treated each other, and he nodded grimly.

"Morven may have been open with his vile vitriol in hopes of segregating the people, but *some* do it more discreetly," Eli added.

"Easy, Eli—we draw enough attention as it is." Vyn's yellow eyes flashed in warning.

"Psh." She nudged Engel onward.

"She's not wrong, though," I muttered quietly to Bas, who shrugged.

The city's centre was just as pristine as the residential quarter. An enormous fountain sat in the middle of the square, surrounded by busy stores. The streets here were a bustle of nervous energy, which I guessed was related to tomorrow's ball.

"Come on." Eli pulled Engel off the main square towards the main entrance to the city. "We'll leave the horses at the stables." Engel snorted, and she winced. "Sorry, boy. I'll bring you some apples from the market to make it up to you?" The beast wriggled his nose, seemingly in acceptance.

"And then where?" I asked.

Her answering smile rendered me speechless for a moment. "You're going to love it."

I did not love it.

It was a small boutique off the main square. The others had gone off to an exquisite-looking bakery on the corner; Ant silently, and begrudgingly, trailed behind me as I followed Eli.

Someone practically assaulted Eli when she walked through the door, pulling her into a firm embrace.

"Yenn—can't breathe!" Eli laughed.

The person stood back, and I saw brilliant green eyes. Not emerald like Eli's, but a springtime green that shone brightly. "Sorry, darling, but it's been *far* too long! Come, come. I assume you're here for the ball?" Eli nodded. "Hmm—I have the perfect dress for you. Though I may have to take it out a little on the hips." Their fingers pinched at her breeches. "Your arse is bigger than I remember."

My eyes widened as Eli slapped Yenn's hand, a laugh escaping her lips. "Your nose will be bigger if you carry on. I actually have a favour to ask." She tilted her head towards where Ant and I stood by the door.

Yenn's brown eyes travelled over me, and they walked to me with unwavering purpose. Flipping their long, black hair over a shoulder, they tapped a finger upon pursed lips.

"Yenn, this is Dracho. Dracho, this is Yenn."

I smiled, sticking out a hand in greeting. "It's nice to meet you, Yenn."

Yenn looked at my hand like it was disgusting, swatting it away and kissing me on both cheeks.

"Hmmm. Lovely," they remarked, scanning me intensely from head to toe. I caught Eli's gaze over their shoulder, feeling like I was being tested.

Yenn's eyes glanced past me, widening as they found Ant. They brushed me aside, reaching a finger out to smooth between Ant's brows. He jerked back in shock, a scowl set on his face.

Yenn tutted. "Honey, stop frowning. You'll wrinkle that beautiful face."

Eli covered her mouth, smothering a laugh.

"Yenn is a dryad," she told us. "They don't identify as man or woman, so would prefer it if you referred to them as they, them or just Yenn."

I smiled widely now; I had already guessed that Yenn was a tree nymph from their forest scent, and I was used to being around people in Tenebris who did not identify as either man or woman. I hadn't expected to encounter that in Stillmere, though.

"How do you manage to be yourself here, Yenn?" I asked, aware it was a personal question.

They smiled, ushering me to a raised platform in the middle of the store whilst taking a thin measuring tape out of their pocket. Coming forward, Yenn yanked my arm up, placing the tape in the crook of my armpit. Automatically, my arm shot back down.

Glaring at me, Yenn smacked me on the forehead with a pencil they'd been keeping behind their ear. My head shot back in bewilderment as Ant snorted.

"Do not move, pretty boy. Still, still—all right?" Yenn scolded me.

I nodded dazedly, utterly confounded by the whole situation. Ant passed me with his natural grace to glance at the suits on the opposite side of the room.

Yenn exhaled, returning to my question. "It has not been without its difficulties. Status over skill is lorded throughout the city. But I made myself indispensable as the king's personal dresser and best suit-maker here. Therefore, I'm allowed to get away with certain privileges."

I nodded in understanding. I scanned Yenn, appreciating the beautiful black shirt they wore, adorned with lilies in different shades of orange. Their high-waisted black trousers fitted to perfection, the wide legs swaying as they manoeuvred around me.

Yenn measured almost every inch of me and Ant. Eli walked around the store, feeling the different fabrics of the dresses hanging along the racks, only glancing at us with mirth whenever Yenn gave us instructions. Ant remained silent, his eyes narrowing every now and again.

"And we're done. Absolute perfection," Yenn stated.

"Um, thank you?"

"Oh, not you, honey. My suits. I can already see them. They're already made, of course; I'll just fit them to your measurements for tomorrow. You will, of course, look fantastic."

"Oh. Well, great. Thank you very much." I smiled.

Yenn's eyes darted over me once more. "You're very welcome. Now," they spun to Eli, "you. Clothes off."

Eli's smile vanished, and she glared at me and Ant as I grinned.

"Oh, right." Spinning back, Yenn started shoving us towards the door. "Out, out!"

"Alright, alright! We'll catch you later?" I called over my shoulder.

Eli nodded as we walked out the glass door, Ant practically sprinting out of the boutique, and I caught the laugh she shared with Yenn as we left for the bakery. Shaking my head, I ran a hand through my hair, wondering what the hell I'd got myself into.

37

⚭

"**I** don't understand why you don't just inform your father you're here. He's likely here already, and he'll have us set up in the palace in no time instead of some cramped inn."

Bas was still moaning about our accommodation as we sat, patrons of said inn—The Spotted Sparrow—sharing a drink together.

"Palace walls always have extra ears," Ant offered.

Roux nodded. "And we don't want to risk running into *anyone*." She looked at Bas pointedly.

"Ah, good point."

Running into her uncle was precisely what I wanted—just not whilst Roux was around.

"Well, I suggest we don't linger here too long before the locals fall prey to their liquor. They don't seem to hold a friendly eye towards us." Taking a sip of my drink, I subtly indicated a couple of customers at the bar who had been eyeing us disdainfully all evening. One man, with a wider build, had a thick scar from his hairline to the corner of his mouth, pulling the skin up tightly so he was constantly wiping at the drool that left it. The second man had long, greasy locks; his dull blue eyes kept roaming over Eli, causing the hairs to stand on the back of my neck. My magick had sensed their animosity as soon as we'd sat down.

Have you picked up on anything? I asked Ant. One of his hands was already resting lightly on his sword hilt, but his face was a picture of nonchalance.

They seem to know of the mage. Quite a significant amount of coin has traded hands for them to rid us of her company. They don't know who tipped them off, only that they'll be paid handsomely, he replied, his tone disgusted.

I sucked in a breath as my back straightened; Eli was the only one who noticed. She leaned in closer. "What's wrong?"

I closed my eyes, shaking my head before turning back to Ant, aware of her watchful eyes. *When?*

They've paid the inn-keep for the room information.

A low growl vibrated through my chest, and I felt Eli tense next to me. They were going to sneak into the girls' room.

We're switching rooms.

He smirked. *Obviously.*

"Do I even want to know what you two are up to?" Eli whispered tightly next to me, her breath sending shivers along the shell of my ear.

I resisted the urge to completely turn my face towards her, brush my nose against hers. "You and Roux are switching rooms with Ant and me."

Her face made it obvious that was the last thing she had expected to hear. "What? Why?"

I looked back to Ant, who just rolled his eyes before nodding.

"Some haven't taken too kindly to Roux's presence here," I murmured to Eli, so close our noses almost touched.

Her demeanour changed immediately, her eyes darkening. I watched her gaze search the tables around us before finding and stopping on those at the bar.

"Change of plan. *You* switch rooms with Roux," she commanded.

"Why?"

"They've been following us since we entered the city—I noticed them in the main square, only there were another two with them. Just in case they're planning on trying all the rooms, it's best we have a plan of attack for us all. I'd rather Antares be with Roux. He's the strongest of us all"—my brows rose— "and that way," her voice lowered, "there's a dragon that can burn them in each room. Not that I advise *that*. Plus, she's still working on her powers. Vyn and Bas will be fine on their own, with Vyn's powers and Bas' strength. Don't you agree?" She gave me a look.

"You're a savage little thing sometimes, Princess, do you know that?"

I think I might throw up my dinner, Ant drawled.

Fuck off. How did you miss the others?

I didn't—they're outside, sitting at a table. Ant yawned, ever with a face of boredom in the face of an easy fight.

Planned on us taking all four by ourselves, did you? I smirked.

Well, adding anyone else into the mix would hardly be fair to them, would it?

I chuckled, earning a confused glance from Vyn.

"Inform the others of what's happening," I whispered to Eli.

She nodded, catching Vyn's eye across the table. His head tilted.

"Ow!" Bas exclaimed, reaching down to rub his shin. "Shit, Eli, what the hell was that for?"

"Sorry, Bas, must've slipped." She gave him an intense look. "It won't happen again. Swearsies."

They both froze for a second, before relaxing back into a casual attitude—too casual. Their eyes kept catching Eli's, but no longer strayed away from our table like a regular customer's would do. They fell into normal conversation, their tone slightly louder than before. Roux's eyes narrowed as she watched them, apparently noticing that something had changed in the atmosphere.

I wrapped an arm around the back of Eli's chair, moving as

close as I could; her intoxicating scent filled my airspace. My nose brushed her cheek as I whispered, "Swearsies?"

Eli swung round on her chair so that her legs now rested between mine. To anyone watching, we would look like lovers, and my stomach dipped at the thought. Her eyes danced with amusement and the couple of ales she had drunk as she lowered her voice, leaning in. "Our safe word from when we were kids, warning of danger. We still use it now."

"Nice."

"Don't sound too surprised. We still need to warn Roux."

Already on it.

"Ant is taking care of it."

Her eyes wandered over my shoulder, spotting him as he leaned in towards Roux.

"She'll be fine," I told her.

"I know." She sounded unsure, watching as a shadow fell over Roux's face. My eyes widened in shock as Ant reached over, clasping the mage's hand and giving it a firm squeeze.

I looked back, catching Eli's equally shocked expression, and chuckled. "Right, shall we head to bed?"

My cheeks heated as I realised what I had said. Eli's silvery laugh rang out; she leaned in. "Yes."

Heat filled the rest of me too. I stood and offered her a hand, and we staggered over to the stairs, the picture of inebriated patrons. The leeches at the bar had no idea what they'd soon be facing.

❧

"Do you think this will work?" Eli whispered.

"Not worried about a few mercenaries, are you?"

Our current position was doing nothing for the tension that had filled my body in the bar. With only one bed in the room, we were lying atop the blankets in the pitch black, my leather over armour removed so I wouldn't get blood on them, but Eli fully clothed —unfortunately—waiting for the scum to make an appearance. I could feel her body heat next to mine, feel every minute movement she made.

She huffed out a quiet laugh. "I meant finding the mage."

"Oh. Well, as Jareth's dignitary, he should be there."

She gave me a small nod.

"You know..."

She rolled onto her side. "What?"

I turned, mimicking her position. "I'm looking forward to seeing you in your dress."

She covered her mouth to muffle her laughter. "Shut up."

"I truly mean it. The last time I saw you in a dress..." Need and hunger filled me as my eyes, able to see clearly in the darkened room, ran down her body—lying there, all curves and olive skin—before returning to her face.

Eli's breath hitched as she caught her bottom lip in her teeth. I nudged forward, and her lips parted. The anticipation that built inside was intoxicating, my dragon fuelling my desire to place my lips upon hers...

For the second time, we were interrupted.

This time it was soft steps outside the door only I could hear. I froze, and Eli followed suit, eyes wide. I nodded. Positioning ourselves so it looked like we were sleeping, I kept my hand near my dagger, Eli slipping one of hers under her pillow.

The doorknob turned with a slight creak; two distinct sets of footsteps sneaked into the dark room. They were almost silent—obviously well-trained—but I could feel the vibrations of their movements. No light followed them in, so they had extinguished the lanterns outside the room. I smirked, a thrill rushing through me as they edged closer to the bed, one heading around to Eli's side. I pushed away my concern—she could handle herself.

I gritted my teeth, listening for the opportune moment to strike and focusing on control of my dragon—the last thing I needed was to transform and destroy the inn. That would surely disturb the locals.

The scrape of a blade being pulled from its sheath rang out, and we struck.

I opened my eyes and turned, coming face to face with a man who blinked in shock as he stood over me, dagger at the ready. I gave him a vicious smile as I kicked out, catching him square in the balls. A pained grunt left his mouth. Grabbing his dagger hand, I jumped up, pushing him back until he slammed into the nearby wall. The crack of bone vibrated through my hand as I smashed his wrist against the wall, the weapon falling to the floor. I wrapped my free hand around his throat, lifting him into the air.

Licking my teeth, I turned. The second man had frozen as he watched my actions, but his terrified eyes went from me to Eli, and he made to draw his own knife.

Eli's hand whipped out with perfect precision, even in the dark, to grip his wrist painfully as she stood, bringing a throwing knife from underneath her pillow and driving it up under his chin. The second mercenary, too, dropped his dagger, choking on his own blood as it ran down his throat and over Eli's hand.

She smiled viciously as she leaned in. "Surprise, you vile *fuck*," she hissed, before ripping her blade out and shoving the man to the floor. She gave me a questioning glance as she felt my stare.

"Princess, I've got to admit—that was incredibly distracting."

She laughed loudly. "There's something wrong with you." She shook her head, wiping her hand on the man's shirt, before nodding towards the man who still struggled against my hold.

"Oh, right." I turned to look at the frightened man in the eyes.

His dirty fingernails scraped me uselessly as he clawed at my hand. A strange feeling clouded me as I realised what I had to do. With a sharp twist of my wrist, the snap of bone sounded out and the man's life was instantly extinguished. I dropped him unceremoniously to the floor, then swallowed the lump in my throat. I didn't even know his name.

Eli's eyes widened slightly. "Well, that was... terrifying."

I jerked my head up to her. "I'm sorry, I didn't mean to scare you—"

"You didn't." She smiled lightly, but I saw her swallow. "I just... never realised how strong you actually were, in your human form."

I chuckled. "But you'd still kick my arse."

Her teeth flashed in an answering grin before we heard feet rushing to our room. Eli tensed; I listened closely.

"It's Ant and Roux," I told her, lighting the bedside lantern before they burst into the room.

Ant checked me over, before taking note of the bodies on the floor. Roux walked closer, her eyes aflame with an unnatural glow as she stared at them, her jaw clenched.

"All good?" Eli asked.

"You were right—two of them tried our room at the same time. They left Vyn and Bastion's room alone," Ant told us.

Nodding, I said, "Well, we'd better let the inn-keep know he'll have some cleaning up to do."

"About that..." Ant started as Bas and Vyn came in.

I squinted as bright golden, black-fringed flames suddenly engulfed the bodies slain on the floor, Eli jumping back with a screech. The magickal flames burnt intensely for a moment before diminishing, leaving nothing but a small pile of ash in each place of each man and no trace of blood.

A chill worked its way up my spine. I'd never seen anything

like that in all my existence from anyone who wasn't a draconi. The intensity of the residual magickal energy tingled along my skin.

"Oh... well, there's that." Bas swallowed.

"I stand corrected," Eli whispered. "*That* was terrifying."

Roux breathed heavily, the effort of such power weighing down on her.

"Roux?" Eli reached a hand out.

"I'll be fine. I just have a—a headache that's—"

Her body swayed as her legs gave out, Eli rushing forward to catch her, and I gripped her shoulders. Bas and Vyn gasped, stepping further into the room.

I checked the mage over, feeling her stir. "She's all right. That was... a lot for her."

Eli nodded, catching my eye. "I'll take her to her room and stay with her."

My dragon pouted, but I smiled as she placed Roux's arm over her shoulder, Bas stepping forward to help. Vyn followed them down the hallway.

Ant closed the door. "It was certainly a surprise."

I hummed in agreement. "That was only an inkling of her true power. I've never felt anything like that, have you?"

He shook his head. "It was almost like—"

"Dragon fire." I had never seen anything else able to turn a man to dust that quickly. It was a testament to how much extra power the ancestors had given her.

He nodded. "I think it's best I stay here with her tomorrow night, whilst you attend the ball. Just in case there are any other stupid attempts on her life."

I nodded. "Good idea. But don't think I can't see your true motives."

He turned away. "I don't know what you mean."

I rolled my eyes. "Anything to get out of wearing a suit."

"Don't be ridiculous."

"Uh-huh," I replied, not convinced.

"But, Dracho," Ant's face turned serious, "she'll need to get a handle on her gifts before she faces the Hollow. We can't risk her being in a weakened state."

My eyes narrowed. "She knows. We all know. That's why I'm helping her."

His smile was tight as he clapped me on the shoulder. "Let's hope your help pays off. Sooner, rather than later."

A beat of silence fell between us, a question burning my tongue. Walking closer to the bed, I rubbed my toe on a flake of ash. "Do you find it easy now? Taking a life?" I asked quietly.

Ant's jaw clenched, his eyes venturing to the ceiling for a moment. "They were evil men, Dracho. They would have killed any of us without blinking an eye." His eyes found mine, brutal and unforgiving. "Yes. I find it easy. To protect those I care about. Do not give it one more moment of your time."

He kicked his boots off, throwing himself onto his front on the bed, taking a deep inhale. Rubbing my eyes, I sighed roughly, mentally bumping Roux's intense magick up my list of problems.

"I know that feeling in your stomach, after your first time. But we don't have time for it. Overthink it tomorrow, Dracho. Get some sleep," Ant said, his voice muffled.

I nodded, though he couldn't see, and laid my dagger down before lying beside him. I stared up at the ceiling for hours afterwards, sleep evading me until the early hours.

38

The innkeeper looked astonished to see us all alive and freshly washed at breakfast the next morning. Ant had a quiet word with him, and his service was suddenly second to none. Plates of bacon, sausages and eggs were laid out before us along with plenty of freshly toasted bread, and everyone took their fill.

Except Roux. Her eyes kept finding mine; I could sense the concern rolling off her.

I wished I could communicate telepathically with mortals without being in my dragon form. I smiled brightly at her, trying to put her at ease. Her worry was understandable; what she had done last night had emanated a power we had never seen. Well, not without the use of dragon fire. I was familiar with the intensity of draconi fire, but this surge in power must have been scary for Roux.

I tipped my head to the door, looking pointedly at her. She gave a small nod before rising.

"All good, little mage?" Bas asked.

Her smile was small, reassuring. "I just need some air for a moment."

I jumped to my feet. "I'll join you. No one should be left alone here."

I followed Roux silently through the streets of Stillmere until we reached the benches surrounding the fountain in the centre of the square. I sat beside her, but didn't speak, allowing her the time to express what she needed.

"I-I didn't know I could do that." Her voice was quiet.

I took in her sorrowful expression. "You were protecting your-self—"

"Not in your room." She swallowed thickly. "They were already gone, but... when I saw them, I felt such anger. Knowing what they had planned to do, without even knowing me. Knowing what they were willing to do to you *all*, just to get to me. The power... it seemed to come so easily—as easy as snapping my fingers. And what surprises and upsets me most of all... I don't regret it."

She tipped forward, burying her head in her hands as if in shame. Moving to kneel in front of her, I took her hands within my own, moving them away from her face.

"I don't regret it either." I held her gaze steadily. "I took life *gladly*, knowing what they were going to do. I don't like killing. But I will if it means keeping you safe—keeping you all safe." My eyes dropped to the ground. "That... that was actually the first man—mortal—I've ever killed."

Roux tensed under my hands as she dropped hers into her lap.

I thought of the words Eli had spoken the night before, even if she had said them as a joke. "Maybe there *is* something wrong with me," I whispered. "Because I feel nothing for the man whose life I took. It's not a life wasted, because at the end of the day," my eyes lifted to meet hers once again, "they made their choice. Their decision to take life if they could. Innocent life—you. So don't you regret it for one moment. I understand that your power scares you, but we're going to get through that—together."

Her breath hitched, a small sob escaping her mouth as she flung herself forward, wrapping her arms around my neck. I froze, my arms held out in shock.

"Thank you, Dracho, for everything," Roux whispered against my neck.

I wrapped my arms around her with a sigh. "It's my pleasure. Now we're alone—I, um... I wanted to say I'm sorry."

Her brows were pinched as she pulled back out of my arms. "For what?"

I swallowed thickly. "For Aion."

Realisation dawned on her face.

"If I had just transformed during my fight with the Ho—"

"Then you would have put yourself at more risk by revealing your secret."

It would have been worth it. If I could have saved...

My thoughts must have been written upon my face; she clasped my hand tightly. "We still have very little knowledge of this thing, so we don't know if your dragon would have been effective at all."

The dragon stirred at that, slightly offended.

"That thing was near Aion for a reason... and I believe it would have happened whether we were there or not. Don't blame yourself for one second, Dracho. I certainly don't."

A weight of guilt lifted from my chest. My eyes stung as I pulled Roux in for another hug. "Thank you."

Her laugh was light, muffled from being pressed against my chest. "Anytime."

❧

Yenn was right: the suit they had made was exquisite. One of the best I'd ever seen. It was a light, supple black velvet which moulded itself to my body. In the mirror, I eyed how the fabric had been tailored to perfection, appreciating the silver details along the edges and pockets.

"Yenn, I have to admit it...you're a genius." I shot them a warm smile, and they rolled their eyes.

"Of course I am, darling." Yenn strolled over, dusting non-existent dirt from my shoulder before walking around me in a full circle. "Very nice. It's good that you are *somewhat* good-looking. Enough to at least pull off my suit."

I suppressed a smile. "When do I get to see Eli in her dress?"

Yenn's brow arched. "When you leave for the party."

Pouting, I looked to my reflection once more, brushing my hair out of my face. "Not fair."

Yenn scoffed. "Just make sure she doesn't do anything to ruin it... like murder someone," they muttered, walking back to the front of the shop.

A dark chuckle escaped me. "I can't promise anything. But I'll give it a try."

From the expression Eli was wearing when I met her outside the inn, it would be an arduous task. I knew she didn't like dresses, but by the stars! She was enlightening—a sinful apparition come to give me forbidden knowledge. I scanned her from head to toe, drinking her in like a man dying of thirst as she sauntered towards me with a scowl on her face.

Her lush lips were a ruby rose; black lined the edges of her eyes, bringing out the green of her irises. She had a braided crown around her head, but the rest had been curled, falling in voluminous waves around her shoulders and resting against the scandalous scarlet fabric that hugged every curve of her body before flaring at the bottom. I wasn't sure what constituted high fashion in Stillmere, but I was positive Yenn's creation would turn heads, even with nobility attending from all over Ruvalon.

"E!" came a booming voice behind her. Eli turned to see Bas and Vyn walking her way.

Vyn took her arms in his hands. "Remember why we're here."

Bas nodded vigorously. "Don't take no shit, E. Get in and get out. You'll be awesome, got it?"

Each giving her a single kiss on the forehead, the duo turned back, heading into the inn. Eli stood staring after them.

I saw her note the confusion in my expression when she turned around. Clearing her throat, she walked forward, coming to a stop a few steps in front of me and looking anywhere but directly at me.

"Well?" Her voice was breathy as she stared over my shoulder, throwing her arms out as her cheeks became pink.

Taking the opportunity to take her in all over again, I blew out a long breath. "You are..."

Her eyes found my chin, not looking directly at me yet, but seeming nervous and expectant as she chewed her cheek.

"*Distracting.*"

Rolling her eyes, Eli scoffed as she pushed past me, heading towards one of the carriages that escorted citizens around Stillmere. I suppressed a groan as I spotted the back of her dress, the low cut of it stopping just above her glorious—

"Are you coming or not?" Her frustrated voice cut off my perusal. I jogged to catch up, helping her up the step of the carriage, shaking away thoughts of throwing her over my shoulder and taking her back to her room. That familiar energy flowed along my skin as she took my hand.

When I had indicated for the driver to go and we started to move, she finally looked at me, that blush deepening for some reason as her eyes travelled all over me, as mine had her.

"Aren't the prudes of Stillmere going to be scandalised by your outfit?" I asked.

She smirked at me. "Do you really think I give a fuck?" I laughed as she continued. "There'll be people here from all over, wearing the fashions of their area. No one will be looking at me."

"I highly doubt that, Princess."

My eyes stayed on her as we sat, the cab jostling as the driver urged the horse up the sloping cobbles before the main gates of the palace.

"All right, so our plan is to find Kanu?" I asked.

Eli nodded. "I want to speak to my father first. Find out why he didn't demand that Kanu be expelled from Ruvalon."

I nodded as the palace fully came into view. It was bold against the darkness that night brought; its white stones contrasted with the red-tiled roof and the surrounding forests beyond the border. The crimson flag of Stillmere waved in the cool autumn breeze, the wings of the grey falcon appearing to move along with it. It all looked as though it had been constructed from an old fairy-tale: a true vision of perfection, much like the residential streets we had seen the day before.

As we passed through the gates, the lanterns hanging from the walls caught my eye.

"The lights are electrical? Why isn't the rest of the city powered?" I asked. From what I'd seen, the city used flames for light.

Eli gave me a sly smile that made her face look sharp. "Proditor saves that for his palace. For himself."

My eyes widened. "By withholding resources, he holds more power."

"Exactly. Deplorable, isn't it?"

I was starting to understand why Eli hated this place. While we had argued over Tenebris—her allegations that we neglected our southern neighbours and denied them assistance—this was differ-ent. The king's decision to withhold such advancements from the rest of his city was a blatant show of his classist values.

There wasn't much written of King Proditor; he had only ruled for a short while. I had read that prior to the Tain, he had been a southern lord in the town of Madain—a town that lay just over a day south from here, and which had been sworn to the then King

Morven. Proditor had never appeared for the final battle, failing to offer Morven his support. That had won him a lot of favour with the humans, and eventually led to him being voted in as King of Stillmere. With no human bloodline entitled to the throne, the nobility of Ruvalon had deemed it the most democratic way to elect a new leader.

But the way he ruled Stillmere, and the attitude of his people, made me wonder. What exactly would we find once we entered the palace?

39

Despite the beauty of the white walls and tiled floors with burgundy accents, the palace was just as cold and clinical as its city. Guests floated around us in clothes of all different colours and styles, chattering animatedly amongst their groups and chugging their champagne, some sets of eyes hovering for a bit too long on the beauty beside me. Violin music reached my ears from further within.

My hand found the small of Eli's back, feeling her tense as I guided her into the reception hall. Spotting a servant with a silver tray of champagne flutes, she stormed over, taking two. I held my hand out for one—and watched her drain them both.

"O-kay." I smiled tightly as two men walked past, eyeing her behaviour with apparent disdain.

Her finger swiped at a stray drop at the corner of her mouth, and she let out a rough, shaky breath. "Trust me... I'm going to need it."

Two loud taps upon the tiles rang out from where a royal guard stood with his staff, at the bottom of the curving staircase.

"Ladies and gentlemen, His Royal Majesty, King Jareth Proditor."

Silence descended as every pair of eyes turned to the stairs and the man descending.

So, *this* was Jareth Proditor. My expectations of the king had been very wrong. I watched the man sway down the stairs and into the room, his luxurious, grey silk robe trailing along the floor behind him along with several guards.

From the way the scholars' texts had described his refusal to help King Morven during the Tain, I had expected some larger-than-life figure to enter the hall. Instead, he was rather unimposing. His build was slight, his robe burying him further, and though his thin face was attractive, it was fixed with a sneer. The people bowed as he passed, though he acknowledged no one. He looked disinterested as he perused his surroundings, his long poppy-red hair swinging with every step; as he approached us, we bowed.

The king slowed, his eyes travelling past me to Eli.

She stiffened, and the uncomfortable charge in the atmosphere made my dragon raise its head. The king eyed her for a few more seconds until she raised her head to look at him, a cruel smirk lifting his thin lips and mirth shining in his eyes. He held her gaze for a second more before turning, completely ignoring my existence, and greeting some dignitaries at the end of the room.

Eli pulled up from her bow, visibly irritated by the exchange as she headed straight for another waiter. I followed silently and watched again as she grabbed another glass and swallowed it all in two mouthfuls. The young server looked on in shock, as if he had never seen a woman drink in such a way. Poor, green boy. She took another champagne flute and downed it to the dregs.

I tapped the server on the shoulder and indicated he should leave—which he did eagerly.

The way Eli's fingers twitched around the glass highlighted how nervous she was, and I felt a flash of amusement. I'd never seen her so... undone. This great warrior-maiden, who rarely showed fear, even in the face of mighty, unknown enemies—was terrified of the bureaucrats.

"I think you should slow down."

"I think you should shut the fuck up. I can't hear myself losing the will to live."

A thrill jolted at me as the word came from her mouth, the language doing highly inappropriate things to my body whilst surrounded by so many people. When I burst out laughing, a few guests close by looked in our direction, and Eli scowled at them.

Feeling brave, I offered my hand, her head snapping down to it so fast I was surprised her neck didn't crack. She looked at it for a moment, before intertwining our fingers and glancing back up at me.

"What are you doing?" she asked, a trace of humour in her tone.

"What do you think? I'm being *distracting.*"

She rolled her eyes. "You're being an idiot."

But she didn't separate our hands, and I enjoyed the feeling of her small fingers wrapped around my own.

"It's just rich folk. Some royalty," I told her.

"It's not just—"

"It's a few hours, and we'll be done."

I could feel the tension in her hand as her eyes darted around the hall. "It's not the—"

"Eliana?" someone called.

Her back stiffened, and her fingers tightened.

My curiosity flared as an attractive man appeared from the crowd behind her, nodding to a couple of guards to stay where they were as he came forward. Concern filled his strikingly blue eyes, his brow creased.

Eli looked at me in panic, and I didn't need to use my draconi senses to hear her heart thundering in her chest. I stepped around her, stretching out my free hand to him.

"Good evening; I'm Dracho. A *friend* of Eli here."

Eli let out an unattractive snort, brought out of her stupor by my choice of words but still keeping her back to him.

The man looked somewhat displeased, his eyes travelling to our interlocked hands before taking my free one and shaking. "Pleasure to meet you," he said. "My name is Jakard—Jakard Proditor."

My hand stopped moving, my eyes widening in shock. I hadn't known Jareth had a son. But of course—he had the same hair colour and angular face as his father. I was even more surprised at how rudely Eli was treating him.

I released him, bowing as I cleared my throat. "My apologies, Your Highness."

"No apology necessary." He smiled tightly, glancing at the back of Eli's head. "May I speak privately with Princess Eliana for a moment?"

She turned now, letting go of my hand. "I don't think that's appropriate."

Now I was definitely curious.

"Please, Eliana?" he practically begged.

How far could I involve myself in this matter? I had to contain my curiosity as people started looking towards us—unknowingly, at all *three* of the future rulers of Ruvalon—and our obvious discomfort. Eli had her arms crossed, and Jakard looked as if he was two seconds from throwing himself to his knees before her.

I decided to try and diffuse the situation. Moving a step closer to Eli, I placed my hand at the small of her back once more, feeling the warmth of her smooth skin. She jumped slightly at the contact, turning to look at me.

"Maybe you two should take this somewhere private?" I indicated the crowd with a tilt of my head.

Eli's eyes constricted slightly, and the emotion I saw there before it vanished made me instantly regret my words. It was hurt. Not at my actions—a deep, tangible hurt that made her want to avoid this man.

Cold settled in my gut at my mistake. She had said no to his invitation for a reason. And essentially, I'd just taken his side.

I looked at Jakard, my nostrils flaring. Whatever this man—this *prince*—had done to her had scarred her. Could it be those scars that caused her to drift from peaceful slumber?

Before I could vocalise my change of mind, Eli took a defeated breath at my side. "I'll speak with you," she said without looking at him.

I grabbed her wrist as she moved away. A second of fright seemed to flash across her face, but whatever she saw in mine made her grace me with a small smile. "I'll be all right."

I sensed the truth in her words, and knew deep down that she was more than capable of taking him out if she needed or wanted to. Releasing her wrist, I allowed my fingers to slide to hers, holding them loosely.

"I won't be far. I'll give you fifteen minutes, and if you haven't returned," I looked at him, "I'll come for you."

Eli nodded before walking past Jakard without a second glance. I knew she tried not to show her nerves, but I didn't miss the subtle way her fingers trembled as she pulled away—in anger or fear, I didn't know.

"Eliana."

She paused.

"I'll be right here."

She nodded again, turning to continue down the hall.

The prince stared at me curiously; as I caught his gaze, he flinched. Whatever he saw, I hoped he took it as a warning.

He turned to follow, and I coughed quietly. Jakard turned, taking in my expression—which I knew wasn't pleasant—and masked his own into one of calm, despite his increasing heart rate.

"If you harm her... you'll answer to *me*," I promised, my voice low and dangerous as my dragon elicited a slight rumble in my chest.

His entire body stiffened, and a flash of fear showed in his eyes. I panicked for a moment, wondering how much of the dragon had shown through, but he seemed subdued, not considering this male a real threat.

Jakard scanned my face as if considering the threat. He must have deemed it genuine, for he swallowed, nodding just once before turning to follow Eli. The two of them disappeared into a side room off the main hallway.

Wondering if my feelings for Eli were affecting my ability to control my dragon, I waited.

40

People-watching—especially rich people—was definitely one of my favourite things to do. I'd spotted Eli's father across the hall whilst I gave her and Prince Jak-arse some space, and I made a mental note of his position, hoping he'd still be there when she returned. I considered approaching him myself, but he was looking rather uncomfortable whilst some pretty redhead ran her hands over the front of his jacket. I thought about rescuing him, but I felt too nervous to talk to him without Eli present. I searched for any sign of the mage—for anyone who looked at all like Bisa—but found nothing.

A server rolled his eyes at another. A gentleman in a very poorly fitting purple suit was loudly telling everyone who would listen how many drams he had made that year from selling his hair loss cure—a tale I found most amusing, considering he was wearing a wig.

"Disgusting, isn't it?"

I glanced sideways to a classy-looking woman dressed in violet, her white hair coiffed tightly. She raised a brow.

"That tramp." She nodded towards the redhead with King Cervidae. "She's throwing herself all over King Cervidae when she's young enough to be his daughter—and engaged to Prince Jak."

"*She's* engaged to Prince Jakard?" *Interesting. Then why did he request a moment of Eli's time?*

The woman hummed. "Foul girl."

I looked uneasily towards the clock on the wall. It had been nine minutes. Tapping my fingers against my champagne, I wondered if I should make good on my promise.

"Excuse me," I told the woman as my dragon urged me on, putting down my glass. Agitation turned my vision red as I marched towards that white door and whatever lay beyond it. *Fuck it.*

I only hesitated for a second before raising my hand to the door to knock, but the raised voices stopped me in my tracks.

"—know, Jak. Your father made it abundantly clear how he felt about me the last time I was here. How he felt about *us*. You don't get to set that clock back! I moved on."

Shock flooded my system. This... *this* was the 'someone' that Bas had briefly mentioned? My mind ran a hundred miles a second, and I smacked myself internally. No wonder she'd been so nervous about coming here. This was why the king had smirked at her like they were familiar. Why she had been so anxious when the prince confronted us—and I'd practically shoved her into the room with him.

Dick move.

"Moved on? Yes, I can see that," he spat back at her.

I heard Eli hiss through her teeth. "You have no idea what you're talking about, so don't you *dare*."

That dismissal stung a surprising amount.

"You don't ever get to question or criticise my choices," Eli went on. "You have no authority in my life, and yet have the audacity to believe you have permission to speak out about *my* behaviour?"

I shouldn't listen to this. I should go. But what if it turned... nasty?

She can handle herself—but I couldn't move a muscle.

It was silent for a moment until I heard Jakard loose a breath. "You're... you're right. I'm so sorry, Eliana. To be honest... I was so overcome by my jealousy that I was incredibly moronic, and spoke out of turn. I can admit when I'm wrong. I'm not my father. Please forgive me."

"I know you're not your father, Jak," she said, calmer but exasperated now. "But you don't get to be jealous. You have no *right* to be. I. Am. Not. Yours. I belong to no one."

I heard the scuffle of feet come closer, and the door swung open before I could move. Eli froze as she spotted me, wide-eyed with my fist still raised.

"I was just—"

"Come on," she commanded, seizing my wrist and dragging me back through the ballroom to the centre of the dance floor.

"Oh," I protested, "I don't think—"

"Take my waist." She swung around, standing opposite me.

"Excuse me?"

She exhaled an impatient breath. "This is a dance floor." She waved her hand around, speaking to me as if I were an idiot. "We dance." She picked up my hands and arranged us into the appropriate stance for a waltz. "It's all right, I'll lead," she informed me.

I didn't like her assumption that I couldn't follow a simple dance. As the music flowed into a new song, I tightened my hold on her and pulled her into a turn. We fell into a graceful rise and fall, swaying as I guided her around the floor, our bodies inching closer.

She looked at me in shock. "Well, isn't this a nice surprise!"

I chose to ignore the obvious insult there. "I'm not completely incapable, you know."

"We'll agree to disagree." Her lips curved into a smile. "Who taught you how to dance?"

I looked over her shoulder as my heart twinged. I contemplated changing the subject, asking what had happened with Jakard. But part of me wanted to let her in... let her know this side of me. My eyes swung back to hers; her brow was creased, questioning.

"My mother."

"Oh." She stared at me for what felt like an age before finding her voice. "Would—would you tell me about her?" she asked tentatively.

I raised my eyes to the ceiling, silent for a moment, collecting my thoughts and pushing down the pain that came with the memories. Slowly, I looked back at the woman in my arms. Her wide, forest-green eyes were full of nothing but empathy, curiosity... and something else. Something that reached out, giving me the strength to talk about what I usually kept silent.

"She—she was the most wonderful woman. The most dependable and wonderful person I knew. She was an amazing queen—she loved all of her subjects. She was everything I could ever aspire to become. Strong, beautiful, wise... and my father loved her like no other."

"She sounds like she was remarkable."

I smiled. "She was." I cleared my throat. "Her sickness came quickly—not long after the Tain ended, actually. No healer could help her, could even detect what it was that would eventually claim her life."

Eli frowned; concern written across her features.

"She... she held on for a few days after it was discovered but—it wasn't a pleasant passing. Wasn't pain-free. It was an awful way for her to go." My jaw clenched as I tried to stem the flow of images that came with those memories. Frail hands covered in creeping black veins reaching out to hold my own, so small and wasted away they looked like they could snap with barely any effort. Her once warm, playful eyes, the colour almost precisely the same shade as mine, begging for her torture to end.

I cleared my throat again. "I think that's what hurt the most. To see such a beautiful and pure creature succumb to something like that... it almost killed my father."

Eli's face was solemn. "I'm sorry you had to experience that so young, Dracho."

"Well, if anyone understands, it's you, Princess."

She looked away for a moment, swallowing, then gave me a bright smile. "Well, she taught you to dance wonderfully."

"Was that a compliment?"

"Don't let it go to your head." She chuckled. "You're an *average* lead."

Laughing, I leaned in closer. "You asked for it." And I pulled her closer, turning us with the music as it flew into a crescendo.

Eli's body jerked as she gripped my shoulder, not having expecting the swing, and she laughed back. Freely and openly. A full laugh, her head thrown back, her eyes squeezed shut.

Breath catching in my throat, I stared unashamedly, taking in my fill of it—of her, like this. I didn't dare blink, for fear I would miss one minute detail changing across her face. Kings, ancients and gods must have fallen across the aeons for such a laugh.

My hand tightened on the small of her back, bringing her closer as we danced in circles around the other couples. Her laughter eased as she opened her eyes, catching my gaze.

"What?" she asked, breathless, amused.

I blinked several times, feeling a faint blush heat my cheeks. "Nothing."

Moving her hand to the nape of my neck, she tugged lightly at the hair there, causing a completely different heat to fill my body. "Um, you were staring?" There was a note of nervousness to her laughter now.

The music changed, leading into a slower song, with couples dancing closer together. I grinned, bringing the hand I was holding up and placing it around my neck to meet her other one, moving mine to rest upon her waist. I heard her breath pause at the new position, but we moved together to the new music towards the edge of the dance floor.

"I've—just never seen you laugh like that before."

Her smile was sly. "Maybe I've never found you funny."

My mouth fell open, but before I could think of a witty reply, a small cough interrupted us. We both turned to see Eli's father. I released her, bowing immediately as my stomach dipped with nerves.

"King Cervidae. A pleasure to see you again, Your Majesty."

The king's eyes took me in knowingly for a moment before a smile tilted the corners of his lips. "Dracho. No need for formalities. Pleasure is all mine, my boy!" He offered his hand, which I accepted gracefully, and turned to beam at his daughter. "My Eliana." He opened his arms, taking her into his embrace and placing a kiss on each cheek. "You both danced wonderfully." She flushed. "I trust your trip has been fruitful?"

"We wouldn't be here if it wasn't, Father," she told him, pulling out of his embrace.

His brows rose. "Oh, really? Then we really must catch up. But not here. Enjoy your night! We will catch up on the morrow."

"Father," Eli stepped forward, lowering her voice, "there was an attack on Aion."

"No!" The king paled, horror filling his eyes. He blinked, then glanced around at the guests near us. He lowered his head. "What happened? Did anyone survive? Is Bisa all right? Are *you* all right?"

Eli nodded, putting a calming hand on his arm. "She is well, but—"

"Actually, not here," her father whispered. "Too many eyes and ears. We shall discuss this privately later." His eyes fell to someone behind us. "Ah, Lys! There you are."

The white-haired woman I had spoken to earlier stepping up to greet the king, kissing him on each cheek before holding her arms towards Eliana. "Eliana, darling."

"Aunt Lys. I've missed you." Eli gave her a warm hug. "This is Dracho." She touched my arm gently. "Draco, this is one of my father's dearest friends, Lys."

The older woman smiled at me. "We met briefly. It's nice to meet you, Dracho."

I took her hand, bringing it to my lips. "The pleasure is all mine."

Lys grinned and gave me a wink, then turned to clasp Eli's arms in her hands. She held her at arms' reach, looking her over. "You've grown into a remarkable woman. Simply stunning. You look more and more like your mother."

Eli looked down. "Thank you."

"Well, isn't this cosy?" drawled a nasal voice.

The redhead who had been flirting with the king before sauntered up to us and ran a hand along my bicep, leaving her arm resting across my shoulders—which must have been uncomfortable, as she was much shorter than me. I looked hurriedly at Eli, but she wasn't looking at me; her eyes were burning holes into the woman.

The newcomer smirked at Lys. "Mother."

Lys smiled back. "Disgrace."

Oh shit.

I coughed out an awkward laugh, stepping sideways out of the woman's touch. Her smile was sly as she tapped my neck.

"Nice tattoo."

I froze, my dragon growling quietly to himself as Eli narrowed her eyes.

She leaned in. "Would you like to see mine?" Her oddly familiar kohl-lined eyes were alight with a secretive glint. Lys made a disgusted noise in the back of her throat.

"Um, no, thank you?"

Her laugh was shrill as she held her hand out. "Illyra. Nice to meet you."

I opened my senses as I gave her my hand, but read nothing from her but a steady heartbeat. A red gem at the base of her throat caught my eye, but I glanced away before she could catch me looking. "Dracho."

She smiled slyly. "So, Eliana, is this your *new* lover?"

I almost choked. My eyes shot to the king, who didn't seem shocked by Illyra's outspoken attitude—but very uncomfortable, shifting on his feet. Eli's nostrils flared, but it was Lys who spoke out.

"Illyra, you can't steal another one."

I was beginning to understand why Eli's break-up with Jakard had been messy.

Illyra tutted. "Shame. I would have liked to have added him to my collection."

What the hell was going on?

"Shouldn't you go and find Jakard?" Lys asked, bored.

"Ah yes, my darling *fiancé*." Illyra's eyes shone at Eli, who showed no emotion.

A tingle worked its way up my spine. I whipped my head around, forgetting the conversation; a flash of white towards the end of the hall caught my eye.

He was here.

The robe disappeared into the crowd as I tried to track his movements, and Ant's words repeated in my head. *I don't believe in coincidences.*

I muttered my excuses and turned to leave, briefly catching Eli's confused expression. I walked briskly through the crowd, anticipation and my magick churning in my stomach. As I turned the corner at the end of the hall, a swish of white disappeared into a side room. I followed.

Just as I reached for the handle, I froze. Should I wait for Eli? Hesitation was never something I had had to worry about before— before the Hollow.

Now...

I took a deep breath and pushed open the door.

41

The figure turned.

The hood of the brilliant white robe was now pulled back; the gold of a belt twinkled in the candlelight. The person I had been seeing wasn't a scholar at all, but a mage. I could see why he usually kept the hood up; a multitude of scars littered his bald head and face.

"Kanu?"

The resemblance was uncanny. The three siblings had the same colour and shaped eyes. But whereas Chief Bisa's and Sizwe's were full of knowledge and kindness, this man's eyes seemed to have been drained of life long ago. My magick hissed in his presence, feeling his stained magick permeate the air. Whatever he had done, it had corrupted the energies he had been blessed with.

He smiled at me, an empty, placating smile.

"Good evening, Dracho. I see my sister has been talking about me. But at last, we meet."

"You know me?"

"Of course. It's my job to know."

I arched a brow. "Your *job*?"

He smiled again, the action as creepy as it was emotionless.

"What exactly is your job?"

"I advise King Proditor—mostly. I also act as a messenger, when it suits him. Lately, I have been finding myself employed as a tracker, of sorts." His eyes flashed at me.

My heart skipped a beat. "A tracker? You've been tracking me?"

His head tilted. "My dear boy, *you*?" He laughed coldly, the sound hollow.

And then it hit me. "Eliana?"

"Ah, you're a quick one."

"Why follow her?"

"The king wanted to be made aware of her movements."

I didn't miss that he failed to specify which king. King Cervidae had put out a bounty for his daughter's safe return, and had been seen talking to Proditor's dignitary...

"You struck a bargain with both kings to relieve your banishment?" I guessed. It was probably the only reason King Cervidae would accept Kanu's banishment being lifted: if he promised to keep an eye on Eli.

His grin was smug.

"Clever. You've been watching Eli... and the company she kept, I presume?" He nodded. "I gather you couldn't follow us into Aion?"

For the first time, emotion seemed to flicker in his eyes. His head lowered, and I thought I saw a small glimmer of despair before he blinked it away. "No. I could not venture there. But I picked your trail up again afterwards."

I stared at him, the fibres of my magick dancing across my nerve endings. He might already know what I was, but the longer I spent with him, the more likely it became. "And... did you learn much, upon your travels?"

He glanced up at me from under his brow, grinning once more. "Now, now, *inyoka*—that would be telling."

The hairs on the back of my neck stood up at the Aioni word for *dragon*.

"And the Hollow?" I asked. My senses reached out, testing his trace of magick, even though I knew he could feel it. There was no likeness between the corrupt traces I had sensed on this mage and the aura I'd got from the Hollow.

His gaze was focused as he stared at me. "I'm afraid I don't know what you're talking about."

Whilst I knew that was a lie, thanks to Bisa, I had no evidence to suggest that he had any involvement with the strange goings-on throughout Ruvalon. Before I could say more, steps sounded behind me. Kanu looked over my shoulder; the steps faltered.

"Dracho?" Eli asked, sounding unsure.

I didn't remove my eyes from the mage. "Let's go."

His mirth-filled eyes glanced at Eli once more before catching mine. "I'll see *you* again, Dracho."

I turned, grasping Eli's hand to pull her from the room. I dragged her along the corridor back to the main hall, her small feet practically skipping to keep up.

"Dracho, what's going on?! Are you all right?"

"I just—I just need to put as much space between you and him as I can."

If he knew who I was—who I *truly* was—and had informed the kings... Well, that changed a lot of things. It meant Tenebris could be in danger.

"Dracho, slow down!"

I stopped by a waiter, scanning the room in a panic as I took a glass of champagne and downed it swiftly. Now it was Eli's turn to look scandalised. I took two more before nodding for him to move along.

"Want one?" I offered it to her.

She shrugged, merely taking a mouthful and placing the glass upon a nearby table. "Now, are you going to tell me what that was about?"

I swirled the cheap champagne around my mouth before swallowing. "That was him."

"H-him? As in—?"

I nodded. "And he knows who—*what*—I am."

Her eyes widened. She glanced around, then grabbed my hand and pulled me through the ballroom and down a hallway.

She took me to a balcony at the back of the palace. String lights were draped along the wooden beams above it, illuminating the white marble tiles below, but it was the view that stole my breath from me.

Despite its issues, Stillmere was exquisite. An enchanting mask to hide the ugliness underneath. Lights shone out below us, gently touching the red acers that surrounded the city. The crisp smell of early autumn was in the air as a slight breeze tickled the hairs at the nape of my neck.

Eli spun on her heel. "Why would you possibly think that?" she demanded.

"He as good as told me... I'm not sure if he's told your father."

"My father?" she echoed. "If Proditor or my father knew, we'd hear about it. There's no way he'd allow you within ten feet of me."

She had a point. If King Cervidae knew of my true identity, he would have had Eli removed from my company. Maybe even try to punish me and Ant for breaching the treaty.

A relieved breath left my lips. At least that was something we didn't have to worry about for now.

"Did you find anything else out?"

I shook my head guiltily. In my panic, I'd completely forgotten our mission. "There's something strange about him. His magick, it's... there's something wrong with it. But honestly, he creeped me out so much I had to get out of the room."

"But you didn't sense any trace of the Hollow?"

"Definitely didn't feel the same. But I think we need to be cautious around him. Find out more before we pursue him."

"All right. So where do we go from here?"

We had no way forward. We'd exhausted all of our options.

Well, not *all* of them.

"I think we stick to our plan. Head to Tenebris and speak to my father."

Eli pursed her lips, chewing on her cheek for a moment. "I think you're right. If anyone is going to have answers now, it's going to be a two-thousand-year-old being."

Squinting, I placed a hand on her forehead. "Are you feeling well?"

"What are you talking about?"

"You just told me I'm right."

She smacked my hand away, but held it firmly as I laughed. She looked down at our joined hands for a moment, brushing her thumb over my finger, my skin tingling.

Releasing me, she moved back against the balcony, smiling. "Well, I suppose there's got to be a first time for everything."

I leaned forward to place my hands on the wall on either side of her, aware of her breath hitching and of how close this brought us to each other. "Are you all right?"

She glanced at me for a second before she looked away. "Of course I am—why wouldn't I be?"

I'd known it would be a sensitive subject. But I wanted her to know that I was there for her—as she had been for me. That she could trust me and talk to me.

"Eli. I put things together. I realise who Jakard is—*was*—to you."

Inhaling deeply, she squared her shoulders before meeting my gaze.

"It was a long time ago. We'd been together for years. I believed he was going to propose, and that it would unite our kingdoms. I was... taken by surprise when Illyra ended up on his arm instead."

Her jaw clenched. "I truly believe Jak didn't mean to hurt me. Or at least—didn't want to. But... the warrior princess from Meridium wasn't good enough for Jareth's only child. Wasn't *lady* enough. The feelings have gone, but the bitterness about the way it happened— that has lingered. I'm stubborn, as you know. I don't forgive and forget. I remember and recover." She was looking at the floor, a faint blush reaching her cheeks, but a smile played on my lips at her last words.

I ran a finger across the edge of her jaw, lifting her chin until her forest eyes met mine.

"You're enough," I told her, my voice lowering to a whisper. "It's unbelievable how *enough* you are."

Her breath caught again, her eyes dropping to my mouth. I tilted my head towards hers, our lips edging ever closer as her eyes fluttered shut.

But...

Not yet. We'd had a few drinks, and this wasn't just about me. I waited, my dragon impatiently roaring at me in a tantrum.

Eli opened her eyes, feeling how still I had gone. She looked up, a crease in her brow.

I huffed. "I want—you know, it doesn't matter what I want. What do *you* want?"

I wanted *her* to say it. To tell me. I needed to hear from her lips that she wanted this—wanted me. The same way I wanted her, even though her body told me she did.

She looked confused, and at a cheer from the banquet hall, her eyes darted away.

"No. Don't look at them. Look at me."

Her eyes shot back to mine, her pupils dilating. I looked down at her parted lips.

"Can—can I kiss you?"

She looked even more confused, and now annoyed. "You... you stopped. If you want to kiss me, why did you stop?"

I moved close enough that our noses were almost touching. "I want—no, I *need* to hear you say that I can." My thumb travelled over her full bottom lip. "That after all my dreams of kissing these lips, I can finally have them. Because the problem is," I picked up a curl of her hair, twirling it around the ends of my fingers, tugging it slightly, "when I kiss you, I don't think I'll be able to stop."

She sucked in a breath as my hand slid along the side of her throat, my thumb feeling her swallow. I waited for what felt like an eternity.

"So don't."

"Thank fuck. I thought you'd never answer," I growled, gripping the back of her neck as I brought her lips to mine.

The sensation sent my magick coursing from my toes up to the top of my head. Eli's small hands moved along my chest to the nape of my neck and into my hair, a shiver running through me as her nails scraped my scalp.

My grip on her waist tightened as I pulled her closer, and when her tongue swiped across my bottom lip, I released a sound I hadn't known I could make. I met her tongue with mine, and she let out a whine that sent all the blood in my body south. We moved gently, as if exploring something new for the first time—her taste of blackberries and champagne, the scent of jasmine driving me wild. If I died tomorrow, I would do so happy in the knowledge that I had been gifted this sensation.

The familiar warmth of my eyes signalled they had changed as my dragon purred in need, urging me to press against her and claim her as mine. She bit gently on my lower lip; a growl escaped my throat.

Enough.

I pulled away, wrenching control back from the dragon, resting my head against hers. My eyes closed, willing away the vertical slits of my dragon form.

"Why did you stop?" Eli asked, husky and breathless, her cheeks flushed and her hair in loose strands. The image did very little to help me maintain any form of control.

I chuckled. "Because we have company."

42

❦

Eli's brow furrowed; her eyes flicked nervously around.

I turned, moving to the side. "You can reveal yourself."

A light, airy laugh sounded before the person I had sensed emerged from around the corner at the other end of the balcony. Her white hair shone under the hanging lights as she made her way towards us. "I apologise for the... intrusion."

I smirked as Eli's face started to match her dress.

"Aunt Lys, we—"

"Were doing what young people do. Never explain yourself, child. Not about what makes you happy."

We avoided looking at each other, shuffling awkwardly under her gaze.

"You missed the official announcement of Jakard and Illyra's engagement. Illyra didn't look too happy about your absence."

"Shame," I lied, still grinning. I much preferred what we had been doing.

Edging closer, Lys took hold of Eli's hand. "I came to apologise for Illyra's behaviour."

"Oh, Aunt Lys. No—"

"Please. The girl has shamed me over and over again with her behaviour over the years. I have no idea why she has turned into the person she has. Maybe if her father had…" She trailed off and inhaled deeply, offering us a tight smile. "Anyway. Forgive an old woman for her rambling. I'm retiring for the evening, so I bid you both an apology and goodnight." With a smile and a twinkle in her eye, she gave a little wave as she turned, disappearing around the corner she'd come from.

I waited for a beat of silence before turning towards Eli. "So… what's the story there?"

"With Aunt Lys?" Eli asked. When I nodded, she blew out a long breath, brushing the stray strands out of her face. "From what I know, Aunt Lys met Illyra's father whilst he was visiting from Eshmnor. They spent one epic summer together, resulting in Aunt Lys falling pregnant… and then he left."

"He just left? Lys never saw him again?"

She shook her head. "Illyra has never met him, and Aunt Lys blames herself. Maybe there was something she could have done to make him stay. I've told her before, his decision was all on him, not on her."

"What was his name?" I couldn't imagine leaving someone after time spent together like that. But intentionally leaving a child without a father—that was despicable.

"I can't recall. Something unusual. Definitely not from around here, anyway. We assume he disappeared back to Eshmnor, or further." Her lip curled in distaste.

"And what is Lys to you?"

A small smile, full of nostalgia and fond memories, transformed her face. "Aunt Lys is my father's oldest advisor. And I mean oldest figuratively and literally." She laughed, turning to look out over the city, clasping her hands together as she situated herself against the wall. "She was really there for us, after the Tain."

After her mother and brother.

"Illyra resented the relationship I developed with her. The

relationship I had with my father. Even though I tried—and I *really* tried—to be her friend, she let her resentment poison her mind."

Eli would do anything for those she cared about. I knew that from the way she had taken Vyn and Bas in, the way she worried so deeply about Roux after such a short amount of time. She cared so much about those around her. I believed her when she said she had tried. I imagined she had tried her hardest to take in the petite redhead who'd never known her father, knowing what it was like to live without a parent.

"She's become worse since Jak. I don't know why; I think there's more there, under the surface. But... I'm tired of trying with her. Does that make me a bad person?"

She looked at me, and I could see the uncertainty in her eyes. Green eyes, framed by thick lashes.

Raising my hand, I cupped her warm cheek. "I don't think you have it in you to be a bad person," I said honestly. "And that," I flicked the end of her nose, earning myself a glare as I stepped away from the balcony, holding out my hand, "is why our plan won't fail."

❧

When I offered to join Eli in a private conversation with her father, she politely refused. I assumed that she wanted to discuss Jak as well, but she did assure me she would speak to him about Kanu, so I gave her some space, without listening in. When they returned to the palace entrance, I tipped my head to the king, and he smiled at me.

We remained silent all the way back in the carriage, finding the rest of the group waiting in my and Ant's room at the inn. They listened intently to the events of the night; Roux especially quiet as I regaled my meeting with her uncle. A gloom seemed to fill the air as everyone came to realise what Eli and I had. Where was left to go?

Well, what a wasted journey. Ant's irritated thoughts reached me as he sat beside me on the floor.

Not completely. I faced Kanu—I won't forget him any time soon.

"So, what now?" Bas asked from the chair in the corner, swirling a cup of wine, his eyes worried as they kept skipping to Roux. I met Eli's gaze; she gave me a subtle nod. Ant caught the exchange, and a curious expression settled on his face.

This was going to be interesting.

Exhaling, I just came out with it. "We go to my home—Tenebris."

Ant shoved his face towards me. "Are you insane!? Pray, what brought on this *ingenious* idea?"

"Union," I replied.

Bas choked on the mouthful of wine he had taken, spluttering droplets down the front of his shirt as his eyes widened, darting between Eli and me. I turned to waggle my eyebrows at her.

Eli rolled her eyes. "Don't be so absurd. Listen, if we're going to get anywhere with this investigation, we need to be working together. Not casting suspicious eyes at each other."

"Well, if I remember rightly, it was *your* father asking if we were the cause of all this," Ant muttered under his breath. "Unknowingly, of course."

Eli only gave him a penetrating stare. "Despite that, Dracho and I discussed how our kingdoms could help each other."

I nodded. "A united front may be our strongest weapon against the Hollow. Especially since we're not clear what we're exactly going up against..." I trailed off.

Vyn's brows were raised. "So you're both going to talk to your father?"

I caught myself before answering, looking over at the brunette. She gestured for me to go on.

"Yes. Tenebris has hidden in the shadows for too long because of an outdated treaty with Ruvalon's kings. It's time for them to learn the truth. It's a sacrifice on our part," I looked meaningfully at Ant, "but worth it if it leads to the prosperity of the continent. The *whole* continent."

After a beat, Bas clapped his hands together, surprising me. "You've got my vote."

I laughed tightly, casting my eyes back to Ant, who looked... impressed?

"I'm actually rather—taken aback. It's very diplomatic of you, Dracho. And just now, you sounded like a leader. You sounded like your father. So maybe this trip has taught you something. Though I can't wait to see your uncle's reaction." He sat back, resting his head against the wall, and I smiled through the knot of emotion in my chest.

"Obviously, we'll have to have discussions with the other leaders after speaking to our fathers. Bisa—"

"Will definitely not be an issue," Roux said. "She loved you all, and it's the least we could do after what you did for Aion. For me." Bas reached over and pulled her into a tight, one-armed hug, causing her to giggle.

My brain drifted away from the current conversation, remembering something my father had said for when I was to venture home.

"Well, if that's all," I stood, stretching, "we'd best get an early night. Tomorrow, we head for Crystalwood."

Vyn immediately straightened. "Crystalwood? Why would we go there?"

"It's the quickest way to Mythhollow."

"Yes—and it's also the quickest way to die."

I smirked. "Not if you know the way."

43

"Are we planning on taking a little detour home on our way north?" Bas asked Eli from atop his steed.

"Most definitely not. My father would be suspicious, and there's no way I'm telling him about Antares and Dracho... not yet, anyway."

Engel snorted as we rode forward, determined to make it as far as we could today. We had left Stillmere at first light, and none of us were sorrowful to go.

Vyn's eyes found mine. "How do we get through Crystalwood?"

I leaned forwards. "Most humans avoid it because of its leaves, but my father told me about a hidden entrance that leads you through the entire forest, straight to the entrance of Mythhollow. It saves us going around."

There was a reason mortals steered clear of the vast forest. Believed to have been created from the tears of an ancient goddess long ago, her name forgotten to time, Crystalwood lived up to its moniker. Hundreds of ash-coloured trees, akin to the weeping willows that grew in Tenebris, lined its grounds, each adorned with thousands of the most exquisite leaves.

Beautiful—but deadly. Each leaf was a perfect, multifaceted crystal that reflected the sun's light in a glorious display of colour.

But every edge was sharper than a knife-edge, and anyone cut by a leaf would continue to bleed, some magickal element to the trees preventing them from healing naturally. Many of the branches hung low to the ground, rendering it almost impossible to manoeuvre through the forest untouched. I'd only ever seen it in sketches in my books, but I'd heard of many a mortal entering, trying to harvest the leaves—only to never resurface again.

Vyn nodded, his yellow eyes flashing with uncertainty. "Whatever you say."

I laughed. "Calm down, that's not even the hard part."

"What's the hard part?" Vyn asked, a note of anxiety in his voice.

I only smiled as I caught Ant's eye.

"What's the hard part?!" he called out again.

"You'll see," I told him as I rode on.

We rode from sunrise to sunset—and again the next day, determined to get off the Still Road and as far from Stillmere and Meridium as we could before anyone noted the direction in which we travelled. Kanu had been playing on my mind, and I found myself looking back frequently, or studying any travellers we saw on the way a bit too closely.

Though I was used to riding by now, my back and thighs ached by the time Crystalwood came into view on the third day, the swaying leaves catching the rays from the late afternoon's last few hours of sun. The others slowed as we neared the forest, allowing me and Ant to lead the way. I kept my hands steady on the reins as we searched for the entrance my father had told me about.

Stick to the eastern border until you come upon a carved tree. It will grant you safe passage through a hidden pathway.

I hadn't asked what the carving was, but I assumed I would know it when I saw it. It had never crossed my mind to ask how or when my father had come to venture inside the forest; I would when I saw him again.

"Dracho." Ant nodded towards the tree line, pulling my attention from my thoughts.

I looked to the ash trees, scanning the trunks until my eyes fell on one just ahead. I gasped and pulled my horse to a stop, throwing myself from it on shaky legs as I approached the tree. Careful not to catch myself on those sharp gems, I lifted a drooping branch, heavy with leaves, out of the way.

It was crudely cut into the bark, probably with a small knife, and it had obviously been there a long time. It was a lovers' heart, the initials 'I' and 'E' carved into the middle of it.

Eli dismounted and joined me, her finger reaching out to trace the edge of the heart. I felt more than saw her look up at my face. "Your parents?"

My heart clenched as I stared at the carving. I gave a small nod. "Eltanin and Irena."

A hand pressed comfortingly upon my other shoulder. Ant gave me a close-lipped smile before stepping back.

"We'll have to release the horses here. They won't be able to journey through the forest or Mythhollow afterwards," he called to the group.

Eli glanced back at Engel. "He's not going to like that." She chuckled.

I reached out, fingertips feeling the rough edges of the letters. I wondered how long this had been here. Had it been done during the blissful start of their relationship? I pictured a younger version of my mother and father standing exactly where I was as they carved out their hopeful declaration of love for each other. A longing I hadn't felt for a long time filled me, but so did warm joy as I remembered their contented days and how lucky they were to have had each other. Releasing a shuddering breath, I pressed my forehead against the harsh bark for a moment before returning to the others.

I watched as Eli whispered gently to Engel, no doubt explaining that it was his time to leave. The others unsaddled their mounts, shouldering our supplies and allowing the horses their freedom before we began our trek through the woods. Throwing her rucksack over my shoulder, I nudged Roux's arm with my elbow.

"You ready for this?"

Her perfect teeth flashed. "A stunning forest no one ever enters, and the city my ancestors helped forge? Can't *wait*."

I laughed. "Let's get moving, then."

Ant stood several feet away, staring intently at a gap in the trees. *There's a magickal barrier here.*

What? I stepped forward.

The pathway would be hard to spot from far away. But those brave enough to venture near, would spot the jagged clearing through the trees, the low-lying branches swaying overhead as the leaves clinked against each other--a small musical bell note sounding from each one as they did. The path was so narrow that we would only be able to travel it in single file. And even if the pathway was found, the magickal barrier would not permit just anyone to enter.

"Feel it?" he asked.

I nodded, now in range of the magick that crept over my skin.

If this is anything like the one in Mythhollow, it only allows those with magick in.

Or people escorted by those with magick, I noted.

He gave one long sigh, then turned to assess the others. "Bastion, come here."

What are you doing? I demanded.

He'll be fine. This barrier feels a hell of a lot weaker than the one in Mythhollow.

Bas stepped forward, looking uncertain. Ant smiled. "I'm gonna need to escort you through."

"Why?" Eli asked sceptically.

Ant looked at her impatiently. "There's a magickal barrier. You can only go through if you have magick, or if someone with magick takes you."

Bas nodded, unconcerned. "Okay, let's go." He held his hand out.

Sometimes, Ant's ruthless nature really scared me. But I didn't want to panic anyone by calling him out.

He could apparently tell how I was feeling. "Wish me luck," he drawled as he pulled Bas forward, not letting go of his hand. I held my breath.

After several feet, Ant stopped. "It's clear."

I blew out a relieved breath. "Eli—" I held my hand out. "Roux, can you grab Vyn's hand? I'm not sure if the barrier will recognise his djinn nature." Vyn immediately shot his hand out for Roux's, the latter smiling widely.

We followed Ant carefully, mirroring his and Bas' steps through the pathway, avoiding the hanging branches of the trees. Silence was our friend; it felt as though our very breath might sway one of them into our direction.

Bas hissed suddenly, and we all froze. He reached up to touch his ear; the ends of his fingers were covered in crimson blood when he pulled them away.

"Shit," Ant muttered.

Bas glared up at a low hanging branch. "That could have cut my fucking ear off."

I laughed nervously and cleared my throat. "Negative of being so tall, buddy."

He tutted. "Any chance you've got a dressing for this, brother?"

Ant nodded. "But a dressing won't do much for that. It's a magickal wound. We need to get you to a healer in Tenebris."

"Dracho," Roux called out from behind me, "let me scoot past."

I obeyed, keeping statue-still as she and Vyn shuffled past me and Eli. The pathway was so narrow that our bodies pressed together as we passed each other. Vyn winked at me, but I noted his white-knuckled grip on Roux's hand.

Once we had switched places, Roux stepped closer to Bas' large back. "Bend down a touch, big guy."

Bas eyed her over his shoulder for a moment, but did as she said.

She brought her hand up and cupped it over the top of his ear. None of us moved, unsure of what she was going to do and wary of the swaying branches around us.

Roux winced. "This may hurt a little."

Bas' shoulders stiffened. "What—?"

A sharp hiss left his mouth as a tiny blaze of black and gold flashed under Roux's palm. It was gone as fast as it had appeared, and when Roux moved her hand, there was nothing but a tiny scar left upon Bas' ear.

His hand explored it carefully as Ant's eyes narrowed.

"You magickly cauterised the wound." He couldn't hide the hint of astonishment in his voice.

She nodded. "It's what I willed the magick to do. I was hoping it wouldn't completely burn his ear off—"

"What the fuck?" Bas exclaimed.

"—but I felt confident that I could do it. I'm sorry, you have a scar now."

Bas' deep chuckle vibrated in his chest as he reached for her hand. "You can scar me anytime, little mage. Thank you."

Roux's cheeks darkened, but a smile lit her face.

"Come on then, let's go—and no one else gets cut. We need to find somewhere to settle before it gets dark," Ant announced impatiently, pulling Bas forward again.

The gaps between the trees did seem larger here—enough for us to continue through, single file, without incident. We continued in silence until we neared the heart of the forest, where the final rays of sunshine struggled to break through the dense treetops.

"There's a clearing ahead," Ant said.

My father told me there would be one. This must be it.

Ant hummed. "We'll camp there tonight. We won't make it much further with the light fading."

The sigh of relief from the group made me smile.

The clearing was large enough to hold all our tents, away from any deadly leaves. This must be the place my father had told me about, and that meant the lake was not too far.

I watched Ant chat quietly with Vyn, a small smile on his lips, as Bas sat telling Roux something which had her laughing hard, her eyes squeezing shut. Strolling over to Eli's tent, I pushed the flap back and popped my head in, catching her surprised expression.

"Come with me? I have something to show you."

She nodded without hesitating.

I searched the back of the clearing and found a small walkway to the left. Grabbing her hand, I pulled her behind me, not bothering to see if the others noticed our departure. We walked in silence through the thinner pathway until it widened.

Eli gasped as she walked past me. The lake was nothing more than a very large pond, but it was the grandest of mirrors, the reflection of the crystals sending rainbow beams through the area. The shorter willow branches above us and beyond the lake created the most extraordinary painting nature had ever made.

Eli stepped closer to the water's edge, making the view even more of a masterpiece as fractured light lit up her form. She stared intensely at the water, which was so still it looked like iridescent glass. Her lips pouted as she chewed her cheek.

Not knowing what she was thinking was the bane of my existence. I stepped forward, unable to take my eyes from her profile.

"It's beautiful." Her expression was unreadable; I froze under the weight of her gaze.

"Extremely." The word left my mouth breathlessly. I coughed. "I

know the forest is deadly, but now I'm here—I'd like to think..."
The words caught in my throat. How could I explain it without
sounding foolish?

"What?" She turned around fully to look at me now, her emerald
eyes swimming with questions that caused my chest to tighten.

The laugh that left my lips was awkward. "Well, I like to think
that those who make it through to see something this spectacular
are... worthy... of it." I stepped closer to her, just wanting her near,
as my voice dropped to a whisper. "If you get through the hardness
and persevere, then maybe—just maybe—you've earned the right to
look upon such beauty."

My stomach clenched as her eyes widened, the corner of her
mouth turning up just enough me to notice. I rubbed the back of my
neck, feeling all kinds of inadequate. "Anyway, I know it sounds—"

Suddenly her hands were on the side of my face, pulling me
down, and her warm lips were on mine.

Shock coursed through me; I stared, wide-eyed. Before I could
enjoy the feeling of her, it was over. A soft, timid kiss—too short for
my liking. She released me and stepped back, her cheeks darkening,
contrasting with the rest of her olive skin.

She started to say something, but I hadn't had enough of her.

My hand found the back of her head, clenching a fistful of her
hair, thrilling at the surprise on her face. I pulled her back up to my
waiting lips, the feeling in my stomach becoming a fluttering in my
chest. I could have sworn she whimpered. A shiver ran through me
as her arms travelled over my chest and around my neck, her fingers
playing with the hair at the nape, touching my mark.

The kiss was all pent-up anticipation and longing. Lifting her, I
pulled her body closer, so there was nowhere that we weren't touching. All I could focus on was how soft her lips were and the way her
addictive scent of blackberries and jasmine invaded all my senses. I

realised the smell came from her hair, and wondered what she used to make it smell that way.

My lips were hungry, intense—as intense as my dragon's reaction, urging me on as I claimed her mouth, making me want more. As if in answer, Eli's lips parted and her tongue brushed my lower lip, asking for permission, which I willingly gave. My heart reacted with a leap, as if jumping into the Pistyll falls from a great height. My entire body tingled as our tongues danced.

Heat flooded me, and started to travel south.

I placed her down and moved my hands to the sides of her face to wrap them in her silky hair. She pulled away abruptly, taking hold of my hands and keeping them still. We stood, foreheads touching, both of us panting slightly. After a moment, Eli pulled back, opening her darkened eyes to look into mine.

A husky groan left my mouth. "Please don't look at me like that."

She giggled—actually *giggled*, the sound of it piercing my chest and provoking a broad smile.

"Why?" she asked, playing coy.

I thought about it for a second, wondering if I dared tell the truth. "Because I'm afraid if you don't, I'm going to find it hard to resist lying you down and taking you on this forest floor."

Her pulse increased as her brows shot up, a blush flooding her neck and cheeks. "Oh."

I threw my head back with a growl. "Please don't make that shape with your mouth either." She had a wicked grin on her face. "Demon woman. Come on."

I held her hand tightly as we headed back to the others.

44

Eli's good mood was a beacon in the darkening forest as we walked back to camp, drifting from each other to re-join the group by the small campfire. My magick swirled in my chest excitedly as Ant shot me a quizzical frown. I happily ignored him, still feeling the bliss of our time together. The conversation between the group remained light, Roux and I exercising her powers a few times before we all wandered off to our own beds for the night.

It was the early hours of the morning when I was abruptly awoken, muted sounds reaching my sensitive ears.

I focused; my dragon was trying to wrench me to my feet as if he already knew what was happening. *Eli.* I quietly left the tent.

A sense of déjà vu surged through me as I hesitated by the entrance to her tent. I entered quietly, finding a scene lit dimly by her lamp very similar to the last time I had witnessed one of her nightmares. But I could only hope that this time, she would allow my presence to calm her.

I eased myself onto the ground next to her; she whimpered, her furs in a white-knuckled grip. I gently reached over to brush an errant strand of hair off her face.

The cold steel of the blade was against my throat before I had noticed she was sitting up, eyes frantic and unseeing.

I remained as still as possible, holding my hands out. "*Eliana.*" Her name was a whispered prayer upon my lips.

Her vacant eyes skittered to my face, wide and glassy from unshed tears.

"It's me, Princess."

She blinked several times before the dagger fell from her hand onto the floor. Her chest rose and fell rapidly. "Dracho?"

I carefully brushed the back of my hand over her cheek as a tear escaped. "I've got you. It was a nightmare—you're safe."

"I'm so sorry." She inhaled deeply, moving back slightly to run her hands over her face.

"Don't ever apologise. Do... do you want to talk about it?"

She shook her head firmly, and I nodded. I started to get up on one knee. "If you need anything, just—"

Her hand shot out to grab mine. "Stay."

"A-are you sure?"

She nodded, eyes flickering over my bare chest. Nervousness filled me, but if asking me to stay brought her any comfort at all, then I would not deny her.

"Scoot over."

She pushed the furs off, and I took in the thin vest she was wearing, her tanned skin slightly flushed. I internally cursed the stars and my male hormones for checking her out whilst she was vulnerable, moving in next to her.

We sat there, our legs pressed against each other for a few seconds; she looked unsure. Determined to make her comfortable, I lay down, throwing an arm out towards her and smiled.

My heart skipped as she gave me an adorable smile in return and lay down beside me, pressing her forehead to my chest. She moved her arm to hover over my stomach, only hesitating for a second before resting it there. Exhaling shakily, I tried to relax as much as I could with this exquisite woman lying in my arms.

"Dracho?"

"Mmm-hmm?"

Her forehead lifted off my chest slightly. "Thank you."

I released her so that I could move back a few inches, wanting to see her face. "Whatever for?"

Her colour deepened, as if she was embarrassed to say the words aloud. "I'm not very good at explaining my feelings. I think that's why people misunderstand me..."

I smirked at her. "Well, from what I've seen, you're able to show your feelings pretty well." Her eyes narrowed in confusion. "When you're very passionate about something, you're able to demonstrate how you feel perfectly."

She rolled her eyes. "I'm not talking about when I'm pissed off."

I laughed. "No, but it's still very distracting to witness."

Her chin jutted out. She tried to shift to smack me, but I pulled her closer, chuckling as I kissed the top of her head.

She pulled back after a few seconds. "I said thank you because no matter what has happened on our journey together, or the differences we've had... you've always been there as a comfort to me." She looked away from my face, her cheeks flaming now. "I guess... I'm just really glad you came into my life."

Gently clasping her chin, I brought her face back towards me, tilting her chin up so I could look at those emerald lagoons, weighing the truth of her words. After the revelation of my identity, I was shocked at how afraid I was. Afraid that she would no longer be a presence in my life, that she would reject me...or worse.

Here, now, whilst it was just the two of us lying together, I could see nothing but appreciation shining in her eyes. I swallowed hard, knowing what I so desperately wanted—but understanding that how we moved forward meant more than just us. It meant change, for both our kingdoms. If this was something we both wanted.

Regardless of any of that, I had to be honest.

I exhaled. "When I first met you, you were such a mystery to me. And when I found out who you were—it was a risk. *You* were a risk. Because I was uncertain what that would mean for my kingdom." I saw the rejection in her eyes as I spoke and gave her a half-smile. "But... I thank the stars they took me your way, because now—Eliana—you're one of the most certain things I've ever known."

Her smile was radiant. A genuine smile, her eyes crinkling, that warmed my entire body and made me want to steal the stars from the sky to see if they held a candle to her.

She glanced down at my parted mouth and bit down on her bottom lip. I tipped my head forward, waiting for her signal that I could once more kiss her soft lips. She pushed herself up towards me to meet me halfway.

The kiss was long and slow as I ran my free hand down her arm, feeling the skin prickle there. She shivered all over, and I could feel her breasts pressing against me through her thin shirt.

This feeling—I would never forget it. My hands possessively roamed over her, greedy and wanting. Elation spread through my entire body as her fingers steepled against my stomach. She pushed closer, bringing a leg over my hip; with mine resting between her thighs, the heat was indescribable as I realised the only barrier between me and the apex of her legs was a thin scrap of underwear. The friction caused a delicious moan to escape her mouth.

The sudden, hushed rumble that vibrated through my chest made her freeze, her eyes finding mine in the darkened tent as she pulled away from that sweet kiss, both of us panting.

"Did you just *growl?*" She laughed softly.

"Just call it animal instinct," I replied, unable to wipe the smile from my face.

She looked at me in wonder for a second. "Dracho... your eyes."

Worry poured over me like a bucket of ice-water as I forced them shut, realising they must have changed. I was trying to will them away when I felt her soft fingers brushing across the skin under my eye.

"Dracho, your eyes are breath-taking."

My eyes shot open, and I heard her heartbeat increase. My chest tightened as I continued to watch her, disbelief and something else warming me. Eli smirked, and I felt her thighs tighten around my leg. I couldn't help the low rumble that gently made its way again through my throat. I started pulling her in again.

"I want to touch you."

Such a simple statement, but one that had the power to end me right there. Desperation consumed me as I became aware of all the points of our bodies touching. I needed to feel her breasts against my bare chest. She must have felt me hard against her lower half; she licked her bottom lip, biting down on it. The action made me twitch in my breeches.

Her fingers moved tantalisingly down my stomach, eliciting a hiss from between my teeth, but I grabbed her hand, ignoring the rage of my dragon. I wouldn't lie with her for the first time on some forest floor with others close by. Not after what she had just shared with me. I would introduce her to my father, romance her around Tenebris. Only then would I take her to my bed.

Her eyes shot to me, that hint of rejection in them once more, and I shook my head. "The first time you touch me will be the first time I take you." I leaned towards her ear. "And trust me, Princess, you'll get your fill of touching me then."

I pulled back, satisfied with the heat that filled her eyes as I manoeuvred her to lie on her back. I brushed her hair away and skimmed my nose along her jaw, peppering kisses along her neck, making my way back to just below her ear. My hand moved over her delicate skin, gently wrapping around her throat so that I could feel the pulse there as her heart started pounding.

I ran my thumb up her throat to the softness of her plump

lower lip, watching hungrily as her tongue darted out to catch it. I looked up, taking in the desire that burned within her furious gaze. I flashed her a half-smile, gripping her chin again and tilting her towards me.

"But I will be touching you," I promised.

She gasped before I caught her lips again with mine.

There was no tentative approach to this kiss. It took only a second before Eli parted my lips by sweeping her tongue across my bottom lip, taking what she wanted. It was like fire and ice, a battle between us for power, but neither of us truly cared who won. We simply consumed, never waning or overwhelming.

She was intoxicating.

Lust roared in me as she bit down gently on my lower lip, and another growl escaped the shackles of the control I was holding on to. I felt the corners of her lips turn up as she pressed her teeth down once more, and I pulled back, huffing as I closed my eyes.

"*Fuck.*"

"Something wrong?"

I opened my eyes, seeing hers dance with amusement as I felt her fingers play with the hair at the nape of my neck. Her pupils dilated as she took in my stare.

"If you carry on like that, I'm gonna have to think twice about fucking you on this floor." Giving her a cocky smile, I narrowed my eyes as I skimmed a finger down her collarbone. "I think you rather like the sound of that, though... *Princess.*"

Her eyes were a raging inferno. "Don't *fucking* call me—"

I relished the choked whimper that escaped her as my forefinger changed course, travelling over her flimsy shirt until it brushed over her nipple. She looked at me, and I couldn't tell if her frustration was still at my use of the nickname or for stopping my ministrations. I couldn't help but beam at her before kissing her again, enjoying her throaty moan. Sliding my palm under the vest, across her stomach, and up, I felt her shiver, her back arching.

Reluctantly, I removed myself from her swollen lips, trailing kisses down her throat as I pulled my hand from her shirt, eliciting a whimper from her.

"*Patience*, beautiful." I chuckled, grazing my teeth over her collarbone. She brought her thigh higher between my legs in a wanton need for friction. I groaned as her hip rubbed against my hardened length, and I knew she could feel it from the way her fists clenched my hair tighter.

I played with the waistband of her underwear, running my finger gently underneath the fabric as her little, breathy pants filled the tent. Instead of dipping further to where she wanted me most, I removed my hand, dropping it to her thigh to glide up the skin there.

Her eyes shot wide open.

I didn't fully comprehend what I was feeling until my hand travelled further up her thigh, my fingertips brushing over pitted and ridged skin. Eli had gone rigid. She gripped my hand to throw it from her entirely as she sat up, causing me to kneel back, the mood sobering instantly.

"D-don't," she stuttered uneasily.

I stared at her, trying to rein back my dragon's urge to tear the furs from her completely, molten fury filling every fibre of my being. Exhaling deeply, I wrestled his urges, eyes closed.

My eyes opened, looking at her squarely. "Show me."

"It's nothing—"

"Show me, Eliana. Please." I hoped desperately that we had somehow reached a point where she trusted me completely. Because I cared—especially about this.

Her brows puckered slightly, but she nodded, though she was clasping the furs so tightly, her knuckles were white again. Slowly, she lowered them past the tanned skin of her legs. Lower and lower, until I could see...everything.

I sucked in a breath, but otherwise contained my immediate reaction.

The thick scar was obviously aged, the silver thread glowing in the low light from the lamp. But the wound had been deep. The jagged edges of it, like the serrated edges of a baker's knife, ran from mid-thigh up to the lace of her underwear. Focusing my senses on the pulse point of her artery, I could see how lucky she was to even be here. An inch lower, and she almost certainly would have bled out.

She started to move the blanket, but I shot a hand out to stop her, gripping the soft fur in my fist as I stared at the scar. A million scenarios swam through my mind. Why had she run away from Meridium? Why did she hide her real name, and why had her father placed a bounty upon her safe return?

"Who?"

"I-I beg your pardon?"

My dragon pressed to comfort her and my free hand reached up to hold her arm gently, but I stopped myself, clenching my fist instead. I didn't want to scare her, not whilst I could feel my draconi eyes flashing with barely contained rage.

I didn't recognise the voice that left my mouth. "Who the *fuck* did this to you?"

She started shaking. "They're—they're dead."

45

I released the fur, allowing Eli to cover herself before sitting comfortably, and hesitated, unsure where to start. My eyes darted around the tent, reminding my dragon that we were in a safe space. That she was safe, and that the culprits were dead.

When he was calm, I looked at her, rubbing the back of my neck. Maybe the best way to go about it was to make sure she actually *wanted* to talk about it. I reached out to touch her hand. "Wh—how did... are you *all right*?"

She brought her knees up to her chest, hugging them close to her under the furs as she nodded. "It was a long time ago. During the Tain."

"Oh." That just piqued my interest further, but I let her tell me in her own time.

She chewed the inside of her lip for a few seconds before huffing and moving her legs so they were crossed in front of her.

"My father is a good ruler," she began, and my stomach dipped in fear. "A *just* ruler. My mother," a small smile slipped over her rosy mouth, "was exceptional. She knew how to work a room of people. Be it guests, dignitaries or common folk, she would just enter and..." Her smile faded as she pulled at a loose thread. "I just remember there being this light whenever she entered a room. And I always felt safe running around after her at the many balls we held... like the naive little girl I was."

She stared down at her lap. "I believed that safety net would stay with me once she left to join the final battle with my father. I was twelve."

I swallowed what felt like a thick stone, unable to speak.

"My mother and father left enough resources to ensure that Meridium and the surrounding areas would not fall to starvation. They had planned it all out." Her jaw clenched. "They were *kind* rulers."

The uncertainty rang out between us, but I allowed no comment to pass my lips. Her nails started to dig into her palm, and I took her hand. It seemed to bring her out of her reverie for a moment.

She cleared her throat before continuing. "I'm not sure what happened. Maybe things didn't go to plan or something..." She sniffed. "One night, a few men broke into the castle. They made their way to my room."

My heart was thundering so hard I was surprised she couldn't hear it. It took everything not to squeeze her hand too tightly as conflicting emotions consumed me. Hatred blazed in my blood and enraged my dragon, but my throat felt choked with an emotion I hadn't felt since my mother's death. I coughed to try and ease it, then was annoyed at myself for making any noise at all.

"I... I thought they brought news from my parents. But they hadn't knocked, and there was no maid with them. I noticed how they were dressed—like commoners. Not guards."

She spoke as if it had happened to someone else. Reeling off words written by an unsuspecting victim, telling their tale of the brutalities done to them. She took a deep breath.

"They dragged me off the bed. Started pulling at my nightgown." She exhaled shakily. "I tried to scream, but they covered my mouth."

I closed my eyes, sucking in a breath, wanting to tell her to stop—worried that I wouldn't be able to control my draconi form, should she confirm the worst—but understanding that she wanted to unburden herself. That she trusted me and needed to share with me this part of her. I would respect that always, and I repeated this internally to my dragon, willing us to calm down.

"The... the wound came w-when he cut my underwear from me."

My dragon's fury escalated. My free hand clenched. She looked at me cautiously, but kept going.

"I was fighting, so he accidentally caught me. When I saw the blood, I stopped fighting. I just... *stopped*. All I could think was, whatever they did from that point didn't matter. Because all I knew was that I was going to die. And I'd never see my parents or brother again."

She took a stuttering breath, looking up at the tent roof and wiping the wet skin under her eyes. I started to rub soothing circles with my thumb into her hand.

"They never got a chance to touch me further. I felt dizzy from the blood loss, but I remember what felt like warm rain falling on my face. When I focused, the man above me had a sword shoved through his chest. The other was already dead on the floor. The one on lookout outside my door too."

She sniffed, squaring her shoulders. Taking in my confusion, she smiled.

"It was Bas... and Connaught. Bas was already living with us at that point, and he used to sneak into my room from a hidden passageway between my wall and my brother's room next door. That night he'd been coming to see me—he was often unable to sleep. His father had left with mine for the war." She took another breath. "He saw the men and rushed off to alert someone, found Connaught at his post. The men had killed the guards that stood at the entrance to my wing."

"They saved your life."

She nodded. This explained why Connaught looked at her the way he did. Why he was so fiercely protective of her.

I huffed. "Remind me to buy them both a drink."

She laughed a genuine small laugh as she squeezed my hand.

Something didn't sit well in my gut. I didn't want to question her, but... I frowned. "You think they were commoners?"

"Yes. Why?"

"It just seems strange that civilians were able to easily take out the princess's guards and sneak into the palace far enough to make it to your royal chamber."

"There was an investigation. Connaught was promoted soon afterwards, and did everything he could to find who was responsible. But we had no idea where the men came from, and with no surviving accomplices to question, nothing was found. When my father returned, he didn't want anyone to know that people had broken into the palace and got so close to the royal family, so he stopped further investigation."

"Have you ever spoken to him about it?"

"Goddess, no. I know deep down he blames himself. So I've never brought it up. Besides..." She chewed her lip.

"Besides?"

"The next day... was the day Volente was destroyed. It was the day my mother and brother died."

"Oh." It was all I could say.

She nodded slowly, as though acknowledging that she had just dropped a huge bombshell.

My fury had subsided slightly; the dragon within reached out, desperate to provide comfort. "That's... that's a lot. I'm so sorry that happened to you, Eli."

She sniffed again, waving a hand. "It's nothing. It was a long time ago. Those men were obviously suffering—"

She stopped when I took her hands gently, bringing them up

to my lips, kissing them lightly. Trying to justify their actions was obviously how she attempted to make peace with what had happened to her.

But those men did not deserve forgiveness, no matter what their motives had been. My dragon fumed. It was not 'nothing' whilst she had to suffer through panic attacks and nightmares. It was obvious she had never truly dealt with what had happened, and I vowed to myself to find a way to help her.

"*You* were just a girl." I stared at her pointedly. She turned her hands over, clasping mine, and gave me a grateful smile. My gut told me there was more there—more to her feelings on the matter. But I wouldn't push her. Not when she had already given me so much. "Thank you. For sharing this with me—for trusting me."

Quirking a brow, she pointed out, "Well, you've certainly trusted me with your fair share."

"I didn't really have a choice in the matter there, did I?"

She laughed. "You did."

I caught her eye, remembering the wendigo. "No, Eliana—I didn't."

Her laughter caught in her throat as she understood my meaning. She tugged on my hands, pulling me towards her. I leaned forward to give her a chaste kiss.

But Eli had other plans. As soon as my lips touched hers, her hands wrapped around my neck, trying to pull me back to the ground.

I pulled away as much as she would allow. "Eli, we don't—"

"Shush, Dracho. I need you."

My dragon purred, and I growled at both of them, battling between what undeniably felt good and what I was sure was right. Continuing our previous activities shouldn't be on the cards now. After hearing her story, I didn't want to risk anything by doing something she wasn't really ready for.

She seemed to hear my inner monologue. "Stop overthinking it, Dracho. I'm fine. I'd just like to return to our previous position."

I pulled back, resting my forehead against hers. "You're sure?"

She gritted her teeth, growling in frustration. "I don't need to be fucking babied or pitied, Dracho. I'm a grown woman. I told you because I *trust* you, and I knew you'd just keep asking questions. What I need," her eyes pleaded with me, "is for you to look at me like you did *before* you saw it."

I was such an idiot.

She was right; her story changed nothing. It didn't change the version of Eli that I knew. It just expanded her world and brought me more into it. I should be honoured that she'd allowed me to be a part of it.

But here I was, ruining it.

I wouldn't apologise. That would be a further insult to injury. Closing my eyes, I took a deep breath. When I opened them, her shoulders seemed to ease in relief. She moved a hand around to my face, running a finger along the skin underneath my eye.

"There you are," she muttered breathlessly.

I huffed out a laugh, wondering how she could accept my dragon like this, when the slitted pupils of my true form must look so unnatural. "Well, it does something to me when you use filthy language like that."

She smiled. "Dracho," she whispered hoarsely, "kiss me." Her tongue darted out to lick her tantalising lips. "*Please.*"

She didn't need to ask twice.

I pressed my body down on top of hers, following her to the floor as I snatched a desperate kiss from her lips. The sigh she released into my mouth was shaky, as if she'd feared I would reject her. *As if I ever could.*

I groaned as her fingernails combed through my hair, scraping lightly against my scalp—she seemed to like doing that. Tearing my mouth from hers, I kissed my way down her throat, relishing the little pants that escaped her as she tried to press her body closer to me. I glided my hand swiftly up her vest, exposing her hardened nipples before covering one with my mouth, rolling my tongue. A sharp gasp left her mouth.

Releasing her, I dragged slow kisses down the expanse of her stomach, feeling it dip as I neared the band of her lacy underwear.

"Dracho, I want to feel—"

I shushed her as I gently spread her legs, settling myself between them. I could see her scar up close now. The wound that could have taken her life. Could have taken her from me.

I shook the thoughts away, leaning down to kiss the puckered skin, hearing a hiss from between her teeth. Skimming my nose up along her thigh, I could feel her heat and relished the whimper from her mouth. I placed one hard kiss against her, over her underwear, before slipping a finger under the sides to pull them all the way down.

Stars above, she was a masterpiece. Skin so golden it would drive the greedy mountain drakes wild—and curves that set an intense, aching heat in my veins.

"You're overdressed." She remained where she was, lying amongst the furs, but her eyes travelled over my chest and trousers hungrily as I knelt before her.

I shook my head at her. "I will be keeping my word. I have no intention of doing *that* right now." My head tilted as I held her gaze. "When I bed you for the first time, it will be somewhere private I can spend worshipping *every* inch of your body. Over every surface."

A sinful sound escaped her as my hand slid down between her thighs, feeling the silky dampness there.

"So... what exactly *will* you be doing now?" she murmured.

I leaned back down, breathing in her addictive scent, then

caught her eye and grinned. "Worshipping one *particular* part of your body."

She jerked, throwing her head back as I brushed my lips over the most sensitive part of her.

"So responsive," I mused as I flattened my tongue, taking a gentle swipe, encouraged by her throaty moans.

I hooked my arms under her thighs to pull her closer as her sighs of pleasure rang out. I pulled away to shush her before feasting upon her, taking everything she would give me as she rocked her hips, writhing against my mouth. My fantasies had done me an injustice, because she tasted better than I could ever have imagined; her breathy moans were the sweetest music to my ears.

I let my tongue dip into her briefly, enjoying the way her thighs tightened around me as her hands clenched in my hair. She bucked up against me before I pinned her thigh down with an iron grip, teasing her with my free hand. I glanced up, enjoying the sight of her coming undone, and placed an open-mouthed kiss on her as my finger slid inside her. I cursed on a long exhalation. She was all tightness and silky warmth, so I added a second and started to pump them rhythmically as she whined.

"*Dracho.*" She moaned loudly.

"Shhh." I told her, and watched as she pressed her lips together tightly.

"Good girl." I smiled, and returned to my task at hand.

Moving my tongue against her a few more times, I curled my fingers and sucked hard. I felt her tighten around my fingers as her back arched, a cry ready to rip from her throat. Without warning, I appeared above her and swallowed that scream with a kiss, letting her taste herself on my tongue as she rode out her pleasure upon my fingers.

Once her breathing slowed, her eyes opened to me, lust-filled but sated. Knowing she watched every movement, I sucked my fingers clean, savouring her delicious flavour and the way her eyes darkened. Her hand roamed down my chest, making my stomach dip as she neared the rock-hard proof of my desire.

I grabbed her hand, shaking my head. "No, Princess, tonight was about you. We have plenty of time. Sleep."

She looked like she wanted to argue, but exhaustion won and she cuddled into my chest instead, a whispered "Thank you" tickling across my skin.

I held her, listening as her breathing evened out and she fell into a peaceful slumber, willing my elation and inappropriate thoughts away so I could join her. I leaned down, pressing a soft kiss to her head, and it wasn't long before sleep found me.

46

My chest was warm. In fact, most of the front of my body was. I moved my head, feeling something tickle my nose.

When Eli moved back, rubbing against my hips, my arm tightened around her waist as memories from the night before flooded my brain. My breeches suddenly became very uncomfortable as I hardened against her bare backside. Only my clothing stopped me from being buried so deep in her, she'd be seeing stars.

Do it, my dragon purred into my ear, urging me to shed the last barriers between us and delve into the velvety warmth I'd merely tasted the previous night. To claim her and mark her as mine as I thrust into her over and over—

Enough! I exhaled roughly, running a hand over her hip.

"Mmm," she mumbled, arching her back and pressing her delectable arse against me. *Not helping.*

She rolled over, breasts brushing against my chest, then froze, her sleepy eyes widening when she saw my gaze. Cautiously, she ran a finger underneath one eye.

"Are you all right?" She frowned in concern.

I let out a strangled laugh—her eyes narrowed slightly—and shook my head. "I'm... I'm having an inner battle with my demon."

"With... wait, do you mean your—your dragon?"

I nodded.

She shifted so she was lying on her stomach, leaning upon her elbows. "Are you suggesting that your dragon form is a separate—being?"

I sucked my teeth, considered my answer carefully. "You know how celestral magick is a living thing, only borrowed, and when we die, it returns to the planet?"

Her turn to nod.

"Well, my transformation magick is a living thing. We are born with celestral magick, but our dragon doesn't actually manifest until we reach our thirteenth year. It's sort of like... two souls living in one body. It's my dragon, and it's also a part of me. But it's still *me*. I'm not exactly sure how it works, but my people can merge with their dragon, become one, so to speak. It merges their power."

"But you haven't done that, or you wouldn't be having an 'inner battle'."

I smirked. "Clever minx. No, I haven't merged."

"Why?" she asked cautiously.

"It's always been expected of me—and I suppose it's something I'll have to do when I take the throne. Those who have merged, like Ant, have a heightened sense of their power. But I felt like *not* merging was, I don't know, holding on to a part of me that was still human."

Her eyes flitted down to the furs. "That must be hard. And... I completely understand. I can see why you'd want to hold on to that."

I smiled, her eyes returning to mine as I moved to tuck a stray piece of hair behind her ear.

She grabbed my hand to halt the movement and swallowed, nervous. "Why were you fighting?"

I looked down this time, chuckling awkwardly. "We had differing opinions on how to deal with our, um, morning *situation*."

"Situation?" Utter confusion crossed her face, making me laugh heartily. I raised an eyebrow before glancing pointedly down to my lap.

"Oh." She leaned toward me, the edges of her lips turned up ever so slightly. "And... what was the opinion of your dragon?"

I didn't need her heated gaze or the excited thrash of my magick to tell me her heartbeat had sped up. I clenched my jaw, trying to maintain a semblance of control. But then she looked up at me with those green eyes, biting her lower lip.

A growl vibrated through my chest, and her mouth parted on a gasp. I ran a hand up her spine, stopping between her shoulders to pull her roughly towards me. I closed my eyes and inhaled deeply, her scent not doing anything to help steady my urges.

"Well?" she pressed, leaning forward with anticipation in her voice as she ran her tongue across my bottom lip.

"He wanted me to take you so hard, you'd scream my name to the stars so loud that no one in Ruvalon would ever question who you belong to," I told her, before smashing her lips to mine.

It was a frenzy of lips, teeth and tongues as we fought for control—a fight I was quickly losing with myself too. I peppered kisses down her throat as she panted, her hands gripping my shoulders.

Dracho. A voice whispered through the lust-filled haze that consumed my mind.

Dracho. It spoke louder as I trailed hot kisses between the freckled valley of her breasts, my free hand going to the band of my trousers.

"Yo, lovebirds! Time to get up!"

A feral snarl ripped through me as I shot up, facing the entrance to the tent. A dark-skinned male stood there, eyes wide and hands open as a gesture of no ill will. My eyes raked over him, evaluating the threat as my breathing started to slow.

"Dracho."

I glanced back to what was mine, seeing she had covered herself with the furs; she was looking fearfully at my hands, shaking her head. My own thoughts started to filter through the beast's rage as shame flooded my system.

Bas laughed awkwardly. "Freaky eyes, man. Anyway, I can see I've interrupted your breakfast"—I heard a smack from behind me and guessed that Eli had buried her own head in her hands— "so I'll let you guys carry on. Keep it down this time, huh? But um, Vyn's chucked some food on."

"Thanks, Bas," Eli mumbled as he left the tent.

You'd better fucking get out here soon.

I realised it had been Ant trying to speak to me earlier. I looked down, and a quiet shock crept down my spine. Deep onyx claws had ripped out through my hands.

I brought them closer to my face, staring for a moment, before flexing my fingers, withdrawing them. The wounds healed instantly. Then it all hit me and I groaned in shame, dropping my head to my knees. Eli, still in her minimal state of dress, scrambled round to me, tentatively touching my shoulder.

"Dracho, what is it?"

"That's never happened before," I admitted. "I'm so sorry, I didn't mean to scare anyone."

"I must admit it was a bit unnerving to suddenly see *claws* where your fingers had been. Especially after last night." She smirked.

I laughed, but ran my hands down my face.

"What?" she asked.

"I never meant for it to go that far. For that to happen. Or with Bas. *Fuck!*"

She grabbed my face. "Hey. At any moment there, did *any* of it seem like it was something I didn't want?"

I shook my head, looking away, but she brought my face back to hers. "Then don't ruin this. Please. I wanted this. Us. All of us—all of *you*. Possessive dragon included."

"But Bas—"

"Bas will forgive you. Blame it on animal instincts."

I snorted.

"You know," she mused, "maybe you're looking at merging the wrong way."

I jerked my head up as if she'd stung me.

"Hear me out. I understand wanting to keep a part of you human. But Antares—well, for the most part—still seems human. And he seems at peace with himself."

I didn't meet her eye, not wanting to discuss this right now. Ant and I had a past that I would not share, not without his permission, nor without the consent of someone else too.

"If it brings peace between you and your magick—stops you from losing control—surely it's worth it?"

She wasn't asking out of fear for herself or her friends. I could tell she wondered purely out of care for my wellbeing. And that was something I had never experienced with anyone else—other than my father, Ant, and Althea. I leaned closer, hesitating only for a second before touching my forehead to hers. Eli froze at the contact, unsure.

"Thank you," I said.

"What for?" she whispered.

"For you." I gave her a quick kiss, taking her by surprise. "C'mon, time to face the music. Then something far scarier."

"What?" she asked, getting to her feet.

"My father."

47

Eli and I dressed and tended to our morning needs in a somewhat awkward silence, but I thought that had more to do with the upcoming meeting with my father than any residual feelings over our nightly activities.

A strange feeling overcame me before I joined the others. I'd never had to apologise to anyone for my behaviour before. I'd never behaved in such a... despicable manner. It made my adrenaline spike just thinking about it.

Embarrassment flooded me as I approached the campfire. They all sat around talking as Vyn fried sausages and slices of bacon from his cool pack. Vyn's eyes flicked up to me; if I hadn't been looking directly at him, I would have missed the slight smile lurking at the corners of his mouth. Roux sat opposite on the ground, leaning back on her palms with one leg resting upon her knee. She sent me a reassuring wink.

I glanced briefly at Ant, but from the glare he was sending my way, I could see our conversation was one we had best have alone.

"Um, Bas, can I have a wo—?"

Bas stood in one swift motion and turned to pull me into a bone-crushing hug. "It's all good, brother." He released me, holding me at arm's length. "All men turn into animals when it comes to their women." His eyes jumped to Roux for a split second, and he cleared his throat. "You just happen to have a bit more beast in you."

A flying sausage smacked the side of Bas' face, leaving behind a trail of fat as it fell to the ground.

"That was one of yours," Vyn declared.

Bas wiped the grease from his face. "Motherfucker."

Vyn elbowed Ant. He took the breakfast roll he was offered, but didn't look away from me.

C'mon, Ant.

He exhaled and looked down, starting to eat. *Later.*

Vyn sent me a half-smile and shrugged.

I breathed out, rubbing the back of my neck as Eli pushed between Bas and me.

"Eat up, guys," she called out, clapping her gloved hands together. "We have a bit of a trek ahead of us. A treacherous mountain—if it even lets us through—and then a meeting with the Emperor of Dragons. No pressure." She huffed.

"Anyone would think you were nervous about something for once, Eli." Vyn glanced up at her from under his eyelashes as he brought his bread roll to his mouth.

Swift as an eye-blink, Eli grabbed one of the throwing knives from her waist and flicked her wrist towards him. Vyn flinched as the blade sprouted from the sausage in his roll.

She strolled up to him, leaning down to remove the knife—and the sausage, taking a bite. "Shut the fuck up."

I grinned as Bas' booming laugh rang out. "Yeah, cause it's like—meeting the parents for the first time, right?"

Everyone glared at him as if daring him to say another word. A muscle in Eli's jaw twitched as she stared him down, and his eyes widened.

Roux stood, walked over to Bas, and patted him on the chest. "Start packing all this shit up, big guy." She winked before turning to Eli, tilting her head in a question, to which Eli nodded. They wandered off together, leaving Bas open-mouthed.

"What? By myself?!"

"I believe that's your punishment, *big guy*." I fluttered my eyelashes at him, and he shoved me away.

"Why, where are they off to?"

"I believe it's called 'girl talk'."

"Ah, you mean they're going to talk about your di—"

"End that sentence, and I'll break your jaw." I crossed my arms. Bas flashed his teeth at me, but avoided my eye.

I let out a resigned breath. Time to talk myself. I caught Ant's eye. *Shall we?*

Let's.

He pushed himself up, following me towards the clearing where the pond was. Vyn gave me an awkward smile that I took as a gesture of good luck, and Bas patted me on the back.

We walked in complete silence. Ant stopped several feet before the water, just short of where I had stood with Eli the night before. He was the picture of stoicism as he stared at the water.

I bit down hard on my tongue before speaking. "Listen, Ant—"

"Is she worth it?" Ant demanded.

I flinched back, my mouth opening. I had anticipated anger—stars, I might have even expected him to take a swing at me—but I had never expected the resigned look upon his face.

"Wh—what?"

"Is she *worth* it, Dracho?"

I looked at the still water and thought over his question. I knew what he was really asking. Would I really put our home at risk for a short fling?

I contemplated our journey—mine and Eli's—since the beginning. Every small conversation, every confrontation and shared dream. The new experiences, fantastical and horrible alike. Discovering each other's secrets and learning to trust one another. The faith we had put in to be vulnerable with each other. The bravery of discovering whether a *real* bond could blossom between us. It was something I'd never experienced with anyone to that extent before.

And then I thought about stepping away. Leaving her behind.

The idea was like a physical punch to the gut. Suddenly it was an easy decision. I *needed* to know more, and I wanted to spend that time with her. I looked at Ant, and knew he could see the resolve in my face.

"Yes... she's worth it all."

He nodded, squaring his shoulders. "All right."

"All right? That's *it*?"

He swallowed. "I can't say I don't have concerns. But I actually agree with the plan you both have. The one you want to present to your fathers. I may be here as your protection, but I haven't for-gotten that I'm also here as your friend." A small smile tugged at his lips. "And I can see that, despite my misgivings, you're happy. That you've changed."

I looked at him. "How much did you hear?"

There was a moment of silence.

"More than I wanted to."

I suppressed a grin.

"I heard her story—I won't tell her. I... understand her a bit better." Before I could answer, he held up a hand. "I'm not saying it won't be complicated. You're future rulers from two opposing kingdoms."

I waved my hands, laughing nervously. "Let's not get ahead of ourselves just yet, eh? Let's just get this meeting with Father out the way first. That's gonna be bad enough as it is." I was dreading it.

"I think he may surprise you," Ant told me.

I hummed, sceptical. Once my father recovered from the shock of seeing my guests and realised what was at stake, I had no doubt he would help us. What worried me was his reaction to having revealed my identity and transformed in front of Eli, of all people.

Most of all, I didn't want him to be disappointed in me.

48

"Tell me again whose brilliant idea it was to put a path *through* the mountain, instead of a path *over* the mountain?" Bas grimaced as he stumbled for the fifth time. "You know, small spaces freak me out a little."

Mythhollow was actually a very well-constructed passage through the mountains, the walls reassuringly sturdy in their solid and smooth grey. We had brought torches, Roux choosing to emit a flame of her own from her hand to light her way. As long as you were careful moving around the rocks and watching the narrow spaces, you could get through safely and quickly.

Ant, surprisingly, broke into a grin. "The ancients'," he said, answering Bas' question. "Further through here, there's a magickal barrier. It prevents anyone without permission from entering."

Vyn faltered. "How does it know who has permission?"

Ant opened his mouth, then closed it. "I... I don't actually know. Magick?"

I pulled up short, causing Eli to stumble into me as my head swung around. "You don't know?!"

"Alright, no need to look so smug." He sent me a rude gesture. "I'll follow up with the scholars."

I smirked. *I bet that's killing you.*

He snarled under his breath, pushing past me in the narrow walkway. *Fuck off.*

I chuckled.

Eli's forehead creased. "What?"

"Ant hates not being in the know." We both watched as he flipped us off again, and Eli grinned. Vyn squeezed past us, rolling his eyes as he walked to catch up with Ant. Behind us, Bas helped Roux step over a pile of small boulders.

"Do you think this meeting will go well?" Eli drew her lower lip between her teeth.

"Nervous?"

"Yes," she whispered, her face flushing as if it took everything to admit it out loud. Which, for Eli, it probably did. My surprise was hard to mask; I wasn't used to her appearing anything other than entirely self-assured.

I took her hand and waited for her to look at me before offering a smile. "I think it will be a big change—for both our kingdoms. But one that will definitely benefit us all. Benefit *all* of Ruvalon. My father will listen. They both will."

She brightened, but then uncertainty clouded her eyes. "Do you think your father will like me?"

"You, oh mighty warrior Princess,"—I laughed, avoiding her punches— "are worried if someone doesn't like you?"

"Don't fucking call me Princess!" she screeched, but a grin was fighting to make an appearance upon her rosy lips. They were so tempting that I ducked down to capture them with my own. She froze for a moment in surprise before relaxing into me.

I pulled away. "Careful, you know I like it when you say *fuck*."

A cough broke us apart. Bas and Roux were standing beside us.

"You guys are so *fucking* cute." He closed his eyes, making pouty lips.

Eli made to step towards him and he hid behind Roux, but I

wrapped my arms around her waist, shuffling her forwards along the tunnel. "C'mon, Princess. You can kick his arse later—in our insane training arena."

Awe transformed her face. "Arena?"

"Well, it's got to be big enough to house dragons."

"You train in your dragon forms too?"

"Of course. If we're not the strongest in our peak form, then what's the point?"

"I suppose that's true. Is that something I could watch?"

I leaned in over her shoulder, my lips brushing close to her ear. "You can watch me anytime you like." I didn't have to see her face to know she was rolling her eyes.

We caught up with Vyn and Ant where the cave opened up.

"The barrier is here," Roux stated. "Do you think it will let me through?" she asked Ant.

"Considering you're an ancestor of the first mages and an Aioni, I don't think you'd have ever been an issue," he told her, not even turning to look at her.

"Gee, thanks, Antares," Roux said drily.

"Technically, you're all here with our permission. So there shouldn't be a problem. It's here."

I stepped up to his side. "You're sure? Where's the rock?"

He nodded to a small boulder. Squinting in the low light, I found it and grinned.

"Rock?" Bas asked.

"We put it here when we were younger to mark the barrier," I explained. "Used to dare each other to go past it. Neither of us ever did."

"Never imagined we'd be bringing mortals back through it either," Ant muttered.

Turning, I took hold of Eli's hand. "All right, I'm gonna take Roux through first and—"

Eli was pointing over my shoulder. I spun, a silent shout on my tongue, as Roux walked right up to the rock and the barrier... and then straight past it.

Ant merely raised a brow, but I glared at her. "Roux. Don't ever do that to me again!"

"You next?" Ant asked, holding a hand out to Vyn.

The djinn's face paled. "Just out of curiosity. What would happen if the barrier didn't let us through?"

Ant and I shared a glance. *Don't*, I warned him.

"The magickal protections in this mountain usually prevent humans from getting this far. From what we understand, anyone not invited would touch the barrier and instantly go insane. However, you're not exactly mortal. So, I can't say for sure."

I rubbed my eyes, pinching the bridge of my nose.

Ant looked at me blankly. "Too much?"

"Just a bit."

Vyn cleared his throat. "All right. But *we* have permission. You're the emperor's son. I'm sure we'll be fine—right?" He looked at me, hopeful.

I shrugged, then nodded.

Squaring his shoulders, Vyn shook his head. "Fuck it." He grabbed Ant by the hand and practically dragged him forward, closing his eyes at the last second as they crossed the boundary. His feet stopped just beyond the rock.

"Vyn, buddy?" Bas called out.

He turned slowly, a smile on his face as he exhaled. "I'm fine."

The group seemed to take a collective breath.

"Right," I offered my hands to Bas and Eli, "let's go."

❧

All I could think about was returning home. There was so much

I had to tell my father, Boone, and Thuban. My guests would be a shock, but I knew my father would come to love them just as much as I did.

The path grew lighter as we came towards the end of the mountain pass. I smiled, my dragon dancing in jubilation. Soon Eli would see the wonder of Tenebris.

"The cave gets a bit narrow before the exit, so be careful," I warned everyone, giving Eli a wide smile and squeezing her hand as I moved ahead. She laughed and squeezed back, sensing my excitement. I turned, pushing through the gap sideways, coming through the other side.

Home.

My throat closed as emotion pricked at my eyes. The palace wasn't too far off; from here I could see Pistyll Falls. I couldn't wait to take Eli on a flight over them.

I watched as she emerged, Roux just behind her. Eli held her hand over her eyes for a moment to adjust to the sudden light, then covered a gasp as she took in the view. Roux rushed past her to the edge of the bridge, sensing the magickal energies in the air. I smiled, feeling them too. With a billowing blast of air from a pair of scarlet wings, one of my brethren flew over the mountain, directly overhead.

"Holy shit!" Bas exited the cave last, staring open-mouthed at the beast above.

Ant's brow puckered as the draconi let out a screech. It was Kalen, one of the oldest members of the Edjer guard and apprentice to my uncle, heading for the palace.

I looked at Ant. *Odd.*

He nodded. *Perhaps we should—*

We heard steps rushing towards us and turned towards the bridge. A familiar figure came running towards us. She stopped a few steps away.

"Dracho?" Her lavender eyes turned glassy with unshed tears.

I smiled. "Althea! I'm glad it was you who met us." We came towards each other to embrace, touching foreheads briefly.

"We were notified that someone had passed through the barrier." She took in my companions, eyes widening in surprise, then glanced to Ant. "Ant?"

He grinned, joining us to embrace Althea. I turned, noting Eli's narrowed eyes, and grinned. "Everyone, this is Al—"

"Dracho. There's no time."

My eyes snapped to her. "What do you mean?"

She only looked at me, as if she couldn't find the right thing to say. My brow furrowed; I had never seen Althea at a loss for words.

The palace bells started to ring. The bells only rang to bring in a new emperor—or to signal an emergency. My heart started to thud with dread.

"Speak!" I demanded.

Ant's eyes travelled over her trembling frame. He took her hand, speaking softly. "What is it, Althea?"

"We've only just found him. It's—it's your father, Dracho."

49

My heart stopped for a beat. I looked back at the group and then to Ant before dropping my bag to the floor and taking off in a run. After a moment, I realised the others were hot on my tail.

But they weren't as fast as me.

I pushed all my strength into my legs, muscles burning as I ran through the main streets to the palace. Citizens gasped as I ran past, murmured concern reaching my ears as they all hurried inside their various homes and places of work. I slammed into a wall at a sharp corner, pushing off to carry on. I should have just transformed and flown, but I couldn't think straight.

The palace gates were open, guards nowhere to be seen. I ran up the courtyard steps, taking two at a time, the wind stinging my face. My magick lurched in my stomach. Something was horribly wrong.

Almost there.

I burst through the ornate palace doors, a copper taste in the air as I heard voices up ahead. My chest heaved as I sprinted to the throne room. There was light at the end of the long hallway; the doors were open. I forced myself to slow my run, my breaths coming in pants. My blood started to run cold, my dragon senses on high alert. The voices quieted upon my approach.

The clash of metal spears upon shields met my ears as I entered. The entire Edjer guard pointed their weapons at me.

"Stop! It is Dracho returned! It is the emperor's son!" Boone's voice boomed out as he rushed to meet me, the guards immediately relaxing into a bow.

The hall was silent. I took the two slain guards beneath the staircase before I looked up towards the dais. Someone had torn the Tenebris tapestry from the ceiling and hung it over the grand throne, hiding it.

The guards parted as I passed them, ignoring Boone, and walked up the carpeted steps. Boone followed, putting a hand on my shoulder. "Dracho—"

I held up my hand. There was something I needed to see.

I noted Thuban and his apprentice, Kalen, off to the side, solemn looks upon their faces, and was vaguely aware of Althea and the others entering the throne room. I reached the top step. The shouts from the guards and arguments from Boone and Ant washed over me as I stared at the tapestry.

My heartbeat quickened as I approached the veiled throne, nausea filling me as I reached out tentatively. Taking a firm grasp of the colourful tapestry that outlined my people's history, I closed my eyes, took one deep breath, and pulled.

He was half slumped, half sitting. Lifeless. His head had fallen onto his shoulder, eyes wide open, jade irises seeming sad. His snow-white hair fell in disarray over his face and arms.

Through the middle of his chest was a winged spear.

I knew that weapon. I remembered thinking that it embodied death itself. Now—now it was embedded so violently through my father's chest that the shaft had snapped. The end with the stone was gone.

I could smell poison around the wound, tiny black tendrils

spreading from the entry point. The sight stirred up unpleasant memories of my mother's death.

"D-dad?" My voice cracked as I towards his still face. A glint of silver caught my eye; there was something pinned to my father's chest.

This can't be happening.

I fought down the vomit crawling up my throat and plucked the item from his chest to get a closer look. My feet shuffled in the silence as I turned to the room. Turned to my *friends.*

Althea was watching from the doors, devastation written across her face. I staggered down from the dais and Ant rushed up the stairs towards me.

"Dracho—brother?"

I opened my palm, staring at what I held, holding it so tightly that its edges dug into my flesh. My chest started to heave with anger, the edges of my sight blurring as blackened claws ripped their way from my fingers. Breathing deeply through my nose, I struggled to keep my human form, closing my eyes in concentration. When they opened I felt them blaze, hotter than any flame, as I showed the pin to the room.

Eli gasped, hands flying to her mouth.

It was a silver stag head with bright, emerald-green eyes. The sigil of Eli's father.

$$50$$

My dragon churned aggressively, magick filling my ears with an overwhelming roar. It drowned out the shouts from the bottom of the stairs. I saw Ant, frozen on a step, in my peripheral vision as I stared at the emerald eyes in my hand. Memories flashed before me. An identity kept secret until it could be no longer, surprising skill in combat for a princess, a coincidental meeting...

My dragon pushed forward, taking over and suppressing my will. "Seize them."

I spoke quietly, but the finality of my dragon's authority felt deafening as the royal guards hurried to do my bidding. Roux stared at Ant in shock or for help, but he looked down upon them before turning his head up to me, unsure what to do.

My mind was clouded. The only clear thought was of emptying the room—giving myself space to think.

"Take them. All but this one." My voice sounded unrecognisable as I pointed to Roux, whose eyes widened further. "But do not harm them. If any of them come to harm, you'll face me."

Bas and Vyn were already surrounded by a dozen guards. Vyn's hands spread, and a small wind appeared within his palms.

"Vyn!" Ant called, holding a hand out as he dropped down a couple of steps, shaking his head. Vyn's jaw clenched, and his hands fisted by his sides. The wind disappeared as fast as it had come, and the guards took hold of his arms.

But they had obviously underestimated Eli.

"Dracho! Please!"

Somewhere deep in my subconscious, beyond my dragon-addled brain, I realised the error I had made. I tried to push past the dragon's control too late. As one of the Edjer guards went to grab her, Eli avoided his grasp, ducking and placing a well-aimed elbow to his jaw. The second grabbed her shoulder, but she had anticipated his move; she followed through under his arm, bringing it behind his back before kicking him forward, so he landed before me on the steps. In any other circumstances, I would have been impressed.

Eli ran towards me, but was caught and held by more guards. She tried to shrug them off, but with their enhanced strength and superior numbers, she stood no chance. She started to shake. "No, you can't do this! Father—my father wouldn't do this! Please hear me, Dracho!"

Her eyes held mine, pleading, but I turned, choking down the suffocating emotion in my chest. I walked up the dais to glance at my father once more, reaching forward to close his eyes for the last time as my dragon tried to numb the pain.

"Take them away," I ordered.

Her screams followed me for hours afterwards.

⁊

"Why didn't you let your guards take me?" Roux demanded icily.

"Isn't it obvious?" I could tell she was pissed at me, but this wasn't the time.

Once Eli and the others had been removed from the throne room, my dragon had forced us out and onto the balcony, transforming and taking flight. I had no recollection of how long and where we'd flown, but we'd needed the distraction.

When I had arrived back in my chamber—my dragon and I both exhausted—Ant and Roux were waiting. I sat in a chair by a table, Ant opposite me, rubbing an ache from his temple. He'd passed on the information Boone and Althea had given him.

The puppet of the Hollow had somehow breached the magickal wards protecting Tenebris just hours before we arrived, managing to get to the palace unseen whilst guards investigated the breach. My father had been with two guards in the throne room when he'd been murdered. There had been no cry for help—no evidence that my father had even tried to defend himself by transforming.

Roux sighed. "I'm not from Meridium, and the magick?"

I nodded dully. Mages could not betray our secret or do anything to upset the balance. Not without risking losing their magick.

"How'd you know that *I* wasn't working with them? Working for my Aunt Sizwe?"

Ant stopped rubbing to look up. I felt my eyes warm as I looked at her. "*Were* you?"

She huffed. "No, of course not—ancestors below, Dracho. But *they* weren't a part of this either."

"And how do you know that?"

"Don't you think it's a bit odd that the day you return with the princess and heir to Meridium, your father is murdered? Seems like the perfect setup to me."

I flinched, pain filling my chest and threatening to choke me. I shook it off. "*I* think it's all a bit coincidental that the day we left Tenebris, we happened to run into said princess in the first place."

"Well, maybe you have a traitor on *your* side of the border." She stood, glowering down at me.

"Don't you dare suggest one of my people would betray Tenebris!" I got to my feet, baring my teeth.

"I've got a suggestion," drawled a voice from the doorway. We all turned as Althea sauntered into the room, her blonde hair swaying behind her. "Why don't we just ask them? It's not like lying would do them any favours at this point. They're already in the dungeons."

"They're in the dungeons?" The words rushed out of my mouth. I felt sick.

Althea raised a brow, crossing her arms. "Of course. Where else would we have put them?" She laughed weakly, looking at Ant, who closed his eyes and shook his head slowly.

This was all going to shit. Turning, I placed my head in my hands, rubbing them through my hair. "I want them moved. Now." Althea's arms dropped, but my look silenced any protest. "I want them placed in separate quarters and guarded."

"Dracho, I'd like to speak with them."

Roux's request rang out like a bell. Of course she would want that. My eyes found Ant for any advice he could offer; he gave an infinitesimal nod.

I exhaled. "All right. You may visit them separately. See if you can gather any information—"

"I'm not your spy, Dracho! They're *our* friends. I'm going to see if they're all right, and if they choose to offer up anything, then I will tell you."

Roux was right, and I cursed myself for even broaching that avenue. I felt all over the place—stomach riddled with guilt for holding them captive, heart refusing to believe they would have had any part in this, and my dragon threatening to tear through me and into the skies in a bid to get retribution.

I blew out a long breath. "Very well. Althea, can you show Roux to her quarters and alert one of the guards to inform her when they've been moved?"

Althea bowed before leaving with Roux. She'd never done that before. I fell back into my seat as I finally realised what my father's death meant.

I was the new emperor.

Cold horror washed over me. A rising tide of fear filled me from head to toe, rendering me the most scared I'd ever been since my mother's illness. I found Ant studying me from the chair opposite.

"Would you like me to go?"

I shook my head vigorously. "N-no. Just..." My breath was shaky. "Please just be here."

"Always, brother."

51

Roux had no information to share with me. Eli had refused to talk to her entirely—I assumed that had more to do with my betrayal than Roux herself. Bastion and Vyn only spoke to tell Roux that I had it all wrong.

I thought a few days had passed since my father's body was moved from the throne room, which had been cleaned, ready for what was coming next. One hour blurred into the next, my head a conflicting mess of memories and thoughts. I had several meetings with the leading families and the mortal council to discuss when my coronation should be held, my father's funeral, and trivial matters, such as making any changes to the palace I wanted.

Disbelief raged within me. How could they talk so casually about everything when my entire world had just changed?

My uncle and a few of the mortal council members found me moments after one of the meetings. Thuban slapped a heavy hand upon my shoulder. "You all right, my boy?"

I blinked a few times, hating their pitying expressions, before nodding.

Thuban sighed. "I know this is a big change for you—one you have been training for, but not for long. If you ever need anything, please know that I'm here."

I nodded again.

His eyes flicked away to the council members for a moment before returning, his hand tightening on me. "You know, you're going to have to deal with the girl."

My eyes narrowed. "Deal with her?"

His nostrils flared. "Her father had yours assassinated. You cannot let this go unpunished."

I glared. "What would you have me do, publicly execute her?"

"It would be a start," he agreed, as if it were no issue at all, and a few members of the council nodded.

My teeth clenched. "I promise I will get to the bottom of his death." I looked each of them in the eye. "But I will not start my leadership by killing those who have not been proved guilty."

I caught the satisfied smile of one of the women before facing my uncle. His eyes darkened before he looked away, grunting.

More guilt stabbed at me. "I know he wasn't just my father. He was your brother too."

"Hm. Well, whatever you decide, I'm sure it will be with the best interests of Tenebris in mind." Thuban smiled tightly at me and left, obviously unhappy with my decision. But I had more pressing matters to attend to.

I didn't get much time to myself over those days, but when I did, I overthought *every* conversation, every movement Eli had ever made in my presence, as I held onto that stag's head pin like a lifeline, begging it to give me answers. Our meeting the day I left Tenebris—had that been coincidence? Did she really feel anything for me? Was all this a cruel ploy? Was I collateral damage in a bigger plot that had been planned for a while? But she had been hunting the thing that had murdered my father.

Hadn't she?

That day, the creature hadn't tried to attack Eli when she'd stepped in front of me. And afterwards, she'd reacted badly towards me trying to attack it. I questioned every minute detail. Why hadn't Father tried to defend himself? How had the Hollow entered Tenebris? If it was a set-up, why would anyone want to frame King Cervidae?

During our final meeting, we received the news that the Hollow had destroyed another village. The village of Cefidan was to the south-east of Chaepstow, not far from Morcroft, whose inhabitants were heading for any safe haven they could find. It meant the creature had returned north—that the threat was growing. I was running out of time.

It was decided then and there that I would personally question Eli and the others in the throne room, and sentence them accordingly. Having them in Tenebris was friction I didn't need in my first days as the new emperor. Whether innocent and removed from Tenebris, or guilty and—

I couldn't even think of the alternative.

So, as the city mourned its beloved emperor's passing, I sat upon the throne, prepared for my first act of judge, jury and potential executioner. It felt entirely wrong that this chair, something so inanimate and lifeless, represented such power within an entire realm. Just because of who sat upon it.

It's just a chair.

I adjusted my position, a sudden burst of laughter making its way up my throat at the absurdity of the situation. Father had never told me how uncomfortable this throne was. But then again, he had always reminded me, *The burden of ruling is never supposed to be comfortable.*

One should never become complacent, as Boone liked to tell me.

Something funny? Ant asked as he ascended the steps, peering at me with mild concern.

I shook my head, realising that to him—and the guards that

stood below the steps—I must look mad. *Just wondering how the hell I'm supposed to do this.*

A heaviness fell over us as we acknowledged my fears. Of ruling. Of doing this without my father here to guide me.

He sighed as he walked over, reluctantly placing a hand on my shoulder. "Be patient."

I raised a brow and snorted. "Be patient?"

"Yes," he replied, like it was obvious, "be patient. With yourself. With our people. You're not going to have all the answers straight away. But we'll learn—together."

I smiled at that. "I knew I chose you as my advisor for a reason."

He stood up. "Like there was any other choice."

"There were many, actually—you were rather far down the list."

He threw his thumb over his shoulder. "Oh, I'll just leave then, shall I? Send one of my *betters* in?"

Chuckling, I flipped him off before getting to my feet, my robe settling around my ankles. "How do I look?"

He eyed me for a moment. "Serious."

"I'm not sure if that's a good thing."

"For what comes next, it probably is."

I exhaled deeply, running a hand over my face.

"They're ready when you are. Let's get this over with." He squeezed my shoulder. "You're doing the right thing, brother. Remember, all this is for Tenebris."

"Then why do I feel like shit?"

Ant's jaw clenched as he shot me a pointed look instead of speaking the words we both knew to be true.

Because of her.

I looked away towards the doors. "Right. Better bring them in, then."

52

"I have some questions for you."

The words were like ash in my mouth. The thought of interrogating those who, only a few days ago, had been my friends, my—

It made my stomach roil, nausea threatening to make me spill my guts.

But my duty first and foremost must always be to my people. To Tenebris. My feelings didn't matter.

Eli, dark hair cascading around her shoulders, stared up at me with a ferocity I had never witnessed in my entire life. If looks could kill, I would have been dead by her emerald eyes a thousand times over, yet all I could think was how truly stunning she was.

Roux walked down the dais uncertainly, but sent them a small wave. Our recent conversations had been awkward. She was staying in a guest room a few floors away from the others, and it seemed she had visited the prisoners numerous times. Bastion communicated to her more than anyone, expressing his fury at being confined.

I felt bad for Roux's position, and I'd told her she could leave if she wished. She refused, adamantly advocating their innocence yet empathising with my delicate position. She knew if I released them, there would be an uproar.

Bastion smiled at her, and a flash of regret coursed through me. I shook my head, returning my gaze to the princess.

"Did you know of, or take part in, the assassination plot against the Emperor of Tenebris?" I concentrated my senses, listening to their hearts.

There was no answer, only a steely look of fury at the questioning. My stomach clenched as I battled with my conscience, trying to train my face into a mask of cold indifference but knowing that my eyes pleaded with her to cooperate.

Kalen, my uncle's apprentice, stepped forward. "The emperor asked you a question." He spat at her back and shoved her roughly to her knees.

"Son of a bitch!" Bastion yelled, trying to shake off the guard holding him. Vyn called his name in warning. My dragon snarled at Kalen, and I was before her before I could stop myself.

Dracho.

I ignored Ant as I glared at Kalen, ignoring his shock and that of everyone around me. Rage burned through me like wildfire, my dragon egging me on to do something. *Perhaps rip his hands from his body. Claim what is ours.*

I spoke to him, but my words were for her. "Unless I say so, no one but *me* makes her kneel."

I waited for Kalen to challenge me; the dragon inside thirsted for that opportunity to burst forth and punish him for daring to touch what he deemed was mine. But Kalen nodded, lowering his head and eyes to the floor as he took a step back.

I removed my eyes from his infuriating face, glancing down at the woman before me. It would never matter that at this point we were enemies, or that she stared up at me with confusion and contempt in her eyes. Despite the betrayal I knew she felt, I couldn't allow someone to treat her in such a way.

I offered her my clawed hand. To my surprise, she took it, getting back to her feet.

I inhaled sharply as I felt that familiar charge when our skin touched, my eyes travelling every inch of her face for any reaction. Disappointment tightened my chest when she showed nothing. I released her and made my way back up the stairs, repeating my earlier question as I took my seat upon the throne.

"No," she answered this time.

I blew out a small breath of relief. Her heartbeat was steady, her body showing no signs of a lie. I repeated the questions to Bastion and Vyn, who answered immediately and also without lying. Ant shifted slightly as he watched the exchange, and Roux's shoulders sagged in relief. But it wasn't enough.

I held up the pin. "Does this pin belong to King Cervidae of Meridium?"

Eli took a deep breath, and I knew she was holding on to what little patience she had left. "My father has a pin that looks similar to that, yes. But without being present in Meridium to check it is missing, your *Excellency*, I can neither confirm nor deny that it is in fact his."

Listening to her steady heartbeat, I noted the use of the word 'missing'. She, too, believed this was a set-up. Why would the king have his own pin left upon my father's body? As a threat? It seemed too obvious. But other questions from the last few days still swirled through my head, and I knew without a doubt she was still hiding something.

I no longer had the time to find out what. I had a kingdom to rule.

"Do you have any idea who would want my father dead?" I had to use every ounce of concentration to stop my voice from breaking on that question.

I could have sworn I saw her eyes soften for a moment. She

blinked. "Many south may have wanted the emperor dead. Everyone believes you to be savage beasts."

Her words were evidently intended to be harsh, and Thuban sucked in a furious breath from the side of the room.

"But," she continued, "I have no idea who would have the ability to control the Hollow."

"Hmm." I was sure that she was telling the truth. My guilt increased exponentially. She, Bastion and Vyn had had nothing to do with my father's death—but that didn't mean her father hadn't.

If I kept them here whilst I sent an envoy to King Cervidae, it could be taken as a hostile action, leading to war. I didn't want to start my new rule that way, and the threat of the Hollow was still bearing down on us with every moment.

I also wanted to protect Eli. Keeping her here would put her at risk.

Well, what are you going to do? Thuban quizzed me from the side of the room, his eyes skipping to Eli. He wouldn't dare ask the question aloud and undermine me that way.

My lips pursed. This decision would not be taken lightly. "Leave," I ordered them. "Now."

"*What?*" My uncle's shock and anger were palpable as he took a step forward, but Ant whirled on him. To question the emperor would not be looked upon kindly.

I kept my full attention forward, choosing my words carefully as I watched Eli and Roux exchange confused glances.

"You may leave, Eliana Cervidae," her head snapped forward, "but remain banished from this realm. Should you dare return *without permission...* you will pay the ultimate price."

Quiet murmurs echoed through the throne room, and my heart squeezed. Was I doing the right thing for Tenebris by letting her go? If I wasn't, I knew in my heart I couldn't face the alternative.

A flash of gold caught my eye: Boone was standing next to one of the stone braziers. I hadn't seen much of him lately; he had been busy taking over duties I should have been dealing with, ensuring the palace still ran smoothly. I knew it was his way of caring. Of helping.

Looking at him for reassurance, I watched his gaze deliberately go from where Eli stood to the doors of the throne room. Swallowing thickly, I searched his face, trying to confirm what I thought he was telling me—that I was making the right decision. Boone had been my father's advisor for centuries, and had far more wisdom than I ever could hope for.

He gave me a small nod.

"Antares, Althea. You shall escort the princess and her crew beyond Mythhollow, then provide them with their belongings and any resources they need for their trip home." I indicated to the guards to release them, not reacting when my uncle stalked furiously out onto the balcony.

"'The Princess?' Her *crew*?" Bastion called, pushing forward once more. I held up a hand when my guards made to grab him again. "Is that all we are to you now, *brother*?" Vyn touched his arm, his lip curling at Ant in an irritated glance.

Bastion was an easy-going man, deeply protective of his friends. He had been kind to me from the moment we'd met, and advised me along our journey. It pained me to see how he looked upon me— as if I was betraying them. I knew, in a way, I was.

But my word would not be sufficient proof of their innocence, even as emperor. Not after Eli's father's pin had been found on my father's body.

Bastion shrugged Vyn off. "No, Vyn, let's hear it. His dad kicks it, they stick a crown on his head—"

"Bastion," Eli warned him as anger flooded me, my self-control reaching its limits. The dragon within froze, considering him.

"—and suddenly he's sauntering—"

The rest of Bastion's words were lost as he suddenly found himself dangling by his neck in mid-air. A feral sound ripped its way out of my throat. Pitch-black claws had once again ripped through my skin, feeling the too-soft skin under them as I applied pressure to his neck, obsidian scales now covering the length of my forearms. For a moment I stared at them in shock. I'd never seen my dragon features take over my human skin without completing the transformation before.

I knew if I were to look in the mirror, I'd also see the thin slits of my draconi eyes staring back instead of my own pupils—which would explain the terror rolling off Bastion, whose hands were scrabbling at my arm.

Vyn stretched out his hands and Ant appeared beside him, grabbing hold of his wrist, silently shaking his head. Vyn gritted his teeth but clenched his fists, suppressing his power again. Roux and Eli instinctively made forward at the same time; I twisted my head in their direction. Eli froze under my gaze, her wide eyes shooting to the scales that covered my arm. I knew Roux wouldn't be an issue—she wouldn't involve herself in Tenebris matters. Her only concern was that someone innocent would be harmed. The lost look upon her face helped rein in my anger, and settled the shame I felt in my gut.

Rolling my neck, I closed my eyes and inhaled deeply. "Let's get this straight. *This*," I motioned to the crown upon my head with my free, scale-covered hand, "was thrust upon me. I didn't ask for it. My father was murdered in cold blood. You were there when I found his body." I stared icily at him. "But yes—stick a crown on my head, and what does that make me?"

I looked around at the guards, allowing myself a dark, cruel grin, as if daring them to answer. My finger tapped my chin.

"Ah yes, I know." I jerked Bastion so close to me that our noses were almost touching. "*The emperor!*"

Bastion's frantic eyes skittered across my face, looking from my beastly eyes to the sharp fangs my canines had become. Horror twisted in my gut, but my dragon soothed me from the inside, trying to tell me there was no other way. My anger and grief, my reaction to all, was necessary. I pushed down how I felt when I looked at Roux, or Eli. My rage was too far gone to let it go.

"Now, if you'd rather, you're more than welcome to take an extended stay within the palace dungeons?"

Bastion struggled but managed to shake his head.

"Good." I lowered him slowly to the ground, just remembering to be gentle, before walking back to the marble steps and stretching out my hand, which was starting to return to my normal skin. "There should be no further business."

I scanned over them, my eyes ending on Eli. She was calm now, cold fury in her eyes. I knew this betrayal would not be forgiven.

The goal with which I had left Tenebris all those days ago had not been met. The dream we'd shared was now broken. *I had failed.*

But I would not fail my people.

"You may leave." They looked around as if expecting one of my guards to attack them at any moment. As if I would go back on my word. I ignored the insult. "Roux, I understand it is a lot to ask, but would you mind staying behind so I could have a word?"

Obviously conflicted, Roux looked to the group and then sideways at me before nodding. Bastion scowled, his mouth popping open as if about to say something before Ant, Kalen and Althea started ushering them towards the exit. Vyn shoved Ant away when he tried to offer a comforting touch, sending him a scathing look. I placed my hands into my robe's pockets, my throat closing with sorrow and regret.

"Eliana."

She stilled as I walked down the steps towards her, turning towards me. I waved off one of the royal guards and the concerned look Ant sent me. The closer I got, the deeper the crease between her brows became. I reached for her hand, glad she didn't notice the tremble of my fingers when she pulled away from me in confusion. Huffing, I grabbed her wrist and placed the pin in her hand. "Take it."

Eli looked down, shock flickering on her face as her fingers tightened around the stag head pin. She slowly raised her head, meeting my gaze. Her eyes clouded over as she spoke, her voice eerily calm. "Take your hand off me."

I immediately let her go, cursing myself internally.

She closed her eyes and took a deep breath before reopening them. "Should you ever venture south, or even vocalise the thought of venturing south again..." Her voice was a breathy whisper as she leaned towards me, her scent of jasmine and blackberries attacking me. "I *will* hunt you down, and bring you more pain than you can ever imagine."

The guards around us reached for their swords; I held a hand up, never removing my eyes from her face. By the stars, she was remarkable. And I was letting her go.

I stared back at her, memorising every detail. The intensity of her eyes; the sprinkling of freckles across her nose and cheeks; the fullness of her bottom lip. I held her gaze, seeing the flash of uncertainty in hers—until finally she turned, leaving the throne room and Tenebris... and me.

"Everyone out. Roux, you stay." I lowered myself onto one of the stone steps, exhaustion threatening to overcome me. This was all too much.

Roux tentatively sat next to me, and nudging my arm. "That wasn't awkward at all." I rolled my eyes. "She—didn't do this, Dracho."

"I don't want to hear it, Roux," I muttered.

"If you'd just talk to her—"

"NO!"

Roux flinched back, stunned. I had never lost my temper at her like that. I leaned forward, my hands burying themselves in my hair, still trembling.

"I'm sorry, Roux, but I-I just can't." My whole body was shaking now. "I've just lost my father, and... I didn't even get to say goodbye. And I don't understand why it looks like he didn't even try to fight back. What's worse is that the man who might have done this is the father of the woman I..."

I trailed off, scared of admitting what I knew deep down to be true. I had sat down to dinner with that man. Shared a toast about a peaceful future for his daughter. Was this what he had meant? Peace, at the expense of murdering my father?

"Didn't they mean anything to you, Dracho?"

My face twisted as I looked at her. "How can you even *ask* me that, Roux?" I shook my head, my throat tight. "I felt like I'd found, I don't know, some semblance of a family with you guys. I just can't process my own thoughts right now when I have responsibilities to attend to. Responsibilities I didn't expect to have for a long time. I *had* to banish them. You saw my uncle's reaction. Even without proof that they were guilty, they never would have been safe here."

"You did it to protect them?"

I nodded. "I hated doing that to Bas. But my emotions got the better of me..." I pinched the bridge of my nose in frustration before lowering my arms, my shoulders dropping in defeat. "Hopefully my people took it as a sign of strength. I know that sounds selfish."

Nothing but understanding shone in her eyes.

"But... can you truly look me in the eye and say that, even if Eli had nothing to do with this, her father didn't?" I looked at her, my eyes stinging she reluctantly shook her head. It only made me feel worse.

A faint smile appeared as she placed a comforting hand on mine.

"*I'm* here, Dracho. And I'm not going anywhere. We'll work this out together. I may not have as much seer blood in as some of my ancestors, but I know your paths will cross again." She squeezed my hand. "As for responsibilities, well... as a future ruler, I understand the fear. I really do. This is our path, whether we chose it or not. Yours just came a little earlier."

I turned my head towards her, thinking that over.

"Being a leader isn't about responsibility or doing great things... it's about making a difference. Helping the *people* do great things." Roux elbowed me lightly. "And I have every confidence that's something you can do."

For the first time in days, I felt warmth inside as I wrapped an arm around her shoulders, giving her a genuine, small smile. "You know, sometimes you sound just like Bisa."

A laugh shook her shoulders. "Well, they don't call her wise for nothing." She rested her head on my chest. "So, what did you want to ask me?"

Butterflies swirled in my stomach as I swallowed hard. "I was wondering... how would you feel about crowning an emperor?"

53

I cornered Ant when he returned from escorting Eli out of Mythhollow, the trip having passed uneventfully.

"Did she say anything?" My heart pounded as I waited for his answer.

He shook his head. "They remained quiet the entire way. They put up no fight. Vyn didn't even look at me."

I had never seen Ant this unsettled. I realised that maybe he hadn't known his own feelings until too late. I felt guilty; not only had I ruined my own friendships, but my actions might have ruined Ant's too.

He cleared his throat and I lifted a hand.

"I don't want to hear I told you so."

He frowned. "I would never Dracho. I know how you felt."

My jaw clenched.

"But what will be done about King Cervidae? You know your uncle won't drop this."

I waved the question away. "I can't think about that right now. First, I need to get through this ceremony."

My coronation breathed down my neck like some ravenous monster. I had exerted all my energy during the meetings on planning an investigation into the Hollow's presence in Tenebris, and then on getting ready for the ceremony.

Ant shifted uncomfortably.

"What is it? Speak up."

"Dracho... you know the coronation will force you to merge with your dragon?"

Irritation spiked through me. "I don't need a reminder."

I had already been worrying about it. If a ruler had not merged already, the coronation to emperor would force the change. Now I regretted leaving it for so long.

"Do you think you're ready for that?" Ant echoed my thoughts.

"Is that a hint of concern I hear in your voice, brother?" I teased, brushing off the seriousness of the situation. His expression hardened as he looked at me, and I rolled my eyes. "It's not like I have much of a choice, is it?"

"You could always abdicate the throne to Thu—"

My dragon raged as I rounded on him, snarling. "Throw away *my* birth right to the commander of my army? I abdicate my throne to no one. Our people will be safe, and *I* will ensure that."

Ant's face turned smug. "There he is." He bowed from the waist, giving an exaggerated hand flourish. I felt a vein throbbing in my forehead.

"Prick."

He chuckled darkly, throwing a finger over his shoulder as he turned to leave. "Well, someone had to give you a kick up the arse."

I met with Roux later that day. We headed to the royal burial chamber, where my father's body would be prepared.

The scholars who had travelled from the Scires—the ancient library situated on a small island to the west of Tenebris—had been startled when I'd asked to prepare his body alone. It was unheard of. But I wanted the opportunity to have a few moments alone with him.

Roux accompanied me as the chief mage performing my coronation. That had also been controversial—that I had appointed my own mage to crown me. Fortunately, since the heir to Aion and direct descendant of the First Mage was the mage in question, the scholars had deemed it a high honour.

Asking Roux to help me with all this had filled me with dread. She'd been through enough, and I didn't want to add more, especially since we were still testing the limits of her magick. But, gracious as ever, she had vowed to be by my side.

Images of my father's body upon his throne, the spear still embedded through his chest, kept flashing through my mind. But when I forced myself to walk into that chamber, to finally look upon him as he lay upon that stone table, he looked peaceful. His white robe had been tied tightly around him, hiding the wound, and any traces of blood and poison had been wiped clean. The scholars hadn't been able to identify the substance.

He almost looked as if he were sleeping, except that when I reached a shaky hand to touch his, he felt cold. I wondered if his soul had already left this plane to wander the Netherworld until he reunited with my mother, or if, like Roux believed, his soul would move on once the funeral ceremony had been performed, his body set alight upon the pyre.

An unyielding tightness formed in my chest as I started to tremble. The grief that I had evaded since his death struck me in this quiet moment: an imposing, insidious force that demanded to be felt. My magick curled in on itself, a small, whimpering thing in the face of it.

I realised that the preparations and daily duties I had been carrying out so far had left me stranded—stuck in this moment of time where I hadn't even truly realised what I had lost. I could feel it now, crowding my heart and shattering my peace as I swallowed, trying to push the feeling down.

The wetness upon my cheek took me by surprise, and I swiped my fingers over my face. The last time I had cried was...

Mother.

That grief doubled. I was alone. Both my parents had been unjustly stolen from me. A raging inferno accompanied the realisation, filling me with an anger I'd never known. Sobs broke through as I dropped to my knees, unable to hold myself up any longer.

Roux was there instantly, a gentle hand upon my back as she lowered herself beside me. I saw my heartbreak echoed in her eyes. She knew this feeling.

"How?" My voice didn't even sound like mine as the hoarse question left my lips.

Her brow furrowed.

"How do you move on from this? How do I carry on?" I choked out.

Her face crumpled. A stray tear escaped the corner of her eye. "We do it for them," she whispered. "Because they'd want us to carry on."

I nodded, closing my eyes, and rested my head upon the edge of the table. For the first time, I gave myself permission to truly feel my pain.

Sobs wracked my body as they came hard and fast. I grieved for what I'd lost, all the things I'd had yet to say, everything they'd miss...

My fingers clung to Roux's shirt as she slipped her arms around me, silent tears falling down her cheeks. There we sat for I didn't know how long, comforting each other. And when our tears had dried upon our skin, our breathing returned to normal, Roux and I set about the task at hand.

Wrapping my father's body for his last journey in this world.

Offerings had been left outside the palace by the people of Tenebris. Offerings of loyalty to my family and offerings for the pyre. There were so many that I didn't know what to do with them all. Thankfully, Boone had promised to take care of them, seeing how overwhelmed I was.

My coronation would be held the day after the funeral, which felt too soon, but the scholars and Thuban thought it best. A smoother transition for the people.

"It's what your father would have wanted," Thuban had told me, his eyes uncharacteristically soft. I knew that he would press me to deal with the issue of Eli's father soon, but it comforted me to know that I had a member of my family close by—someone who had grown up with my parents. I wasn't completely alone.

But I still felt it was happening too quickly.

A great pyre had been built upon the throne room's balcony. The room was full of people, thousands more lining the streets below. They sang together, an old lullaby of sorrow, their voices a beautiful chorus over the city. As Boone passed me the torch and I lit the bonfire that would return my father's body to dust, the people celebrated his life and accomplishments. All mourned openly, including me.

Watching the flames, I felt the memories take up residence in my heart, sadness and finality settling within me as I realised no more would be made. I bowed one last time to Eltanin the Wise.

"Goodbye, Father. Go safely on your journey through the darkness." *And maybe I'll meet you and Mother again one day, in the starlight.*

54

"Are you ready?"

A shaky breath left my mouth. "Tad nervous."

"I'd be more worried if you *weren't* nervous." Ant smirked, his eyes travelling the length of me. "You look good."

We stood in the throne room as I put on my father's royal robe, the soft velvet, a heavy weight upon my shoulders. When my father had worn it, it had seemed to be as light as a feather. I suddenly realised that was only how he'd made it look. "I feel like a child playing dress-up."

A nostalgic smile appeared on Ant's face. "I remember when we used to steal your father's robes, pretending to be the emperor as we ran about the palace."

I shoved a hand through my wayward locks—they had grown over the course of our journey in Ruvalon. "It didn't feel as heavy then... It's not pretend now." Our days of recklessly running around were over. Everything was different now.

"No," he agreed. "It's very real."

"What if I'm awful at it?" I voiced my insecurity quietly, staring at the flames as they swirled in the braziers.

Ant stilled, his sharp eyes flicking to me. "There's no way

you could be, Dracho. You're too determined and compassionate for that."

The words rushed out before I could stop them. "But what if I'm not ready? I was supposed to train for years before ascending the throne. Now I'm the youngest emperor ever. How am I supposed to lead them in this uncertain time? With the Hollow, and the precarious position we've been left in with Meridium? I need to find out who murdered my father, or the people will think I'm completely incompetent. *How* am I supposed to do it all?"

"You get up every day and work hard."

"That's really helpful," I scoffed.

His chuckle was deep. "I mean, that restless, hungry energy you have in abundance—you use that every day to fuel you forward. You always tackle everything head-on, so continue to do the same. Though you do need to work on your impulsivity."

I sniffed indifferently. "I have no idea what you're talking about."

"Of course not. You might as well have publicly declared your feelings for *her* when you put Kalen in his place."

"I was... going through a lot of emotions at the time."

"Uh-huh." The look he gave me was thoroughly unconvinced. "What are you going to do about her father?"

I blew out a long breath, my dragon growling softly as I rubbed the back of my neck. "I haven't decided yet."

He nodded, looking towards the door as attendants entered. "Are you ready?" he asked again, and this time the words had an additional weight.

My impending coronation and merging pressed down upon me. I had no idea what was going to happen once I merged. I had spoken to Ant and Althea about theirs, but it differed for everyone. They described a charge of power as they became one with their dragon and a feeling of heightened emotion, but also wholeness. Before the last couple of weeks, the thought had terrified me.

Now, despite my racing heart, the thought of two separate parts of me coming together also gave me some relief. Whilst everything around me seemed out of control, maybe this one thing would help me feel like I had a grasp on some of it. My draconi form was a part of me; what could I fear from it?

"I am," I told Ant.

Whatever he saw in my eyes must have reassured him. He nodded, strolling down the steps. "I'll fetch your little mage, then."

Less than half an hour later, the throne room was packed for the ceremony, with barely any room to move between people as they all looked up towards me. Thuban, Boone and Ant watched from the side of the dais, whilst the leading families and Mortal Council stood front and centre of the crowd below. Roux was in a ceremonial robe to my left; she flashed me a smile before taking her position at the top of the steps. I stared intently at her back.

Here we go.

"To the people." Her voice rang out, clear as a bell as she stood before them—a queen in her own right—performing this for me. Many of my fellow draconi had stared in awe when they saw her, starstruck. "Today I present unto you Dracho Celesta, first of his name, your undoubted emperor. Here is your wisdom, your royal law, your defender in all things." She turned to face me, motioning towards the throne.

This was it. After this, there could be no turning back. But I owed stability to the people, to my friends... and to myself. A vision of emerald eyes flashed before me; I shook it off, my heart pounding as I took my seat, lifting my chin high.

Roux's steps were silent as she picked up the crown of Tenebris—a crown forged in dragon fire, a crown my father had hardly worn. The points, curved like my own claws, stood proudly from the band, the black metal catching the light. Roux stood behind me, holding it a few inches above my head as she continued.

"Dracho Celesta, will you promise to defend Tenebris for all your days? Use law, justice and mercy in all your judgements? And do your utmost to bring prosperity and peace to the kingdom? All this do you promise to do?"

"I promise I will." There was no hesitation or quake in my voice.

"Stars blessed you, Dracho Celesta, and today anoint you with a crown of glory and righteousness. May you lead your people in the way wherein they should go. I now crown you, Emperor."

There was a moment—just a split second—when I heard the rough exhalation leave Roux's lips, and I felt nothing as she placed the crown upon my head.

Then she removed her hands.

Small gasps broke out around the throne room as they witnessed first-hand my merging. The floor vibrated with a pulse of energy as immense pressure built within my chest before spreading through the rest of me, my fingers trembling. The magick flowed from the top of my head to the tips of my toes, the sensation causing them to curl. My dragon form reached out to fill every cell in my body, that pleasant warmth spreading over me as I felt my power increase.

My head tipped back as my eyes closed, succumbing to the complete sense of oneness. My body thrummed as I felt the magick touch every bone, every strand of hair—felt it flow through me to the throne below. I heard Roux's small gasp behind me; my eyes opened, flicking to the dragons carved into the stone of the throne, watching—fascinated—as they turned from jade to silver. The rug and banners that adorned the hall transformed from jade to black.

I twirled a lock of hair between my fingers, admiring the silver-flecked blackness of it. The change was a shock, but the new colour reminded me of my dragon, just as my father's white hair had matched his own.

I didn't know what I'd ever been afraid of. I didn't feel like I'd lost anything by merging with my dragon. There was no longer he and I, two warring factions in one body. We just were.

I *was* the dragon.

As I looked over my people, the anger, sadness and pain which had been pushed down since my father's death started to build. Cold fury became white-hot rage. I could no longer think of a valid reason to hold it back.

I cracked my neck from side to side as I stood, feeling taller as I walked to the top of the steps, holding my hands out.

"My beloved people of Tenebris." My voice—deeper now—rang out, silencing the chatter of the crowd. "The time for commiserating *will* end. The time for action is near. I promise to you, the treason against my father will not go unpunished."

People started to mutter in agreement; I heard Roux shift her feet.

"We will not stay silent whilst those who oppose us assassinate us in our own home. I vow that you shall have my protection until my soul journeys from this plane. I will be just and merciful, but I promise you..." My eyes blazed as I scanned the crowd, the excited tension in the air building. "In the name of justice, I will venture south to find those responsible." Some cheers broke out. "And they will wish for the end before I *ever* grant them mercy."

The jubilation from the crowd was music to my ears as I smiled out at them, feeling the press of my fangs against my bottom lip. As I turned my head, I caught the wide smile of my uncle and Boone's concerned frown. My eyes skipped sideways to glance at Roux. Hers were wide with fear.

My low tone was as dark as the dragon form that swirled viciously beneath my skin. "This I swear to you!"

So... we're heading back? Ant's thoughts were unsure.

I gave him a smile that bared my fangs as I watched the people celebrate before me.

Yes. We're going back.

PRINCE OF THE ANCIENTS

G L PRESTON

Thank you for reading *Prince of the Ancients: Book One of the Stag and Hollow Chronicles*.
Please share your feedback on social media using my hashtags and handle:
@Authorglpreston
#princeoftheancients #pota
For exclusives on future projects and offers, don't forget to sign up to my mailing list on:
www.glpreston.com
If you enjoyed this book, please consider writing a review with your honest impressions on Amazon, Goodreads, or the platform of your choosing. Your feedback is incredibly valuable for helping independent authors like me to reach a wider audience.

Acknowledgements

Well, that was a rollercoaster ride of emotions!

A few people made this book eminently more readable than it would have been. The biggest thank you, to my beautiful editor Emma O'Connell, who helped me unravel issues with the storyline and whose hilarious notes encouraged my faith in this story. She also fed me home-made cakes and made the best cup of Earl Grey tea ever! Not only did I discover an amazing editor, I made a new friend! I shan't forgive you for leaving me and Wales, but I thank the stars I found you and your beautiful family!

My two amazing beta readers, Beth and Brit. Your feedback was so essential in improving my story. Brit, my Bookmother and member of the three Bookstateers (Erin & Cass) — the three of you kept me sane during those months leading to publication. I have loved every teaser, every laugh, every compliment on my accent, and discussing everyday life. Thank you from the bottom of my heart. Sometimes strangers become the best of friends!

To Jodie, Holly and Zoe, members of the COC, and my besties from high school, Sarah, Kell and Nell—thank you for your unwavering support and for being the best hype women ever (Also for taking me out for cocktails when needed and reading spicy scenes in public!).

To Matt, for being an amazing encouragement and inspiring me with your own words and ideas when I first started.

My beautiful Mammy, thank you for reading the first ever draft of my story (even if you did skip the spice!) and for your unconditional love and support. You give so much to everyone, never taking—it would take more than a lifetime to pay back everything you and Dad have ever done for me but know that I appreciate it more than you know. I love you forever.

To my little brother and sister, for always making me laugh, and being the best siblings anyone could ask for.

To Grandad, for showing me what it meant to have a good father figure when I was a very little girl and needed it most, and for igniting my passion for stories, with your tales of Bernard the cat. To Nannie, for always letting me stay up late to watch Touched by an Angel, for all the times you let me bake with you, and the times you stroked a troubled little girl's hair until she fell asleep.

To my little demons, this book would have been finished a lot earlier if it weren't for you two—but I wouldn't change you for the world. You are the most beautiful, clever and tenacious children I know. When you are older, I hope this story inspires you as much as books have inspired me.

To my husband, thank you for supporting me and pushing me through this writing journey. Thank you for being an insightful first editor, helping me decide what my Dracho would do in certain situations and for listening to my brain-storming sessions over tea. Thank you for encouraging my ideas, giving me time to myself to write, and knowing when I just needed a hug after a long day.

Finally, to *you*. The reader. I cannot express in words how grateful I am to you. When I was growing up, fantasy books were an escape from the real world. Some stories I read saved me, and my mental health. If I can inspire just *one* person, and make them feel the same way...it will all be worth it. For the stories we read, and the dreams that follow, never forget them.

Photo by Jack Harper

Gem has tried many things in her lifetime, but writing has to have been the best. She is a wife, and a mother to two beautiful daughters, but she's also been a Law graduate, a designer, a photographer and an artist. When she's not writing, she loves gaming, and discussing Marvel or Harry Potter theories with anyone who will listen.

In 2015, Gemma was diagnosed with Intracranial Hypertension, a rare disease that involves a build-up of pressure in the fluid surrounding her brain. She pushes for education on the various symptoms that accompany this disease, including potential blindness and severe headaches.